CHILD

OF THE

COVENANT

KIM GRAVELL

CHILD

OF THE

COVENANT

Book two of the *Dark Places* sequence

Matador
9 Priory Business Park
Kibworth Beauchamp
Leicestershire LE8 0RX, UK
Tel: (+44) 116 279 2299
Fax: (+44) 116 279 2277
Email: books@troubador.co.uk
Web: www.troubador.co.uk/matador

ISBN 978 1784620 998

British Library Cataloguing in Publication Data.
A catalogue record for this book is available from the British Library.

Printed and bound in the UK by TJ International, Padstow, Cornwall
Typeset in Bembo by Troubador Publishing Ltd

Matador is an imprint of Troubador Publishing Ltd

MIX
Paper from
responsible sources
FSC® C013056

For all my sensei — both in and out of the dojo — and especially for Michael Neill. "What one person can do" turned out to be this.

CHAPTER 1

Gwyn scowled at the dead woman standing beside her desk. The promise she had made to her, over quarter of a century ago, had niggled at her all night.

You've left me with a problem, Anne.

Oh, I don't think so. He's come back to you, hasn't he?

Built from sunlight and memories, Anne Morgan settled one hip on the corner of the desk and took a long lick from the ice cream cone that had appeared in her hand. Gwyn caught the whiff of suntan lotion and the mingled salt and mud smell of Aberaeron harbour at low tide. Far-away, she fancied she could almost hear the metallic clink of rigging and the cry of seagulls.

That's not what I meant, and you know it.

Lacing her fingers behind her head Gwyn leaned back in her chair and glared balefully at her friend as though she suspected the apparition she had conjured of teasing her.

I've been thinking. We talked yesterday; not about that exactly, but about other things, about what happened with Monty and – well – maybe it's time. Maybe he should know.

Know what – that James isn't his father? How's that going to help him?

I'm not expecting it to help him. To be honest, I don't know what it's likely to do to him.

It had been that uncertainty, as much as the promise she

had made to Anne, that had stopped her saying anything to Aidan yesterday, but she had found that it hadn't stopped her thinking about it.

I think he has a right to know.

You didn't have a problem with him not knowing before.

'Anne—' Gwyn found herself growling the name aloud and stopped. Deliberately she made herself relax.

You know how I felt about it, but it was your choice. He was your son and I respected that. But he's an adult now. She sighed, wondering why she was having this particular conversation with a long dead woman in her head. Was there really any point? She could tell Aidan that James Morgan wasn't his father but she couldn't tell him who was. That was the one detail Anne had never confided in her. Thinking about it now she was surprised to find it still hurt.

Why would you never tell me Anne?

The one time she had pressed her friend on the subject Anne had flown into a fury. *'He's dead! Gone! What does it matter?'* Amidst the near-hysteria that had followed Gwyn had never learned whether Anne had meant her words literally. It seemed more likely that – for whatever reason – the relationship had gone sour and Anne was wiping the man in question out of her life. It scarcely mattered. In the face of Anne's absolute refusal to tell, and still grieving and broken from her own loss, she hadn't had the will to pursue it any further.

There was nothing to tell, Gwyn. You didn't know him – none of you did – and he was gone before I had the chance to tell him.

The voice in Gwyn's head now was calm but offered no new insights, leaving her no nearer a decision as to what – if anything – she should tell Aidan regarding his parentage. Maybe

Anne was right and it was only a problem if she made it one.

The sound of stealthy movement behind her interrupted her reverie.

And there's another problem that needs sorting.

Gwyn rolled her eyes heavenwards as the change in light told her someone had stepped between her and the bull's-eye glass panel in the centre of the front door. She knew that someone was Marcus Eldritch. Nor was she surprised by the soft slur of sound as the door was carefully opened and then, just as quietly, pulled to. To some extent she had been expecting it. With a resigned sigh she looked at her PC screen and the text she hadn't updated for over half an hour. *Spotting the Early Signs of Dementia* simply wasn't high on her list of priorities right now.

Oh, that any of us might live long enough to get it, she thought. And then, *Mal is going to kill me if I don't get this finished.*

She saved the document and stood up.

Oh well.

As she suspected, Eldritch had not gone far. He stood in the corner of the garden, staring out over the slate and limewash wall up towards the head of the valley. Gwyn walked over to join him. Without taking his eyes from the hills, Eldritch said, 'The car keys are still on the table if that's what you're worried about. I'm not about to pull another disappearing trick on you.'

'Who's worried? I disconnected the battery last night.'

That got his attention. He glanced at her sharply and she could see he wasn't quite sure if she was joking. He opened his mouth to say something, clearly thought better of it and shut it again, turning his attention back to the view. She wondered if he had been watching the buzzard that gyred lazily over the head of the valley, a tiny circling speck in the pale blue sky, but when she looked she realised his eyes weren't following the movement. In fact he didn't really seem to be focussing on anything he saw. It was more as though he was listening, as if the thin breeze carried the sound of voices to him and he was straining to make them out. For a moment Gwyn listened too, but she could hear nothing beyond the not-quite-silence of a normal autumn afternoon so she left the hills to mind themselves and looked Eldritch over instead.

They had spent an uneventful day. Eldritch had slept late, still drained from his encounter with the avatar – though the lethargy that had lain like lead on his bones was lifting – and after breakfast and an hour of increasingly fidgety wakefulness, she had agreed that he could get up and take a shower. The corners of Gwyn's mouth twitched as she stifled a smile. It wasn't that she had been deliberately wicked, but Eldritch's repeated assertions that he was absolutely fine and her own equally dogged insistence that he would very quickly find out otherwise if he pushed himself too hard had been in danger of escalating into a full-scale row. So when she had thrown her hands up and told him to go take the damned shower if he was so certain he was up to it, he had been halfway out of the bed before he remembered two small but vital details. Not only was he completely naked under the bedclothes but he also had no idea where his clothes were. Gwyn had watched that realisation hit him as he had retreated behind a hastily grabbed armful of quilt. While Eldritch might just about live down the fact that she had been the one to undress him – after all he had been barely conscious at the time and in no state to prevent it – he wasn't brazen enough to walk through her house clothed in

4

nothing but his dignity, even supposing his strength didn't give out halfway across the room and pitch him full-length upon the floor as she had warned him it might. The smirk took full control of Gwyn's lips. Despite the patina of bruises and dirt, he was still a good-looking man and she had taken a certain delight in his dilemma, letting him sweat for a few minutes before she relented and fetched the dressing gown that Aidan had brought with him the previous night.

As it turned out they could both argue that they were right. Gwyn admitted that Eldritch looked – and presumably felt – a lot better for having that shower, but she had been deadly accurate in her prediction that it would take more energy than he expected and much to his chagrin he had had to lie down afterwards, dizzy and weak-kneed, while she redressed his shoulder. By tacit agreement neither side claimed victory over the other.

They had talked a little – of the cats and of writing, of the generations of her family who had lived in the valley and of the relative merits of living in the town or the country; safe, inconsequential things – and then Eldritch had drowsed and Gwyn had got on with her work. After lunch she had given him the clothes that Aidan had left for him and tactfully withdrawn. When she had tapped on the bedroom door half an hour later she had found him stretched out once more on the bed, fully clothed but fast asleep. Looking at her watch now she realised that had been almost two hours ago.

The clothes weren't too bad a fit, Gwyn thought as she flicked her eyes over Eldritch's lanky form. He had rolled back the cuffs of the brushed cotton shirt to disguise the fact that the sleeves were too short. Unable to do anything similar with the jeans he had compromised by pulling them as low as possible on his hips. He still managed to look as though he was wearing his younger brother's clothes, but at least he had something to wear. If it had been left to her the best she could have offered him was one of her London marathon t-shirts – they tended to be sized to fit even the largest runners and would probably fit over some of the more bizarre fancy dress costumes as well – and a sarong. She covered an amused snort with a small cough. No doubt Eldritch would be much happier when he and Aidan had retrieved his things from Mrs Vaughan's guest house that evening.

'When I've been staring at the computer for too long I'll come out here and look at the hills instead,' Gwyn ventured. 'It's surprising how often the phrase I've been looking for will just drop into my head after a few minutes in the fresh air.'

She glanced at Eldritch to see if he was listening and then looked a second time more closely, her dark brows drawing down, making her thin face seem more elfin than ever. It wasn't the sight of the bruises, just visible under the collar of his borrowed shirt and already beginning to fade to an ugly yellow, or the way he hugged his right arm into his chest, more as if he were cold than to take the weight off his shoulder. What worried her was the weary, pinched look that had returned to Eldritch's face and the way his brow furrowed as if with discomfort or grief. Even as Gwyn watched him, Eldritch raised a hand to his face, rubbing the skin above his eyes with thumb and forefinger as though massaging away a headache.

'The fresh air is meant to be helping you, not making you ill,' she commented, not bothering to mask the concern in her voice. For a moment Eldritch said nothing. He tilted his face towards the sun like a bruised and storm-battered flower, seeking warmth. Then he spoke and his voice was soft and with no trace of the defensiveness that had filled it moments earlier.

'I can hear it, Gwyn; yammering in my brain. I can't make out what it's saying yet, but if I listen hard enough it's there.'

The shock of hearing him use her name almost outweighed the realisation of what he was talking about. Gwyn's automatic reaction was to tell him not to be so stupid and to stop listening, but then she realised what else it was about Eldritch's voice that had shocked her and her protest died on her lips. Just for a moment Eldritch had sounded pleased. Gwyn took a deep breath and then let it out very slowly.

'Is that a good thing?' she asked, her voice carefully neutral, watching him. His eyes were closed now and the expression on his face had twisted until there was no doubt that it was pain that contorted his features. She could almost feel him stretching out his senses as he answered her.

'Its thoughts wash over me.'

Gwyn held her breath. Eldritch's shields were paper thin and it was all she could do not to slap her own around him and cut off the link he was seeking.

'Scarlet tides of anger and pain… and hatred… such a deep, visceral hatred.' His deep voice was distant, as if he spoke to her from the far shores of nightmare. He paused, his head turning like a questing hound's.

'They colour my vision and I feel them stealing over me.' He paused again, drawing in a sharp breath and his voice changed as he exhaled the air almost like a moan. 'It hurts so much I think it's going to stop my heart.'

Gwyn had heard enough.

'Stop it!'

Her hand clamped around Eldritch's good arm and she stepped in front of him, putting herself physically and psychically between him and that demonic influence. For a moment she thought he was going down as he rocked backwards, his eyes flying open to show only the whites rolled back in his head, and she moved to catch him, but as she did so he snapped back from wherever he had been. He stood looking down at her, dazed as a sleepwalker, his sides heaving like a broken-winded nag. Very carefully, aware that the slightest lapse of self-control would let her voice spiral up the octaves until she was shrieking like a fishwife, Gwyn said, 'I don't think you should try that again. Not until you and your shields are an awful lot stronger.'

Not until Hell freezes over and Satan starts commuting to work on ice skates.

Eldritch looked at her, his eyes still shocked and otherworldly. He blinked and nodded slowly and Gwyn hoped that he was agreeing with her rather than just trying to clear his head.

'I can stop it for you. You still don't have much strength for shielding, but I can do the same for you as I've done for Aidan; create a crystal seal that will stop it reaching you.'

Eldritch's head came up almost as though she had slapped him.

'No!' he said, just a shade too quickly. 'No. Dear God, I wish that were an option, but I need to be able to feel it.'

His eyes were haunted and Gwyn was certain there was something about the contact with the demon that had scared him but, as the silence stretched between them, she realised he wasn't going to say any more.

'If it gets too much, tell me,' she said, knowing that her words were inadequate but uncertain whether to offer help or a warning. Neither, she felt, would be welcomed.

'I will,' he agreed, but he looked away swiftly, without meeting her eyes. Gwyn took her hand from his arm. She knew he was lying. She just didn't know why.

'So, how long have you been able to hear the demon? And, if you can hear it, why the whole charade about needing to find where the avatar had been to be able to track it?'

Gwyn handed Eldritch a shot glass of brandy and watched over him while he drank it down. The kettle was on again – she was beginning to feel as though she was running a café, she was making so much tea recently – but her guest had looked in need of something stronger than Earl Grey to settle his nerves. Eldritch handed the empty glass back to her with a tiny smile.

'I don't normally drink much, you know,' he said, neatly sidestepping her question.

Back inside the cottage he seemed more himself, although Gwyn had to remind herself sharply that even now she didn't really know the real Marcus Eldritch. Even so, she recognised the pattern of wry humour that he used to deflect any question that came too close for his liking.

'Don't worry, I'm not planning on getting you drunk and then taking advantage of you,' she countered, going along with him. Eldritch sighed theatrically and his shoulders slumped.

'And I thought my luck was finally in.'

Despite herself Gwyn laughed at the sheer ridiculousness of that statement, but she would not let him off the hook.

'The demon?' she prompted.

Eldritch pushed his hair back from his eyes. Freshly washed as it was, it simply fell straight back.

'I didn't know until I stepped outside that I could still hear it.'

He accepted her sceptically raised eyebrows without reproach. 'Honestly, I was only going out to get some fresh air.' He waved a hand at the PC spiralling through its screensaver of endlessly forming pipes behind her. 'I crept out because I didn't want to disturb you when you were working.'

Gwyn sucked thoughtfully on her lower lip, but chose to accept this version of events for the moment.

'So when did you first realise you could hear it?'

Eldritch looked unhappy.

'It was after the fight with the avatar. I'm not quite sure when it started. I don't think it was Saturday night, but I'm not sure – things were a bit hazy – but in the forest yesterday I had this...' He groped to find the right words. 'This sort of buzzing in my ears. I didn't really think much about it. I've had a sense of the demon's presence more or less since I came to Llancathan. It's like the heavy feeling you get in your head before a thunderstorm.'

He cocked his head on one side, looking at her to see if she understood and she nodded.

'It's not something you could pin down as coming from anywhere in particular. Yesterday I just assumed it was more of the same, maybe a bit louder, but then the avatar had been close by.'

He gave a little lopsided shrug at that flawed logic.

'But it wasn't there when I woke up and I didn't give it a second thought. It was only when I went outside and I realised I was hearing it again that I understood what it was.'

'Can you hear it now?'

Gwyn wasn't surprised when Eldritch shook his head. She had guessed as much from the way his whole demeanour had changed within moments of his re-crossing the cottage's threshold. It was as though a weight had dropped from his shoulders. So the wards could keep it out, whatever it was that the avatar did to him.

'No, thank goodness. It's not a nice feeling.'

'You seemed to be courting it when you were outside,' Gwyn pointed out bluntly. Eldritch had the grace to look embarrassed.

'That probably wasn't the brightest thing to do,' he acknowledged, his lips twisting briefly into a look of self-reproach. 'Don't worry, it's not something I plan on repeating for a while, but when I do I'd like you to sit in the circle with me as back up.'

Gwyn wasn't sure which surprised her more – the fact that Eldritch seemed to be heeding her advice or that he had effectively just asked for her help. Before she could think of a suitable rejoinder he added, 'If this link lasts, I'm fairly certain I can use it to pinpoint where the demon is breaking through.'

CHAPTER 2

'So, do we pick up an Indian or a Chinese tonight?'

Eldritch looked nonplussed as Aidan pulled up in the little car park beside Saint Cathan's Church.

'I'm sorry?'

'Do you fancy an Indian or a Chinese?' Aidan asked again. When Eldritch still didn't answer he went on, 'We had a Chinese last night so do you want an Indian tonight? We could have fish and chips, but The Fryer is closed on a Monday and I've always avoided Jenner's since the Food Standards Agency found the dead Alsatian in his freezer.' Aidan paused and looked at Eldritch curiously. 'What did you think I was suggesting – a prostitute?'

Eldritch felt rather overwhelmed by all this information.

'It never crossed my mind,' he said, somewhat unconvincingly. 'But if you ask that question around King's Cross you might find you get more than you bargained for. An Alsatian? Didn't they close Jenner's down?'

'No.' Aidan made it sound as though the idea was ridiculous. 'There was some talk about the RSPCA trying to get him for cruelty, but when it turned out the dog was dead before he put it in the freezer that didn't stick either.'

Eldritch looked at Aidan, trying to work out if he was joking. If he was, the Welshman could make a fortune playing poker for there was no sign of it in his face.

'Indian would be fine,' he concluded weakly. 'Do you and Gwyn live on takeaways?'

'Whatever gives you that idea?'

'Oh, nothing. Except that this will be the third night in a row that you've had one.'

Aidan thought for a moment as he led Eldritch down the footpath alongside the church.

'That's not strictly true. We didn't get the one on Saturday — other things intervened.'

Eldritch was silent, seeming to study the blocky, slate-clad shape of Llancathan's eponymous church.

'I'm sorry about that,' he said softly. 'And I haven't even thanked you for what you did. You or Gwyn.'

Aidan shrugged negligently.

'Don't worry about it. We demon hunters have to stick together.'

This time Eldritch could hear the humour lurking beneath the soft burr of accent.

'You can buy this one to make up for it.'

'Gwyn's not the best of cooks, see,' Aidan elaborated as they perused the menu at the Bombay King and placed their order. 'She wouldn't let you starve — well, not once she'd remembered you were there she wouldn't, although she does tend to get caught up in her work and forget what time it is — but she's a bit too pragmatic where food's concerned. She's just as happy to eat it raw as bother cooking it.'

'Lunch was quite normal.' Eldritch didn't want to disagree with Aidan over what was clearly a long held position, but he didn't feel comfortable belittling Gwyn, even when it was clear that, for all his comments, Aidan regarded the older woman with a great deal of affection. 'We had soup.'

'Oh yes? What kind?'

'Tomato. Straight out of a can.'

Aidan whistled appreciatively.

'You are honoured.' He held the door for Eldritch. 'Next you'll be telling me it was hot.'

Eldritch turned to respond, but Aidan was no longer paying attention to their conversation. He was looking across the road to where three young men lounged at a trestle table outside the Black Lion. Eldritch had been in the pub – he had met Andrew Holmes there – but something about these three would have made him think twice about going inside. He didn't need to hear Aidan's softly muttered, 'There's trouble,' to understand that the small group was best given a wide berth. All three were strong and thick set – the word that sprang to mind was "powerful", an adjective that was often over-used, but which seemed uncomfortably appropriate for these three. None of them were overly tall, he thought, although it was difficult to judge while they were sat down, but they radiated the kind of solidity that would not have looked out of place in a rugby squad. One was dressed in dark green farmer's overalls, the sleeves rolled up to reveal the corded forearms of a man well used to hard manual work. The other two – brothers if their shared sandy hair and rather similar faces were anything to go by – were in work-stained jeans and t-shirts, seemingly impervious to the growing chill in the air as evening came on.

They had noticed Aidan, for the one in overalls shouted at him across the road and the brothers half-rose from their seats, gesturing obscenely. It seemed to Eldritch that one word from the farmer – for it was clear that he was the group's alpha male – and they would have been across the road, spoiling for a fight, but without his permission they contented themselves with hurled abuse.

'Hey, Cripple! You found yourself a new boyfriend?'

'You don't want to hang around with him, mate. The last sod he went with killed himself.'

Hoots of laughter and more gestures accompanied the words.

'They reckon he couldn't get it up anymore.'

'Ignore them.'

Beside him Eldritch felt Aidan tense, his breathing short and angry, but he kept walking, ignoring the jeers and catcalls that followed him down the street. As they passed the market hall and crossed to turn down a narrow side street the raucous calls faded away behind them and, in the comparative silence, Eldritch felt his own breathing even out. He was aware that his palms were sweating and he rubbed them self-consciously on his jeans. Aidan said nothing, but his face was pale and rigid though Eldritch thought that was due more to anger than any fear of physical violence. He swallowed, uncertain what to say. Perhaps Aidan felt his discomfort for he glanced up and the hardness was already passing from his eyes.

'Sorry about that. This town has more than its fair share of village idiots.'

With that he seemed to dismiss the incident from his mind.

Eldritch envied him his self-composure. Now the initial shock of the encounter had worn off, he found he too was angry and upset on Aidan's behalf.

'Cripple?' He looked at the athletic young man walking

beside him. It was hard to imagine anyone who looked fitter. 'Forgive me if I'm missing something, but that doesn't seem a particularly accurate insult.'

The side street was little more than a car's width of tarmac running between the two rows of terraced houses, their neatly painted front doors opening directly onto the road, their broad slate doorsteps forming a tripping hazard for pedestrians trying to avoid passing traffic. But at this time of evening there were few cars and none that wanted to use this narrow thoroughfare. As they walked, their footfalls echoed back as a dull patter from the brick and slate walls. Or at least Eldritch's did. The wizard noted that Aidan moved almost soundlessly and he wondered if that was simply because he was wearing trainers or because he was listening for the sound of running footsteps behind them. Eldritch decided not to ask and Aidan stayed silent, but as they emerged into Oak Street the younger man said quietly, 'It isn't. Not anymore.'

Aidan said nothing more on the subject until they left the Llancathan View Guest House. Although Gwyn had phoned the little hotelier to let her know that her errant guest had turned up on her doorstep, Mrs Vaughan seemed relieved to see Eldritch in the flesh and insisted on hearing the story of what had happened from him. It was all too easy, she agreed, to get lost when walking on the hills and he was lucky that he'd crossed tracks with Aidan otherwise who knows what might have happened to him. Eldritch nodded solemnly and endured the subsequent lecture about the dangers of going out on the hills unprepared with good grace while Aidan did his best not to choke as he held back his laughter.

'But it's an ill wind that blows no good,' Mrs Vaughan

concluded, 'and this young man will show you all the wild places you need to be able to describe in your book.'

'Yes, he's shown me one or two already.'

Behind Mrs Vaughan's back, Aidan looked fit to burst.

There were a few minutes spent haggling over the bill as Eldritch insisted he should pay for the full stay he had booked and Mrs Vaughan swore she would do no such thing as rob a guest. In the end they reached a compromise that left them both quietly convinced that the other was daft not to accept what had been offered and then Eldritch went upstairs to gather his things.

On the pavement outside the guest house, Aidan paused and took the bag from Eldritch, slinging it lightly over his shoulder. His good humour seemed restored by the encounter with Mrs Vaughan so it took Eldritch a moment to work out what he was referring to when he said, 'It happened in the second year of senior school. I was pushed down the main stairs.'

He spoke so casually that Eldritch could scarcely believe he had heard correctly, especially when Aidan continued.

'I broke a few vertebrae – amongst other things – ended up having to have a rod put in my spine. For a while the doctors weren't sure that I'd walk again. As it was, I spent the next six months in a plaster cast from chest to hip, so cripple was a pretty good description of me for a while.'

He noticed Eldritch's shocked expression and flashed a grin that seemed to say, "this really is ancient history".

'Griff swore he wasn't there at the time.'

A touch of cynicism invaded the grin, inviting the observer to make of that what he would, but still Aidan seemed remarkably unbothered by the story he was recounting.

'Claire Maddock said I'd been larking around after rugby practice, showing off to her on the stairs, but she was going out with Griff so I don't know, she'd probably have said anything he asked her to. I certainly don't remember her being there. What I do remember is hearing Griff and his gang shouting in the corridor, then the next thing I know I'm lying at the bottom of the stairs and there's a voice somewhere above me saying that I'm going to be a cripple. Then someone kicked me in the back and after that it's all black until I'm waking up in hospital two days later. The headmaster said I was very lucky Griff had been working late in the library and found me.'

Aidan snorted derisively.

'Griff never spent a minute longer than he had to in the library and he certainly never worked late. He copied all his projects from Claire or whoever else he was going out with at the time.'

'I take it that Griff was the one in the overalls?'

'Yeah, that's him. He's not changed much.'

'So who were the two Rottweilers with him?'

That raised a peal of appreciative laughter from Aidan.

'The dogs of war? Rod and Alec Owen. The three of them were pretty much a unit at school. Griff was the brain – well, he's got more than the pair of them have – and they were the muscle. They still hang out together, giving people grief. It's best to ignore them.'

And Eldritch could believe that he meant it. As a child Aidan had weathered the broken bones, as an adult he would be damned if he would deign to notice the name-calling. Eldritch felt a new respect for the younger man.

That didn't, however, diminish his sense of relief when they

18

turned the corner into Market Street and saw that the table outside the Black Lion was vacant. A litter of abandoned glasses marked their passing, but Griff and his cohorts were gone. Eldritch relaxed a little at the sight. He hadn't relished the thought of another confrontation. Though it hadn't been aimed at him directly, the venom of their earlier abuse had disturbed him and he was glad they didn't have to run that particular gauntlet again. Yet if Aidan shared his concerns he gave no sign. The table warranted barely a glance as he cut across the street, heading purposefully for the gilt and flock wallpapered warmth of the Bombay King and the promise of supper. Eldritch scrunched himself a little deeper into his borrowed fleece and decided Aidan had the right idea. He lengthened his stride to catch up.

Waiting for him on the other side of the road, Aidan asked, 'Feeling cold?'

'A little,' Eldritch conceded. It was probably four or five degrees cooler here than it would have been in London and the light breeze had stiffened so that, for him at least, the autumn evening now felt decidedly chilly.

'English softie,' Aidan muttered, entirely without malice. 'That's how I came to take up karate, you know.'

Following the jump in the conversation, still Eldritch couldn't help but ask, 'Because of the cold?'

Aidan gave him a pained look.

'Because of Griff. The physio recommended I did something that would work the whole body, improve my coordination and build up my core muscle strength again. She suggested t'ai chi, but there wasn't a club nearby so my mum,' there was just the faintest hesitation on that last word, 'took me to karate instead.'

An odd smile blossomed on Aidan's face.

'I don't suppose she really understood the difference, but it turned out to be the best thing she could have done. I doubt that many clubs would have let me train, not the state I was in, but the sensei at the local club is incredible. She knows the human body like you wouldn't believe and she was very understanding. I think she saw me as something of a challenge.'

'She?' queried Eldritch. 'That's unusual isn't it? I thought most karate instructors were men.'

'Most are – even these days – which should give you some indication of just how good Sensei is. Looking back it's hard to describe just how lucky I was to have had her as an instructor.'

Aidan's voice sparkled like a child's describing Christmas morning.

'Not only did she let me train but she worked me absolutely to my limits. From the word go she refused to talk about what I couldn't do – she could see that for herself. What she was interested in was what I was capable of and she made damn sure that everyone else in the club took the same approach, me included. She wouldn't stand for self-pity in her dojo and she wasn't going to accept anything less than one hundred percent commitment. If she thought I wasn't trying hard enough, so what if I couldn't do press-ups? She'd make me do squats instead or extra punches and as soon as I could manage one thing she'd try me with something harder. All the time she was stretching me, making me work. I'd go home almost in tears some weeks, but I'd go back the next lesson absolutely determined to be able to do what she'd asked me to do and somewhere along the line I realised that I was enjoying it.'

He grinned and for a second Eldritch caught the fierce and savage joy burning in the heart of Aidan's soul, something akin to the wild elation that he himself found in his magic. Perhaps there were more people who had experience of what Aidan felt – at least martial arts could be practised openly – but there was still that same indefinable sense of being set slightly apart, of having touched something that only a very few could reach and fewer still could understand and make it their own. The look was gone in a second, but its echo remained in Aidan's voice.

'If anyone's responsible for my not being crippled, it's Sensei.'

'Didn't Gwyn help?'

Eldritch wondered if he had misunderstood and Aidan and Gwyn didn't have the years of shared history he had assumed. Aidan paused as he stepped up to the Bombay King's door and his hand fell away from the ridiculously large brass doorknob. He turned back into the street, seeming momentarily taken aback, his head tilting to one side as he considered the question, in a gesture that was so very like Gwyn's.

'Yes, I suppose she did.'

He sounded hesitant, almost as though he hadn't given much thought to the part she had played in his recovery.

'I don't remember much about the first days after it happened – they must have been using some pretty heavy drugs on me and then there was the operation.'

He shook his head as though clearing the fog of the anaesthetic from his brain.

'I was washing in and out like the tide, but she seemed to be there pretty much any time I was awake. I didn't give it much thought. Gwyn was always around and Mum was working so it just seemed logical that she was there. She'd joke that she was healing me while I was asleep. I sort of believed her at the time, but when I got older I thought everything she'd told me about healing was rubbish.'

Aidan bit his lip and Eldritch wondered what it was about that change of perspective that the younger man wasn't sharing. He would have been on the cusp of adolescence when the accident happened; a time when it was natural to abandon the trusting acceptance of childhood for the questioning, doubting nature of the teenager. Yet he had the impression that there was more to it than that, but he didn't know the young man well enough to feel he could ask. Aidan scuffed the side of his trainer along the pavement. He wasn't about to say so out loud, but Eldritch thought he could see the admission that he had been wrong in that almost unconscious gesture.

After a moment Aidan continued, 'Whether or not she worked any healing on me, she certainly helped with all the physio when I came out of hospital.'

Something about that memory conjured a brief, sweet smile.

'She was forever throwing things for me to catch to improve my reflexes.'

The smile broadened into a self-mocking grin as if Aidan suspected he was sounding sentimental.

'Come on,' he said, reaching once more for the door. 'Dinner's getting cold.'

As it was, their order wasn't quite ready although the young woman who appeared behind the counter, like a *djinni* summoned by the sound of the opening door, assured them it would not be long. Aidan stood at the counter, idly flicking through the pages of the local paper, working his way backwards from the sports section to the headlines, while Eldritch found himself a seat in the corner where he could lean back and surreptitiously rest his head on the wall.

His shoulder was beginning to ache and, much though he would never have admitted it to her, he suspected Gwyn had been right when she suggested he should wear a sling to keep the weight of his arm off it. As it was, he could feel the muscles across his upper back tightening up and the knock-on effect was that he had a headache building. There was a break in the rhythmic turning of pages as Aidan found an article worth reading and Eldritch took advantage of the diversion to knead his fingers into the back of his neck unnoticed. Then he slumped a little deeper into the moulded plastic, shifting so he could rest his right arm across his stomach without it looking too obvious that he was supporting it. He made a poor invalid and found it faintly embarrassing that his body couldn't simply shrug off the injuries he had received although – having seen them properly in the shower that morning – he realised his recovery so far had been faster than he had any right to expect.

The sound of Aidan's voice made Eldritch look up and he realised that some minutes had passed. Not only was their meal ready but, despite his earlier comment, Aidan must have already paid for it, for the young woman – Nav, he thought Aidan had called her earlier – was handing him his change.

'I didn't realise it was past your bedtime,' Aidan commented with a glance over his shoulder towards Eldritch, dashing his hopes that his little siesta had gone unnoticed. He picked up the takeaway in one hand and Eldritch's bag in the other and then paused to eye up the way Eldritch was sitting.

'If that's hurting you'll take more weight off it if you put your hand under the elbow to support it.'

So the careful subterfuge with the arm hadn't worked either.

'It's just a bit stiff,' Eldritch tried to sound dismissive.

In truth his shoulder wasn't so bad, but the buzzing in his head made him wonder if he might risk an "I told you so" from Gwyn if there was a chance of getting some aspirin from her. Aidan nodded in a way that suggested the entire sequence of thoughts had shown clearly in Eldritch's face, but all he said was, 'You might find it helps anyway,' and let the matter go. Eldritch levered himself out of the chair and made himself useful by opening the door.

He tried suggesting that he could at least carry the takeaway, but Aidan merely smiled and said it was no bother and somewhere between the Bombay King's door and the footpath leading down to the church Eldritch decided to swallow his pride and take advantage of the fact he wasn't carrying anything to follow Aidan's advice about his shoulder. He felt slightly ridiculous, walking down the street with his right elbow cradled in his left palm, as though he were making a public statement of his injury, but, other than Aidan, there was no one else to see and pass judgement and to his surprise it did indeed make his shoulder more comfortable. They walked in companionable silence, neither feeling the urge to make conversation and as they came to the footpath Eldritch dropped wordlessly behind Aidan. Though the path was supposedly wide enough for two people to walk side by side, the somewhat overgrown shrubbery to the left and the closeness of the churchyard wall on the right meant the reality of doing so required both parties to be close friends or for neither of them to be carrying anything.

As he followed Aidan, Eldritch couldn't help but wonder what he had done to deserve this level of acceptance. He thought he should feel uncomfortable with this gentle cosseting except he knew instinctively that Aidan wouldn't throw it back in his face at some later date. Nor, he realised, would Gwyn. For all her prickliness and her uncanny ability to get under his skin, when she gave her help she did so ungrudgingly and with no conditions attached. It occurred to him he could even have asked her to help him that morning when he had stood in her shower and wondered exactly how he was going to wash his hair when he couldn't raise his right hand above his head. In the end he had managed well enough one-handed, but the thought of asking her to help in such a situation amused him, except... except he wouldn't have known what to do if she had said yes and – knowing her – she would have had no compunction about doing so. Eldritch felt a slow burn of heat in his cheeks that made him glad Aidan couldn't see his face. It would have been very difficult to explain exactly what had caused that blush.

Idly he wondered what Helen would have made of Gwyn. For no reason he could put into words, he thought the two women would have liked each other, though they were as different in character as they would have been to look at. He imagined the pair of them, pictured them sizing each other up, and in his mind Helen turned and grinned at him, mischief in her flower fairy eyes as though she had been eavesdropping on his earlier thoughts and was teasing him over his discomfort.

Contemplating the unreasonableness of his wife and Gwyn ganging up on him in his own mind, Eldritch barely noticed the pathway opening out. The first indication he had that they were back at the car park or that Aidan had stopped in the middle of the path was when he walked straight into him. It was also his first indication that they were in trouble.

CHAPTER 3

Aidan barely seemed to notice six feet something of wizard hitting him in the back and it was Eldritch who staggered away from the impact, his embarrassed-sounding apology failing to cover the mixture of irritation and resignation in Aidan's voice as the younger man growled, 'I don't believe it.'

For a fleeting moment, Eldritch thought Aidan's words had been aimed at him and he was opening his mouth to give an explanation for his inattention when his eye was drawn by an out-of-place movement to the middle of the car park and a figure in green overalls lounging against the side of Aidan's Land Rover. Eldritch's mouth shut with an almost audible snap. Automatically he looked round for the two missing people he knew instinctively had to be there. He didn't have to look far. As Griff crossed his arms and leaned back against the driver's door, in a gesture of casual arrogance, Rod and Alec Owen appeared from the sidelines like bit players joining the master villain on stage.

'Oh you must be joking…'

Eldritch looked from the three figures to Aidan and his voice tailed off. The expression on Aidan's face removed all possibility that this was anything other than deadly serious. Aidan looked very calm, but there was a steeliness about his eyes that Eldritch had not seen before. For a moment he was simply glad that that expression wasn't being directed at him.

Without taking his eyes off the three men, Aidan asked, 'Is there anything valuable in this?' lightly hefting Eldritch's bag in his hand as though judging something by its weight – its importance perhaps or its potential as a weapon. Eldritch glanced at the black duffle.

'My laptop, but it's security marked so it wouldn't be worth stealing.'

There was a grin lurking in Aidan's voice that was entirely missing from his face.

'I don't think that's what they have in mind.'

As Eldritch digested Aidan's meaning, he wasn't sure whether to be appalled or amazed.

'Are you kidding?' He tried to interject a little reason into the situation. 'But you know who they are.'

'Oh yes.'

'So you'd be able to report them to the police.'

'That won't take away their satisfaction at having kicked my head in.'

'But surely they wouldn't…' Eldritch stopped short, remembering just what Griff and his gang had proven capable of in the past, and amended his words. 'Not in front of witnesses though, surely?'

The eyebrow nearest him quirked upwards.

'Why not? It's our word against theirs as to who started it and in case you haven't noticed we're outnumbered on the witness front – there are three of them. Besides,' Aidan added, the grin disappearing from his voice, 'I don't want you getting involved.'

Eldritch let that last statement slide by him.

'What about CCTV?' he tried.

'In Llancathan? Now you're the one who's joking. There's so little trouble here we still get the local bobby patrolling on foot on a Friday night. They might as well put a camera up in Santa's Grotto – there's more chance of a riot there than there is in Llancathan.'

'But—'

'No buts.'

Finally, Aidan took his eyes off his opponents and looked at Eldritch.

'If anything kicks off, I don't want you in the middle of it.'

His expression was deadly serious. 'Go into the church. If you're worried about your laptop take the bag with you. If not, don't bother, they're not likely to try and take it. Just get inside, tuck yourself down between the pews and stay there; out of sight, out of mind. I don't think they'll bother to try and find you.'

'Three on one isn't good odds,' Eldritch pointed out, his chin coming up stubbornly.

'It's a damn sight better than three onto two when I've got to watch your back as well as my own,' retorted Aidan with brutal honesty. He flicked an appraising eye over Eldritch and shook his head. 'You'd manage to slow Griff down for about as long as it took him to shake your blood off his fist.'

Eldritch flushed angrily.

'I could go back to the takeaway. Get them to ring the police.'

'No.'

Aidan's swift glance took in the few vehicles in the car park, assessing and dismissing them. There was another Land Rover, older than the Red Kite one and looking twice as dilapidated, but while Griff would drive a 4x4 – it was a necessity, not a luxury, for most farmers – his would be a big thug of a car, not a beaten-up work horse. In the same way, it was unlikely that Rod or Alec Owen would be seen dead in either the rusty little Fiesta or the Volvo sporting a collection of stickers proclaiming "I slow down for horses" and "A dog is for life – not just for Christmas", not unless they had adopted them as some form of protective camouflage. He shook his head.

'Once they've finished here they'll head back into town down the footpath. I don't want them tipping you over the churchyard wall just for the fun of it on the way past.'

Eldritch glared at him.

'What about you?' he ground out. The corner of Aidan's mouth quirked into the briefest of smiles.

'Don't worry about me. Things have changed a lot since second year high school. So long as we don't go near any stairs I'll be fine.'

The joke was feeble and Eldritch didn't feel much like laughing. He looked away, his hands clenching impotently by his sides, as he fought to rein back the frustrated anger that would have had him lashing out verbally at Aidan, but his head snapped round when Aidan said quietly, 'Besides it may not come to a fight.'

Aidan regarded Eldritch's shocked expression. 'You seriously think I'm going to fight them?'

'You're not?'

Aidan shook his head, seemingly genuinely surprised that Eldritch would think that of him.

'No, I'm not. Well, not if I can help it. We're going to walk past them, get in the landy and drive off and they can call us all the names under the sun without it making a blind bit of difference.' Aidan said it so confidently that, for a moment, Eldritch was almost prepared to believe it was a possible option. 'Of course, they may have other ideas,' Aidan continued. 'In which case... well, if one of them is daft enough to take a swing at me, he's going to regret it.'

For a moment Aidan's eyes were hard and cold again, but then he turned back to Eldritch with a shrug. 'But it won't be me who starts it.'

There were many things that Eldritch could have said in response, comments about blind optimism and flying pigs came to mind, but he held his tongue. Nothing he could say would change the situation. Aidan filled the silence with a bright, daredevil grin.

'Come on. Let's go see what we can get away with.'

They walked slowly across the tarmac, Aidan keeping his eyes on Griff, but still aware of Rod and Alec moving out to either side. Griff himself made no move; he knew his prey had to come to him. Aidan knew it too. When he was close enough not to have to raise his voice, he stopped and carefully put Eldritch's bag on the floor, flexing his fingers as though he were resting his arm from the weight.

'What do you want, Griff?' he asked, his voice perfectly neutral. A light dew was falling, darkening the tarmac, and the evening air smelled of damp and the evergreens in the churchyard. While he might be capable of fighting, it wasn't something he wanted to do.

Griff pushed himself upright, his face darkening as though he resented Aidan's attempt at reasonable dialogue.

'What I want, Cripple, is some answers. My neighbour had

eight ewes slashed on Saturday night. I want to hear what you know about it.'

If Aidan was surprised by the question, he kept it from his voice.

'Only what's in the paper and a lot less than you from the sound of it,' he replied evenly.

The answer seemed to annoy Griff. His chin came down, tucking into his neck like a prize fighter's and he jerked forward a step, stabbing a finger towards Aidan.

'Don't you lie to me. Where were you on Saturday night?'

Aidan took a deep breath. He guessed 'That's none of your business' wasn't the answer Griff was looking for but he said it anyway. He wasn't naïve enough to think that meekly submitting to the interrogation would change Griff's mind if he had already decided he wanted a brawl.

'Your car wasn't outside your house,' Griff challenged again, almost as though Aidan's response hadn't quite registered.

'So what?'

'So what were you doing? Holding 'em for Pretty Boy there to bugger?'

Eldritch flinched at that, but Aidan had been the butt of so many sheep appreciation jokes over the years that the crude suggestion left him untouched.

'Yeah, that's right,' he agreed amiably. He made a mental note to introduce Eldritch to Matt and some of his more ribald contributions to the field of farmyard humour.

'So why'd you slash 'em?' Griff's voice was angry and insistent, demanding an answer. His whole body bristled with pent-up aggression, but still he made no move against Aidan. Aidan too was getting irritated, but he kept it from his voice and his posture.

'I didn't. And if the police want to talk to me about it, I'm happy to do so, but I'm not arguing the toss with you.'

He took a good look at Griff and wondered how long the man had been drinking. It wasn't just idle speculation; Aidan was confident his reflexes were faster than Griff's and alcohol would slow the farmer down further. But it would also make him more belligerent and less sensitive to pain, meaning it would take more than a broken nose or bruised ribs to knock sense into him. Well, so be it. It was worth understanding from the start that this was likely to get ugly. He might be an inch or so taller than Griff now, but he was several stone lighter. If an attack did come it would be like standing in the path of a freight train.

Around the car park the first streetlights were beginning to come on, their glow reflecting yellow in the whites of Griff's eyes and giving his skin a sallow, unhealthy cast. At least, Aidan thought, with a surprising degree of charity, he hoped that it was the sodium lights that were responsible. Either that or Griff was heading fast towards liver failure. It was a depressing thing to see in a man less than a year older than himself. Aidan sighed and made his decision. Picking up Eldritch's bag again he turned to walk round the front of the Land Rover.

'Get out of the way, Rod,' he said flatly to the man who stepped up to block his path. He moved confidently as though fully expecting his old classmate to give way and for a moment it seemed he would. Then Griff barked, 'Grab him!' and several things seemed to happen almost at once.

Aidan sidestepped Rod's lunge, dropping Eldritch's bag and the takeaway with equal disregard and wheeling round to give the man a solid kick in the small of the back to help him past.

From the corner of his eye he saw Griff bending to snatch something from beside the Land Rover's front tyre and his blood scalded with adrenalin as he realised exactly what it was. He saw the pickaxe handle coming up and spared the breath to yell, 'Run!' at Eldritch, but didn't dare look to see if he had obeyed as he was already turning to face Griff. At the same time, Rod had regained his balance and was turning back towards him while Alec, always the slower of the two brothers, had unfrozen and was charging at him from the other side. It was Sunday's training session all over again, but this time with weapons and malice.

Aidan gathered himself for the onslaught, poised and ready to turn, to block, to fight. Except that none of the three reached him. He felt the air crackle with power and knew in that instant that Eldritch hadn't run. Against all his training, he cast a horrified glance over his shoulder and saw Eldritch, white-faced and wild-eyed, raising his right hand. The world seemed to freeze. Aidan shouted, 'No!' not so much because he cared about the others but because he did care what would happen to Eldritch if they died in a welter of Levin fire. Then Griff screamed and dropped the pickaxe handle as though it had become red hot. He stared at his hand in horror and then cried out again, clutching at his stomach as his knees buckled. Rod was also staggering while Alec clung to the side of the Land Rover, his face white and terrified. Eldritch stepped forward.

'Run!' he commanded, in a voice like Lucifer's, devoid of compassion or mercy. 'Run before I choose to make this permanent.'

His eyes swept the three men, raking them like fire and Alec whimpered and then turned and ran. A second passed and Rod bolted after him. Only Griff remained, still on his knees like a reluctant penitent, his eyes feral with hatred and fear. Spittle gathered at the corners of his lips as his mouth worked convulsively but no sound came save for the heavy rasp of his breathing. Eldritch raised his hand again and Griff crumpled forward, his scream ringing out across the car park.

'That's enough!'

Aidan stepped between his friend and his enemy and anger flamed in his voice.

'Stop it or you're as bad as he is.'

He turned to Griff, but if he expected thanks none were forthcoming. As the farmer slowly straightened from all fours to kneeling he looked up at his ex-classmate with a depth of hatred in his eyes that stopped Aidan in his tracks and held him there, rigid. Eldritch had hurt Griff and the floored man would pay the Englishman back tenfold should he ever get the chance, but nothing could balance the account for what Aidan had just done. Aidan had shown him mercy and that was unforgivable.

A tiny, barely heard sound behind him snapped Aidan from that strange, wordless communion. He dipped his head in the briefest of bows, acknowledging the raising of the stakes between him and Griff, then he turned back to Eldritch, still edgy with adrenalin and ready for further confrontation. But the sight that greeted him wiped his anger away. He had seen this before. Not with karate; though there was adrenalin aplenty in tournaments, they were too well regimented for there to be any visceral sense of danger and since school he had never been involved in a fight outside a dojo. Instead it had been on a climb out of Llanberis, when a missed handhold and a cam failure had resulted in a sixty foot drop before the second anchor point had held and arrested the lead climber's fall. Shaken, but essentially unhurt, Ben had gathered himself together and re-climbed the section as confidently as if he had been velcroed to the rock and the group had finished the climb uneventfully, trading the lead between them and pausing at the top for energy bars and a chance to admire the views out over the Menai Strait before reversing their route back down. But back at the cars, as they stripped off their harnesses, joking and swearing and re-living each handhold of the climb, Ben had looked at his rack of camming devices and wires and had sat down suddenly beside the rope bags, trembling uncontrollably as the reaction finally hit him. So it was now with Eldritch.

The tall man stood with his arms wrapped around his chest as though assailed by sudden cold, his long body wracked by shuddering. Ashen-faced, he looked sick and dazed and not just a little frightened.

'Whoa there!'

Aidan grabbed him, scared he would fall without support, and pulled him close, talking to him as he might to one of the club juniors.

'Easy Tiger, the fight's over now.'

The feel of the body shivering convulsively under his hands made him consider briefly whether his own calmness wasn't the more unnatural of their two responses. It occurred to him, somewhat belatedly, that it might be quite reasonable for someone to be scared rigid in the face of impending violence – even someone who habitually dealt with demons and avatars and the Lord knew what other nightmare creatures.

The physical contact seemed to reach Eldritch in a way that Aidan's voice alone hadn't. Slowly the shaking subsided and the grey eyes focussed once more, turning to him in confusion.

'Aidan?'

The voice had lost its satanic overtones. It was his friend's again but blurred around the edges as though it had travelled untold distances to reach him.

'Are you okay?'

Eldritch's hands came up, grasping Aidan's arms as if seeking reassurance.

'Am I okay?' Aidan wasn't sure whether to laugh or cry. 'I'm fine. We're both fine,' he stressed, having the sense to keep the proviso, *in so far as neither of us has been worked over with a pickaxe handle*, purely within his head. He took another look at Eldritch's eyes, decided they really were focussing now and released him. The wizard shook his head slowly like a man stepping out of a dream.

'When he picked up that baseball bat...'

It was a statement that would be equally offensive to American sports fans and Irish navvies the world over – *quite an achievement*, thought Aidan, *even for an Englishman* – but Eldritch was oblivious to his mistake and Aidan didn't bother to correct him.

'I thought...' Eldritch stumbled over the words. 'I wanted to...'

He was unable to bring himself to say any more. Shame brought the first flush of colour back to his cheeks and he looked away, no longer able to meet Aidan's gaze. Aidan thought he understood.

'You think I'm going to bawl you out because I'd told you not to get involved? Because you stepped in when you saw someone about to go for my head with a pick-handle and now you think maybe you overreacted?'

Eldritch shook his head. 'No. It's not that,' he protested, his voice sounding deeply unhappy. 'It's…'

He stopped again and Aidan could almost see the mental gears shifting as he changed his mind about what he would say next. Finally, Eldritch shook his head. 'It doesn't matter what I thought,' he said wearily.

'You idiot.'

There was amused affection in Aidan's voice. If Eldritch had been one of the karate regulars he would have accompanied the words with a cuff round the head or a mock punch or two, just to show he was joking, but he didn't think the tall man would understand that as a gesture of camaraderie so he settled for a grin instead.

'When I said I didn't want you getting involved I was talking physically. It never crossed my mind that you could wade in magically. What the hell did you do, anyway? I didn't think you had enough energy left to turn on a light bulb.'

He hadn't missed how easily Eldritch had fallen asleep in the takeaway. At the time he had found it amusing. Now he berated himself for not being more concerned. Eldritch drew himself up, rubbing a hand across his face as though wiping away the last cobwebs of a dream.

'I threw pain.'

He managed to avoid looking at Aidan's face as he said it.

'You did what?'

The comment made no sense to Aidan.

'I didn't have the strength for a Levin bolt so I threw pain at them.' Eldritch sounded almost sheepish. 'It's sort of the same thing, but it's more mental than physical.'

Aidan eyed him suspiciously.

'Let me get this straight. You can make people think they're in pain when they're not?'

'Well, yes. I mean the pain's real enough, but it's in their mind, not their body. They're not actually hurt.'

The implication of that hit Aidan.

'Christ!'

He wheeled round, but Griff was gone. He turned back to Eldritch breathing heavily.

'It might have been useful to have known that last piece of information a bit sooner,' he said, but it was more a comment to himself than a criticism of Eldritch. He was the one who had turned his back on an opponent. If he had ended up wearing a pickaxe handle through his head as a result it wouldn't have been the wizard's fault.

'So Gwyn can take pain away and you can give it to people?'

Aidan shook his head in mild disbelief. The world was getting stranger by the day. 'You make a fine pair.'

Eldritch shrugged noncommittally and immediately looked as though he wished he hadn't. Aidan took hold of his arm and firmly steered him round to the other side of the car.

'Tell you what,' he suggested, as he unlocked the passenger door – like Llancathan and its lack of CCTV cameras, Aidan's vehicle harked back to bygone times – central locking had yet to be thought of when it rolled off the production line. 'Let's not tell Gwyn about any of this.'

Eldritch offered no resistance as Aidan ushered him firmly into the haven of the Land Rover's passenger seat. The deep body tremors had ceased, but he still felt shaky and he was grateful for the opportunity to sit quietly and do nothing while Aidan retrieved his bag and the takeaway. Wearily he let his head drop back against the headrest and closed his eyes. He knew, and Aidan must have guessed, that this was partly a reaction to using his power again. He was still a long way from being fully recovered and it had hurt to use the energy channels he had overstretched on Saturday. But there was something else. Something he had stopped short of sharing with Aidan, something he hardly dared acknowledge to himself. For a few seconds, as the power burst from him, he had genuinely wanted to hurt Griff and the two brothers. Not just that, but he had wanted to feel them squirm and beg him for mercy, grovelling at his feet and promising him their very souls if that was what it took to buy his favour and then to feel their blood bursting from between his fingers as he crushed their throats. Unnoticed, Eldritch's hands twisted into fists in his lap at the violence of the memory. Had he listened to that strange siren voice in the back of his head, he knew he would have killed them, ripping them apart with his power – even if it had killed him in the process. And if it hadn't, the carnage wouldn't have stopped there. In the depths of his soul he knew he would have turned on Aidan next. Eldritch clenched his fists tighter, his knuckles whitening, as a single shudder wracked his body at the thought. He felt sickened and degraded – defiled even – by the thoughts and the emotions that had seethed through him when he had reached for his power. But the worst thing, the thing that ran like ice through the marrow of his bones and turned his heart to ashes, was that part of him felt excited.

CHAPTER 4

When she opened the door, Gwyn took one look at their faces and asked in a resigned tone, 'Who's going to tell me what happened this time?'

Aidan and Eldritch exchanged glances; so much for secrecy.

'We ran into an old school friend of Aidan's.'

'Griff Howell,' Aidan expanded. 'Complete with Rod and Alec Owen, naturally.'

Gwyn's face tightened at the names.

'They seemed keen on a rather more physical reunion than most,' Eldritch continued.

Gwyn glanced pointedly at Aidan's knuckles.

'You didn't?'

'No, I didn't,' he responded indignantly, managing to inject just the right level of hurt into his voice as if to ask how she could possibly think such a thing of him. Then he grinned maliciously and jerked his head at Eldritch. 'He did.'

Gwyn's back stiffened and she turned on Eldritch, but whatever version of "you should know better" she had been about to reproach him with died unspoken as she got a good look at him. She settled instead for narrowed eyes and a toss of the head.

'You two aren't safe to be let out on your own,' she declared, making it sound as though they were two schoolboys caught scrumping.

'Hey, we didn't start it,' protested Aidan, determined to defend their innocence. 'And besides, there were three of them, plus a pickaxe handle.'

Gwyn gave him a quelling look and then, lest he think she had forgotten his part in the escapade, she turned back to Eldritch.

'Dare I ask what you did?'

'I threw pain. As far as Griff was concerned he had a sudden attack of appendicitis. Likewise his two friends.'

Gwyn pursed her lips and considered this. It seemed she was no stranger to the concept for she asked none of the questions that Aidan had raised. At length she smiled grimly and there was a certain satisfaction in her voice as she said, 'I can't think of anyone who'd deserve it more.'

She looked more closely at Eldritch, her expression changing as she tilted her head to one side, examining him like a curious bird. 'You weren't really in a fit state to do that much, were you?' She shook her head and sighed. 'You'd better have some painkillers now and I'll do some more healing with you later, when you're ready for bed.'

From somewhere Eldritch managed to conjure a wolfish grin.

'Life gets better and better,' he said, putting away his tiredness and leering suggestively. 'Do I get a goodnight kiss as well?'

'You'll get a crack round the head with a goodnight cup of cocoa if you're not careful,' Gwyn muttered, slapping him down. Then her expression softened. 'Thanks for looking out for him,' she added.

It was a strange council of war. They sat at the kitchen table — that being the only place all three of them could sit — with the plates piled in the sink and a faint smell of curry hanging in the air and Eldritch's Ordnance Survey map spread on the table between them. Kali curled in Eldritch's lap, much to the wizard's bemusement, while Yard Away Cat sat like an Egyptian statue by the back door.

'So, we still need to find out where the demon's manifesting.' Gwyn laid the problem in front of them, tactfully avoiding any explicit suggestion of time having been wasted since she and Eldritch had first reviewed the situation. The tall man nodded in silent agreement, leaning an elbow on the table and cupping his chin in his palm as he surveyed the map bleakly. On his lap Kali started purring as he absently stroked the soft fur behind her ears.

'I don't understand why it's not broken through yet,' he confessed, puzzlement drawing his dark brows down as he looked at the evidence outlined on the map. Opposite him, Gwyn gave him a basilisk glare.

'Thank all that's merciful that it hasn't,' she retorted, as though she had heard in his words a desire for that manifestation to take place. Eldritch glanced up at the sharpness in her voice, but reacted with nothing more than a rueful smile.

'Tell me about it,' he agreed. 'And yet we know that it's gathering power through the avatar.' His smile faded, his face turning thoughtful. 'It's almost as though something is preventing it.'

He gave a small lopsided shrug, acknowledging Gwyn's raised eyebrows and her unvoiced scepticism at the idea.

'No, I don't see what could be doing that either. It was just a thought.'

He shook his head, dismissing the possibility and returned to those things they could be sure of.

'These are the incidents I know of.'

Long fingers swept over the scattering of neat red crosses that covered the map. They spilled out northwards across the forestry lands bordering the reservoir and southeast to the hill pastures around Tair Fferm. Gwyn nodded, having seen this once before, but Aidan stared at the map in appalled fascination.

'So many,' his voice came out as a shocked whisper. 'I had no idea.'

'There's no reason why you would. Not unless you made a point of recording them. Spread over twenty-six years – and that's pretty much how long this has been going on – you wouldn't see a pattern. Accidents happen all the time and even with a local legend there's not many people will attribute them to a supernatural cause, not seriously anyway.'

'You should have heard some of the old biddies at John's funeral,' Aidan commented sourly, remembering the two carrion crows he had encountered, but Eldritch shook his head, unconvinced.

'People say all sorts of things without necessarily believing half of them.'

'It's best that they don't,' Gwyn interjected softly. 'Everyone loves a ghost story, but it's the fact that they're fantasy that makes them enjoyable. It's alright to be scared because it's not real, it's not dangerous. If they knew the truth,' she indicated the map with its scattered crosses like so many grave markers, 'they'd be terrified.'

Aidan looked again at the map, this time paying more attention to the grouping of the crosses. Eldritch said they were all connected with the demon, but there was no obvious pattern, no clear epicentre of events that screamed out that this was where the manifestation would happen and, while on paper the area they covered might seem quite small, in reality it was depressingly large. Not only that but much of it was rough terrain, forest and upland pastures that were fit for sure-footed sheep but not so great for people to search over, even if it was clear what they were looking for.

'Talk about a needle in a haystack,' he growled, frustration spilling over into his voice. It wasn't that he had expected a grid reference, but somehow he had imagined they would have a clearer picture than this. All his experience of search and rescue told him they faced a nearly impossible task.

He turned back to Eldritch, sat at the head of the table like a particularly rough-looking refugee in his obviously borrowed clothes and three days of stubble that was fast reaching the point where it would have to be called a beard. He wouldn't want to bet which Eldritch would be more relieved to unpack; his own clothes or his razor.

'So if this is all you had to go on when you went after the demon on Saturday what the hell made you so certain you were going to find it?'

He had meant his words as a question rather than an accusation of incompetence, but when he saw Eldritch's expression harden he knew that that was how they had been taken. He could almost see the walls going up behind the other man's eyes.

'I wasn't. But this was the best information I had and given that the demon's influence had already led to at least four suicides that I could trace — five if you count Thom Hughes, although I think he killed himself when he realised what the demon had made him do to his family – I didn't feel I could wait to find out more.'

The glacial gaze flicked across to encompass Gwyn.

'I still don't,' he said and now there was a note of challenge in his voice. 'With that sort of power it won't be long before it manages to summon someone to it, someone it can take as a host. Anyway, it worked. I found the avatar.'

'I think the avatar found you,' Gwyn commented. Her voice was a careful study in neutrality, almost pointedly so, and perhaps it was that very lack of intonation that Eldritch took offence at for he stiffened and Aidan felt the palpable increase in tension. He raised his hands as though he would physically separate them.

'Okay, let's not get bogged down with semantics. At the very least we have two more encounters we can add,' he said, doing his best to find something positive to focus on before Gwyn and Eldritch went for each other's throats.

'We know the avatar was here at the hut.'

He put a finger on the map.

'And we know where you fought it.' He caught the look on Eldritch's face and swallowed a sigh. 'Don't tell me; there weren't any street signs.'

On the other side of the table Gwyn had the grace to cover what might have been an unhelpful snort with a cough.

'I headed northwest from the bird of prey centre car park,' Eldritch said precisely. 'I'd been walking for half an hour, maybe slightly less when I found the avatar.'

There was just the slightest emphasis on those last words.

'Hmm.'

Aidan concentrated on studying the contour lines, choosing to let the emphasis pass him by unremarked. Wonder of wonders, so did Gwyn.

'Over that kind of terrain you wouldn't have gone much more than a mile, a mile and a quarter at the outside, so it must have been somewhere around here.' He tapped the map. 'Thanks,' he added as Gwyn marked the points with two neat crosses. The three of them leaned forward to survey the results.

'It doesn't help much, does it?' Aidan conceded. 'Is there nothing else we could look for that would help us find it? I mean, what causes a demon to break through into this world anyway?'

He looked at his companions. Gwyn in turn looked at Eldritch, silently deferring to him. The wizard eyed her suspiciously as though he suspected her of mocking him, but then he sighed, perhaps remembering that he was amongst friends.

'Demons awaken when the boundaries of their realm are broken or disturbed,' Eldritch said slowly. 'But you need to understand that the Unseen Realm links to our own Mortal World in many ways. Some of those boundaries are physical and when the elements they're made of are broken or changed – a tree chopped down, a river dammed – the boundary may thin to the point where a demon or some other creature is free to come through. Other borders are defined by a moment, a point of change; the change between one season and the next, between morning and night... at those times the border between the two worlds grows thin and at certain times it becomes thinner than at others. The passing of the old year into the new at the end of October – I'm talking about the old calendar now – is still understood as a time of thinning, even by those who would deny any such beliefs. At times like that if the right things are done then it's possible to move from one world to the next. It has been known for people to do it purely by accident. Sometimes it happens from the other side as well.'

He rubbed a hand over the back of his neck.

'In this case I think it must have been a physical change that weakened the boundary. Otherwise all the incidents would have happened at the same time of year.'

'But if the Black Dog's been around for years and that's how long the demon's been waking then we're looking for something that changed over a quarter of a century ago! What use is that? I wasn't even born then.' Aidan threw his hands up in frustration. 'So, what do we do? Wander round the hills and hope it will turn up again?'

Eldritch didn't answer immediately. He steepled his hands together in front of his chin and looked across the table at Gwyn. She shook her head, her expression troubled.

'I don't think this is a good idea. It's too soon.'

When Eldritch made no response, she added, 'You said as much yourself.'

'Look at the map.' Eldritch's gesture encompassed the scatter of crosses as though they were all the argument he needed. 'What choice do we have?'

'There's always a choice,' Gwyn insisted.

'Not in this there isn't.'

Eldritch shook his head, his long hair flicking across his face, like the mane of a wild horse. He pushed it back irritably, his eyes never leaving Gwyn's.

'Not for me. Look at them. Every one of those crosses

marks a tragedy; a maiming, a killing, a suicide. And with every one of them the demon has grown stronger. Each time what it did next was that little bit worse. Its last victim was a young man with no conceivable reason for taking his own life. I don't know why it's not manifested yet, but I do know that when it does – when it takes a host – we've lost it. And all those ruined lives are going to be as nothing compared to what happens next.'

He exhaled, a weary, bitter sound, and when he spoke again there was a note of reproach in his voice as though he felt Gwyn's opposition was a personal betrayal, one that he couldn't quite understand.

'You know that too.'

Gwyn said nothing, but her lips narrowed dangerously.

'We have to do something.'

'You're not up to it.'

Their words clashed across each other like rapiers and for a moment Gwyn and Eldritch glared at each other across the table. If the wizard's eyes were as cold and desolate as the Atlantic then hers were the unyielding emerald of the Arctic pack ice. Neither seemed likely to back down.

Watching the exchange with some bemusement, Aidan wondered if stubbornness had been declared a competitive sport. Not only did he guess that this "yes, I can", "no you can't" argument could continue for some time but from the tension sparking between Gwyn and Eldritch he feared it was quickly going to become very personal. Yet he could see quite clearly what presumably the two protagonists could not; that Gwyn wasn't being deliberately contrary – she was genuinely concerned for Eldritch's safety – and that Eldritch, though convinced of the need for whatever course of action he had decided upon, was scarcely more comfortable with the risks than she was. Whatever it was that his friends were arguing over – and yes, Aidan realised that somehow in the last forty-eight hours he had come to count both the fierce-tempered witch and the insular wizard as friends – it worried him greatly that both of them were afraid of it.

'Would one of you tell me what the hell it is we're talking about?' he interjected, the prickly sense of unease adding a sharpness to his tone. 'We're all on the same side here. Let's try to remember that, shall we?'

Gwyn huffed as though she might disagree with that statement, but said nothing, crossing her arms and shifting back in her chair as if distancing herself from the conversation. In the small room her very silence was like a challenge – *say it then and be damned*. Looking from her to Eldritch and at the stubborn anger suffusing his face, Aidan thought there was a lot the wizard might like to say, but for once he opted for discretion. When he did speak his voice was surprisingly calm.

'We don't have to go wandering the hillsides now; we can do better than that. Since the fight with the avatar I've been able to hear the demon. I think I can use that to find where it's breaking through.'

A stillness seemed to settle over the room at his words, as though everyone in it was collectively holding their breath.

'What do you mean, "hear the demon"?' The skin between Aidan's shoulder blades crawled with a deep sense of unease. 'You mean there's a voice in your head that's talking to you?' Unconsciously he drew back, away from the wizard.

'No!' Eldritch's denial was immediate, his eyes flaring wide as though the idea both frightened and revolted him. He swallowed convulsively, and then seemed to gather himself.

'No,' he repeated, his voice calm again. 'It's not like that, it's…'

He stopped, gestured vaguely like a man groping for the right words.

'It's not words precisely, it's more like emotions.'

'Like throwing pain?'

Aidan had meant it as a joke – a half-teasing reference to their earlier conversation – as much to cover his own apprehension as anything, but for a second the horror was back in Eldritch's eyes. Then he laughed shakily.

'Something like that,' he conceded, but he looked away, not meeting Aidan's gaze.

'You'll need to work from a circle.'

As if she had never opposed the idea, Gwyn's tone was brisk and practical. Eldritch swung round to face her.

'Does that mean you'll help me?'

'Did you really think I'd leave you to do something this crazy on your own?'

When Eldritch didn't answer she snorted.

'Oh, for goodness' sake! I may not like the idea but I can see you're not going to be talked out of it. Better that I help now than I end up having to pick up the pieces when it all goes pear-shaped.'

Gwyn's tone was caustic but from long familiarity Aidan judged there was no real heat behind the words. Perhaps Eldritch understood that too for there was the hint of a smile in his response though he did his best to hide it.

'Thank you.'

'Huh, you can thank me later when you've tried this ridiculous stunt.'

'Let me get this straight,' for his own clarification Aidan waded back into the conversation. 'You're going to try and find the demon based on where your sense of it is the strongest?'

'That's the idea, yes.'

'Okay.'

He considered this, deliberately putting to one side any questions of what such sensing might entail. He didn't understand the arcane details – to be honest he wasn't entirely sure he wanted to – but the idea of using that sense as a means of locating the demon? As far as he could see that was essentially no different from getting a fix on a locator beacon in order to find a lost climber. And that was something he did know about.

'You realise you'll need to do this… whatever it is you're going to do, from several places in order to pinpoint a location, otherwise all you've got is a direction to walk in. Even then you're likely to end up with an area of probability rather than an exact spot.

'I'm guessing that, however good your radar is, it's not going to be absolutely accurate and the difference of a degree or two could leave you half a mile away from where you need to be.'

He placed his hands on the map, fingers touching in a V.

'Instead of your lines intersecting here, if you change the angles even slightly,' he moved his hands to demonstrate, 'then they're meeting up over here instead. You're in the right area, but you're still going to end up searching. The only way round it is to take repeat bearings; the more you do the smaller the area where they all overlap. That will give you the best chance.'

'Unfortunately, that gives us a problem.' Though she spoke

quietly, Gwyn's tone brooked no argument. 'I understand what you're saying, Aidan, but this isn't something we want to be doing multiple times.

'I'm not thinking so much of the physical stress,' she added, quashing Eldritch's protest before he had a chance to voice it, 'although it's something to be borne in mind. What we don't want to do is risk alerting the demon to what we're up to. Even working from within a circle, the more times we do this the more chance there is that it will sense us.'

'What happens then?'

'Who knows? Maybe nothing.' Though his words were accompanied by a casual shrug, the vertical frown line pinching the skin between Eldritch's brows gave lie to that verbal bravado. 'Then again maybe it sends the avatar against us. Circle or no circle, that's not going to be pleasant, as you well know.'

'Nice.'

Aidan tried to ignore the sudden sick feeling in the pit of his stomach. 'Okay, I can see why that might not be a great idea, but it doesn't change the fact that you need a minimum of two readings. Like I said, without that all you've got is a direction to walk in.'

There was silence as Gwyn and Eldritch digested this information and its possible consequences.

'This afternoon, when I realised I could hear the demon I was in the garden here. It was definitely coming from down the valley.'

'Down the valley's not a terribly precise direction,' Aidan pointed out. 'That variation of one or two degrees? It makes a huge difference, remember.'

Eldritch gave him a tight smile that suggested he had thought as much.

'It was just a suggestion.'

'Don't dismiss it just yet.'

Surprised, both Aidan and Eldritch turned to look at Gwyn. Drawing her feet up she tucked her chin onto her knees and regarded them speculatively.

'You weren't looking straight down the valley,' she said. 'You were to start with, yes. But as you spoke of hearing the demon, you turned.'

She paused, examining the image in her mind; the tall man standing in her garden in his borrowed clothes, the autumn sun bright on his face and whispers of madness swirling round his brain.

'As you connected with it, you changed; your voice, your posture, everything. And you turned.'

She turned her own head in a slow, precise sweep to demonstrate.

'You locked onto it and when you did you were facing the Lady Stone.'

'The Lady Stone?' Eldritch queried. He shot Gwyn a sceptical look, but it was Aidan who nodded.

'The Lady Stone. Up on the far side of the valley, it's a big chunk of rock standing out on its own.' The smile that had been lurking in his voice spread to the corners of his lips, quirking them up into a wry grin. 'When I was a kid, Gwyn used to tell me stories about how Lady Alwyn would meet there with her witches and they'd sit up all night and watch the stars. The stories changed over the years; it was a look-out point, a hiding place, the back of a troll caught out by the dawn; all sorts of things but somehow the name's always stuck.'

He turned to Gwyn, his eyes still dancing with memories, but his voice was serious.

'Are you sure?'

'Oh yes.'

Under the sleeves of her shirt, her skin prickled at the recollection and she shivered, running her hands over her arms. 'I'm sure.'

'Okay, so if you show me exactly where you were standing we can take a compass reading, but for now this is roughly what you're looking at.'

Using the edge of the breadboard as a ruler, Aidan drew a line across the map from the tiny grey square marking the cottage to the little curled symbol denoting an outcropping of rock, and beyond.

'That's your first bearing. Your second needs to be taken from one side or the other of that line.'

'Could we use the hut?'

Aidan was a little surprised by Gwyn's request, but he shrugged.

'Sure. It's far enough off the line that you should get a decent triangulation. Any particular reason why?' He was afraid it would be something to do with the avatar's presence there.

'I'd prefer somewhere private for what we're going to do.'

'You're not planning to work skyclad, are you?' Eldritch interrupted with a leer.

Gwyn rolled her eyes.

'No and I hope you don't intend to either.'

'That's another of my illusions shattered.' With a regretful shake of his head Eldritch turned to Aidan who had watched the exchange with bemusement. 'Private's best so we won't be disturbed. The last thing we need is to have a stray hiker tripping over the circle. And of course,' he added with typical gallows humour, 'if things go wrong and the avatar does show up, having four solid walls around us is a definite plus.'

'I plan to use incense when I cast the circle,' Gwyn stated. 'Scent is a good way of marking the boundaries. It's the oldest sense, the strongest sense, to bring you home if you stray.'

At Eldritch's quizzical look, she went on. 'If there's a chance we're going to have to search for the manifestation site you might want to try scrying for any details you can pick up.'

'Scrying for a demon? I'd have thought you'd consider that far too dangerous.'

'I do, but it will be a lot less dangerous doing it from a circle than trying it on the fly in the woods when we're looking for the site and we realise we can't find it.' She regarded the wizard balefully from across the table. 'And don't tell me you wouldn't try it because I know you would.'

Initially, Aidan was content to sit on the sidelines of the conversation, amused to listen to Gwyn and Eldritch's verbal sparring. It was giving him a whole new perspective on his former guardian. But as the details they were discussing grew increasingly arcane, he lost interest. With nothing to add he got up, prepared to do his bit for the joint cause by washing the dishes, but as he collected together the debris of empty cartons he saw the newspaper he had picked up at the takeaway.

'There's something I meant to ask you about.'

He opened the paper and spread it on the table between Gwyn and Eldritch.

'There were eight sheep butchered on Tom Owen's farm at some time on Saturday night. Would that explain how the demon got the power to re-manifest the avatar?'

'Sweet Lady!' Gwyn's hand went to the string of turquoise beads encircling her throat. Eldritch's curse was less delicate.

'That would probably do it,' he said grimly. A thought struck him. 'This is what Griff was asking you about, isn't it?'

'Yes. His house is on the lane leading down to Tom Owen's farm. It says in the article he told police he'd heard a vehicle late on Saturday night, but hadn't thought anything of it at the time.'

'And he seriously thinks you could have done it?'

'No, I think that was just a good excuse to have a go. Not that he's ever needed one, but any farmer – even Griff – is going to go a bit crazy over something like this, especially when it happened almost in his backyard.'

'It's a shame he didn't get it together to go out and look when he heard the car,' Eldritch said sourly. 'It would have saved us a run in with the avatar.'

Unconsciously he rubbed a hand over his shoulder.

'So now we know for sure that someone's far enough under the demon's influence to be feeding it power. That settles it. We have to find out where it's manifesting.' He flicked a wry smile towards Gwyn. 'Best bring plenty of incense. It seems we're going scrying for the demon after all.'

CHAPTER 5

'Are you ready for this?' Gwyn looked at the man sitting opposite her, cross-legged, his hands resting lightly on his knees, the palms upturned and open. His face was calm, but she could see the long body was strung with tension, like a drawn bow. To her left she was conscious of Aidan, sat similarly cross-legged, his expression watchful. He had some inkling of what they would attempt here, she had briefed him carefully on his role, but he could only begin to guess the dangers that awaited them if this went awry.

'You know what I said about trusting you with my life?'

Eldritch's grey eyes sought hers, his voice a soft thread of sound against the silence of the hut.

'I said I hoped it wouldn't come to that,' she replied, remembering all too vividly his torn and battered body sprawled across her lounge floor. His life had lain in her hands then whether he willed it or not, but today he was placing it there deliberately. She would have reached out and touched his wrist, offering reassurance, but such a gesture carried with it the implication of weakness, perhaps even of fear that he was unequal to the task ahead, and Gwyn knew better than to bring even the suggestion of such things into a circle, no matter how innocent the intent.

'I think it just has.'

He managed a grin for her, but it did not reach his eyes.

For all his bravado, she could tell that Marcus Eldritch was scared. He had been joking in the car, throwing up a smokescreen of wry humour. The wisecrack comments had come thick and fast to start with, but as the forest closed in around them the humour had faded and died. In its place had come an odd, unholy enthusiasm for the venture that she did not like but suspected was just another way of covering his unease, like a coward's bullying bluster. Not that she thought he was a coward; just someone who knew – better than most – what could happen if this went wrong.

Even that had left him as they came to the hut and he had sat in silence, watching as she went round the cabin, sweeping the floor, gathering up the little smudges of sulphur and salt and the small black disc of obsidian discarded against one wall, obliterating the smeared blood with salt water. Then she had ritually cleansed the space with incense and fire. The room smelled of it now, of amber and herbs, rose petals and sandalwood, ground together and carried burning around the room. Mingled with that pungency was the sweetness of lavender and beeswax – her smells, her grounding – for more than anyone else's, it would be her strength that kept them safe this afternoon.

She and Eldritch had talked at length about how they would do this. Long after Aidan had gone home they had continued debating the risks back and forth between them, considering their choices until even the seriousness of what they discussed could not keep Eldritch's eyelids from drooping. They had spoken more as she sat in the chair by his bed, her hands stretched over his chest, scarcely an inch away from the warmth of his skin, channelling strength and healing into his bones.

'Are we crazy to be doing this?'

Eldritch's eyes had been dark and heavy with sleep, but his voice was restless even as he sank towards oblivion and she heard the uneasiness he had kept from it earlier.

'Perhaps,' she conceded. 'But you said yourself that it has to be done and, much though I hate to agree with you,' she treated him to a smile that was positively impish, 'I do think you're right. The situation with the demon is only going to get worse and the longer we leave it the more dangerous this is going to be. So we'll do this together and we'll take every precaution we can.'

He turned his head to look at her through slowly closing eyes and she felt the warmth of his breath on her fingers.

'Thank you.'

'So.' Gwyn exhaled all extraneous thoughts along with that breath, turning her mind to harmony and calling into being the circle of light she had woven around them.

'Gatherer of Souls, Watcher on the far horizon…'

As she began her invocation, she felt the energies in the room change, her own small powers rising to meet and merge with that which was beyond her simple human frame. She reached out, sending her words and her intention out into the world, placing the three of them and the circle she had wrought in that greater protection. The whispered echo of amen came back to her from Aidan and Eldritch as she completed her prayer and brought her awareness back fully within the circle.

For a moment Eldritch's eyes linked with hers, but she could not have said what emotions lurked in their grey depths. Then he nodded, the slight movement breaking that link, and his lids slid closed. Like her he had the discipline to pass into trance in a matter of heartbeats. Without need for ritual or relaxation, it took no more than a measured exhalation of breath and he was there on its borders. Now she watched the tension ease from his body, his breathing lengthening, his pale face grown motionless and blank, as he sank deeper, awaiting her instruction. His life was in her hands indeed.

'Eldritch.'

There was no visible change in his body, but she felt his attention turn to her as she spoke his name, like the pricking of a hound's ears at the far off sound of a war horn.

'You know that you are here, safe and grounded within this circle of my making.'

The subtlest feeling of assent came from him and Gwyn felt a small smile tug at the corner of her lips. Agreement between her and the wizard was a rare enough thing that she held it in her mind for a moment like a luck token, a good omen that they were starting in accord on this. Letting a little of that smile warm her voice, Gwyn continued.

'I want you to take a moment now to sense its boundaries. I have wrought them about you with candle flame and fire, laid them out in smoke and incense. I have marked them with the scents of sandalwood and lavender, rose and amber so that you can know this as a place of sanctuary, of peace and safety. No harm can befall you here.'

In that, at least, Gwyn was confident. It was what might happen to Eldritch as he searched beyond the circle that worried her, but she had no power to influence that so reluctantly she consigned it into the hands of the Lady and resigned herself to leaving it there. Around her she was aware of the web of Eldritch's senses spreading out into the circle, familiarising himself with it on a psychic level, grounding himself for the search. They brushed lightly against the edge of her own aura, like a cat making its presence felt, and she felt a twinge of amusement as she realised that, for all his earlier apprehension, Eldritch was keen to begin.

'Very well then.'

Gwyn focussed her attention once more on Eldritch's mortal form, taking in the slow rise and fall of his chest, the peaceful stillness of his face.

'As you sit here within this circle, I want you to become aware of all the different sounds you can hear. As you listen to them you can begin to pick out the sound of the demon in your head. I want you to focus on that now.'

She watched carefully, but there was no change in the regular measure of his breathing, no sign of distress and she wondered briefly if her circle had isolated him from that uncanny link.

'Nod your head when you can hear it.'

Very precisely the dark head dipped and Gwyn felt a little thrill of relief. She had no desire to try this without the protection of a circle, but she knew that was what Eldritch would propose if this didn't work.

'Good. Now concentrate on your awareness of the demon. Focus on it and sense which direction it is coming from.'

Gwyn held her breath as Eldritch's head swung slowly from side to side as though he were trying to pinpoint the source of an audible sound. Then he stopped, as if his attention had been caught by something over her left shoulder. Gwyn resisted the urge to turn and look, knowing there would be nothing there for her to see, but from the corner of her eye she saw Aidan glance sharply in that direction before turning his focus back to her and Eldritch.

'Are you certain you know which direction your sense of the demon is coming from?'

Eyes still closed, Eldritch nodded again. Had he been awake he would have scowled and no doubt accused her of doubting him, but in his state of trance he was content to do as she wished.

'Then point to where that is.'

Slowly Eldritch's right arm rose, as if pulled by an invisible string fixed to his wrist. The hand hung limp until the arm reached shoulder height and then the wrist slowly straightened until his long fingers were pointing into the distance. Aidan noted the bearing on his compass and then leaned forward and drew a chalk line on the floor. Only once he had signalled to her that he was satisfied did Gwyn tell the wizard to put his arm down, watching as his hand sank back to rest on his knee as though he were a marionette under her control. That was the straightforward part of what they had set out to do. Now came the difficult part: using Eldritch's link to the demon to find out more about where it was breaking through.

Though the search had been Eldritch's idea, Gwyn was very aware that it would be her command that sent his spirit questing into the darkness. She felt the weight of that responsibility take hold of her, remembering how shaken he had been after making contact with the demon's thoughts the previous afternoon. Theoretically it was her choice now whether or not they continued and yet, in reality, she knew there was no choice at all. Eldritch had asked for her help, but not having it wouldn't be enough to stop him. If they didn't do this now then sooner or later he would try it on his own and that wasn't something that Gwyn wanted on her conscience. She huffed out a breath, half in annoyance, half in resignation, for the knowledge that she had been outmanoeuvred didn't make it any easier to accept. Still, none of that conflict showed in her voice as she addressed Eldritch once more.

'Now you are going to travel out from the circle, following your awareness of the demon like a path that leads you to where it is breaking through.

'It's alright,' she promised, praying that it would be so. 'You'll only be a heartbeat away from the safety of the circle. You can return any time you wish by following my voice or your own senses, but for now you're going to travel along that link and tell me what you can of where the manifestation will take place.'

In the silence that followed her words, Gwyn watched the restless movement of Eldritch's eyes shifting beneath lids like finest porcelain. She could only hope the risk he was taking would pay off whilst watching like a hawk for any sign that things were going awry. After a moment she asked, 'What can you see?'

'Darkness.' Eldritch's voice was little more than a breath, the rich, warm tones pared away leaving only a sibilant whisper that barely carried to her ears. 'All around me is darkness.'

Beside her she heard the amused huff of Aidan's breath and saw him raise an eyebrow, clearly conveying what he thought of the helpfulness of Eldritch's revelation, though he carefully wrote it down. Gwyn spared a second to smile in return, but she was puzzled by the response. It was mid-afternoon. Wherever Eldritch had travelled to it shouldn't be dark. Not unless the demon's portal was in some way linked to a specific time and Eldritch had somehow tapped into that fact. With that in mind she asked, 'Is there any light at all – starlight or moonlight perhaps?'

She could almost sense Eldritch questing around.

'No… nothing. Just darkness.'

'That's alright.' Gwyn made her voice reassuring, as though that was exactly what she had wanted to hear rather than the beginnings of a riddle.

'And in this darkness, what can you feel?'

'Cold.'

Across the circle from her, Eldritch's body shivered and she saw gooseflesh rise on his forearms where the cuffs of his shirt were rolled back.

'The stones breathe cold. It seeps out from them. Ancient and venerable, older than the ice, the stones endure in the cold.'

Another shudder wracked his body, hard enough to make his teeth chatter together. Gwyn scowled, uneasy that he should react physically to what he was experiencing in spirit.

'Listen to me, Eldritch. Your body is safe within this circle. The cold cannot touch you. It is nothing more than a shadow brushing across your senses. You are warm and safe.'

The latter might not be entirely true, but at least his shivering stopped.

'Can you feel the air moving? The wind on your face?'

'No. There is nothing.'

Gwyn suppressed a growl of frustration.

'Is there anything else you can sense?'

But the answer that came back was the same.

'There is nothing.'

As his voice trailed off, she thought that was all Eldritch would say, but then he stiffened.

'There is only the demon.'

Gwyn froze, the hackles rising on the back of her neck.

'Eldritch,' she warned. 'Remember that you can return to the circle at any time.'

But if he could hear her, he chose not to respond. His face a mask, he intoned, 'I hear it thinking. Its thoughts are mine.'

'Gwyn...' Fear made Aidan speak up when he had agreed he would stay silent.

'Just write,' she snapped, cutting him off, unwilling to shift any of her attention from Eldritch. Unwilling to do anything that might upset the delicate balance of concentration and power. She felt her pulse racing, her chest tightening so that her breathing became shallow and fast. With all her heart she wanted to end this, wanted nothing more than to tell Eldritch to finish this astral exploration and return to his body. Instead she forced a long breath past the constriction in her throat and said, 'Tell me what it is thinking.'

'It remembers the grubbers in the dirt.'

The wizard paused and Gwyn wondered if he was trying to interpret those inhuman thought patterns, to translate swirling tides of unworldly images and emotions into words. Then he continued and Gwyn's chest locked solid, her heart turning to ice within her as she heard his voice change.

'They come into the darkness, seeking, seeking. The taste of their dreams awakens me. I burn them. I consume them. But in their cunningness they bound me.'

As he spoke Eldritch twisted as though he sought to free himself from some invisible shackle. His breathing quickened.

'Sacrifice,' he moaned, his head rolling from side to side. 'Death and fire and the long sleep.'

'Eldritch!'

'They come again with their petty hatreds, their anger and jealousy and lusting.' Eldritch panted the words as though each one took an effort to speak it. 'I feed on them all and the wards cannot hold me.'

There was a savage jubilation in his voice that hardened to bitterness.

'I rise, but one stands against me. Death and binding once more.'

His words tailed off in a long animal moan, his face momentarily contorting in anguish as he shared the demon's memories. For a second he went very still and then his features relaxed. Softly he began to speak again.

'But the Covenant weakens. I wake. I rise. Soon. Soon.'

The longing in Eldritch's voice was palpable. His body swayed from side to side, his chest heaving as though he fought to drag air into his lungs.

'That is enough,' Gwyn proclaimed. 'Return to the circle, Eldritch.'

Eldritch shuddered, his head dropping forward onto his chest as his breath left him in a long groaning sigh.

'Come back now.'

Slowly Eldritch straightened, the movement careful and deliberate as if too sudden a shift of position might make him lose his balance.

'No.'

As his head lifted, his eyes opened, but if anything looked out through them it was not Marcus Eldritch. For what seemed an eternity those unblinking eyes regarded Gwyn. Then whatever it was that was in possession of Eldritch spoke.

'You are known to me, witch-woman. Your tame warlock, your pathetic wizardling is mine. I claim him through the spilling of his blood and through his pain and by the hooks I have trailed in his flesh.'

Gwyn returned the stare without flinching, refusing to be cowed, though Eldritch's eyes had turned the sulphurous grey of a pre-storm sky.

Oh hell!

But though Gwyn's thoughts were a tangle of prayers and curses, there was no hesitation in her voice when she spoke.

'No!'

CHAPTER 6

Held in the cradle of the demon's mind Eldritch dreamed. Or at least the small segment of awareness that remained to him held fast to the hope that he was dreaming. The alternative was too terrifying to contemplate. A blade of obsidian flame pierced his shoulder pinning him in place while chains of bale-fire trailed around his limbs, burning him, his flesh searing under their touch. He had walked into the furnace willingly at the behest of the witch, following the voices that sung like sirens inside his head and now, having done so, he was trapped. Yet, through the endless waves of agony, he knew one thing; he had only to submit – to surrender his soul to the demon – and the torment would cease. Weakness would be replaced by power, pain would be washed away on a sea of blood and replaced by pleasure so intense that it would itself be a glorious never-ending pain. He would endure forever in an ecstasy of torment. The words wheedled their way into his brain, sweet and tempting, bright as magnesium and burning like phosphorus as they slid between each synapse, corrupting every thought. Stubbornly he fought against them recognising them as lies. He would not endure. He would die; the first in a long series of deaths that would begin as soon as the demon took his body. But the demon knew of his resistance and it twisted him upon a rack of pain until his spirit screamed and he longed for the dissolution of his flesh and his soul if only it would bring oblivion.

And amidst it all Helen was there, her fingers a burning caress along his skin. She dripped honeyed poison into his panting, gasping mouth and followed it with kisses as his body convulsed beneath her. Golden scaled snakes coiled in her hair, striking at him with jewelled fangs. She was the most gorgeous creature he had ever seen.

'Come to me,' she whispered, her breath hot in his mouth. 'Yes...'

It was more of the demon's trickery but he was beyond caring. He leaned forward into her caress, straining to reach her, his arms twisted behind him by the chains that dragged him back from her and suddenly those chains were no longer bale-fire but cool silver and between him and his demon lover was another woman. Smaller than the demon, her body thin and plain against the wanton voluptuousness of the demon's curves still there was something about her that drew the eye. Black hair cascaded down her back like nightfall and starlight coalesced on the pallor of her skin.

'No. You shall not have him.'

She spun and from her hand a million scintillating droplets flew in a trail of star fire, forming a barrier between her and the demon. Her face was lambent as she turned towards him casting fire around him and across him, the droplets burning like ice as they fell across his skin. Eldritch howled in torment, struggling to free himself, desperate now to reach the demon's embrace but the star fire had become a net around him, its threads scented with sandalwood and rose, lavender and beeswax. The threads closed closer and closer until he could see nothing beyond their light. He screamed aloud as his world dissolved into coruscating starlight but the name that came to his lips was, 'Gwyn!'

There were voices, warm and familiar and — though he couldn't quite place who they belonged to — their very presence was comforting. Floating in darkness he followed the flow of words absently, not even trying to make sense of what was being said but simply letting the sounds eddy around him, soft and reassuring as a lullaby.

'So you really think he was referring to a mine?'

'It would make sense; the darkness, the reference to the "grubbers in the dirt". That could be how the demon would have perceived the miners.' Somehow the tone conveyed a shrug to Eldritch's disjointed consciousness. 'It's a starting point anyway and more than we had to go on before.'

'But the map doesn't show any mine workings around there.'

'I know, but the tunnels must run for miles. I'd bet on there being one if we could find it.'

The voices faded, eddying away as Eldritch's mind drifted. He caught some comment about Jenny and a lamb and then something else about a library, but it made little sense and he was content to let the noise wash over him, a gentle reminder that there was a world out there, waiting for him to join it when he was ready.

'He will be alright, won't he?'

The first voice drifted back into his awareness. Perhaps it was the concern sharpening its tone that made it register with him. For a moment he wondered, in a vague, disjointed way, who the voice was referring to and if he too should be worried for them.

'Yes, he'll be fine.'

Ah, that's alright then. Reassured by the calm certainty in that second voice he let the conversation slip away.

'He was channelling the demon. It hadn't possessed him.'

'There's a difference?'

'To start with, yes, but it's not a route you want to go down. You open a channel for a demon thinking you can control it and you don't notice that each time it's a little easier to make the connection, each time the boundaries blur a little further. Before you know it the thoughts in your head, the little ideas you start having, they're not yours at all – they're coming from the demon. It's a very fine line between channelling and possession and there's no chance to step back once you've crossed it.'

There was silence for a while.

'It said it had claimed him.'

'Yes, it did, but I don't think it meant today. I think there was some kind of link created through the avatar when they fought, when it bit him. What with his hearing the demon in his head and the way he set off the wards on the house, there's something there. And today – we'd agreed he'd try and find out more about where it was breaking through, but he wasn't meant to link with it. I'd like to know whether he intended to do that or if it just happened.'

'Because it could happen again?'

'It shouldn't, not if he's careful with his shielding, although I'm beginning to wonder if that link's allowing it to reach him even through his shields. That's pretty worrying if it can and it means he's going to have to be doubly careful. But my wards block it so I should be able to create a seal that will help. Even so we daren't risk doing anything like this again.'

Time blurred and the world drifted away again. Then a hand touched the side of his neck, solid and warm. It brushed his cheek and he caught the faint scent of incense as that familiar voice said, 'There we are. He's starting to come round.'

Was he? But whether it was the words suggesting it or it was simply time for it to happen, awareness of his body was indeed flooding back and it wasn't an entirely pleasant experience. Without opening his eyes Eldritch said, 'I think I'm going to be sick.'

Whatever response he might have expected to that statement, laughter was not it. But laughter was what he got. Laughter followed by a very firm, 'No you're not. Just take a sip of this and you'll be fine.'

A hand lifting his head made it easier to comply than to resist. He gagged at the sticky taste of coffee, liberally laced with sugar and brandy, but it was either swallow or choke and his body chose the former. There was only one person who would do that to him. Gwyn. Somehow the thought was immensely comforting.

'Are you trying to get me drunk again, woman?'

Eldritch wasn't sure he managed to shape the words correctly, his tongue seemed not entirely under his control, but they generated another laugh, throaty and warm and perhaps a little more relaxed than the first.

'Only in your dreams, wizard.'

'Feeling better now?'
'I'm fine.'

The response came automatically but then, because it was Gwyn who had asked, Eldritch paused to consider the truth of that statement. Certainly the nausea he had felt on waking had passed swiftly enough under the onslaught of sugar and caffeine. In fact, apart from a renewed ache in his shoulder, which he put down to sitting for an hour with his arm unsupported, he felt better than he had for some time, not least of all because the odd migraine-like pressure in his head had gone. Leaning back against the doorframe he breathed in deeply, allowing the cool afternoon air to chase the last dregs of incense from his lungs.

'Honestly.' He flicked her a swift grin as though to say, *would I lie to you?*

Gwyn eyed him sideways.

'No strange desires to go round sacrificing virgins?'

Eldritch pursed his lips.

'No more so than usual. Anyway, Aidan tells me they're in short supply round here. Why?' he asked his face lighting with sudden interest. 'Do you know where I might find some?'

'No.' For a moment the twinkle in Gwyn's eyes was positively wicked. 'But personally I've always found virgins to be overrated. So,' she added, her voice becoming more businesslike as Eldritch blushed, 'do you remember anything from this afternoon?'

The change of tone had Eldritch mentally shifting gears. His grey eyes closed and a frown line wormed between his brows as he tried to dredge up some recollection of the events of the last hour. He had a fleeting image of snakes and another of a woman who might have been Gwyn – except her hair had been longer and her skin had shone like mother of pearl – but even as he tried to make sense of the impressions they faded away like smoke and he was left with nothing. He opened his eyes and looked back at Gwyn, sitting on the floor like a schoolgirl with her knees tucked up and her chin resting on her folded hands.

'Not a thing,' he said, shaking his head.

Aidan turned from where he was checking over a climbing harness and looked at him incredulously but Gwyn simply smiled as though she had expected no other response.

'That's usually the way with trance,' she said, directing her comment towards Aidan. 'The medium doesn't remember a thing of what happened. That's why it's so important to make a record of everything that's said.'

If anything Aidan's eyebrows rose even higher at this and he muttered something under his breath that Eldritch couldn't quite catch though, from the way she rolled her eyes, clearly Gwyn had.

'I take it it worked, then?'

He raised a hand to brush the hair back from his eyes and stopped, looking in surprise at his wrist.

'When did I get the hippy bracelet?'

A rope of polished rose quartz spheres, smooth and regular as pearls, was looped across his watch. Gwyn's lips twitched in a hastily suppressed smile. Suspicions aroused, Eldritch's gaze dropped to his right wrist.

'Bracelets,' he amended, scowling at the strand of amethyst chips that sat alongside the plain copper band he habitually wore as though it were a personal affront. He held his wrists out in front of him, regarding the bracelets dubiously. They looked like the sort of thing Gwyn usually wore; indeed he would have sworn she had been wearing something similar that morning.

Alright for her perhaps – women could happily deck themselves with strings of crystals and more besides and no one would look twice – but they made him feel ridiculous, as though he were wearing fancy dress. All he needed now was a headband with some arcane symbols and he could set himself up as Marcus the Mysterious, reader of fortunes and tarot cards. He shuddered inwardly at the thought but as he moved to slip the bracelets off his vision shifted and for a second he saw an image not of crystals but of chains and spancels made of burning green fire. He blinked and the image was gone as swiftly as it had come but when he looked up he saw that Gwyn was watching him closely. Slowly he let his hands drop into his lap and Gwyn nodded.

'Think of them as a little extra protection.' Like her eyes, Gwyn's voice was half teasing, half serious. 'Best leave them on until we get home.'

CHAPTER 7

Standing near the top of Penglais Hill, its pale stone frontage rising up from a surround of manicured lawns and neatly clipped evergreen hedges, the National Library of Wales was an imposing sight. Gwyn watched Eldritch taking it in as they walked from the car park.

'Welsh architecture isn't all about castles,' she commented as he stopped in front of her, hands thrust in the back pockets of his jeans, and craned his head back to take in the height of the walls.

'But you can see where they got their inspiration from,' he countered, eyes scanning the tall, narrow windows and the sheer expanse of wall between them. It wouldn't take much imagination to turn such a weight of stone into a fortress.

'Very impressive.' A smile tugged at his lips as he nodded approvingly, giving the building its due. 'And what a fabulous view.'

He turned his back on the vast stone edifice to look out over the town, laid out below them in neat blocks of whitewash and red brick and charcoal-grey roofs. Two headlands framed the view in scrubby trees and heathland to the left and a dark mass of evergreens to the right while beyond it all, its grey-green waters stretching out to melt into the sky on the horizon, was the vast sweep of Cardigan Bay, bright in the early morning sunshine.

'To hell with the research,' he grinned down at his companion, 'it's worth coming here just to see this place.'

Gwyn shook her head in mock reproach, sending her dark hair snaking across her shoulders.

'So much for the man who claimed to be a Ph.D. student.' Then she relented, unable to stop her own delight bubbling over, and she answered his grin with one of her own. 'Just wait until you get inside and see the books!'

They walked along the wet tarmac path towards the front steps, the dew still thick on the grass and glinting on the spider webs covering the knee-high hedges. Beneath one of the wooden benches two herring gulls, massive in their grey and white plumage, mewled and squabbled for possession of some titbit, their thick yellow beaks jabbing like bayonets, but beyond that the morning was quiet. No traffic sounds filtered up from the town. At 9:25am what passed for a rush hour in Aberystwyth had finished and – well used though it was – only the most enthusiastic frequenters of the library would trouble to queue outside its doors before it opened. The one person doing just that turned to greet them as they walked up the sweeping steps to the massive front doors.

'Good morning,' Aidan's greeting was as sunny as the weather. 'Everyone okay?'

His bright hazel gaze touched briefly on Eldritch's wrists.

'Fine, thanks.'

Eldritch made a not-quite casual move to straighten his shirt cuffs, realised what he was doing and stopped himself. 'I'm looking forward to spending this lovely morning locked in a library with a heap of dusty old books.'

The grunt as Gwyn poked him none too gently in the ribs could be heard across the gardens.

If the green uniformed porter was surprised to find three people waiting outside the doors when he opened them he made no comment, simply wishing them a good morning and directing them to go to the reception desk if they needed readers' tickets. Gwyn already had one but Aidan and Eldritch dutifully went and completed the necessary forms. The receptionist, a cheerful man in his early fifties smiled encouragingly at their respective moans when they learned the process included having to have their photographs taken.

'It won't hurt a bit,' he reassured them as they stood in turn against the strip of white wall to face the camera. 'And while it's digital you can have a look on the screen before I print it and if you think it's that bad I'll take another one.'

He turned the monitor to show Eldritch a picture that made him look more like someone who would burn books than read them. Eldritch groaned and shook his head.

'It'll do.'

Another shot was unlikely to make things any better. He took the white plastic card the receptionist handed him and slipped it into his shirt pocket.

'Show that to the librarians upstairs and they'll sort you out. What is it that you're interested in?'

'Anything on the local lead mines. I'm researching them for a family history.'

'Books and texts are in the North Reading Room. I expect you'll want to start there. Turn right at the top of the stairs and the porters up there will show you where you need to go. And when you want a break from your research there's the Pen Dinas restaurant on this floor.' The cheerful smile broadened and he gave a conspiratorial wink. 'They're open for drinks and snacks now and they'll start serving lunch at twelve.'

The porter stationed at the top of the stairs confirmed the receptionist's directions, pointing them along the corridor to where a large wooden counter blocked further access. Beyond it was a sign which read, "North Reading Room". Rather disconcertingly there was a second sign below it stating, "No access during refurbishment". As they stopped to consider this a young woman came through a side door, carrying a box file and some loose-leaf papers. Seeing them she leaned over the counter and called out, 'We've got customers, Mike,' and then turned back with a smile. 'He'll be right with you.'

Gwyn stopped her before she could walk away.

'Can we not get into the Reading Room at the moment?'

She pointed to the sign and the young woman shook her head.

'No, not while the building work's going on, I'm afraid. We're hoping it will be finished by the end of the year.'

The latter was added as though that knowledge would somehow lessen the inconvenience to their visit today. Gwyn chose not to respond by asking where they could wait in the meantime. Instead she said, 'But we can still access the collections?'

'Oh yes. It just means you'll have to use the desks out here. It can get a bit crowded sometimes but you should be fine this morning.'

The librarian cast her eyes over the row of tables lining the far side of the corridor, empty save for a scattering of PC monitors and keyboards.

'There are some more desks in the annexe but it gets noisy

in there if people start using the photocopiers so I wouldn't recommend it. Don't worry, Mike will sort you out.'

With that she headed off down the corridor. Aidan turned his head appreciatively to watch her go.

'If you'd told me librarians had changed that much I'd have been a lot keener to come here,' he said, admiring the swaying silk skirt as the woman walked away and the considerable length of leg between its hem and her sharp-heeled ankle boots.

'Tell me about it,' murmured Eldritch. 'It was knee-length tweed and sensible shoes last time I looked.'

'Can we focus a little please?'

'Oh, we're focussed,' Aidan sighed.

Fortunately a discrete cough behind them spared the need for Gwyn to respond.

'What can I help you folks with?'

The slightly sardonic cant to Mike's eyebrows as his gaze swung from Gwyn to encompass Eldritch and Aidan was the only indication he gave that he had noticed the impact his colleague had had on the two men. Even so Aidan found himself momentarily tongue-tied.

'Ah, er… yes.'

'Lead mines,' said Eldritch firmly, as though dragging his thoughts back from somewhere else entirely.

Mike looked at them as though he had hoped for slightly more information and then turned back to Gwyn.

'Do you all have readers' tickets?' he asked her, managing to add a silent, "*Are these two even capable of reading?*" to the end of his question. Wondering the same thing herself Gwyn presented her ID.

'We're looking for anything on the old lead mines in the

Llancathan area,' she explained as Aidan and Eldritch hastily produced their cards for inspection. 'How many mines there were, where they were sited. Ideally we'd like plans of them too, plus any records or accounts from when they were operational if you have anything like that.'

Mike nodded his understanding.

'We have all sorts. Books, journals and original newspapers are here, maps and film copies are in the South Reading Room, but it's all in the online catalogue. Find yourselves a work station and you can look it all up and request what you want to view and then Sal or I will bring it to you. It's about a forty minute turnaround.'

By tacit agreement they chose the table furthest from the counter and Mike's watchful eye and settled themselves at one end. Gwyn withdrew a sheet of paper from her notepad and put it on the table between the PCs.

'Jenny gave me the names of the local mines she remembers from the museum but she said there could well have been others that they didn't have material from. Some mines only operated for a year or so. If the seams turned out not to be as rich as the owners had thought, or they ran into technical problems, they'd close the mines down and dig somewhere else. I suggest we start with a general search on lead mines in central Wales and see what comes up. We can always narrow it down but I don't want us to miss something.'

She cocked her head at Aidan and Eldritch but when neither of them suggested an alternative approach she pulled a keyboard towards her and started typing. 'Let's see what we get.'

There was a pause as the request was processed and then Gwyn blinked in surprise.

'Three hundred and eighty-nine documents,' she read from the screen. 'That's a few more than I was expecting. I wonder what we'll get if I add Llancathan into the search.'

Her fingers flew across the keyboard but when the results came back she sighed.

'Three. Oh well.'

'It's more manageable,' suggested Eldritch.

'But not terribly helpful.'

She scanned the descriptions.

'Text relating to the transfer of assets between a Captain Reynolds and a Mr Taylor; mineralogy reports relating to the lead mining companies of Cardiganshire 1847-1937, as acquired by the British Geological Survey; and a set of accounts for the Tan-y-bwlch mine.'

She checked her piece of paper.

'That's one of the ones that Jenny mentioned so I suppose that's something.'

Gwyn sat back in her chair and looked thoughtfully at the computer. 'I think we have to go back to the original list and see what we can find in there. The records wouldn't necessarily be cross-referenced with Llancathan so it's not to say there isn't anything. I'd just hoped we might cut it down a little.'

'Look on the bright side,' Aidan commented. 'At least there are records there. And if they've kept things like accounts and transfers of assets surely they'll have kept plans as well.'

Gwyn shrugged.

'Well, we'll find out, but you're right – it's a promising start and we won't have to look at everything. We should be able to discount a lot based on the descriptions and then request anything that sounds worth a closer look.'

'Okay.' Eldritch pursed his lips. 'So if I pull up the same list I can work backwards from three hundred and eighty-nine while you start from the beginning. What about you, Aidan? Do you want to take the middle hundred?'

Aidan shook his head.

'No. I printed some stuff off the net last night, from the Welsh Mines Preservation Trust. I'm going to see if I can tie any of it up with the workings shown on the OS map. At the very least I might be able to come up with some more names for you to look out for.'

Aidan pushed the map and his papers across the table and stretched, arching his back and squeezing his shoulder blades together until the muscles cracked. At the other end of the table Gwyn and Eldritch were still busy scanning the PC screens. He had been aware of them breaking off every now and then to confer in hushed tones, or the odd flurry of typing as they requested an item but so far no books had materialised. His own research had yielded one positive – an additional name for them to look out for – plus one that might be of interest. It was a small step but he had the feeling that small steps were all they could reasonably hope for. Besides, enough small steps would take them where they needed to go. He stood and stretched once more, the movement attracting Gwyn's attention. She looked at him over the top of her screen.

'Anything?' she asked. By way of an answer he slid the map over to her, leaning across the table to point out what he had found. Eldritch half rose from his chair so he too could see.

'These workings here,' Aidan tapped the map. 'They're part of the Greenfields mine. These others could be from the

Glynafon. The report said they were close to each other but it wasn't clear in which direction. It could just as easily be these ones here,' he slid his finger away from the reservoir, 'which would put it outside the area we're looking at. Still it might be worth checking if you come across any references to it.'

'Nice one.'

Eldritch nodded his approval and Gwyn smiled.

'Well done. That should be a big help.'

Aidan shrugged dismissively but secretly he was pleased with what he had managed to find.

'We'll see. There may not be anything on either of them. Listen, I could do with a coffee. Do either of you want one?'

'We can't all go. If there's no one here when they bring the books we've requested they'll just take them away again.'

Gwyn turned to Eldritch.

'I'll stay, but you go if you want to,' she offered. For a moment Eldritch looked tempted but then he gave a small shake of his head.

'No, it's alright. I'm getting into the swing of this now – if I break off I won't want to come back. Wait till we've gone through the list and then I might grab one.'

Gwyn rested her chin on one upturned palm and gazed up at Aidan.

'You go. We might as well do this in shifts.'

The Pen Dinas restaurant was empty so Aidan took his coffee and a Danish pastry to a sunny table underneath one of the tall windows looking out over Cardigan Bay. It was a lovely view and the coffee was good – freshly brewed and strong – but he didn't linger over it. He didn't want Gwyn or Eldritch to feel that he was leaving them to do all the work. He wouldn't have broken off for the coffee at all except he hadn't had time for breakfast, forgoing it so that Sula didn't have her morning walk shortened by the fact that he had overslept. That had been a consequence of trawling the internet until nearly two in the morning, searching for anything he could find on the old mines. Staying up that late might not have been ideal but his success this morning proved it had been worthwhile. It had also been quite an eye-opener. Aidan shivered as he recalled the descriptions of the conditions the miners had worked and lived under. Men died falling from the long shaft ladders they used to reach the working galleries. More lost limbs or eyes in the frequent accidents with blasting powder. Even for those that escaped such perils, life expectancy was short. Poor ventilation and the long hours breathing in silica-laden dust, combined with the wet and the cold of their underground existence, meant that the miner who lived to see forty was considered old. The cold hand of tuberculosis claimed many of those who did not die underground. Looking out at the bright October morning Aidan could barely imagine how the world must have seemed for those men who earned their living locked away in the dark and the dust, hammering away at the rocks. It had been a life that was short, brutal and bone-achingly hard. And unbeknownst to them, somewhere in that darkness, a demon had been waiting.

He was halfway up the stairs, taking them two at a time, when a voice behind him made him stop and turn.

'How's the research coming on?'

It was Sal, the librarian who had greeted them outside the Reading Room. She of the short skirt and the long legs. Aidan stopped and waited for her to catch up with him, making a conscious effort to keep his eyes on her face as she came up the stairs to join him.

'Mike tells me you're interested in the old lead mines.'

Aidan nodded, not sure what more he could tell her. Then, remembering Eldritch's words to the receptionist, he added, 'Eldritch is researching the ones round Llancathan for a family history.'

'Oh? I didn't realise he was Welsh.'

'He's not, but his great-great-something or other grandparents were,' Aidan lied, ad-libbing furiously. 'He's an old friend of Gwyn's so we thought we'd come with him and help him get started.'

He stopped as she came level with him, finding himself caught between a liar's urge to avoid eye contact and the realisation that dropping his gaze would leave him open to an entirely different accusation. The thought made him wonder if Mike had said anything to her about that earlier indiscretion and he winced. But either it hadn't been mentioned or she took such things in her ankle-booted stride, for all she said was, 'That's good of you. Too many people seem scared of libraries these days,' and awarded him a smile like a badge of honour. As they reached the top landing she turned to him again and said thoughtfully, 'It may not be relevant but would you be interested in seeing the books that came out of the Miners' Chapel? Mike probably didn't think to mention them as they've not been catalogued yet, but we've a couple of boxes of them.'

'The Miners' Chapel? I didn't know there was one.'

'Well officially it was the Greenfields Wesleyan Chapel but I suppose because it was built for the miners that's how it became known. It was deconsecrated about five years ago and then, when it was finally sold, the new owners donated the books from its schoolroom to the library. To be honest, I don't remember there being much about the mine itself. The books were for the local people to read and learn about the world. They covered a fair mix of subjects.'

She flashed another smile that told Aidan quite clearly that in her world all books were considered objects of love.

'You never know, you might find something interesting in there.' Without waiting for a response she added, 'It's quiet at the moment. I'll bring them over for you.'

There was a definite smirk on Eldritch's face when he saw just who was walking along the corridor with Aidan.

'Had a pleasant break?' he whispered as Aidan slid into his seat.

'We met on the stairs. She was asking how the research was going,' Aidan replied, rolling his eyes heavenwards in response to Eldritch's suggestive leer. 'And she's going to bring me some books that haven't been catalogued yet,' he added smugly. Eldritch waggled an eyebrow at him.

'Really? Sounds like you've made quite an impression on her.'

From behind Gwyn's terminal a voice murmured, 'Come up and see my book collection, little boy,' in a throaty Mae West tone that made Eldritch's smirk widen still further.

'Behave. The pair of you,' Aidan warned.

'Yes sir.'

Eldritch ducked his head in mock obedience and the sound of typing resumed from the other side of the table, accompanied by a low and rather wicked chuckle.

The cardboard box of books that Sal brought to the table minutes later proved to contain as eclectic a mix as she had promised. As he lifted them out, one by one, Aidan was both fascinated and amused by the titles; *A History of the Embassy to Abyssinia, Livingstone's Journeys in Africa, A Treatise on the use of Steam in Engineering.* He held each one in his hand, taking in the yellowing pages and the worn cloth bindings, faded and greying along the spines where years of sunlight had bleached away the reds, greens and dark blues that were visible elsewhere on the covers. He thought again of the miners; young men of his own age, working six days a week in the darkness of the pit. Men who, on their one day off, didn't go up onto the hills seeking fresh air to clear their lungs of the grey dust from the mines, but came instead to the chapel to attend the services and to read these books and learn about places they had no hope of visiting. When a trip to Aberystwyth might be an annual treat and Cardiff would seem like another world, how could they comprehend Abyssinia? As he thumbed through the black and white engravings of Livingstone's meeting with "the natives", Aidan pictured the hands that had previously turned these pages and felt a strange connection with those ghosts of the past, combined with an overwhelming sense of humility when he considered all that he had that they had not.

There might be nothing here of relevance to their search for the demon but Aidan was loathe to put the box to one side without at least looking at each of its treasures, for treasures they were. Like Sal he loved books. His earliest memories were of his mother reading to him, adopting different voices and expressions for each character in the rich casts of Middle Earth and Narnia, of Kipling's India and of Earthsea and all the other worlds that she brought to life for him, long before he could read the words for himself. Gwyn too had joined in his indoctrination, introducing him to different authors and other worlds. She was the one who brought to his awareness the savage beauty of poetry. The hairs on the back of his neck still rose when he thought of the first time he heard her read the opening lines of R.S. Thomas' *Welsh Landscape*.

> *To live in Wales is to be conscious*
> *At dusk of the spilled blood*
> *That went to the making of the wild sky,*
> *Dyeing the immaculate rivers*
> *In all their courses.*

The words had conjured pictures of conflict and long ago battles, of small, fierce warriors with their spears and their round shields facing off against towering armoured knights and had cemented in him a lifelong love affair with language and the written word. So while Gwyn and Eldritch were immersed in the books they had requested Aidan allowed himself the indulgence of picking through these other volumes and imagining the lives and the times of the men who had read them.

Not all the books in the box were text books. There were prayer books too and Bibles with crumbling leather covers. Aidan peered into each, looking at the front pages with their names and dates in thick, neat copperplate. Even more so than the text books these were a link to that long ago congregation. Some had clearly been handed down through generations of children making him wonder what had become of the last recipients that they had ended up on the shelves of the chapel library rather than in someone's home.

As he picked up one small, black-bound tome a newspaper cutting slipped down from between the back pages. Aidan opened the cover and removed it, intrigued as to what news item had been folded between the pages of a Bible. The yellowed cutting was stapled to a piece of notepaper, itself discoloured with age, and had been taken from the top of a page bearing the legend *Cambrian Times* and a date of 12th September 1987, the year before he had been born. Aidan looked at the article curiously. It was the report of a car crash that had happened the previous day on the A483 near Welshpool. Accompanying the text was a grainy picture that looked as though it had been cropped from a holiday photograph, showing a Mr William Wynn-Jones smiling at the camera. Aidan hoped he had been enjoying himself for the article told how he had died when a drunk driver had ploughed into his car. Mr Wynn-Jones had lived in Bristol and had been staying at the Llancathan Arms hotel. He was believed to have been visiting the area for pleasure. There were a few more details of the road conditions at the time of the accident and a police plea for any witnesses to come forward, but little more beyond that. Aidan re-read the article wondering what it was that had made someone keep it. Presumably that someone hadn't been a relative of the dead man – if the journalist was to be believed William Wynn-Jones had been unmarried and had left no surviving family. Perhaps it had been someone connected to the unnamed second driver or even a witness to the crash. Intrigued, but sensing it was a mystery that would have to remain unsolved, Aidan carefully re-folded the cutting but as he did so he noticed writing on the notepaper to which the article had been stapled.

Folding the clipping to one side Aidan read the few lines that it had hidden. The writing was neat and not hard to decipher, the letters formed with round, almost childish loops, but when he had finished he stared at the page for some time before re-reading the words, not sure he could believe what he was seeing. Then he turned the page over and looked once more at the face of the man who had died. There was nothing remarkable in the photograph, certainly no indication that within a short while of it having been taken it would be used in an obituary. In fact there was nothing to indicate that William Wynn-Jones was in any way special. Nothing at all except for those few handwritten lines. Finally Aidan got to his feet and took the paper over to Gwyn and Eldritch.

'I think you should see this.'

Placing the cutting on the table between them he waited while they both read it. Then, when they looked up at him with almost identical *so what?* expressions he folded the newspaper back and showed them the notepaper underneath and the words written there.

The Covenant is broken. The last Child of the Covenant is dead. The time of the Beast is at hand and who can say what will happen? Will it arise from the pit and devour us or will it call us to it in the darkness one by one? I fear for us all.

Gwyn was the first to speak.

'Sweet Lady,' she whispered and even someone unfamiliar with Gwyn's personal pantheon would have been left in no doubt that it was a prayer she offered with those two words. 'The demon spoke of a Covenant. Now we know it exists… or rather that it *existed,*' she corrected herself.

'But this man wasn't a lead miner,' Aidan protested. Like her he kept his voice low but it didn't conceal the frustration behind his words. 'He was a computer programmer from Bristol. Besides, the mines closed down long before he was born. Hell, they probably closed down before even his grandparents were born.'

He gestured irritably at the paper, torn between the conviction that he had found a vital piece of the puzzle and an inability to see how it could possibly fit.

'A *Child* of the Covenant,' Gwyn said thoughtfully, refusing to be perturbed by the truth of what Aidan had just said. 'To me that suggests the binding was secured through a bloodline.'

She looked at Eldritch for confirmation. 'Would that be possible?'

For a moment Eldritch seemed not to have heard her or at least he chose not to answer.

'Child of the Covenant,' he turned the words over on his tongue, his eyes distant, his expression thoughtful. 'I've heard that somewhere recently. Or read it, maybe.'

He frowned, struggling to place the memory.

'Eldritch?'

The wizard started, looking across at Gwyn as though he had only just registered that she had spoken.

'Sorry. Bloodlines – yes, technically it's possible to tie a binding or a ward into a bloodline. It would take an awful lot of power though, more than could normally be raised by one person.'

Aidan watched Gwyn consider this. He could almost see her drawing into herself as she did so. She was piecing something together, he realised, and whatever it was she didn't much like it. When she finally spoke he realised why.

'Do you mean the sort of power that would be released by a death?'

The whole room seemed to grow still around them and Aidan felt the hairs on the nape of his neck lift. On the other side of the table Eldritch stiffened, staring at Gwyn with eyes that were suddenly glacial and hard. Aidan offered up a swift prayer that Sal wouldn't decide that now would be a good time to bring that second box of books. He glanced swiftly over his shoulder but neither librarian was visible at the desk so there was no one to overhear their conversation.

'You're talking about sacrifice.'

If anything Eldritch's voice was colder than his eyes. He might not have put it into words but his tone was accusing, questioning what she knew of such things. Gwyn shook her head, a sharp negating movement, but let the apparent accusation and Eldritch's distaste go without comment.

'Self-sacrifice,' she corrected him firmly. 'One man's willing death. Although it's true that others died as a result of his actions,' she conceded, 'whether or not he intended that.'

For a long moment Eldritch's eyes remained locked on Gwyn as she returned the fierceness of his stare with a level, peridot gaze but finally he sat back in his chair, his breath leaving him in a long sigh. He kneaded the bridge of his nose with his fingertips as though he was fighting off a headache and perhaps there was a tacit apology in that bowed head, or at least an acknowledgement that he had overreacted. Finally the wizard looked up at Gwyn and if not all the hostility had gone from his face at least it was no longer directed at her.

'A binding given power through self-sacrifice,' he mused. 'Heaven help us.'

'Why so surprised? Do you think you're the only one who's ever put the common good ahead of self-preservation?'

From anyone else it would have been a rhetorical question. Only Gwyn could ask such a thing as though she genuinely wanted to know the answer. Only she would then add, 'It bought two generations of safety.' before Eldritch had even drawn breath to respond, leaving the implied corollary – *which is more than can be said for what you managed* – hanging in the air between them.

Aidan understood neither the magical implications of what Gwyn had suggested nor the tension it had generated between her and the wizard. He groped for some kind of explanation, wanting to make sense of it. Even more he wanted to break the prickling silence that followed her last words.

'I don't get it. Sacrifice? Self-sacrifice? What are you talking about?'

He looked at his two companions but a cold barrier had dropped behind Eldritch's eyes and his face was closed. He turned away from Aidan's enquiry without a word. Instead it was Gwyn who spoke.

'There is power in death Aidan. We all know it instinctively. Throughout history religions the world over have petitioned their gods through sacrifice. These days we speak of sacrifice in terms of giving something up for the greater good but we rarely think of the actual giving up of life. The power in such an act is too raw, too horrifying, to sit comfortably with our safe, sanitised world so we've hidden it, turned our backs on it. We can pretend we don't believe in it – that's if we dare acknowledge it at all – but it hasn't gone away. It's hidden not lost.'

She paused, watching his face, watching the impact of what she had said settle over him. Then she continued. 'I believe that someone in that mine knew about the demon and realised there was only one way he could stop it manifesting. A man of power sealed the tunnel where it was breaking through, bringing the roof down to close it off and binding it with the power of his own death. Whether he intended to kill others when he did so, we can't know. At the very least he must have known it was likely that men would be caught in the cave-in. I doubt he could have engineered a way to empty the mine and remain there himself.'

Her face grew troubled, her eyes dropping to her hands, small and neat where they rested on the keyboard and there was sadness in her voice as she went on. 'It would have been a terrible decision to make, perhaps some would say it was a decision he wasn't entitled to make, that it wasn't his place to take innocent lives with him, even if it was the only course of action he could see. Does the end justify the means?'

Her eyes met his again as she spoke, making the question personal, then she shrugged dismissing it as of no consequence. 'We could debate it forever and a day, but there we have it. One man's willing death and the unwilling deaths of half a dozen others and the rift was sealed once again, the beast subdued and forced back into its sleep.'

'You sound very certain,' Eldritch's voice was grudging but if he was still smarting from the sting of her earlier remark he had at least listened to what she had to say and seemed willing to consider the merit of her idea.

'I am,' Gwyn's voice was definite but calm. There was no knife hidden in the space between her words. 'Look at this.'

She turned the screen on her PC and pointed to the record she had been about to request from the library archives.

'An account of the dreadful explosion in Greenfields lead mine on 9ᵗʰ of November 1910, by Edward Evans of Bwlch-y-gle.'

There was a pause while Eldritch thought about this. He swept a hand through his long hair as he regarded the screen.

'So you think that instead of this being an accident the explosion was caused by a wizard caving in the tunnel to trap the demon?' The dark brows drew down as Eldritch wrestled with the prospect. 'That he created the Covenant and that our computer programmer from Bristol was his last descendent?' He favoured Gwyn with a doubtful look. 'It seems rather a long shot.'

'Not when there's a William Wynn-Jones listed amongst the dead, it doesn't.'

Eldritch shrugged.

'That could be a coincidence. There must be hundreds of Wynn-Joneses around, surely?'

Like Gwyn he seemed to have refocused his attention on their hunt for the demon for his disagreement was targeted at the argument rather than the woman voicing it. Gwyn shook her head.

'I don't think so. It's not a surname you come across that often around here. In fact I can't think of a single Wynn-Jones in Llancathan.'

'And of course you'd know all of them.'

Gwyn contrived to look down her nose at Eldritch – no mean feat considering that, even sat down, he was inches taller than her.

'This isn't London; we know the names of the people living round us, but you can check in the phone book if you want to be sure. Strangely enough William's not a common name around here either. People used to say it was unlucky but I never heard an explanation as to why.'

'Perhaps we've just found it,' Aidan chipped in, nodding his head at the PC screen.

'Perhaps we have.'

Gwyn looked at him, her head tipped to one side like a blackbird regarding a particularly juicy worm, then seemingly out of nowhere she added, 'Anne wanted to call you William.' Her voice was soft as she spoke of her friend.

'What?' Aidan looked at her appalled. 'Why on earth would she have wanted to do that?'

Gwyn laughed at the horror in his voice.

'Honestly, Aidan. It's a nice name. You might think it's a little old fashioned perhaps but there's nothing wrong with it. She said it was a friend's name.'

For a second her smile faltered, replaced by the kink of a puzzled frown, but whatever thought or memory had struck her Gwyn chose not to share it and, after a moment, she visibly put it to one side, a wicked look stealing over her thin, pixie face.

'James wouldn't hear of it.'

Aidan almost choked, his eyes widening in disbelief.

'You mean I actually agree with him on something? That's

got to be a first.' He shuddered theatrically. 'Who'd have thought after all these years I'd finally find something I was grateful to him for.'

Eldritch was listening to the exchange with a faintly amused expression. He leaned back in his chair, a long scarecrow of a man, and favoured Aidan with a wry smile.

'James was your father?'

Aidan nodded, his face sour.

'I take it that the two of you didn't get on terribly well.'

'That would be one way of putting it,' Aidan's tone added all the detail that was necessary. 'Another would be to say that he loathed the sight of me. The feeling was mutual, by the way,' he added fiercely, sensing sympathy behind the amusement and wanting no part of it. 'I don't know why he ever decided to have children. He made it pretty clear it wasn't something he enjoyed.'

'To be fair that was your mother's choice,' Gwyn interjected softly. She regarded him with inscrutable jungle-cat eyes. 'And perhaps not such a bad one.'

Before he could move out of range she reached across and ruffled his hair, her expression deliberately impish, teasing him away from the darkness.

'Families, eh?' Eldritch commented as Aidan batted Gwyn's hand away, growling in his throat like one of her cats. 'That's why God gives us friends to make up for them.'

He winced as he rolled his shoulders under the black denim of his shirt and straightened up, his face serious once more. 'So, I wonder what brought William Wynn-Jones here from Bristol. If he was the last Child he won't have been visiting family.'

'Would he have come back because of the Covenant?'

Aidan asked tentatively, aware that his ignorance on the subject meant he might be asking something very foolish. 'I mean, how do these things work? Do the descendants have to go back to the scene every few years and re-consecrate it somehow?'

The suggestion earned a rare uncomplicated grin from Eldritch.

'Scattering incense and dancing naked under the full moon round the site of the binding?' the wizard asked, laughter warming his deep voice. 'It's a nice thought but a little tricky if the binding took place half a mile underground. No,' he dismissed the image with a regretful shake of his head. 'It's actually far simpler than that. The binding is tied to the bloodline. It's like the "till death us do part" in a wedding vow except it's not the death of the person making the vow that ends it. A Covenant says "this will endure while any child of mine lives". It goes on until the death of the last direct blood descendent; child, grandchild, great-grandchild and so on. If that's really what happened in 1910 and our William Wynn-Jones was a relative of the man who died in the mine I guess he'd be what...' His brow quirked as he did a quick mental calculation, 'His grandson?'

'And the Covenant would last that long?'

'Oh yes. Eventually they weaken as the bloodline becomes diluted over the generations, but seventy-seven years – two generations – isn't so very long.'

'1987,' Aidan mused. 'Twenty-six years. The timing fits in with the first sightings of the Black Dog.'

'Except that William can't have been the last Child of the Covenant.'

Aidan started as the quietly spoken words cut across his like a rapier. Gwyn had been so silent that he had almost forgotten she was there. Eldritch too seemed equally surprised although whether that was due to what she said rather than her sudden interruption was a moot point. The tall man swung round to face her, questions in his eyes, as though he suspected she was being deliberately perverse.

'But it fits with the timings Gwyn,' Aidan protested, unsure why she should disagree. Opposite him Eldritch said nothing, but he knew the wizard's attention was focussed on Gwyn. There was a sudden watchfulness about him betrayed by the stiffening of his muscles and the way he shifted his weight forward, no longer sitting back in his chair but poised, waiting. Gwyn continued as if she neither noticed nor cared about the impact her words had had on the energies in the room.

'It does,' she said leaving Aidan puzzled as to how she could agree with him on that and yet not accept that the Covenant had ended with William. Almost as though reading his thoughts Gwyn gave a little half smile. She glanced at Eldritch and the smile took on the hint of a challenge.

'But it doesn't fit with what the demon told us.'

Not waiting to see if they understood she picked up her notebook and read, 'But the Covenant weakens. I wake. I rise.'

She eyed them over the pages and then closed it with a snap, as if to underline her point.

'If William was the last of the bloodline surely the demon would have said the Covenant was broken.'

Eldritch rubbed his chin thoughtfully as he considered her words.

'Whoever wrote that note seemed to think that he was,' he said slowly. 'And the article makes no mention of any family. I can't see any journalist worth his salt missing the chance to mention a grieving widow and children.'

Gwyn shook her head.

'They wouldn't necessarily know,' she countered smoothly. She paused then laid her key card on the table. 'Not if the child in question was illegitimate.'

Eldritch said nothing but she must have read either doubt or disapproval in the tightening of his lips.

'Oh come now. People do have them you know – even computer programmers. He might not even have known about it himself. A brief affair or a holiday romance.' Her eyes flicked from Eldritch back to Aidan. 'It's perfectly possible.'

'But if the bloodline wasn't broken why do the incidents with the Black Dog start with William's death?' Eldritch asked, his tone suggesting that he didn't expect her to have an answer. Gwyn threw back a question of her own.

'What would happen if William died before his child was born? The bloodline would be unbroken but for a time the Covenant would rest on an unborn child.' Again she glanced at Aidan. 'Surely that would weaken it?'

Eldritch opened his mouth to comment and then shut it again. He scowled at Gwyn but under the tangled forelock of his hair his expression was thoughtful.

'So the Covenant weakens sufficiently for the demon to be able to create an avatar. Then, when the child is born and the Covenant strengthens, it's still able to use the avatar to source power from this world and slowly it increases its strength despite the Covenant.'

He sat back in his chair, his eyes never leaving her face. Then he gave a small laugh and said incredulously, 'You have the most convoluted way of thinking I've ever come across.'

Gwyn dipped her head as though acknowledging a compliment.

'It would fit though, wouldn't it?' she pressed him. The wizard sighed and leaned forward, propping his elbows on the table and resting his head in his hands either conceding defeat or simply wearied by the conversation.

'Yes,' he agreed at last, his voice reluctant. 'It would fit.'

He stayed there for a moment longer then scrubbed his palms over his face and raised his head, ready to contemplate the world and the witch anew.

'So, an illegitimate child,' Eldritch tested the words, toying with the idea. 'Well, I suppose you're right. A bloodline isn't like a legal inheritance. It passes to the children regardless of whether they were born inside or outside marriage and people do have them.'

'Do you?' asked Gwyn, mischief clear in her face.

Eldritch jerked upright sharply, regarding her with a small frown of disapproval.

'None that I'm aware of,' he said primly, his lips compressing into a thin line as if shocked by the impertinence of the question.

'Ah – that you're aware of.'

'Do you?' he countered but Gwyn parried the enquiry with a swift grin.

'No. And I would be aware of them.'

Aidan watched the pair of them with a tolerant smile, amused by the verbal sparring, but there was a puzzle lurking in the back of his hazel eyes. With his head in his hands Eldritch hadn't seen the look on Gwyn's face when he had answered her question about the Child. But Aidan had. It wasn't the cat got the cream expression he had expected of her having wrung such an admission from her adversary. Instead what he saw was something more akin to grief or fear, as if what she had heard had somehow confirmed her worst nightmare. For a second her eyes had turned towards him and in that moment he had had the oddest feeling that her fear was somehow connected with him – which made no sense at all – then she had looked away and the moment was gone, leaving him wondering whether he had imagined it after all.

As if she felt the weight of his thoughts Gwyn turned her head, leaving off her baiting to smile at him and he could read nothing untoward in her expression. She ran her hands through her hair, lifting the dark swags of it off her shoulders and twisting them into crazy tasselled knots on either side of her ears, seemingly unaware of how daft it looked. For a moment he wondered if the clowning around was a deliberate distraction then he dismissed the thought as ridiculous.

'Well boys,' Gwyn's smile reached out to both of them, warm and encompassing as a hug. 'I think it's time we took a break and worked out what we need to do next.'

Gwyn made a point of searching out Mike before they went to tell him they were going down to the restaurant and to ask him to hold on to the research they had ordered. While she did so Aidan collected together the chapel books and tidied them away into their box. As he picked up the last Bible his eyes were drawn to the text at the top of the open page.

And he laid hold on the dragon, that old serpent, which is the Devil, and Satan, and bound him a thousand years,

> *And cast him into the bottomless pit, and shut him up,*
> *and set a seal upon him, that he should deceive the nations*
> *no more, till the thousand years should be fulfilled; and after*
> *that he must be loosed a little season.*

The two verses from the Revelation were underlined in soft pencil. Aidan shivered as he replaced the fold of notepaper between the pages and gently closed the Bible trying to ignore the goose flesh crawling up his spine. He didn't count himself a Christian, in fact he didn't admit to any religious leanings beyond a vague belief that there had to be something outside the human experience, but even in a secular world it was hard to grow up without absorbing something of society's beliefs and the ancient words touched a chord within him. What would Sal or Mike think when they eventually came to catalogue the books? Would they read the cutting and its cryptic note and leave them in place or would they choose to discard them? He paused in the act of putting the Bible back in the box and turned the little black bound volume in his hand, running his fingers over the ancient leather binding. Behind him he could hear the soft murmur of Gwyn and Mike talking over by the desk. There was no one else near, Eldritch having wandered off to look at the South Reading Room. Deliberately Aidan opened the Bible and retrieved the cutting, carefully sliding it out of sight amongst his own notes. Then he put the Bible back with the other books and went to join Gwyn.

CHAPTER 8

'So how are we going to find them?'

Eldritch gave Aidan a quizzical glance over the remaining bite of his bacon roll. The smell of freshly cooked bacon had engulfed them as they entered the restaurant and it had only taken Aidan's rather feeble excuse of "well, it is nearly lunchtime" for all three of them to succumb to temptation.

'Who?' he asked.

'The missing Child and whoever wrote that note of course.'

Aidan thought it should have been obvious.

'We don't.'

Eldritch shook his head and frowned at Aidan almost as if to ask why on earth they would do such a thing.

'But surely they could help us...' Aidan's voice trailed off in the face of Eldritch's intensely sceptical look.

'I doubt it.'

There was more than a little arrogance in the wizard's tone. He wiped his lips with a paper napkin and added dismissively, 'We have no way of knowing who wrote the note and the only hope we have of finding William's illegitimate child is if his name appears on the birth certificate. My guess is that it doesn't or else the journalists would have found it.'

He paused as if to give Aidan the chance to dispute this view but his expression said clearly he himself had no doubts. Aidan scowled unhappily but he had to concede that what

Eldritch had said was true. He glanced at Gwyn, hoping she might have some insight he hadn't considered, but she simply shrugged.

'He's right.'

'Besides, what help can they give us? There's no guarantee that the Child will have any power and even if he does the likelihood is that he's completely untrained. What good is that?'

Eldritch crumpled up the used napkin and dropped it onto his plate as though similarly discarding the thought of the Child and the note's author as well. Aidan felt a stab of irritation. The casual dismissal reminded him uncomfortably of the Englishman's attitude when they had met above the Bite. Since getting to know the wizard Aidan had found reasons to excuse that behaviour but it crossed his mind now that perhaps he had been a little too ready to forgive. There was a side to his friend's character that wasn't very likeable. It also occurred to him that Eldritch had been wrong about his need for help that night and he wondered if he might be just as wrong now. But it wasn't an argument he wanted to go into. Not when he had no clues, no ideas, nothing in fact other than a gut feeling that told him the identity of the Child had to be important. So he shrugged in turn and muttered, 'It was just a thought.'

But there was something else that the wizard had said that had piqued his interest.

'Why wouldn't the Child have any power? Wouldn't he have inherited it?'

'Not necessarily. Power is inherited, yes, but it's not unusual for it to skip generations.'

Mercurial as the British weather Eldritch's attitude had changed and there was no hint of his earlier arrogance in his response. Whether it was because the wizard no longer felt he was being challenged, Aidan wasn't sure, but Eldritch surprised him by adding, 'Neither of my parents had power although my uncle – my mother's brother – did. I was taught by my grandmother.'

'The one who gave you the ring?' Aidan asked, remembering. As if in answer Eldritch's fingers strayed almost unconsciously to touch the chain around his neck.

'Yes.'

A hundred memories resonated in that one word. He was still for a moment, grey eyes focussed inward on some private image.

'By God she was a hard taskmaster.' A brief, sweet smile softened his angular face, taking the sting from his words. 'How about you?' he asked, turning to Gwyn.

She laughed, a soft huffing of breath, as though sharing a joke with him.

'Much the same. My mother understood about power but she had none of her own. All my training came from my grandmother.'

She took a sip of tea and added nonchalantly, 'Oh, and a month with an Indian yogi when I was four.'

'What?'

Aidan's eyes looked like they might stand out on stalks he was staring so hard at Gwyn. Even Eldritch seemed taken aback by her casual pronouncement.

'I don't suppose you knew I was born in India, did you?' Gwyn continued innocently. Her expression was deadpan but the twinkle in her eyes gave away her delight at their astonishment.

'You think your father was feckless? Mine was a student my

mother met in Goa. They had a brief affair and nine months later I was born.' She directed a wry gaze at Aidan. 'Think yourself lucky that you were going to be named after one of your mother's friends,' she challenged. 'Mine named me after the house they were staying in.'

'I didn't realise your name was Indian,' Eldritch said, with more tact than Aidan would have given him credit for, given all he had endured at Gwyn's hands that morning, and certainly more tact than he himself could have managed.

'Oh no, it's Welsh alright, well sort of. The bungalow belonged to an ex-pat couple. They used to run a vegetable stall on Newtown market, would you believe, until they dropped out and retired to Goa. I don't think either of them actually spoke Welsh but they called the bungalow Gwynyfa. It was supposed to be the Welsh for "paradise", except they spelt it wrong, but apparently my dad liked it – said it sounded like a Welsh version of Guinevere.'

The cant of Gwyn's eyebrows spoke volumes as to what she thought of that.

'Gwynyfa,' Eldritch tried the sound of it and nodded as if agreeing with that earlier judgement. 'It's a pretty name.'

Gwyn's eyes narrowed fractionally as she tried to work out if he was teasing her.

'Anyway,' she continued, 'that's where my name comes from. It's also why I spell Gwyn with a Y not an E.'

Seeing the confusion on Eldritch's face she explained, 'Gwyn spelt with a Y is a man's name. It should be spelt with an E for a woman. It confuses the hell out of people when they contact me on the basis of the copy I've written and they're expecting to talk to a man.'

'But far be it for you to be contrary,' murmured Eldritch with a slight smile. Gwyn carried on as if she hadn't heard him.

'It's not a bad thing sometimes. Technical writing used to be a very male dominated field. I'm convinced I picked up some of my earlier commissions because editors thought I was a man.'

'J.K. Rowling used the same strategy,' observed Aidan, finally trusting himself to say something that wouldn't earn him a clip around the ear.

'Hmm… sadly I don't earn her sort of money.'

'How long did you live in India?'

'I spent my first four years out there. We travelled around a lot, staying at various ashrams while my mother sought enlightenment. I'm not sure she ever found it but it certainly wasn't for the lack of trying. Every few months we'd be off somewhere new. Then, when I was four, a yogi told her that I was a source of disruptive energies and I needed to be trained by someone who understood the powers I had. That was it. The next thing I knew I'd been packed off to Wales to live with my grandparents.'

'Nice.' Eldritch made a face at such a gesture of maternal closeness.

'It was a long time ago.'

Gwyn dismissed it with a twitch of the lips but Aidan wondered if the four-year-old Gwynyfa had been quite so stoical. Perhaps she had been for Gwyn added, 'Besides, the yogi was right. I needed to be trained.' And the smile those memories conjured mirrored that of Eldritch as he had remembered his grandmother – sweet and almost ethereal.

'She's still out there, in Darjeeling. She sends me cards occasionally – for Diwali – and I send her Christmas cards back.

She's settled down now but the group she's with doesn't encourage visitors. I last saw her oh, about five years ago. We met up at a little hill station town called Mount Abu. A curious little place but lovely and cool after the plains. It was June at the time. She was enjoying herself studying Ayurvedic medicine. Maybe she inherited some of Nain's healing after all.'

Gwyn's gaze swept between the two men and her smile was wry.

'You're right,' she said, picking up her tea cup and looking at Eldritch over its rim. 'All families are weird. It's the only normal thing about them.'

Eldritch laughed sympathetically, pushing a hand through the thick brush of his hair, and Aidan wondered what stories he might have to tell, this man who refused to be known by his given name. The three of them made an odd grouping – odder still if one knew what had brought them together – but the feeling of camaraderie that flowed between them gave him confidence to voice the question that had gradually been shaping itself in his mind.

'So if power's inherited, where did mine come from?' he asked softly, his eyes dropping to the smooth grain of the tabletop. 'I mean, I know it's not much, not compared with you two but what I did, on Saturday, when the avatar came…'

He hesitated, suddenly diffident as he sought the words to express what he had experienced.

'I didn't know what I was doing but it felt as though something in me did, like it was an instinct taking over.'

He looked up, shyness giving way to an awkward defiance, but neither Gwyn nor Eldritch sought to contradict him.

'There was no suggestion of power in either of your

parents?' Eldritch asked, his deep voice thoughtful but not challenging. Aidan shook his head.

'There wasn't, was there?'

He glanced at Gwyn for confirmation. She smiled but there was sadness and something else lurking in the back of those clear peridot eyes.

'Your mother − bless her − was a lovely, kind woman but she had no magic. As for your father…'

She stopped and for a second Aidan had the strangest feeling that she was on the verge of saying something very different but eventually she said, 'James never showed any sign of having magic. Neither did his parents − not that I'm aware of. I never knew your other grandparents to be able to say about them.'

'If you could ask you'd probably find that one of them showed traces of power.'

Eldritch scrubbed a hand across his chin. He had been clean-shaven that morning but already a heavy shadow of stubble was darkening his jaw. His thin lips quirked in an unspoken acknowledgement that what he suggested might not be possible.

'Then again it could just as easily have been a great-grandparent. I wouldn't let it worry you,' he concluded.

'I guess not,' Aidan agreed reluctantly, disappointed with the answer but recognising its essential truth. He drained the last of his coffee but as he did so his expression changed.

'You knew though, didn't you Gwyn?' he said abruptly, putting the mug down on the table and staring at her. 'You knew.' His voice changed as he moved from question to certainty. He was right and the startled look on her face confirmed it.

'Aidan, I—'

Aidan cut her off. He realised then what it was that he had just seen in her eyes – a sense of knowing, of having seen this coming.

'When we talked, after John's funeral, I asked you why you'd told me about shrieks and things as a child and you said you'd thought I might be able to sense them. But you wouldn't tell me why. You thought I'd inherited power, didn't you?'

'Ah,' Gwyn relaxed. 'That wasn't to do with your parentage. I told you how I had to heal your mother when she was pregnant.'

Aidan nodded but said nothing, waiting for her to continue.

'I thought that being exposed to that level of power might affect you. Not that it would hurt you in any way,' she added quickly, holding up her hands to reassure him, 'but that you might be more sensitive as a result. That's why I tried to teach you about the Unseen Realm when you were younger. I had no reason then to suspect you would inherit power as well, but now...'

A small, one-sided shrug encompassed everything they had discussed.

'I think it's fairly clear that you have, whoever it's come from.'

She paused, absently tracing a finger through the crumbs on her plate, like a diviner searching for omens amongst the entrails of a sacrifice. Then she looked up at him and there was a promise in her ancient forest sprite eyes.

'When this is over we'll see if we can work out who it was.'

'So, if we're not going to try and find the Child what are we going to do?'

With the origins of his power at least partly addressed by

Gwyn's promise Aidan's thoughts circled inexorably back to their original discussion. He looked at both his companions for an answer but it was Eldritch who spoke.

'Exactly what we originally planned to.'

There was no hesitation in the wizard's response. He leaned back in his chair, tipping it back onto two legs so far that Aidan half expected Gwyn to snap at him.

'If we accept that the Covenant is connected to the original William Wynn-Jones,' Eldritch shot a look at Gwyn, 'and I think we can take it that it is – then we know that the demon is breaking through somewhere in the tunnels of the old Greenfields mine. If we pull up the article about the explosion with luck it will give us some indication as to where in the mine the original breakthrough happened.'

Aidan nodded cautiously, following the other man's logic but unsure where it got them.

'And then what?' He gestured helplessly. 'Even if we can find plans – hell, even if we find one with a big X marks the spot and "here be demons" written on it – what good is that going to do us?' Aidan stopped short as he saw the look on Eldritch's face. 'Oh no, tell me you're not seriously thinking of trying to get into the mine.'

Eldritch dropped his chair back onto four legs and leaned forward with a swift, pantherish movement, his previously relaxed expression suddenly deadly serious. 'We have to. That's where the demon's breaking through. That's where it has to be stopped.'

Aidan shook his head.

'That's impossible.'

Eldritch's eyes narrowed as he favoured Aidan with a hard look.

'Why is it impossible?' he demanded, his voice taking on a dangerous edge and once again Aidan was reminded of their confrontation in the forest. He sighed and made a conscious effort to relax. He didn't relish the role of killjoy but someone had to inject some reality into this discussion. What Eldritch had in mind was sheer lunacy.

'Because the entrances to the mine workings are all sealed off,' he explained patiently. 'Those that weren't blocked when the mines were closed have long since been bricked up by the county council. They don't want curious hikers wandering into the workings and falling down the shafts.'

'That's the main entrances,' Eldritch argued. 'What about ventilation shafts or other ways in?'

'They'll have been done as well. The ones on common land will have been sorted by the council. Those on private land will either have been capped because the farmers don't want their livestock falling down them or they'll have been used as handy places to dump all their rubbish. Either way you're not going to be able to get down them.' He saw the frustrated anger building in Eldritch's eyes and added quietly, 'I'm sorry, I'm not deliberately trying to be awkward. I'm just telling you what we're going to find.'

Eldritch's jaw tightened, his lips compressing into a thin, hard line as he considered what Aidan had said.

'There must be another way in,' he said stubbornly, glowering at the younger man as though force of will alone could get him to retract his words. Aidan returned the glare with a level stare of his own, refusing to be cowed.

'We can check the plans,' he conceded, but his tone made it obvious that he doubted it would do them any good.

Eldritch's eyes glittered dangerously and Aidan thought the wizard would argue but instead he turned his head and stared out of the window. Aidan eyed him silently for a moment, exasperated. He was under no illusion that Eldritch was admiring the view. Even without Gwyn's sensitivity he could feel the simmering roil of emotions barely held in check behind that angular profile; the sense of frustration – of being thwarted by circumstance – and the determination to find a way round the deadlock. Another man might have paced, seeking release in movement, but Eldritch was motionless, the energy of his emotions condensing within his tall frame until Aidan felt as though he stood at the base of a snow slope in the moment before an avalanche. He glanced at Gwyn, curious to see what she made of the Englishman's stubborn refusal to listen to reason, but wasn't sure how to read her raised eyebrows and the tiny shake of her head unless a combination of *give him space* and *what an idiot* made sense.

Aidan wasn't sure it did but even as he was debating what he could do about it Eldritch turned back and regarded him balefully. It seemed to Aidan that, framed in the dark curtain of his hair, the Englishman's face was paler, the shadows under his eyes more pronounced than they had been moments before.

'Alright,' a look of grim resignation pulled at the corners of Eldritch's mouth as he spoke. 'Always supposing that what you say is true and we can't get into the mine itself then we need to know where the entrances are – the tunnel entrances, the air shafts, all of them – and then each one will have to be sealed individually against the demon.'

He looked from Aidan to Gwyn as though daring them to challenge him.

'To survive in this world a demon has to take a physical form. So normally it will seek to manifest in the presence of its chosen host — someone it's already opened a channel to, someone it knows it can easily possess. It will call that host to it. But if no one can get into the mine because it's sealed our demon won't have that option. Instead it will be forced to leave the mine in its ethereal form and find a host and that's going to be the first poor innocent it comes across.'

Eldritch paused, his hand coming up almost unconsciously to cover his mouth as though the very thought of what he had said sickened him. For a second a storm of grief and anger played across his face, then he swallowed convulsively and said, 'I can put spells on each of the entrances that should trap the demon if it tries to pass them.'

Aidan looked at the wizard curiously, wondering why there was no trace of satisfaction in his voice, no indication that he had just solved the problem of their having to access the mine. At the very least he would have expected a return of that cocksure arrogance that the Englishman did so well but instead Eldritch sounded ineffably weary, so much so that Aidan felt a cold prickle of uncertainty replace his initial sense of relief. There was something wrong, something he was missing.

'What is it?' he asked without thinking and then kicked himself mentally knowing that Eldritch would never tell him. But to his surprise the wizard raised his head and the ghost of a brief, tired smile tugged at his lips.

'Spells like that take a lot of energy. It's going to be like drawing the veil on your cabin on each of the entrances. Not only that but they'll have to be renewed almost daily.'

The grey eyes sought Aidan's, their direct gaze seeming to

ask if the younger man understood what he was saying. Then the wizard sighed and shook his head.

'I don't know how long I can keep that up for. If I start setting the spells too soon I'll catch the demon when it manifests but there's every chance I won't have the strength left to stop it. But if I leave it too late it will escape from the mine and take a host and it will be the scenario with Nigel Granger all over again.' Beneath the tangled black forelock Eldritch's expression was bleak. He scrubbed a hand through his hair and when he spoke again his voice was heavy with resignation. 'It would be so much easier if we could reach the spot where it's breaking through.'

'I think you're forgetting something.'

Eldritch turned at the sound of Gwyn's voice.

'Such as?'

'You're not doing this on your own. I can help you.'

One elfin brow slanted upwards as she read the puzzlement in his eyes.

'What do you think I've been doing these last few days if not feeding you energy? Oh, and let's skip the, *I can do this on my own* routine, shall we?' Gwyn silenced Eldritch's response before he had barely opened his mouth. 'You've already as good as admitted that you can't – and there's no shame in that, given what it entails – but the point is you don't need to.'

A smile took the sting from her words and Eldritch's expression changed from indignation to surprise as she reached out in an unexpected gesture of comfort and laid her hand on his arm.

'Let's see what we can find out about the mine first and then we can decide what we need to do to tackle the demon.'

CHAPTER 9

Achingly beautiful the first notes of Beethoven's Moonlight Sonata spiralled into the shadowy darkness. Brown glass caught and refracted topaz lamplight, sending myriad splinters of honey and amber across Aidan's face as he stretched out full-length on the sofa, beer in hand, and contemplated his notes on the Greenfields mine. Having something finite to look for had made their second search far simpler and the records had turned out to be more informative than they could have hoped. Aidan pulled one sheet from the half dozen fanned out across his chest and angled it to the light. Bless Messrs Johnson and Fitzsimmons who had thought to document the extent and prosperity of their holdings and the mine supervisor, Captain Trent, who had described in such detail the development of each new working, noting depths and dimensions alongside the tonnages of ore that were raised from them. How his niece in Colwyn must have delighted to receive his letters – Aidan smirked slightly at the thought of what that stiff Victorian gentleman had presumably considered to be riveting correspondence – but within their pages lay sufficient details to map much of the mine's layout.

Aidan re-read the notes, double-checking the written descriptions against the plan he had created from them and superimposed on the modern OS map. It had been an interesting exercise mapping horizontal miles of tunnels onto contours and hillsides and by no means all the shafts and workings Gwyn and Eldritch found mention of were shown on the modern map. It would be his job to find them, to guide the three of them to where the old records said these entrances had to be. Their success would depend on the accuracy with which he could take them to the locations he had calculated. Aidan took a long swallow of beer and smiled grimly at the coordinates he had noted on the map. Accuracy would be important but not all their problems lay in finding the ruined workings. If the records were to be believed at least one of the main drainage adits came out on private land. He stared for a while at the patterns of light dancing within the glass, mulling over that unexpected complication. They might get away with one visit unnoticed but somehow Aidan couldn't believe that Griff Howell would fail to notice, or take kindly to, their repeated presence on his land.

After a while Aidan turned from his notes on the tunnel layouts to read once again the account of the disaster that had claimed the lives of six men. In a report written for a local journal Edward Evans, a contemporary of the miners, recounted how work had been proceeding in a newly opened section of the mine when an explosion had caused a massive cave-in, bringing down the tunnel roof and entombing the men. Though there were no survivors to bear witness to the exact circumstances, experience suggested a misjudgement in the handling of the blasting powder had caused the tragedy and blame had quickly fallen on William Wynn-Jones who had been in charge of laying the fuse. In itself it was not an unreasonable conclusion but what shocked Aidan was that Evans publicly claimed it had been no accident. According to his account signs of far older workings had been uncovered in the days preceding the explosion and William Wynn-Jones had been heard repeatedly protesting that the area was unsafe. Evans noted that Wynn-Jones had gone so far as to approach the foreman – not just once, but on several occasions – to try and dissuade him from following their course and when the foreman had openly ridiculed the idea Wynn-Jones had claimed that disaster would follow any attempt to open up those ancient tunnels. Evans was quick to suggest that the humiliated Wynn-Jones had deliberately tampered with the blasting powder in an act of sabotage designed to vindicate him and his perverse beliefs. Even couched in the archaic, almost formal language of the journal Aidan could taste the bitterness with which the words had been written yet it seemed that Evans was not alone in his belief. At the end of his account he made mention of a benevolent fund set up by Captain Trent to provide for the dependents of the deceased miners. All the beneficiaries were listed but no member of William's family was among them. He had been twenty-eight. Even without knowing of the existence of the Covenant it was inconceivable to Aidan that he hadn't been married. Long after he had finished his beer he lay staring into the semi-darkness wondering what had become of the widow and any children that William had left behind.

Eventually Aidan got up and fetched another beer from the fridge. Then he took out the old newspaper cutting and looked again at the face of the last William Wynn-Jones. It was an ordinary face, nothing especially attractive and showing signs that at thirty-seven William was turning chubby, but the smile was warm and friendly. This William looked like the sort of man who would have made friends easily and kept them for life. *Had he known?* Aidan wondered. Was that why he had come to Llancathan; to visit the site of his grandfather's sacrifice? Or had it been pure coincidence that had brought him there?

'Did you have any idea what your grandfather did?' he asked that silent, smiling face. He looked for some trace of knowing in the dead man's eyes.

'Did they tell you he was a hero or did they never even mention his name?'

He fell silent, brooding over the injustice of Edward Evans' account. Was that why the family had moved away, to escape the shame that clung to William's memory? While his wife could in no way be held responsible for what had happened it was easy to guess that she might have been shunned as a result. Aidan could imagine the whispering behind her back, the things the children would shout in the street. As for her children, they would grow up being told not that their father was a hero, but that he was a murderer. Aidan's chest tightened with an almost palpable sensation of pain as he considered the likelihood. A deep sense of pity for that first William overwhelmed him.

'Was that all your sacrifice earned you?' he asked the shadowy figure he saw in his mind's eye. 'Did you think it was worth it?'

And out there somewhere was another young man – though he knew it was biased somehow he couldn't think of the Child as being a woman – much the same age as him who, without knowing it, was tied to this ancient battle. Did he have powers that he couldn't understand or had his legacy left him untouched? He shook his head.

'You're best out of it.' he told him.

Maybe Eldritch was right. Maybe the identity of the Child didn't matter, that what was important was their own strength of arms, but even now Aidan found himself scowling, as rankled by his recollection of Eldritch's attitude now as he had been in the restaurant. It was the same with the author of the note. While part of Aidan could understand his friend's complete focus on what they had to do and his refusal to waste time and energy on anything so unlikely to help them, he wanted to know more about the people who had encountered the demon before. Who had they been? What had they felt? He felt a kinship towards them and a sense of closeness that made Eldritch's casual dismissal not only unpalatable but also incomprehensible. How could he not be intrigued by them? How could he not want to know who it was who had watched through the years, tracking the fate of the Children of the Covenant? Aidan picked up the newspaper cutting and its accompanying note again, turning the yellowing paper over in his hand, trying to get a sense of the man behind it. Who had written those despairing lines, seeing the impending conflict mirrored in the Bible's end of days? A contemporary of the original William Wynn-Jones – though he would have been an old, old man by the time of the last William's death it wasn't impossible – or had the task of watching been handed down through another family as the Covenant had passed through William's?

With a small sigh Aidan put the cutting aside, accepting the likelihood that he would never know the answers to those questions but seeing that as no reason to give up asking them. One day he would look into it further but today – and he grimaced as a glance at his watch confirmed it was indeed past midnight – he needed to be up at the hut by eight, to set up for a morning on the ropes with the Hafren Youth Club. Barring unforeseen accidents, or the possibility that he might intentionally hang one of the youth club tearaways, the plan was that he would then meet Gwyn and Eldritch to go in search of the remains of the Greenfields mine. He scrubbed a hand across his face and yawned. Hormonal teenagers or equally temperamental adults – neither would be much fun if he didn't get some sleep first.

Looking back Aidan would wonder how they could have been so stupid as to assume that the demon would wait meekly for them to trap it in its lair, but at the time no such thoughts disturbed him or raised the hackles on his neck. He called Sula to him and went to bed.

He dreamed that he stood in a tiny kitchen, smaller even than Gwyn's. A woman stood there too, her back turned to him but still close because of the confines of the room. With hesitant fingers he reached out and touched the nape of her neck where the few wisps of hair were escaping from the bun into which she had wound the thickness of her plait. Her hair was mousy brown, plain in its colour but so soft to the touch. It tickled his face when they lay together in their small bed. The woman flinched at his touch and he snatched back his hand as though burnt.

'I have to do this Sarah,' he said. 'I have to. There's no one else.'

She turned then to face him, slowly, as though she were reluctant to look at him. He could see she had been crying, that the tears were very close to the surface even now, but she was doing her best to keep them from spilling over. Looking at her he was aware of how much he loved this woman. He wanted more than anything to take her in his arms and hold her there for an eternity. Instead he was going to desert her.

Sarah crossed her arms over the swollen mound of her belly. Two more months of waiting and they would have the child they had so longed for. How could he contemplate doing anything that would stop him seeing their child born?

'Do I have to beg you not to go, William?'

Her skin was so pale it seemed almost transparent, the blue tracery of veins showing too close to the surface, scarcely covered by flesh that had grown ever thinner through the months of her pregnancy, yet there was nothing but strength in her voice.

'Sarah...' his voice trailed off as he saw the look in her eyes. She knew what he had chosen and there were no sweet words he could offer her, nothing he could say that would ever blunt the pain of that choice, not even the truth, yet he offered it to her anyway. Insufficient though it was it was all that he had.

'If I don't stop the creature there's no one else who can. Men will die, Sarah.'

'You'll die,' she countered with unanswerable logic. He tried again.

'If I couldn't do anything – if this beast was going to take my life and yours, and Thomas' and Gwylym's, old Edward's and all the rest – and not one of us could do anything about it, but there was one man who could, a man who lived in another village maybe, who had the power to stop the creature – what then? We'd pray that he'd help us. We'd pray that he'd follow the path that the Good Lord walked before him and lay down his life to save us, wouldn't we?'

Her chin tipped up and she didn't answer but he knew she had heard him. Very gently he reached out and took her thin hands in his own, feeling the swollen shape of the knuckles, already starting to stiffen and knot from a lifetime of hard manual work. He smoothed his fingers over the work-reddened skin, his own hands calloused and rough but infinitely tender as he raised her fingertips to his lips and − mercy of mercies − she let him.

'But it's not a stranger from another village who has the chance to save us. It's me.'

He kissed each one of her fingers in turn, trying to memorise the shape of them, the taste of them, the sweet sensation of her skin under his tongue.

'I'm the one who can do something. I can put a stop to it. I can cast the beast back into its pit and bring the walls raining down upon it.' He tried not to feel her stiffen as he spoke. 'I can save Gwyndaf and the rest of the boys. I can make sure Megan sees her Tada at the end of the day.'

'But you don't care that it's your own child who'll grow up without a father? You don't care that my heart will break, that you'll be killing me when you walk out of that door?'

Sarah did not snatch her hands away but slowly she withdrew them, pulling them down to her apron. He let his go with them and when she bunched them into fists he slid his up to encircle the thin prominence of her wrists, holding them loosely because he could not bear to let her go.

'It won't stay in the mine, cariad. It will call people to it. One by one, they'll go, without any knowing of what's wrong and without anyone able to fight, and it may be our child that goes to it.'

He looked into the pale winter blue of her eyes and tried not to see the red of her earlier tears.

'I can stop it now – it's only just waking. It's not as strong as it will be, but if I wait it will get stronger and in time I won't be able to. It has to be now. It has to be today.'

He reached for her properly and this time she didn't resist him. He pulled her close, feeling the thinness of her shoulders. They barely had enough to eat now, what would she and the child do? Surely the chapel would look after her? He lowered his face to the top of her head, breathing in the scent of lavender that clung to her hair and the smells of soap and cooking. Sweet Lord, he wanted her, one last time before he went into the darkness. He held her fiercely. Were he able to he would have crushed her flesh into his, melding them into one being that could never be divided; him, her and the child growing within her. She was crying now, her tears soaking his pit shirt, and his own were running freely to meet them.

'Promise me you'll not forget me,' he whispered.

She raised her head up.

'How could I ever forget you William? I'll love you 'til the day I die.'

'Promise me you'll tell the child about me?'

She buried her head in his shoulder and, if she answered him, her words were lost in the sound of her tears.

'She's not here.'

If Aidan was surprised that it was Eldritch who opened Gwyn's front door he was even more surprised by the man's words.

'Why not? Where is she?'

Eldritch shrugged, winced and rubbed his shoulder absently, as though it had twinged rather than caused him real pain.

'She went for a run,' he said in a rather bemused tone of voice, stepping aside to let Aidan come in. 'Don't ask me why. She was up half the night working, or at least every time I woke up I could see the light from her PC under the door. To be honest I'm not sure she went to bed. She looked pretty wrecked this morning.'

Aidan was surprised to hear something akin to concern softening Eldritch's voice.

'After breakfast she said she had something she needed to think through so she was going for a run.'

Aidan pulled a face.

'She's probably working out how to organise some article she's writing.' He gestured at the disarray of her desk as though it proved his point. After a moment's consideration he pushed enough papers aside to allow him to prop one hip on the corner, leaving Eldritch to choose which cat he was going to fight for possession of an armchair.

'And she can do that while she's running?' Eldritch looked at Aidan sceptically. With the air of one who had learned his place in the household pecking order he elected not to sit but leaned his tall frame against the wall, hooking his thumbs in the front pockets of his jeans. 'She's been gone a couple of hours. How far can she run?'

'Gwyn? She runs marathons. Yeah, I know you'd never believe it to look at her, but she does. If she's got it into her head to think something through by running she could be all the way to Rhayader before she stops for breath.' Aidan grinned at the look on Eldritch's face, somewhere equally between horror and admiration. 'I'll be annoyed if she has though,' he continued. 'We've got five hours of usable light before we'll have to call it a day. It's going to be a stretch to cover all the ground we need to.'

He glanced at his watch. 'Did she say where she was going or how far she was planning to run?'

'No.'

Eldritch shook his head.

'She had all her kit on but she went off in her car. I thought she must be going to a running track somewhere or a gym.'

Aidan shot him an amused look.

'Not round here. She'll have gone up on the hills somewhere or maybe round the reservoir or into the forest. You're sure she didn't mention anywhere?'

'To be honest she didn't say much at all before she went. She seemed pretty distracted.' Eldritch frowned as though something about that memory disturbed him. After a moment he added tentatively, 'You don't think anything could have happened to her, do you?'

Aidan made a rather uncharitable noise.

'It's more likely that she's got her head wrapped round a commission and she's forgotten what time we agreed we'd meet. It wouldn't be the first time.'

He sighed, trying not to let his irritation get the upper hand. There was nothing to do except wait for Gwyn to come home in her own good time.

'I've got a spare pair of boots for you in the car. You might as well try them on while we're waiting, see if they fit.'

He pushed himself upright but stopped as he heard the

sound of a car in the lane. Eldritch turned to the window.

'Here she is,' he announced, as the old blue hatchback pulled up outside.

'About time,' Aidan muttered as though he had been waiting for hours rather than minutes.

But although it was Gwyn's car it wasn't Gwyn who got out of the driver's seat. Aidan's first thought as he opened the door was, *what the hell is Bethan Hughes doing driving Gwyn's car?* Then he froze, all conscious thought splintering as he realised she was in uniform. He barely noticed the police car pulling up behind the hatchback, all his attention was on Bethan. As she reached the garden gate he saw the look on her face and felt the blood drain from his own. His hands went icy cold and the world swayed until a strong arm caught him round the shoulders. A tiny whine of pain escaped him but it was all the sound he could make while his mind screamed, *no, not Gwyn!* in a medley of horror and fear.

'Aidan, I'm so sorry.'

He could barely hear Bethan's words over the pounding of blood in his ears.

'I've got some terrible news about Gwyn.'

CHAPTER 10

They went straight to the hospital. If anyone had ever driven the thirty miles to Aberystwyth faster Eldritch would not have wanted to be their passenger. By the time they hit the A44 he had serious doubts about being Aidan's and as the miles fell behind them and they climbed the moors around Plynlimon, the silvery tumble of the Wye far below them and the road hugging the steepening mountainside, he commended his spirit to whatever benevolent deities might be listening and abandoned himself to fate. Aidan drove like a fury; tight-lipped and white-faced, his eyes never leaving the road. On hearing Bethan's news Eldritch had immediately suggested they take his car, thinking that Aidan would be in no fit state to drive, but Aidan had refused.

'You don't know the roads,' he had snapped as he flung himself into the Land Rover and it had been a simple choice between going with him or being left behind. Except for an icily vicious 'Shut it!' when he had tentatively suggested that Gwyn was in good hands, that had been the last thing Aidan had said to him and for his own part Eldritch felt disinclined to say anything that might take Aidan's mind from the road. Beyond prayer there was nothing to be done except to sit there, white-knuckled, and silently hope that all three of them made it to Aberystwyth alive.

Bronglais hospital was an unprepossessing sprawl of concrete buildings scattered on the slopes of Penglais Hill just below the splendour of the National Library. Eldritch hadn't realised why the streets had looked familiar until he saw the brown tourist information signs. Then he found himself overcome by a sense of disbelief that yesterday he could have been here with Gwyn, admiring the views and teasing her about her passion for books, and now he was back under such very different circumstances. He tried telling himself that that irritating contradiction of a woman would be fine but every time he did he saw the look the policewoman had given Aidan and in his heart he couldn't help but fear the worst.

Heaven only knew what must be going through Aidan's mind. That the young man was hurting was obvious but he had retreated behind an emotional brick wall and Eldritch wasn't sure he had the right even to try to break it down. All he could do was be there to offer whatever support Aidan needed, and to keep on offering whether it was accepted or not. Then, when they knew the best or the worst that would come of this, he would settle the matter by destroying the demon. That much he promised himself as he followed Aidan at a near run across the car park.

Faced with the clinical green walls and sterile hospital smell that enveloped them the nervous energy that had sustained Aidan up until that point seemed to desert him. He stormed through the doors of the A&E department and then ground to a halt in the foyer, standing and gazing around him as though he had lost all sense of purpose. Eldritch put a hand on his shoulder.

'We'll ask at reception,' he said, keeping his hand there and steering the younger man towards the desk.

'Oh dear God,' Aidan whispered. He clasped a hand to his mouth, his face suddenly beyond pale, and turned away sharply but not so fast that Eldritch missed the shine of tears in his eyes, swiftly blinked away. Eldritch dropped his gaze to the floor, giving Aidan the space to compose himself, but he too was shaken. The nurse who had shown them to Gwyn's bedside, tucked in a side ward, had warned them that her injuries were serious but nothing could prepare them for seeing what those words meant in reality. Almost against his will his eyes were drawn back to the still figure in the bed.

The black mane of hair, spreading out across the pillow, was almost all that was recognisable of Gwyn. Her entire face was swollen, the skin mottled red and black with bruising where her attacker had hit her repeatedly. Over the horror of the bruising a row of stitches ran from the corner of her left eye towards her ear, the little tufts of black thread like a parody of Frankenstein's monster above the incongruously cheerful blue and mustard check of the hospital gown. Eldritch closed his eyes briefly, drawing in a shuddering breath, and then forced himself to look again at the raw and battered flesh, mentally acknowledging each injury, each insult to her body, as if by doing so he could somehow take some of the burden of them from her. The policewoman had said that, having beaten her unconscious, Gwyn's attacker had dragged her body some way from the road and dumped her, effectively leaving her to die. That she had been found was due solely to a sharp-eyed farmer on her way to check on her stock who had glimpsed the fluorescent yellow of Gwyn's running jacket in amongst the gorse and blaeberry bushes and decided to investigate. If Marion Taylor had been in more of a hurry to get to her ewes Gwyn might have lain there unnoticed for days if not longer. By then it wouldn't have mattered who had found her.

Who did this? Eldritch did not have to think hard to find an answer. He knew – though he had no proof and certainly nothing he could share with the police. This was the work of the demon's agent, that unknown human intermediary who had been behind the slaughter of Tom Owen's sheep, raising power so that the demon could re-manifest its damaged and defeated avatar. His half-healed shoulder stabbed with remembered pain as he thought of what he had been through and how that hard won advantage had been stripped from them by that unknown person's wiles. That had been bad enough, but now this! Once more they had been out-manoeuvred. He watched Aidan fumble as he took Gwyn's hand in his own, the young man's normally sure movements rendered clumsy by his desire not to disturb the cannula running into the back of her hand, and felt a hard seed of anger growing inside him. An alternative to the bitter helplessness he felt when he looked at Gwyn's supine form, he welcomed it, letting it grow. They would pay for this, he promised himself. Whoever was responsible, he would make them pay. He felt the hot seethe of his blood and in that moment he could imagine the instant when he blasted the life from them. Closing his eyes he let himself anticipate the warm pleasure of revenge.

'She's always been there for me,' Aidan spoke softly but the tenderness in his voice reached Eldritch, lifting him from the dark violence of his thoughts. 'Even when I hated her – when I blamed her for not being able to save Mum's life – she never turned away from me.'

Aidan's eyes never left Gwyn's face as he spoke. He ran his thumb across her knuckles, stroking her fingers, the gentle caress keeping time with the slow rise and fall of her breathing, wordlessly encouraging her, letting her know he was there.

'I don't know why she did it. I don't know *how* she did it. Anyone with any sense would have packed their bags and left me to it the moment I turned sixteen. I must have made it pretty obvious that that was what I wanted.'

'That's probably why she did it – just to spite you,' Eldritch said dryly. Amazingly that raised the ghost of a laugh from Aidan, as it had been intended to. He glanced up briefly as Eldritch continued.

'I've not known her long but I don't think I've ever met anyone else as stubborn as she is.'

'You don't know the half of it.'

The trace of a smile crept into Aidan's voice as he turned back to the bed and Eldritch dared to drop his hand onto Aidan's shoulder, squeezing it briefly in a slightly awkward gesture of comfort.

'She'll be alright you know,' he said, trying to instil his words with all his faith, all his belief that nothing would stop this crazy, dynamo of a woman for long. Aidan nodded, the smallest of movements, as though he didn't quite trust his voice to answer but after a moment he turned back to Eldritch, his hazel eyes dark and intense.

'Can you help her?'

It was a question Eldritch was completely unprepared for. Taken by surprise, shocked and disconcerted, at first he didn't know how to respond. At least Aidan hadn't asked "will you help her?" with its implication that power could be used like a fairytale magic wand to set everything right if he would but choose to wield it. *If only that were the case.* Eldritch swallowed,

135

his mouth suddenly gone dry as the feelings of helplessness he thought he had banished returned to swamp him. *Don't you think I would if I could?* He wanted to shout, but he couldn't bring himself to throw the angry words in Aidan's face, knowing that such venom was just an echo of his own impotence and frustration. Aidan must have read the hesitation in his eyes but he did not back off.

'You're a wizard,' he said, with flawless logic. 'You have power. Isn't there anything you can do to help?'

It was not a child's petulant demand for miracles – life had long since taught Aidan that even if such things might happen they could not be summoned to order – but an adult's request that they consider all avenues of help. Yet still Eldritch felt himself held hostage to that child's hopes and fears and when Aidan's eyes caught his it was he who looked away first.

'Yes, I'm a wizard,' he agreed, 'but I'm not a healer. If I were I wouldn't be here now. The demon would have taken me, not Helen.'

He shot Aidan a haunted, hunted look, as he searched for the words to explain the impossibility of what he was asking. But Aidan didn't wait for him to find them. The young man's nostrils flared.

'So you're saying you won't even try?'

The quietness of his voice did nothing to offset the venom in his tone as he rounded on the wizard. He eyed Eldritch with something akin to contempt.

'What's wrong? Are you scared the demon's going to get you now?'

Eldritch held onto his temper with difficulty, swallowing down his initial response. Keeping his voice low in deference to their surroundings he said, 'What I'm saying is that I don't have the skill – the knowledge – to do anything. I wouldn't know where to start.'

'Gentlemen?'

Aidan was opening his mouth to reply, and from the look on his face his words would have been ugly, but the query stopped him in his tracks. There was just enough steel injected into that one word to make it clear that the speaker was aware of the brewing argument and would tolerate no such thing on the ward. Aidan's expression went through an odd metamorphosis from embarrassment to anxious hope as he looked past Eldritch to the newcomer. Eldritch turned slowly, schooling his own face into something more agreeable than the angry scowl he had shown Aidan. He was surprised to find himself facing a woman several years younger than himself. From the authority in her voice he had expected someone more of Gwyn's age, not a woman who appeared to be barely into her thirties. For an instant the woman's expression hardened and he realised she had seen his double-take and understood the reason behind it but in less time than it took him to think it she had covered that flash of irritation with a professional smile.

'I'm Doctor Carmel, the consultant looking after Miss Hughes. Are you relatives?'

Aidan was already scrambling to his feet and stepping forward, anxious for news.

'She's my, that is she was…'

He flinched visibly from his use of the past tense, correct though it was.

'She used to be my guardian.'

The doctor nodded once as though filing the information away and then looked at Eldritch enquiringly.

'I'm a family friend,' he said with a self-deprecating smile. 'I was visiting when we got the news of what had happened.'

He took a half step backwards, turning away slightly so it was obvious that he was deferring to Aidan. Much though he wanted to hear what the doctor had to say it was Aidan she should be speaking to. He had no claim on Gwyn. If Aidan missed that slight repositioning the doctor did not.

'I see,' she said and there was the smallest softening in her eyes as she turned back to Aidan.

'How bad is it, doctor?' Aidan didn't waste time on niceties. There was only one thing he wanted to know. Eldritch could sympathise with that because he wanted the same thing. The doctor seemed to understand.

'Surprisingly, given the ferocity of the attack, her injuries aren't as extensive as was initially feared. That's not to say that they're not serious,' she added quickly. 'She has a fractured skull and her scans show that there is bruising to the underlying tissue. That's not surprising in a case like this but realistically we won't be able to determine the extent of any damage until she regains consciousness.'

'You're talking about brain damage.'

The doctor considered Aidan with a dispassionate gaze then she nodded.

'Yes, I'm afraid I am.'

'Is it likely?'

'The paramedics recorded her as unconscious when they reached the scene.' Doctor Carmel studied Gwyn's charts. 'That was four hours ago and so far her responses haven't changed.'

She looked down at Gwyn and sighed. 'Basically she's unresponsive, even to pain. That's not a terribly good sign.'

Eldritch listened as Aidan questioned the doctor further. They spoke of bleeding into the subarachnoid space, of compression and concussion and of microscopic arteries and lacerations of the brain. The terms were mostly meaningless to Eldritch but he could read all he needed to know in the steady whitening of Aidan's face and the way he chewed at his lip as he listened to each answer. After several minutes the wizard had heard enough. He cast a glance at Aidan and drew himself up, making his decision.

'This bruising that you've mentioned, doctor, is that the main problem?'

There was a moment's silence, as if both Aidan and Doctor Carmel were surprised by the interruption, then the doctor turned towards him.

'The problem isn't so much the bruising but the associated swelling. I'm sure you know yourself that if you have a bruise the area around it swells.'

She frowned as she spoke, her eyes narrowing slightly as she looked at him as if trying to make something out and Eldritch guessed she had noticed the bruises still visible under the collar of his shirt. He resisted the impulse to tug it closed and after a moment Doctor Carmel continued.

'Because the brain is contained within the skull the swelling causes pressure which in turn can damage the tissues further.'

She eyed him carefully as if gauging whether he was following this. 'We're monitoring her and if necessary we can operate to release that pressure.'

'Trepanning,' whispered Aidan, his face so pale that it seemed he might faint or throw up at any moment. The consultant turned to him with a raised eyebrow.

'Exactly.'

'So is there nothing that can be done to reduce the bruising itself?' Eldritch pressed, drawing the woman's attention back to him. Her lips thinned, rather as though she felt she was being asked to repeat herself.

'You need to understand that a bruise is a form of wound. When blood is trapped in the tissues, rather than lost – either externally through a cut or internally into one of the body's cavities – what you end up with is a bruise. We can administer various drugs to limit any further bleeding but once that bruise has formed it's up to the body's own healing mechanisms to clear it. That takes time.'

'So there's nothing you can do.'

Doctor Carmel's tone became distinctly glacial. 'We can do a lot. As I've told you we're monitoring her and if the swelling gets too severe we'll operate, but as far as actually reducing the bruising that's already there, no. To do that we would need to be able to turn back time and stop her receiving the injuries.'

She looked down her rather elegant nose at Eldritch, treating him to a glare that even Gwyn would have been proud of. Eldritch held his hands up placatingly.

'I'm sorry, I didn't mean to imply you weren't doing all that you could. I just wanted to be sure I understood the situation.'

He bowed his head, pressing his steepled hands to the bridge of his nose, thinking deeply. Finally he raised his head and looked at the doctor, licking his lips as if suddenly nervous.

'I want to...' he hesitated, shooting a glance at Aidan who

was watching him intently, 'to pray for Miss Hughes' recovery.'

To his surprise the doctor took that in her stride.

'Yes, of course. We have a chapel, or there's a non-denominational quiet room you can use if you prefer.'

Her gaze had fallen to his wrists and Eldritch realised she was looking at the crystal bracelets Gwyn had given him. He coloured and for a second time had to force himself not to adjust his clothing under her scrutiny.

'I'd rather stay here,' he told her. 'If that's alright?'

'I see.' The doctor managed to convey a weight of disapproval in those two words and Eldritch wondered what she was expecting him to do. Did she think he had a sacrificial goat hidden somewhere about his person?

'Well, so long as your prayers,' there was just the slightest inflection on the word and Eldritch could almost see her picturing that goat, 'don't involve anything physical or disruptive – no burning incense or chanting for example – then I suppose there's no reason why not.'

Her lips tightened primly and then to his utter surprise her expression softened.

'We don't object to people petitioning the higher powers on behalf of our patients.'

With that she turned to leave but then swung back with one final word of caution. 'Just remember that God moves in mysterious ways when He's performing his wonders and our nurses are one of them. They need to monitor Miss Hughes' condition. I would ask you to make sure you don't get in their way.'

Eldritch watched her walk away, professional and self-assured and totally at home in this environment that made his own skin creep. With a faint sigh he turned back to the bed to find Aidan watching him closely.

'My,' he said, ducking his head to avoid the scrutiny, 'that went well. Do you think she's gone to check the manual on witch burning?'

He made a play of pushing the hair out of his eyes, waiting to see how Aidan would respond.

'Not a chance. She's going straight to the stores to check they've got enough kindling.'

CHAPTER 11

Eldritch sat by Gwyn's bed and took her hand in his, contemplating what he was about to try to do. He knew that Gwyn worked with her hands stretched out above the area she was going to heal but he was uneasy about doing the same. It wasn't that he was squeamish but the idea that a lapse of concentration might lead him to knock the swollen and battered flesh, causing her pain or worse, was not one he felt comfortable with. As he intertwined his fingers with hers he prayed that this would work instead. Gwyn's hand was surprisingly warm but the fingers were limp and flaccid against his own, and very different from the strong, sure touch he remembered. Indeed, try though he might, he could get no sense of Gwyn inhabiting this broken cage of flesh. Could it be that there was nothing of her left? Resolutely he turned away from the thought, refusing to accept that that might be the truth. He couldn't – wouldn't! – believe that. He hadn't told Aidan but he was hoping Gwyn's presence would somehow guide him, leading him to understand what he needed to do. Lord knew he had little idea of what he would do otherwise. Eldritch held Gwyn's fingers a little tighter. *Don't let me down woman!*

Even as he thought that he turned his attention inward, reaching within for the bright source of his power. He had done so without thinking on Monday, when those three thugs had set upon them in the car park, and it had hurt although that fact had barely registered until after the event. Three days later he was pleased to find the pain was no longer there. There was stiffness, like an overstretched muscle or a newly healed scar, but as he relaxed even that dropped away as the power flowed up from his core. This also was Gwyn's doing, the result of the hours she had spent healing him. Eldritch smiled a little at the thought of the time she had insisted on working with him, much of it in the face of his protests that he no longer needed her help. Helen had once told him that he made a lousy patient, and he suspected he had given Gwyn good cause to agree, but with luck that healing would serve him now as a link to her. The thought gave him the confidence to take the next step. He straightened in his chair and, as he closed his eyes, he gave Gwyn's fingers a final squeeze.

'Okay woman, let's do this,' he murmured to her under his breath. But when he reached out, stepping his awareness across the divide between his body and hers, he found nothing there.

After a while Eldritch opened his eyes. He wasn't sure how long he had been out of his body. It felt like minutes but from the expression on Aidan's face he guessed it had been longer. He straightened and rubbed his free hand over the back of his neck, taking refuge for a second in that gesture, as he wondered how he was going to explain what he had found to Aidan. But Aidan wasn't going to give him time to make his mind up.

'Well?' he asked, shifting anxiously in his seat, and in that short breath of sound Eldritch could hear all the hope that Aidan couldn't bring himself to express in words. The hazel eyes were full of unasked questions and Eldritch dropped his gaze unsure what to say. He stared down at Gwyn's battered features, his dark brows squeezing together as if in pain or confusion.

After a moment he leaned forward and very gently laid Gwyn's limp hand back onto the sheet beside her body. Quietly, almost thoughtfully, he said, 'I couldn't reach her. She's gone.'

The sharp gasp of breath from across the bed jerked his head up. Aidan had gone very still, shrinking in on himself like an animal in pain.

'What? What is it?' And then Eldritch realised how his words had sounded. 'No, no! I don't mean it like that. She's not *gone* gone, not brain dead,' he amended hastily, cursing his own clumsiness. His brain was churning but that was no excuse for the shock he had just given Aidan. 'Oh hell! Sorry.'

He realised he was babbling and shut up, glad that there was a bed between them. From the look on Aidan's face the young man didn't know whether to kill him or kiss him. Neither option was desperately appealing.

'What then?' Aidan ground out after a moment. His expression said that the explanation had better be good. Eldritch pressed his hands to his temples, screwing his eyes shut as he tried to order his thoughts. Taking a deep breath he started to speak, his sentences clipped and fragmented as he sought to explain something that he wasn't sure he had felt but which he desperately wanted to believe.

'I couldn't reach her. She's... I don't know... withdrawn somehow.'

His eyes sought Aidan's, willing the young man to understand.

'I think she's in some kind of self-healing trance. There's a barrier there.' He sketched a wall in the air with his hands and

145

then gestured helplessly. 'I couldn't reach her through it and I didn't think it was a good idea to try to force it.'

For a long time Aidan stared back at him across the bed, saying nothing. His face was still chalky and tight from shock, but the little frown line between his brows showed he was considering what Eldritch had said.

'Is that possible?' he asked eventually. 'She's been unconscious since she was attacked.'

'No, we don't know that.'

It felt like taking his life in his hands to disagree with Aidan now but Eldritch soldiered on regardless. 'We know she's been unconscious since she was found, yes, but she may have been conscious before that.'

'Enough to start to heal herself?' Aidan was sceptical. 'It's not something I know much about but the one time she mentioned it to me she said it took a lot of discipline.'

He worried the corner of his lip between his teeth, considering the matter. Finally he said, 'If it were possible do you think it might explain why she's not been responding?'

Eldritch shrugged, feeling the eggshells under his feet as he spoke. He didn't want to build false hope but given what he had just experienced it seemed feasible.

'There are plenty of religions where people go into a trance and can do all sorts of things to themselves because they can't feel pain.'

He sighed. 'But I don't know. I'm not a healer.'

The lift of Aidan's eyebrows said that he had made that point before and Eldritch managed a half smile. 'I'd like to think that it's not as bad a sign as the doctor believes.'

'Is there any way of telling?'

Aidan looked at the fragile figure in the bed, clearly wanting to believe but not quite daring to do so.

'I'm sure there is, but I don't know.' Eldritch nodded at Gwyn. 'No doubt she'd be able to tell us.'

His lips tightened briefly in something akin to exasperation, as though he considered Gwyn to be withholding the information deliberately. Despite the seriousness of the situation Aidan couldn't help but smile, amused that even with one of them unconscious there was no let up in the cat and dog squabbling that Gwyn and Eldritch managed to spark from each other. In a brighter voice than he had managed since they left Swn-y-gwynt he asked, 'So what can we do to help her?'

On the other side of the bed Eldritch stretched and rolled his shoulders.

'She may have it all under control,' he suggested.

Aidan scowled at the casual response, as though the wizard had come right out and said he couldn't be bothered to help, but before he could protest Eldritch smiled and added, 'But there is one thing I can do that I think will make a difference. At least I'd like to give it a go.'

If Eldritch's words took Aidan by surprise what the tall man did next shocked him more.

'Should you be doing that?' he queried as Eldritch slipped the rose quartz bracelet from his left wrist. He remembered the deadly seriousness with which Gwyn had taken those strings of semi-precious stones from her own arms and put them on the unconscious wizard's. A prickle of unease teased the skin between his shoulder blades but Eldritch grinned wickedly, as though he had heard the concern in Aidan's voice and was amused by it.

'Don't worry, I've got another one.'

He held up his right wrist to display a flash of amethyst chips.

'They were just a precaution anyway,' he added, his voice dismissive. 'I don't need them now, my shielding's fine.'

For a moment he looked at the second bracelet as though he might remove that also but then he pushed it back under his cuff. Aidan was surprised how relieved that made him feel.

'So what are you going to do?'

Eldritch turned the rose quartz spheres in his fingers and looked at the figure in the bed. His grin turned positively rakish.

'I'm going to give her some of her power back.'

Despite his initial concern about the bracelet Aidan was intrigued, drawn in by the rich enthusiasm in Eldritch's voice.

'How's that going to help?' he asked, curiosity replacing any lingering feelings of disquiet. Eldritch's smile broadened. For a moment he was a showman with his cure-all bottle of snake oil.

'The one thing I do know about healing is that it takes a lot of energy. So I'm going to give her more to draw on.'

'But why the bracelet?'

'Because, while our self-sufficient neighbourhood witch has walled herself off from the world, I can't give her power directly. But if I use this as an energy sink...' He weighed the bracelet in the palm of his hand, 'the power's there for her to tap into if she needs it.'

'Just like your ring,' Aidan said, understanding.

'Exactly. And because the bracelet's hers she's already attuned to the crystals so it should be easier to make a link to them for her.'

With his eyes closed and his mind sunk lightly into semi-trance, Eldritch ran the rose quartz pearls through his fingers, feeling the energy matrix of the stones set about with the lines of protection that Gwyn had placed upon them. He smiled inwardly, confident in what he was doing. Having worn them for two days these stones were already familiar to him – this would be a straightforward working. So… Cupping the bracelet in the palm of his left hand he placed his right hand over it, feeling the quartz grow warm against his flesh as if even now it burned with a life of its own. He allowed himself the smallest feeling of satisfaction as he considered the energy it would hold when he had finished with it, but first he had to construct the web of power in which that energy would reside.

Bel for Sanctuary, Mir for Silence and Serreth for Stillness. That was what Gwyn had told him of the sigils she would have used to evade the avatar, so very different from his own approach. Amidst the bitter recollection of pain and exhaustion the memory of her words was diamond sharp in his mind, carrying with it that precious insight into how Gwyn's world was ordered. Eldritch considered that understanding now, turning it in his mind as his fingers turned the bracelet, lingering over the facets of it as he might a precious gem. It was important that this matrix of energy be built so that it fitted the way that Gwyn handled power, so that its usage would be natural and effortless for her. That would be the one challenge he faced with this working; to create that intimacy, that binding, out of the little he knew of her. With that in mind, one by one he called upon all of his senses, remembering Gwyn through each of them, from the touch of her hands – strong and competent as she slathered comfrey over his shoulder – and the tones and accents of her voice, to the smell of vanilla and lavender that clung to her hair and the sight of her glimpsed through a half open door, curled in her armchair with a book and a lapful of cats. Carefully he brought each element of her from his memory, little vignettes of sight and smell, touch and hearing, until at last he felt he held some small understanding of her essence.

He would use Keth then, for strength, for that was at the heart of what he wished for her, but teamed with that he would bring the sigils of lightness and of joy, Herat and Kel. In his mind he saw Gwyn whole and strong, dancing like a wood sprite in her garden, with her crazy hair billowing around her like a storm and her eyes flashing like dark emeralds. *Let it be so,* he breathed sending his consciousness down into the stones, bearing with it the essence of that vision. As his mind formed the shapes of each sigil his hands moved infinitesimally, tracing their lines and binding each one into the heart of the crystals, taking them and shaping them into vessels into which he could pour his energy, suffusing them with warmth and life. *Let it be as I make it.*

For the second time that afternoon Eldritch opened his eyes to find that Aidan was watching him. This time he managed what he hoped was a reassuring smile even as he reached across the bed for Gwyn's hand. With his mind still within the borderlands of trance he slid the bracelet onto her wrist and set a link from it into that strange walled off emptiness behind which he hoped she was waiting. Then, sitting back in the chair, he loosed his grip on his power, letting it subside into the marrow of his bones. As the sense of otherworldliness faded from him he filled his chest with a long, deep breath and let his physical body relax, knowing he had done all he could. When Aidan asked, 'Is that it?' he had to stir himself to answer.

'Hmm?'

'What, no fireworks, no mystical chanting…'

Eldritch cracked open eyes that had been sliding towards shut and considered Aidan.

'No incense?'

The twitch of Aidan's eyebrows confirmed it; he was being teased.

'You should know better,' he growled, straightening up and trying to resist the urge to yawn. 'The link's made, the power's there for her to use.'

Then, because he hadn't missed the fragility lurking underneath Aidan's show of humour, he added, 'She'll be okay Aidan.'

Just for a second the confident façade slipped and he saw the fear haunting Aidan's eyes.

'Can you be sure?'

Eldritch nodded as he settled himself more comfortably in the chair.

'She's there behind that wall, don't you doubt it.'

They continued to sit, one on either side of Gwyn's bed, waiting. Aidan held Gwyn's hand, his voice a soft murmur as he spoke to her. Eldritch closed his eyes, trying not to eavesdrop on that very private outpouring of feelings. He was aware of time passing, marked by the regular coming and going of the nurses monitoring Gwyn's condition. Every half hour one appeared to go through the same ritual of checks and tests. Eldritch amused himself, picturing them as stylised figures on some grand Bavarian clock face, appearing each time with the same precise movements, the same data recorded. And each time the ritual ended with Aidan asking how Gwyn was doing. Each time the answer was a variation on "stable" and the nurse would disappear back into the mechanism of the hospital while the murmur of Aidan's soft monologue would start again. So it went on. After the second time Eldritch moved his chair back from the bed so the nurses could step past him unhindered.

'Are you okay?'

Eldritch jerked his eyes open, wondering for a moment if he had fallen asleep.

'Of course,' he said, automatically, not quite certain he had registered the question properly or if it had even been directed at him.

'You look kind of... grey.'

'Grey?'

'Yeah. You know, washed out.'

'Thank you for that vote of confidence.'

He pushed the hair out of his eyes in the vain hope that doing so might make the world less blurry and sat up straighter, uncomfortably aware of a crick in his neck and that his buttocks were numb from being sat too long unmoving on the hard plastic seat.

'When did you last eat?'

'What?'

For a moment Eldritch couldn't understand what Aidan

was on about but though the question made little sense he felt obliged to answer it anyway.

'Oh, er breakfast I suppose.'

'Thought as much. Low blood sugar,' Aidan pronounced with all the gravity of one of the hospital consultants. Eldritch sagged back into the chair with a groan as he watched Aidan pick up his jacket and rummage through the pockets.

'Not more Kendal mint cake,' he protested, raising a swift grin from his companion. Aidan reached into another pocket and withdrew a familiar white and red wrapper.

'I have some if you want it,' he offered, laughing again as Eldritch's mouth turned down in disgust. 'But I was thinking more along the lines of coffee and a sandwich from the café. If it's still open,' he added, glancing at his watch. 'It's gone seven o'clock. I hadn't realised it was so late.'

Eldritch looked at his own wrist for confirmation – neither had he. Perhaps he had been asleep. He scrubbed his hands over his face and then up through his hair, turning the move into a stretch as he tried to ease the kinks out of his body. Aidan watched him with an air of thoughtful consideration. After a moment he said, 'I suppose we should be going.'

His eyes strayed to the figure in the bed and his expression turned wistful. Despite his words it was clear he was reluctant to leave.

'Not for my sake,' Eldritch interjected. He shrugged dismissively. 'I'm used to hospital chairs. I can sit in these things for hours.'

A slight moue of regret twisted his lips, though whether it was at the implication that they might end up doing so or because of some memory his words evoked, wasn't clear. Either way Aidan didn't pursue it. He simply shook his head, his gaze lingering on Gwyn like a physical caress.

'No, someone will have to feed the cats and I need to rescue Sula.'

Still he didn't look up. It was as though he was committing every nuance of Gwyn's living form to his memory. Eldritch waited silently, watching him watching her. He felt he knew that look, that desire. He had been there himself with Helen.

'I can go back and do all that if you want to stay.'

It might have been the unexpected gentleness in Eldritch's voice or perhaps it was simply the recognition that he wasn't being left to cope with this alone but Aidan's eyes were suspiciously bright as he looked up and he swallowed heavily before he spoke.

'Thank you,' he said and his voice was tight and choked. Then the moment passed and he was back in control. He ran an appraising eye over Eldritch's lanky form and shook his head.

'You don't know the road and at the moment I wouldn't trust you not to fall asleep at the wheel. No, it's alright,' his voice became firmer as Eldritch started to protest. 'You've done what you can and the nurses seem to think she's stable so there's nothing more we can do just by being here. I'll come back in the morning but for now we should go.'

He summoned a crooked smile. 'I'm surprised they haven't thrown us out yet anyway.'

As Eldritch shrugged on his jacket Aidan bent down and kissed Gwyn lightly on the forehead.

'We're going now, Gwyn,' he told her, his fingers reaching for her hand, lifting it from the sheet and holding it lightly as he spoke. 'I'm going to feed the cats so don't you worry about them. You just concentrate on getting better and I'll be back to see you tomorrow, okay?'

He paused as though against all odds she might finally respond, stirring like a sleeper at the sound of his voice, but there was no change in the steady rise and fall of her breathing, no flicker of movement discernible behind her swollen eyelids and, after a few moments, he gently released her hand. Straightening up he answered Eldritch's silent regard with a small, self-conscious shrug. There was no need to explain.

'They say that hearing's the last sense to go when you loose consciousness,' Aidan commented as he fiddled with the zip on his jacket. He didn't raise his eyes or look at Eldritch as he spoke, almost as though he was talking to himself.

'There are lots of stories about people who've been in comas responding to their favourite music or to the sound of someone reading to them. When I come back in the morning I'm going to try that, see if it helps.'

Finally Aidan looked up, glancing swiftly at Eldritch his eyes at once defiant and anxious. He paused, waiting for some reaction.

'What do you think?'

Eldritch gave a noncommittal shrug, looking from Aidan to the still figure in the bed. He shook his head.

'I'm no expert but if they say that sort of thing helps then you should give it a go.' He rubbed his jaw thoughtfully and a sudden mischievous look softened his face. 'Of course, you know what she'll say when she wakes up, don't you?'

His dark brows quirked upwards and without waiting for

an answer he put his bunched fists on his hips and scowled dramatically at Aidan, his head jutting forward, his grey eyes intense under the fall of dark hair.

'I'd have healed myself sooner, but what with the nurses poking at me every half hour and then some damned fool reading poetry to me, it completely ruined my concentration.'

It was an appallingly bad attempt at a Welsh accent but Aidan couldn't help but smile, buoyed up as much by Eldritch's confidence that Gwyn would come through this as by the likelihood that her first comment would be a complaint about the way she had been treated.

'You don't think I should try poetry then?'

Eldritch returned the smile but after a moment it faded and he turned away, hugging his arms across his chest as though suddenly cold.

'You know I won't be able to come with you,' he said quietly.

Aidan nodded, his mouth slipping from a smile into a thin line of resignation.

'I know.'

He had expected as much but it still hurt to hear Eldritch confirm it. He looked down at Gwyn's bruised and fragile form and then again at Eldritch's turned back. For a moment instead of charcoal-grey wool he saw the pale nacre of scars adorning the wizard's shoulders and the way his body had twisted and strained, helpless under the avatar's lash. Aidan swallowed heavily, closing his eyes against the image. Inwardly he railed against the circumstances that forced him to this, yet he knew he had already made his choice, as had Eldritch. It didn't make it any easier. Guilt lying like ashes on his tongue he asked, 'Will you be okay?'

Eldritch laughed, a short exhalation of breath that was devoid of humour, his back still turned so Aidan could not read his expression.

'I can read a map you know,' he said, deliberately misunderstanding.

'That's not what I meant.'

Again Eldritch laughed, the sound of it ironic, almost mocking. Finally he turned back to face Aidan, a half smile playing across the saturnine curl of his lips. *Does it make any difference?* he seemed to ask, his eyes daring Aidan to answer with the truth and for a heartbeat it was as if they stood once more above the Bite, facing off hostile and defensive. Then Eldritch sighed and the cold glitter passed from his eyes as he relented.

'I don't know,' he said and shrugged, as if the matter was of no great importance. He could have said *of course,* but it would have been no more believable than his attempt at nonchalance.

'What about the avatar?' Aidan persisted, refusing to be diverted. Eldritch pulled a face.

'I beat it once, I can do it again.'

At Aidan's raised eyebrows Eldritch inclined his head, acknowledging the unspoken point but still he refused to be drawn. 'We'll see. It may not come to that.'

CHAPTER 12

In the dark the road seemed even more perilous than it had in daylight, despite the fact that this time Aidan was keeping well within the speed limit, a blessing for which Eldritch offered up heartfelt thanks. He was conscious of tight bends and the narrowness of the safe band of tarmac tucked between the dark, grasping shapes of trees and sudden open drops. Long stretches of Armco barrier guarded the worst of these but in many places there was nothing more than wire stock fencing, that would do nothing to stop a car, and in some places not even that. He might not have admitted it but deep down he was very glad that it was Aidan at the wheel. This wasn't a road to drive for the first time in the dark. Smothering a yawn the wizard fought the urge to sit back in his seat and go to sleep, knowing that Aidan too must be tired. Instead he kept up a steady stream of conversation, not sufficient to take Aidan's attention from the road but enough to help the pair of them stay awake.

As the road turned left over a narrow, stone-walled bridge the sweep of headlights illuminated the slate name plaque of a house set back from the road, almost on the river's edge; Bwlch-y-felin.

'How on earth do you pronounce that?' Eldritch asked. 'Bwelch ee felin?' he attempted tentatively, rhyming the first word with squelch. Beside him Aidan laughed in genuine amusement.

'Firstly it's *velin* with a V,' he corrected. In the darkness

Eldritch couldn't see the smirk on his face, but it was clearly audible in his voice. 'In Welsh a single F is pronounced as a V.'

'Oh how stupid of me not to have guessed. Any particular reason?'

'It's simple enough; there isn't a V in the Welsh alphabet.' Eldritch snorted.

'There don't seem to be many vowels either,' he commented sourly. 'Go on then, how do you pronounce it?'

'Book-ah-velin. It means mill pass.'

Eldritch turned in his seat to study Aidan's profile. There was no hint that the young man was winding him up.

'How in God's name do you manage to get *book*—,' he ignored the choked off snigger his attempt to reproduce the nuance of Aidan's accent earned him, 'out of B-W-L-C-H?'

Aidan cleared his throat. 'It's just the way it is.'

'Bloody daft if you ask me,' Eldritch muttered.

'No worse than English,' Aidan countered. When Eldritch only grunted sceptically he added, 'Gwyn had a cat once. She called it Fish.'

Eldritch considered this for a minute but it still left him bemused.

'And your point is?'

'She spelled it the way the English would. G-H-O-T-I.'

Aidan turned his head briefly from the road and smirked at Eldritch.

'Someone should tell her that her spelling's worse than her taste in names.'

'Ah, but she was spelling it phonetically; GH as in cough, O as in women and TI as in potion. Put them together and you get Fish.'

There was a long silence as Eldritch digested this.

'I still think Welsh is a weird language.'

Aidan flashed him a Welsh archer's salute and laughed.

They drove in silence for a while as the road climbed steadily then, seemingly out of the blue, Aidan said, 'I know the government wants to be seen as doing its bit for the environment by clamping down on 4x4s – which is pretty stupid if you ask me because you can't get a sheep trailer on and off a field round here without one – but sometimes I think there's a case for making people prove they need them.'

Eldritch looked at him as if to ask where this had come from and Aidan jerked his head backwards.

'There's some idiot behind us in one of those big 4x4 pickups. He's been with us pretty much since we left the hospital and if he drives any closer he's going to be in the boot.'

He glanced in his mirrors again and said caustically, 'I'll bet the damn thing's never been off road in its life, he just likes driving something bigger than everyone else.'

As he spoke he slowed down for a tight bend.

'He's dropped back a bit now,' he muttered, returning his full attention to the road as it opened out again before them, but then he swore as the pickup's driver flicked his lights onto full beam and accelerated up behind them.

'Christ! What a place to overtake.'

Aidan flung a hand up to shield his eyes from the dazzle in the mirrors.

'You go ahead, you moron, and good riddance to you.'

But although the pickup pulled out it didn't overtake them. Instead there was a sudden jolting thud as it swung in viciously and slammed into the Land Rover's rear wing. The Land Rover bucked under the impact and Aidan fought to keep them from pirouetting as they started to skid. He almost had it, felt the wheels starting to grip again, when the pickup hit them again and suddenly they ran out of road. He felt the jolt as the front wheels hit the curbing. There was no Armco barrier there to stop them, just a crazy web of shadows and silver that the headlights cast in the trees. Aidan felt the springs compress as they landed and the whole car start to tip as the land fell away sharply to the right. There was time to yell an almost incoherent 'Hang on!' and then everything became spiralling madness. Through the windscreen he saw a pinwheel of light and tree limbs as he was thrown against the side door. He felt something give and his last thought was that if the door went he'd be crushed beneath the vehicle as it rolled. Then there was only blackness.

'Come on Aidan, talk to me. Wake up and give me a verse of "Land of Our Fathers" or whatever you lot sing to drown your sorrows when we beat you at rugby.'

From a distance Aidan registered the voice as one he recognised but felt disinclined to respond. Irritating though it was the intrusion was far enough away that he could ignore it if he chose to. Suitably comforted he settled again into the warm darkness waiting for the sound to recede into nothingness. It didn't. When someone began slapping his face he became really annoyed. Without opening his eyes he made a grab for where he guessed his assailant's wrist to be and was rewarded by a surprised yelp.

'If you don't stop that I will rip your arm off, take the soggy end and shove it all the way up to your hepatic flecture.'

He gave the arm a small twist so its owner would realise he could do exactly that, eliciting another sharp intake of breath.

'And,' he continued in the same reasonable tone, still without opening his eyes or releasing his grip, 'if you don't know where that is, I will draw you biologically accurate diagrams to explain. Now leave me alone.'

The response was a curse that, in other circumstances, would have impressed him with its inventiveness, but for now Aidan was interested solely in the fact that the slapping had stopped.

'Listen to me you pigheaded Welshman. The only thing stopping this car rolling down the rest of the mountainside is a very small tree. Now by all means you can stay in here. Your skull's probably thick enough to survive the impact but – and I appreciate this is only a personal opinion – I think it would be a good idea to get out.'

It was the tone the words were delivered in that persuaded Aidan that this time he should listen. There was fear there, he realised, underneath the posturing and the caustic bite of sarcasm, and fear was not something he associated with that particular voice. Resigned he cracked his eyes open. Everything seemed to be at a peculiar angle and ineffectively lit by a single headlight beam bouncing back from rocks and trees and refracting crazily through the starred and shattered windscreen.

'What the…'

Memory hit him.

'Oh Christ!'

'Prayer is good,' Eldritch said, with his eyes never leaving Aidan's as he leaned across the front seat, 'but movement would be better. Very gentle and careful movement,' he qualified. He himself was absolutely motionless. 'I'm not sure how secure we are.'

Still Eldritch made no attempt to shift position. After a second he added, almost as an afterthought, 'By the way, I'd appreciate it if you'd let go of my arm now.'

'Huh?'

Aidan looked down at his left hand, swore and dropped Eldritch's wrist faster than if the man had just announced he had leprosy.

'Sorry,' he muttered, belatedly realising exactly why Eldritch had been holding himself rigid. 'Oh hell, that's your bad arm too. Sorry!' he apologised again as Eldritch straightened, his hand coming up to rub not his wrist but his shoulder. Aidan winced guiltily. Thank goodness the wizard had had the sense not to struggle. In his half conscious state he could have inflicted some serious damage without fully realising what he was doing.

'It's alright,' Eldritch said, shaking his head, although the grimace as he lowered his arm suggested otherwise. 'Damn.'

It was his turn to wince as he flexed his wrist, pulling back his sleeve to show where the amethyst chips had dug in all the way round it.

'I'll say one thing for you, there's nothing wrong with your grip.'

He eyed the dented flesh wearily and then slid the bracelet off, dropping it into his lap as he rubbed at his wrist.

'You're the one to worry about. I know you've got a bump the size of an egg where you've whacked your head but I couldn't tell if you'd done anything else. Do you think you're okay?'

Aidan had already been through a swift mental checklist.

He could wriggle his toes, clearly his reflexes were working well enough and he couldn't feel blood anywhere. His chest ached and now Eldritch had mentioned it the whole side of his face felt stiff, but no more so than after taking a good punch.

'Yes,' he said with utter confidence. He started to move and let out an involuntary yelp as pain stabbed through his side and chest, bringing him up short. Eldritch lunged forward, bracelet and wrist forgotten as he grabbed him, holding him still.

'What is it?'

In the feeble light Eldritch's features were little more than a collection of shadows but Aidan could hear the concern in his voice. Cautiously he tried moving again. Expecting it, the pain wasn't really that bad. Certainly he had had worse.

'I think I've popped a couple of ribs.'

He remembered hitting the side of the door before everything went black.

'Still it beats a flail chest from the steering wheel.'

Cracked ribs he could cope with; he had done so before.

'It's okay,' he added, sensing Eldritch's frown even in the dark. 'You can let go. It's nothing to worry about. You wanted me to move carefully? Trust me, I'm going to be doing exactly that.'

He took a measured breath, letting himself feel the pain and judging just how much it would limit him. Then he asked, 'How close to the edge are we?'

'I don't know but I wasn't kidding about the tree. Spindly little thing, but we've not shifted since we hit it, so it's obviously tougher than it looks. Same could be said for a few things round here I guess.'

Aidan sighed and straightened up from scrutinising his vehicle, his breath catching slightly as his ribs pinched. He clamped his arm tight against his side and tried to keep the pain from his face before Eldritch saw. The wizard had been hovering like a mother hen from the moment they had eased themselves carefully from the Land Rover and Aidan was finding his patience beginning to fray under the unlooked for attention.

'There'll be no moving her without a winch,' he muttered glumly, stating the obvious in the hope that it might divert some of Eldritch's concern away from him. 'I suppose I'll have to call the AA.'

'Forget the AA,' Eldritch replied with a degree of feeling that had Aidan looking at him in surprise. 'You need to call the police. That car rammed us deliberately and it didn't stop.'

Aidan grunted noncommittally, shifting his feet in a vain attempt to find a position that eased the ache in his ribs and head. Though he knew Eldritch was right an interview with the police was the last thing he wanted right now.

'And you need to go to hospital and get that looked at.'

Make that the last thing he wanted right now besides going to hospital.

'It's only a couple of ribs,' he protested, not for the first time. Eldritch eyed him critically.

'I'm talking about your head. You were completely out of it back there. You need to get yourself checked over.'

Aidan chose to ignore that. So far as he was concerned there was nothing wrong with him that a couple of aspirin and a good night's sleep wouldn't put right, but he knew the police, like Eldritch, would see things differently. There was also another reason why he didn't want to involve them.

'This was the demon's doing wasn't it? First the attack on Gwyn and now this.'

Eldritch regarded him thoughtfully, his grey eyes almost silver in the pale cast of moonlight, his hair falling in a dark web around his face.

'Don't think you're getting away with not calling the police just by changing the subject.'

His voice was light but his eyes narrowed in warning. Aidan ignored both the words and the accompanying frown.

'Well?' he asked again.

Eldritch's lips thinned momentarily in annoyance and for a long while he was silent, looking out past the dark bulk of the Land Rover, wedged halfway over on its side against the tree, and beyond, following the line of the hillside as it dropped away sharply to the valley bottom far below where a faint glitter marked the presence of flowing water. Aidan followed his gaze. It occurred to him that, had the tree not been there to stop them, the Land Rover wouldn't so much have rolled as bounced when they hit that steeper section and the roof that had taken a couple of turns and barely crumpled would have been mashed flat by the time they reached the bottom. It was a sobering thought.

'It's trying to stop us.'

Aidan started as the sound of Eldritch's voice broke the stillness. The wizard had been silent for so long that he had given up all expectation of his question being answered. Eldritch nodded reluctantly as he spoke, as though the admission were being dragged from his lips.

'But at least it proves that it can't have manifested yet – if it had there'd be no reason for all this.'

He gave a sharp, barking laugh as his gaze pulled back to survey the stranded vehicle.

'Strangely enough demons don't tend to be big on revenge. What they want is pain and misery.'

He threw a grim smile at Aidan who wondered what this counted for if not exactly that and Eldritch laughed again darkly as if reading the thought in his face.

'Not from a distance, like this,' he said, 'but up close and personal. A demon wouldn't have attacked Gwyn and then left her for dead; it would have smashed her brains out against a rock. The same with this. A demon might run you off the road but it would want to see the look in your eyes as it shoved a match in the petrol tank while you were trapped in the wreckage.'

As he spoke his voice hardened, and his face, gaunt and angular in the dark curtain of his hair, turned vicious. Then he stopped abruptly.

'I'm sorry...'

He looked away quickly as if embarrassed by the violence of his words and Aidan saw his shoulders stiffen under the charcoal wool of his jacket, sudden tension curling his hands into fists. How much of this knowledge, he wondered, came from personal experience? But it was not something he could ask. After a moment the wizard took a deep, steadying breath and in a voice schooled to icy calmness he continued.

'Oh yes, it's the demon that was responsible. This was done by someone it's managed to influence; someone who wouldn't need much persuasion to attack a woman while she's out running or run another car off the road. Don't feel sorry for them Aidan, just call the police.'

Aidan shoved his hands deep in his jacket pockets, digesting what Eldritch had said. For all his reluctance to do so he knew he was obliged to inform the police of the accident – his lips twisted in a humourless smile at the misnomer – and yet, as his fingers closed around his mobile he paused, holding back. As the silence stretched between them he turned to Eldritch.

'How bad will it get? If the demon gets out and takes a host – how bad will it be?'

'Ah. I was wondering when you might ask that.'

Eldritch's grin was fleet as a mountain hare and for a moment it seemed that he would retreat as he so often did into humour, shying away from any serious answer. But the moment passed and with it any trace of laughter. Pinching the bridge of his nose, he bowed his head over his fingers and briefly closed his eyes. When he opened them again his face was bleak. It was the face of a man who, presented with tomorrow's paper, had read his own obituary.

'We're not talking Armageddon, if that's what you're thinking.'

An attempt at a smile brushed the corners of his mouth, like a reflex encouragement, but it could not reach his eyes.

'Unless it goes berserk it may seem as though nothing has changed – not at first and at least not to anyone outside the host's circle of friends and family – but from the moment it manifests everything the demon does will be focussed on sowing discontent and unhappiness, pain and sorrow.'

Eldritch's voice sank almost to a whisper and he dropped his head again as if he could no longer bear to look out over the surrounding hillside. When he spoke a great sadness weighted his voice.

'The demon's power will grow as it feeds. The more misery and suffering it can engender the more it can feed off the negative emotions and the stronger it will become. Slowly its shadow will spread. There will be more like your friend John; suicides, accidents, families will tear each other apart over stupid, pointless things. All the meanness of spirit, the uncaring, casual violence that marks the worst in people will come to the fore and no one will realise or care. None of it will seem linked together, no one will be able to point and say, *that's when it started*, or *that's where it comes from,* but life in these valleys will become very bleak. Darkness and desperation are the things a demon feeds on. They will be the only things that flourish in its presence.'

'Is that what happened with Helen, with your wife?'

Aidan wasn't sure he had spoken out loud until he saw Eldritch's face twist in pain. The wizard nodded briefly, his Adam's apple bobbing in his throat as he swallowed convulsively.

'I should have known,' he whispered. 'I should have realised sooner than I did. She was never cruel, never malicious, but after that night…'

His words tailed off as though he couldn't bring himself to voice the details of what had happened and Aidan guessed he would say no more. He was trying vainly to think of something he could say, some grain of comfort he could offer, when to his intense surprise Eldritch said, 'She killed Paul.'

His voice was soft, the simplicity of his words only serving to emphasise the grief that edged every syllable. 'Her brother,' he added. 'He was diabetic. The demon bided its time, waiting until they were alone and then it used its magic to overpower him. All it took was one simple injection and then it sat there taunting him as it watched him die. She told me how she'd done it... at the end.'

At the end. In the hollowness of the wizard's voice Aidan heard the echo of what he could not say, that the end he spoke of had been the battle royal in which he had driven the demon from his wife's body.

'You want to know what it will be like if the demon takes a host?' Eldritch asked, finally lifting his head, his eyes seeking Aidan's. There was neither irony nor exaggeration in their quicksilver depths. 'It will be as though the sun has gone out.'

'*Mor ofnadwy yw y lle hwn!*' Aidan breathed the ancient words, exhaling the mournful sound of them into the night air. For a moment they seemed to hang there, as much a part of the dark hillside as the voice of the wind amongst the bracken.

'I beg your pardon.'

'*Mor ofnadwy yw y lle hwn!* How awful is this place! It was written on a plaque behind the pulpit in the Miners' Chapel, the one that box of books came from at the library. There was a book of local history in with them with a picture of it. "*Gwylia ar dy droed pan fyddech yn myned i dy Dduw. Mor ofnadwy yw y lle hwn!*" Roughly translated it means "Watch your step as you enter God's house. How awful is this place!" When I read it I thought they must have been using awful in the old sense of the word, as in full of awe, awesome, awe inspiring. Maybe they weren't.'

Eldritch thought about this and then he smiled, brief and bittersweet, as if in that moment he had put all that he had just spoken of behind him. 'If I were a miner I think I'd go with the current meaning. It must have been a pretty grim existence. I can't imagine why anyone who worked down a mine would want their children to do the same.'

He shivered and wrapped his arms across chest as though chilled by more than just the night air.

'To know that you'll probably die in your fifties, if you even make it that far, coughing up bits of blackened lung.' He shuddered again but more theatrically this time. 'Why wish that on your kids? I couldn't understand the fuss when they closed down the pits in the eighties. People should have been celebrating.'

For a long time Aidan was silent, his face thoughtful as he regarded the wizard. Eventually he said, 'The Miners' Strike was before I was born. I can't say I even remember the aftermath of it — not really — I wasn't old enough, but I'd keep that view to myself if I was you. Not so much round here, we're farmers mostly — it was wool that made these valleys rich, not just lead and never coal — but go down to Merthyr and they'd still lynch you for saying that.'

Aidan woke to sunshine streaming in through a crack in the curtains. It wasn't something he was used to, especially not at this time of year when he had normally been up for several hours before it got light. Irritable and muzzy-headed he threw a hand over his eyes and rolled over, only to be brought up short by a white-hot stab of pain through his chest. With a groan he flopped back, reaching out and fumbling for his alarm clock. It took him two attempts to make sense of the figures, his eyes unaccountably blurry as he held the small plastic cube in front of his face and tried to focus. 10:20am. Aidan let his hand fall back across the bed and lay there as if crucified. Blearily his eyes returned to the curtains, but there was no mistake. It was very definitely daylight outside. He groaned again.

'But I never oversleep,' he protested out loud, perhaps to the imp that seemed to have taken up residence somewhere behind his forehead – the one with the drill that it was currently applying to the inside of his temples.

Slowly it came back to him, the memory of two o'clock in the morning and how he'd given up trying to get to sleep, fed up with the fact that every time he did he would turn onto his side and the pain in his ribs would wake him again. Irritable and sore he had finally admitted defeat and gone down to the kitchen to take some of the painkillers he'd been given at the hospital. He smiled with a certain grim satisfaction at the thought. At least the doctors he had seen had been as blasé about his bang on the head as he had been – much to Eldritch's disgust – they wouldn't have prescribed their little pink pills otherwise. Effective little critters – the pills that was, not the doctors. Had he taken only two of them? Aidan wasn't sure although he was starting to think that it might have been a bad idea to chase them down with a tumbler-full of whisky. He was surprised he'd made it back to bed... oh yes, he'd been intending to get dressed. Somewhere between returning upstairs and retrieving his clothes from the floor it must have seemed like a good idea to get back into bed and nature – aided and abetted by the pharmaceutical industry – had taken its course.

The thought brought another groan and he swallowed dryly. He had little memory of the rest of the night beyond vague recollections of fractured dreams. He thought he remembered hearing Eldritch calling out and Sula barking, sharp and urgent, on the little landing between the two bedrooms, but thinking of it now the substance of that memory felt no different from those of the endless black tunnels he had run down, heart thudding against his ribs, alternately hunted and frantically hunting, and he had no idea whether he had dreamt that nocturnal disturbance or if it had been real. Strangely Sula wasn't in her customary position at the foot of the bed. He raised his head and looked just to be certain although he knew she would have made her presence known the moment he showed any sign of waking. Had he shut her in the kitchen when he went down to take the painkillers? If so she would be desperate to be let out by now. Guilt gave him the momentum to push himself upright, swinging his feet over the edge of the bed and sitting there for a few seconds while his body got used to the idea of being vertical.

'Bloody hell!' he moaned, scrubbing a hand over his face and glaring at the bedside clock. Not only had he neglected Sula but he had meant to go back to the hospital to be with Gwyn. He groaned and dropped his head into his hands. He hadn't even made it as far as her house to feed the cats. Another thought struck him and he raised his head, taking in the stillness and the deep silence of the house all around him. A thread of ice traced its way along his spine and his heart sank.

'Damn it, no!' he protested, as though words could make a difference now. 'We agreed.'

His voice was at once both angry and plaintive but as the silence came creeping back in the wake of his words he knew there was no denying it. Despite all common sense and contrary to what they had agreed as they waited on the roadside for the police to arrive, Eldritch had taken it into his head to go out onto the hills on his own.

CHAPTER 13

Aidan padded down the stairs, barefooted and still in his sleep rumpled t-shirt. There was nothing he could do about Eldritch and little he could do about Gwyn, although he promised himself that he would phone the ward as soon as he retrieved the number from his wallet, but he could at least look after Sula. So preoccupied was he, his mind vacillating between penitence and angry disbelief that Eldritch would be stupid enough to risk going anywhere near the mine workings alone, that he didn't register the smell of coffee until he opened the kitchen door to find Eldritch sat at the table surrounded by a spread of maps and papers and bits of arcane paraphernalia.

'What the hell are you doing here?' he demanded, his surprise coming out as anger. 'I thought you'd gone off to find the mine.'

Eldritch stared at him, grey eyes surprised and puzzled by the outburst.

'But we said we'd go this afternoon,' he protested, his voice reasonable despite Aidan's tone. Aidan ignored this.

'You could at least have woken me up,' he muttered petulantly.

'Believe me I tried,' Eldritch started. As Aidan continued to glare at him he added, 'Well, okay, I'm joking, but I've looked in on you twice and each time you've been dead to the world. I didn't try to wake you because you looked as though you needed the sleep.'

'You don't look so great yourself.'

Aidan had meant it sarcastically but even as he said it he was noticing how the autumn sunlight highlighted the deep lines around Eldritch's eyes and he felt his anger drain away. Eldritch's face held the worn, pinched look of a man who had taken no rest from the sleep he had had which made Aidan wonder if he had heard the wizard calling out during the night. Under his scrutiny Eldritch passed a hand over his face.

'I'll live,' he said, offhandedly.'I let Sula out into the garden,' he added, changing the subject. 'I hope that's okay. I didn't think she'd take too kindly to me trying to take her for a walk.'

Aidan grunted a slightly less than gracious thanks under his breath and dropped onto the other kitchen stool, reaching across the table to test if there was any coffee left in the pot.

'It's fresh,' Eldritch commented, unselfconsciously rearranging the scatter of papers to give Aidan some space.

'So what *are* you doing?' Aidan asked, spooning sugar into his coffee. He was curious to note there were four long quartz crystals placed on the map. It took him a moment to realise they were aligned to the cardinal points. Eldritch's antique sapphire and diamond ring lay in the centre of that little group.

'It's an experiment,' Eldritch conceded. 'How certain are you that these are where the mine entrances are?'

He indicated the points that Aidan had carefully marked amongst the salmon pink curves of the contour lines. Aidan looked at the map and then at the wizard.

'You and Gwyn were the ones who came up with the mine layout. These are as accurate as they can be based on what you told me.'

'Hmm.' Eldritch picked up the ring, drawing the chain

between his long fingers as he studied the map. 'That's what I thought.'

Aidan took a sip of coffee, his interest piqued despite himself.

'What's that meant to mean?'

Eldritch smiled inscrutably.

'Watch.'

Looping the chain around his right middle finger Eldritch held his hand out so the ring dangled freely above the map. It swung slightly for a few moments but gradually the movement decreased and it settled into stillness. Once it had done so Eldritch began to move his hand over the map. Aidan was surprised to see how steady the ring remained but as it crossed the map it suddenly started to spin. Eldritch drew his hand back and the movement of the ring slowed and stopped. Again he extended his hand and, as it came over the same section of the map, the movement of the ring started again.

'You're doing that deliberately,' Aidan said, his eyes travelling from the spinning ring to the outstretched hand and then to Eldritch's face. Eldritch raised a challenging eyebrow.

'Try it yourself if you want.'

Aidan eyed the wizard sceptically, making no move to take the proffered ring.

'Well, if you're not doing it, then what does it mean?'

Eldritch lowered his hand, letting the ring settle on the map and coiling the chain around it.

'Something's happening here.'

He tapped the map where the ring had swung wildly. Aidan surveyed the map.

'Something with the demon?'

Eldritch shrugged eloquently. 'I think so.'

'But none of the mine entrances we know of come out there.'

'I know. Interesting, isn't it?'

There was a certain wry humour in the wizard's voice.

'I'll tell you what's more than interesting.' Aidan scowled at the map. 'You know where that is, don't you?'

Eldritch favoured him with a one-sided shrug and a look that said clearly, *other than a hill in mid-Wales?* Aidan sighed.

'No, of course you don't, so let me tell you. That's more or less the edge of Griff Howell's land.'

'Ah.' Eldritch's saturnine face tightened in understanding. 'Not somewhere we want to go wandering then. A pity, because I think we need to.'

Aidan looked at Eldritch dubiously.

'Let me get this straight. We're already going to have to go onto his land to look for a possible shaft entrance over here, and then you want us to come all the way over here to check this out as well?'

'Actually, I was going to suggest we check this first. If we can find out what's happening there we might not need to check the other sites.'

'But how will we know?'

'That,' said Eldritch, enigmatically, 'depends on what we find.'

Aidan waited to be enlightened but Eldritch merely sat there, weathering his gaze, his face inscrutable as a stone-carved idol. Privately Aidan wondered if Eldritch was being secretive or if the wizard had no clearer idea what had caused that psychic ripple over the map than he himself did. Finally, when it had become clear that no further explanation would be forthcoming, he drained his coffee and put the cup to one side.

'Okay,' he said, making his decision. 'I need to make a phone call and then we'll talk about how we tackle this.'

'Is everything okay?' Eldritch asked as Aidan came back into the kitchen. The wizard's voice was carefully neutral but his eyes betrayed the knowledge of who it was Aidan had been phoning. Not that it took any great Holmesian skills of deduction to work it out. Given the circumstances there was only one phone call that Aidan was going to make that morning. A brief tilt of Aidan's head showed that he had heard the wizard but he said nothing as he returned to his seat at the table. In his absence Eldritch had cleared the detritus of coffee pot and cups to the sink and secreted away the long crystal points and the delicate antique ring so that only the map remained there in splendid isolation. Aidan sat, absently smoothing over its creases with a finger.

'She's had a comfortable night but there's no change in her level of consciousness,' he responded after a minute, giving Eldritch information without actually answering his question. 'They're going to do some more scans so it would be best if I waited to see her until this afternoon.' He conjured a brief, tight smile. 'I'll go over this evening.'

'I can manage on my own if you want to be there,' Eldritch offered but Aidan shook his head.

'No. No way. There's too much that can go wrong if you're on your own.' He dropped his gaze back to the map. 'Gwyn's being looked after,' he said after a moment. 'Going over earlier won't make any difference.'

He didn't look up as he spoke, tracing the flowing contour lines round and round the shape of a hill as if learning it by rote, but his unhappiness showed in his voice as though this was a decision he didn't much like, even if he felt it was the right one to take.

'I need to go and see to the cats but then we'll go.'

'Aidan…'

'No.'

Finally Aidan glanced up at the wizard and the look in his hazel eyes was desolate. *Don't turn this into an argument. Please.* Out loud he continued, 'We need to do this and if Gwyn was here that's what she'd be telling us. She'd understand.'

Grey and hazel eyes locked and for a moment it seemed that Eldritch would argue but then he nodded slightly. Perhaps he had understood that unspoken plea for his expression changed and a deliberate smirk spread slowly across his face. He looked pointedly at Aidan's bare legs and raised an enquiring eyebrow.

'I hope you're going to get dressed first.'

Aidan stood in the centre of the small lounge and looked around sadly. The familiar jumble of papers on Gwyn's desk, the books on the windowsill, their pages marked with fluorescent post-it notes, a solitary tea cup abandoned beneath the branches of the weeping fig, the casual ephemera of Gwyn's existence, all waiting – like the cats – for their mistress to come home and give them purpose once more. A nudge against his leg drew his attention and he looked down into a pair of huge absinthe eyes. Having successfully gained his attention Kali yowled pitifully. Aidan bent carefully, mindful of his ribs, and picked her up.

'She'll be back soon,' he promised her, burrowing his fingers into the soft fur behind her ears. 'Another couple of days and she'll be home, just the same as always.'

He swallowed the sudden lump in his throat, hoping desperately that what he said was true. Kali butted her head into his hand and made a plaintive chirp of sound as though adding her own side to the conversation. Aidan smiled wanly.

'I hope so, cat. I hope so.'

He looked again at Gwyn's desk. Eldritch had said she had stayed up late working and that suggested a deadline looming. Being self-employed himself Aidan had a professional respect for business commitments. He was only grateful that Red Kite Training's diary was empty at the moment although thankfully that was a function of Matt's imminent return to New Zealand for his younger sister's wedding rather than an indication of the normal health of the business. While Matt was enjoying a three week round of barbecues and parties, catching up with friends and relatives, Aidan had planned some rest and relaxation of his own but the mountains of Snowdonia would still be there to be climbed another day when he was done with demon hunting. Disappointed clients tended to be far less forgiving.

He gave Kali's head one last rub and set the Burmese down, considering what he could do to help. Presumably somewhere in that pile of notes and papers was the name of an editor waiting for Gwyn's article or at least some clue as to the journal she was writing for. If he was lucky there might be a phone number he could call. He picked up the top page and scanned it but no numbers leapt out at him. By the look of things it was a shopping list although he guessed that not many people would include rose quartz, frankincense and powdered hyssop alongside the more mundane cat food, tea bags and milk. The thought raised a wry smile – even Gwyn's shopping lists were idiosyncratic. Still smiling Aidan put the paper to one side and picked up the next, scanning it without success for any sign of a name or telephone number. It crossed his mind that this might take a while and he hoped that Eldritch would forgive the delay but as his eyes skimmed over the next sheet of paper he stopped, all thought of such matters gone from his head. Reaching behind him he pulled up Gwyn's office chair and sat down re-reading the scrawled green writing, his expression turning from interest to puzzlement and then to shock.

On the page Gwyn had drawn out a family tree, starting with William Wynn-Jones. His marriage to Sarah Rees had produced a single child, Henry William, who had gone on to marry Elspeth Carson. Their one son had also been called William and from the date of death written beneath his name Aidan realised that this was the William Wynn-Jones whose obituary he had found. There was no wife's name written beside this William. Instead Gwyn had drawn a dotted line to the name Anne Morgan and below that, circled and with three large question marks beside it, was his own name. It took Aidan a moment to comprehend what Gwyn was suggesting but the line below made it clear. She had started with his birthday in June 1988 and worked backwards, writing out the months. The ninth month was September. He stared at the dates and then reread everything on the page but, far-fetched though it was, there was no other conclusion he could come too.

Gwyn thinks I'm William's child.

Aidan felt his hands go cold with shock. For a moment the room seemed to spin around him as the implications of that one sentence hit him. But why? Why would she think that? The dates might fit but so what? Had his mother told her that he wasn't James' son?

'I don't know why he ever decided to have children.'

'To be fair that was your mother's choice.'

Gwyn's response suddenly took on new significance.

'No, this is crazy.'

He made to screw up the paper and stopped. Did he care if James wasn't his father? No, but... *But what?* He asked himself. Was his own sense of identity so wrapped up in his father's that this had rocked the very foundations of his world?

'Illegitimate children... people have them you know.'

Aidan tossed the paper back onto Gwyn's desk. A sense of anger was growing in him, replacing the cold shock of discovery with a slow burn of rage, not so much at what he had discovered but at how he had found it out. Part of it was impotent fury at his mother although the cool dispassionate part of his mind understood it wasn't a subject that would have been easy for her to bring up, *'I had an affair dear, your father isn't who you think he is...'* but mostly it crystallised around the woman he had, until recently, found it so easy to hate.

'Dear God, Gwyn! You've got a lot of explaining to do.'

His voice was almost a shout, startling loud in the silence of the little cottage.

'Were you going to bother to tell me?'

He was still staring at the paper when the soft snick of a key in the lock broke through his circling thoughts. He spun round just as the door opened and a mop of salt and pepper hair appeared around it.

'Anyone home?'

Chris Edward's face broke into a broad smile as he spotted Aidan.

'Oh, it's you Aidan. I saw the car and I wondered if it was Gwyn's friend, Mr Eldritch, isn't it? Kath and I thought one of you would stop by this morning so I'm glad I've caught you. Kath's gone off to yoga but she wants you to know that we'll take care of the cats. Save you having to come over and do it.'

He paused, his smile disappearing, as he continued more diffidently, 'It's a terrible business what happened. You don't expect anything like that round here. Is there any news?'

Aidan shook his head.

'Not much. She's stable and they're doing more scans this morning. I thought I might take one of her books over this evening and try reading to her.'

That had been his intention but he no longer felt like doing so. Chris smiled again, not hearing that in his words. He reached down and picked up Kali who had stood up on the arm of the chair, butting her head against him as though he were a long-lost friend.

'That's a good idea,' he agreed, nodding thoughtfully. 'You know if there's anything we can do to help, anything that needs doing, you only have to ask. We'd like to go and see her too, but I wasn't sure they'd be allowing people in other than family. Not that she's got much of that.'

'Just the cats.'

'And you,' Chris corrected him firmly. 'She always did think the world of you Aidan. It's good to see the pair of you talking again.'

Framed in his white Vandyke beard Chris' wide, rather

sensuous mouth formed again into its characteristic smile. Aidan turned away quickly so that Gwyn's neighbour wouldn't see his own much colder expression.

'*Ddu!* What happened to your face?'

'Ah.'

Aidan started, embarrassed, having forgotten the plum coloured bruising standing out across his temple and cheekbone. What indeed?

'Some idiot tried overtaking us on the mountain road back from Aber last night. He misjudged it, pulled back in and clipped the landy's rear wing. Sent us over the bank.'

'No! Some of the youngsters today shouldn't be driving – no offence like. Was he drunk?'

'I don't know, he didn't stop, but the police reckon he must have been. So, if you see a big silver pickup with a scrapped up front bumper and green Land Rover paint over it let me know will you.'

'You should have a word with Edward down at the garage.'

'I will do. I'll be seeing him anyway. I'm hoping he's going to beat the dents out of the landy for me. That's if it's not a write off. The police were going to arrange for its recovery today.'

'You rolled it?'

Aidan nodded.

'Twice I reckon, based on how far down the slope we ended up.'

He thought he remembered the first roll and the start of the second. The tree had saved them from the third.

'*Ddu Ddu*, man. It's a good job you were in a landy – sturdy buggers.'

'I think it was the roof rack as much as anything.' Aidan was more comfortable discussing the impact on the car than on himself. 'Acting like a roll cage.'

Chris nodded thoughtfully.

'Even so, someone was looking out for you.'

'You could say that,' Aidan agreed readily. *But probably not in the way you're thinking.*

'Well,' said Eldritch, shoving his hands into his jeans pockets and regarding the hillside below them, 'I don't think we need go searching for what the demon's been up to.'

Beside him Aidan muttered something softly under his breath. Amused Eldritch glanced sideways and said, 'I hope that's an indication of surprise and not a request.'

The young man had been preoccupied, withdrawn even, since he had come back from Gwyn's. Something to do with that visit had unsettled him but he had refused point blank to talk about it, leaving Eldritch to surmise that it was renewed concern for Gwyn prickling his conscience. He had tried suggesting that Aidan go to the hospital and leave him to find out what was happening on the hillside but Aidan wouldn't hear of it and eventually Eldritch had had to accept that decision. But although Aidan had been with him in body his mind had most certainly been elsewhere. He had brooded silently in the car, mostly staring out of the window and only giving cursory directions when they were needed. When they left the car and took to a sheep track across the hillside Aidan had broken his near silence, asking questions about the nature of the Covenant and about inheritance of power which Eldritch had answered patiently but without coming any nearer to understanding what it was that had upset the young man. Yet whatever it was that had, up until that moment, been consuming his mind, Aidan was fully focussed now.

'It's neither,' he replied, his eyes not leaving the hillside. 'It's a technical term. A technical term for a bloody big hole that's appeared where two weeks ago there wasn't one.'

'Fair enough.'

Eldritch nodded amicably. Aidan's description might lack finesse but it was essentially accurate. In the floor of the narrow valley below them a hole big enough to swallow a car stood out like a fresh scar against the pale greens and greys of the upland landscape.

'Shall we go down and take a look?'

On closer inspection Eldritch was forced to revise his estimate of the hole's size. *Hell, it's big enough to swallow a bus,* he thought, *should one just happen to be passing.* He left Aidan and walked a little further around the rim, looking down into the pit. Perhaps twenty feet below him the grass and bracken that had – until recently – been part of the hillside were visible at the top of a slide of mud and rock that filled the bottom of the hole.

'Something like this happened over at Welshpool last summer after all the heavy rain,' Aidan commented, eyeing the raw edge of the pit where tufts of the coarse sage-coloured mountain grass clung precariously, sticking out into space. 'It just appeared overnight in someone's garden. When they went to bed they had shrubs and a lawn, when they got up the next morning they didn't.'

'And some people complain about mole hills,' Eldritch tutted and shook his head.

'The council evacuated half the street in case the hole got

any bigger. They blamed it on subsidence round an old mineshaft.' Aidan looked across at Eldritch. 'This is new; the grass is only just starting to die round the edges. Could the demon have done it?'

Eldritch didn't answer immediately, still staring into the pit. Shading his eyes against the low afternoon sun he thought he could make out a darker area at the bottom of the scree slope of debris, something amidst the tangle of shadows and rock and dark, wet earth that looked as though it might be another hole, one that led off into a far greater darkness. He was stepping closer to get a better look when, from the other side of the pit, Aidan's voice jerked him back.

'Hey! Don't get too close to the edge. You don't know how stable it is.'

'What?'

Eldritch's head came up and he looked about him, freezing in place as he realised that less than a foot beyond his boot tips the grass suddenly vanished. One more step with his mind distracted and he would have gone over the edge. Very deliberately he stepped backwards away from the rim.

'I wasn't going to,' he lied, aware of the sweat sliding down his back and of the sudden frantic pounding of his heart. 'I'm just…'

His voice tailed off. What *had* he been about to do? He had a sudden image of a shape coagulating out of darkness, glittering and shimmering somewhere within an endless dark tunnel and all at once his head was filled with a nameless, wordless longing as if something down there was calling to him. For a moment he was aware of nothing more save for a strange, innocent wondering what would happen to him if he chose to jump.

'Eldritch?'

With an almost physical effort Eldritch tore his attention away from the pit and its multi-layered shadows. Meeting Aidan's gaze across its gaping maw he took a deep breath and shook his head, dismissing the strange phantoms from his thoughts.

'I'm just looking,' he finished lamely. He peered again, narrowing his eyes and shifting sideways to try and get a better view but once again he was frustrated by the angles and the patchwork jumble of dying plants and mud and crushed grey rock. Part of him still wanted to get closer but he fought the inclination, Aidan's warning and some deeper sense of caution holding him back.

'There's something down there.'

He pointed as Aidan came round to join him.

'At the bottom, where all the rock and mud have slipped down. Can you see where I mean?'

Aidan squinted towards where Eldritch was pointing, twisting and tilting his head as he too tried to get a clear view of what lay hidden in the shadows.

'It's hard to make out. Hang on a sec.'

A good deal more circumspect than the wizard had been Aidan knelt and then, rather stiffly, stretched out full-length along the ground. Eldritch watched anxiously, all but holding his breath as Aidan cautiously leaned forward a few precious inches and peered over the edge, but something akin to excitement put the concern from his mind when, after a moment, Aidan looked back over his shoulder and said, 'I think you're right.'

He turned back to the pit, contemplating it for a few more

moments and then inched himself backwards. Only when he was safely away from the edge did he roll over and look up at Eldritch. For a moment they stared at each other, neither of them caring to say what they had discovered.

It was Eldritch who broke the silence. He swallowed against a mouth suddenly gone dry and said, 'I need to get down there.'

He had tried to keep the eagerness from his voice, guessing that Aidan would neither share nor understand it, but the wary look Aidan shot him told him he had failed.

'To ward it?' Aidan asked, his own voice neutral.

'If needs be,' Eldritch demurred. 'This is too big an area to seal.' He gestured at the hole but his eyes were fixed once again on that patch of deeper shadow. 'But if that does lead into one of the tunnels—'

'Going into it could get you killed,' Aidan cut across him. He clambered to his feet, wincing as the movement jabbed at his side and glowered at Eldritch as though that too were his fault. When Eldritch made no response Aidan's expression turned to one of puzzlement.

'Why? Why do you need to go into the mine? I thought we'd settled on you warding the entrances and trapping the demon when it tries to escape?'

'That was only ever an option while there was no way for anyone to get into the mine. But if that's a new entrance there's nothing to stop a potential host getting down there.'

'Except the fact that they'll need a whole heap of ropes and caving equipment to do it.'

Eldritch shook his head.

'That's not the point. Look, the demon's close to manifesting, I can sense it. If I can reach it before it does so it will be a lot easier for me to stop. The idea of setting traps for when it's free of the Unseen Realm and it's trying to leave the mine was only ever a fall-back. It's too energy intensive to be anything other than a huge risk, especially now I'm doing it on my own. I'm not ignoring the danger of going into the mine, I'm sure you're right to be concerned, but even so I promise you it will be safer to stop the manifestation in situ than to try and deal with the demon once it's broken through.'

'I still don't see how it's going to call anyone to it when it's down a mine,' Aidan protested, throwing his hands up in disgust. 'Even if we were to try and get down there – and I'm not saying we're going to – you don't know the first thing about caving. At the very least you'd need a couple of hours on the ropes course before you'd be anything like safe to try. So what if it manifests and tries to call a host to it? There's no way anyone's going to get down there without the right equipment.'

'And if the host it calls just happens to be one of your mountain rescue friends?'

Aidan rolled his eyes.

'How likely is that?'

Eldritch shrugged and shifted slightly, putting his back to the thin wind that had sprung up out of nowhere. He pulled his jacket closer around his chest, cold now as he always seemed to be since that first night in the forest.

'I don't know,' he admitted. 'But it's a risk I'm not prepared to take.'

He looked at Aidan, willing him to understand. When it seemed that Aidan didn't Eldritch said at last, 'Don't you see? If it takes a host I'm going to have to kill someone to stop it.'

CHAPTER 14

'What difference would it make if we had the Child with us?'

Eldritch looked up from the rough sheep track they were following and glanced across at Aidan, his expression one of amused tolerance.

'You're not back on that again?'

Aidan shrugged and said nothing but he continued to watch Eldritch as they walked, his eyes on the other man's face, waiting for him to answer the question. Eldritch raised an eyebrow.

'It wouldn't make any difference. We don't know if the Child has any power, let alone if he knows how to use it. Anyway,' he added, with faultless logic, 'we don't know who the Child is.'

'But what if we did?' Aidan persisted.

The briefest flash of annoyance tightened Eldritch's face and he put his hand up and absently rubbed at his shoulder. He had felt tired and achy all day and, though that had eased a little during the hike up here, he realised he had stiffened up standing in the cold wind and now his shoulder was starting to trouble him again.

'But we don't,' he insisted. His brows pulled down as he saw the look in Aidan's eyes. 'Do we?'

Aidan pulled a face.

'Gwyn thinks it might be me.'

There. He had said it. He turned and kicked out at a stone bordering the sheep track, watching as it skittered across the close-cropped grass rather than meet Eldritch's astonished look.

'She'd worked out a neat little family tree – I saw it on her desk this morning.'

'But you know who your father was.'

'Do I?' Aidan turned sharply, rounding on Eldritch, his expression belligerent. 'Do I really?'

Eldritch flinched back and Aidan swung away with a muttered apology and carried on walking.

'I know who I thought my father was, but as Gwyn said, people do have bastards,' he spat the final word.

'Even when they're happily married?' Eldritch asked softly, falling back into step beside him.

Aidan was silent as they laboured up a steep stretch of path. As the ground flattened out again he said, 'I don't think they were. I was still pretty young when he left but… well, kids pick up on these things.' He shook his head regretfully. 'It would sure as hell explain a lot about his attitude towards me.'

All of a sudden he was seeing James Morgan in a new light; Anne Morgan too.

'Mum must have said something to Gwyn otherwise why would she even consider it, but why didn't she tell me? And why didn't Gwyn say anything?'

'Maybe she was going to. If she'd only just worked it out she might have been planning to tell you when she got back from her run.'

'I don't mean now. Why didn't she tell me before, about James and the fact that he wasn't my dad?'

Eldritch let out his breath in a long sigh.

'That's one to ask her but maybe she promised your mum that she wouldn't?' he suggested.

'Huh.' Aidan's disgusted snort said all he thought about that. 'She's been dead nine years. How long are you obliged to keep a promise to someone who's dead?'

Eldritch bit his lip and a flicker of something long suppressed showed far back in his eyes but if he had an answer he did not care to share it. Instead he said, 'I may be wrong but I got the impression that you and Gwyn weren't exactly on speaking terms for most of that time.'

They carried on in silence, Eldritch with his shoulders hunched against the cold and Aidan with his head down, hands stuffed deep into his jacket pockets, lost in thought. They had crested the hill and were descending towards the distant strip of tarmac and Eldritch's car when he finally looked up.

'Is there any way of telling?'

'Telling what? Oh, you mean if you're the Child?' Eldritch considered this. 'Not that I know of.'

He took a hand from his pocket long enough to push the windblown strands of hair back from his face and added, 'It means one thing though. There's no way you're coming down the mine with me.'

'What?'

Aidan stopped in the middle of the path and rounded on the wizard, his face a mixture of shock and incomprehension and the hard, ugly seeds of resentment.

'I'm assuming you don't have any children,' Eldritch continued patiently. The comment seemed so irrelevant that the angry tirade Aidan had been about to unleash died unspoken in his throat.

'No, but…'

'Then the demon only has to kill you and the Covenant's broken. It's free to manifest.'

For a moment the world seemed to stand still; even the restless breeze that had been at their backs since they had turned away from the pit ceased as Aidan stared back at the wizard, his jaw dropping as he took this in. All day he had brooded over the implications of his being the Child yet he had forgotten this most fundamental of truths – that if he was the Covenant now resided solely in his blood.

'Could the demon know who I am?' he asked softly, his face reflecting more curiosity than fear. The question raised a wry smile from Eldritch.

'It certainly seemed to know who we were last night.'

'But that could have been the same as the attack on Gwyn. It knows we're the opposition so it's trying to take us out – all of us,' Aidan reasoned. 'Not just me.'

Then his chin lifted and he looked at Eldritch with a new firmness in his expression.

'Anyway, it doesn't matter. "The Covenant weakens. I wake. I rise". Remember that? We know the demon's getting powerful enough to manifest regardless of the Covenant. You said as much up there.'

A jerk of his head indicated the pit, hidden away on the far side of the hill.

'It's going to be able to escape soon anyway. It doesn't need to kill me to do it. What really matters is that you can't get into the mine on your own.'

Eldritch's eyes flicked heavenwards as if inviting comment from some higher power.

'It's only a twenty foot piece of rope to climb down. I think I can manage that on my own.'

But Aidan shook his head.

'That's just to get down to the tunnel. The workings where the accident took place are on the twenty-five fathom level. I think you're forgetting the hundred and fifty feet of shaft you're going to have to climb down to reach them, and that's if there are no cave-ins or flooded sections to have to work around.

'Besides, you said yourself you need another power source. I may not have much training but if I'm there surely you can tap into mine.'

'Absolutely not.'

Eldritch had listened quietly as Aidan pointed out the physical obstacles that the mine presented and if he hadn't greeted the comments with enthusiasm then at least there had been a grudging acceptance in his flint-grey eyes. But at Aidan's final suggestion the thoughtful look vanished and his expression hardened.

'Power might have been an issue if I was going to have to keep all the entrances sealed until the demon manifested but the whole reason for going down the mine is so that I can strengthen the boundary and stop that happening.' He glared at Aidan. 'And I can do that on my own.'

'But what if the demon does manifest?' Aidan asked.

'It won't,' Eldritch's voice was coldly certain as though he had dismissed any possibility that he might be unable to stop it. 'But if it did I'd want you running as fast as possible in the other direction, not wasting time trying to share power with me. I won't need it and I don't want you putting yourself at risk just because you think I might.'

Aidan blinked at the vehemence of Eldritch's tone but his

immediate reaction was one of concern rather than anger.

'What about the avatar?' he asked quietly. 'When Gwyn first told me about the demon she said you'd have to destroy the avatar first or drive it back into the Unseen Realm. She was worried that that would take so much power you wouldn't have enough left to seal the boundary afterwards.'

'Oh, she was worried, was she?'

Eldritch shoved the hair back from his face impatiently and scowled at Aidan as though he had made a direct challenge to his competence.

'Well she's wrong.' As Aidan started to react to the bluntness of that statement he added, 'For the simple reason that the avatar's served its purpose once the demon is ready to manifest. It's no longer needed so the demon will have reabsorbed it.'

Aidan raised an eyebrow.

'You've thought of everything, haven't you?'

'Believe me, I've been thinking of very little else for a long time. Look, I appreciate what you've said about getting through the mine and you're right – you know how to do it and I don't – but the demon is my field. I know how to handle it and I really don't want you putting yourself in danger unnecessarily.'

Unexpectedly Eldritch's expression softened. The corners of his mouth twitched in the beginnings of a smile as he thought of something and he gave Aidan a knowing look.

'You remember when we met Griff and his Rottweilers? You were pretty adamant that if there was going to be a fight I was to stay out of it. I didn't like it—'

'You didn't stay out of it either.'

'Maybe not,' Eldritch conceded, his smile becoming wry, 'but you were right.'

He paused and pulled the collar of his coat a little higher.

'The point is that this is the same sort of situation. Yes, you have power but no matter how willing you think you are to open yourself up so I can share it, without training there's no guarantee that when you need to you'll be able to do it. It would be like me thinking I could pitch into a fight with no training just because I wanted to help.'

'That seemed to work quite well, if I remember rightly.'

'Aidan...' Eldritch gave an exasperated sigh. 'The middle of a manifestation isn't the time to find out it's not going to work.'

'Not that it's going to come to that,' Aidan reminded him, sarcastically. Then, against all odds, he grinned. 'I don't know why we're even discussing this. Okay, I promise no heroics.' His expression turned positively wicked. 'But unless you know someone who can lend you a set of caving equipment you're not going anywhere in that mine without me.'

It would take a lot of equipment. Back in Aidan's kitchen they pored over the notes of the mine layout, amending and annotating the rough sketches they had drawn previously to make sense of the descriptions of that subterranean world of tunnels and shafts. As they worked Aidan jotted down what they would need.

'That's one hell of a distance,' he said, moving a coffee cup so he could put two pages side by side and compare their descriptions of the precipice known prosaically as Number Two shaft. 'Normally I'd single rope a drop like that but you don't have the experience and we don't have the time to teach you. So, we're going to have to use ladders. It's a good job we've got enough. I'd hate to have to explain to Chris Parker why I wanted to borrow some from the Moles.'

'The Moles?'

Eldritch raised an enquiring eyebrow as if Aidan had just proposed going to the fairies at the bottom of the garden for his caving equipment.

'The Montgomery Moles. They're our local potholing club.'

'Potholing.' The wizard shuddered theatrically at the word, his lips turning down as though he had tasted something sour. 'Why anyone would do that for pleasure is utterly beyond me.'

The distaste in his voice raised a small smile from Aidan but he forbore to comment.

'I can pick this stuff up from the centre before we go up to the ropes course.'

When Eldritch looked as though he might protest Aidan said, 'I wasn't kidding about you needing some training before we do this. Even using ladders it's going to be tricky enough. I don't plan on teaching you caving by numbers in the pitch dark.'

Eldritch subsided, his hand straying up to rub his shoulder and Aidan's slight smile became a frown.

'You keep doing that. I thought it was getting better.'

'It was. It is,' Eldritch corrected himself. 'It's just a bit stiff after yesterday, that's all. All of me is,' he added ruefully. 'Anyway, it's you and your ribs we should be worrying about,' he countered. Aidan pulled a face.

'I've done worse things in worse shape,' he said dismissively. Eldritch looked sceptical.

'Worse than fighting a demon half a mile underground? You'll have to tell me one day.'

'Over a pint in the Unicorn, tomorrow night,' Aidan promised. 'Listen, I think I know all the kit we're going to need now, so I'm going to go over to the hospital. Are you coming?'

Unfooled by the casual tone Eldritch shook his head regretfully.

'There are some things I need to do to prepare for tomorrow.' He adopted a stern expression. 'You drive carefully. I don't want my car written off too.'

He looked at Aidan and the teasing died from his eyes.

'Give her my love,' he said quietly.

Aidan was silent for a moment and then he smiled, a sad-sweet expression that acknowledged more than his words.

'I will.'

Doctor Carmel was sat at the staff desk when Aidan walked onto the ward. She glanced up at the sound of his footsteps, quiet though they were, and he saw the look of recognition on her face followed swiftly by the little double take as she took in the bruising around his temple and cheek. One elegantly shaped brow winged upwards though she was far too polite to make any mention of it. Instead she smiled widely at him, getting to her feet and coming out from behind the desk, her hand extended towards him.

'Hello,' she said. 'I was hoping you'd stop by this evening.'

She had a sure, light grip and Aidan found himself returning both her handshake and her smile with more enthusiasm than he had initially felt at the sight of her.

'Is your friend not with you this evening?'

The doctor tilted her head quizzically, looking past Aidan as if expecting to see someone behind him. Thrown by the unexpected warmth in her voice it took Aidan a few seconds to realise who she meant, but then it clicked.

'Eldritch? No, he couldn't make it this evening. He's er... working.' He paused, curious. 'Why, is the kindling all ready to go?'

'Excuse me?'

Confusion crinkled the doctor's smooth olive-skinned brow and Aidan winced, hardly able to believe that he'd said that out loud.

'Nothing,' he muttered, feeling a blush spreading from the back of his neck and up over his face. 'Sorry, it's a private joke. Not even a very good one. Forget it.'

'I see.'

There was a moment's hesitation as the doctor considered this but then her smile returned.

'It's a shame he's not here because I rather feel I owe him an apology. I think his prayers,' – a subtle tweak of the eyebrows accompanied the word – 'may have done some good.'

Aidan realised with surprise that the doctor's gentle mockery was aimed at herself. He found himself warming to the woman behind the consultant's white coat.

'How? What's happened?'

'Well…'

Doctor Carmel paused as if to gauge his likely reaction to her story.

'Before Miss Hughes went down for her scans this morning one of the nursing team thought it would be a good idea to remove the bracelet he left with her. So it could be put somewhere safe you understand.'

'And?'

'And when he tried to take it from her wrist she sat up in bed and told him to take his hands off it. In no uncertain terms I believe.'

Laughter danced in the back of her espresso-coloured eyes at the recollection.

'You mean she's awake?'

All the chaotic mix of emotions that Aidan had experienced in the last twenty-four hours – anger, fear, grief – crashed over him and were wiped away by a burst of relief that left him light-headed and struggling to breathe around the jubilant whirl of feelings churning around behind his breastbone. He caught at the corner of the desk to steady himself, aware that a manic grin had taken control of his face and not caring.

'Not exactly.'

Doctor Carmel's voice sobered him as quickly as a bucket of iced water. He stared at her, shocked and startled and not a little hurt by this unexpected backtracking.

'When Stephen let go of the bracelet Miss Hughes simply lay back down again and she's remained unconscious since.'

'So she's really no better?'

The giddy rush of delight curdled in his stomach at the doctor's words and Aidan sank down onto the desk, careless of the piles of paperwork or the black and silver serpent coils of a stray stethoscope poking out from underneath a back copy of *The Lancet*. His head bowed, he stared at the floor. The grey linoleum under his feet seemed the colour of ashes.

'That's not what I meant.'

Doctor Carmel's hand on his arm was light but reassuring, rather as her handshake had been earlier. Aidan raised his head to meet the doctor's steady gaze.

'Although I can't guarantee anything I'd say there are significant grounds for optimism in that response. Her scans were quite positive too; the swelling is diminishing and there are no signs of it having caused damage to the underlying tissues.'

She gave his arm a small squeeze and then said firmly, 'Of course, if she's not improved in the next twenty-four hours I may risk another attempt at a braceletectomy.'

The suggestion conjured a small huff of laughter from Aidan, even as he realised that that was what the doctor had intended.

'Be careful if you do; she's very fond of that bracelet. It's one of her favourites.'

'Really?' The doctor regarded him in surprise. 'I thought it was your friend's.'

'What, Eldritch's?' Aidan's smile broadened at the thought of what the wizard would say to that. 'No, he was just holding onto it for Gwyn while she went running.' Something made him add, 'He's more a precious stones type when it comes to jewellery; diamonds, sapphires, that sort of thing.'

Doctor Carmel pursed her lips, considering this particular insight, and then she smiled appreciatively.

'A woman could like that in a man.'

When he had read her notes that morning Aidan had seriously wondered if he would ever want to see Gwyn again but at the sight of her lying in bed, fragile and still as a porcelain doll, he felt the last dregs of his anger seep away and he realised he would give anything to be able to talk to her about what he and Eldritch were planning to do.

'It's not the mine so much Gwyn...'

And indeed it wasn't. The mine he felt he could cope with; it had, after all, been created for men to work in and with the plans they had drawn and the descriptions gleaned from their research he had as clear an idea of its layout as he could ever hope for; certainly more than he would have expected had he been exploring a new cave system. While climbing was his real passion Aidan knew he had enough caving experience to deal with anything marked on those maps.

'I reckon with an hour or two on the ropes course I can teach Gandalf enough so that he won't be a complete liability when we're down there. I mean obviously I'm going to have to keep a close eye on him but if the shafts have stayed clear we should be okay.'

Of course if that wasn't the case... Aidan paused as he considered the likelihood of flooding or the possibility of cave-ins. If they encountered either of those it might be that they wouldn't be able to reach the old workings. His teeth worried at his bottom lip at the thought. Greenfields mine had closed in 1912; that was a long time for tunnels to stand empty and unmaintained. There were very good reasons why mines had pumping engines and it wasn't beyond the realms of possibility that the deeper workings would be underwater. Aidan sighed. The only way they were going to find out was if they came off the ladder in Number Two shaft and found themselves knee-deep in water – or worse. He made a mental note to go back over the maps when he got home so he knew what alternative routes they might take if they found their way blocked. Like teaching Eldritch some basic caving techniques, it wasn't something to be left until they were underground. Once more he wondered how the tall wizard would manage. He remembered the look of exaggerated horror on Eldritch's face at the mention of potholing but he was reasonably certain that the Englishman would take it all in his stride. They would have to be extremely careful but on the whole the physical aspects of the descent had him no more apprehensive than if tomorrow's venture had been planned for a natural cave. No, it wasn't the mine itself that was troubling him.

'It's the demon...'

Even saying it aloud brought a surge of adrenaline that set his heart pounding and he felt sweat break out on his palms. He slipped his fingers free of Gwyn's and wiped his palms on his jeans.

'React like this tomorrow son and you'll be the one falling off the ladder, never mind Eldritch,' he murmured, shaking his head at his own foolishness. He would be no use to anyone if he was sweating so much he couldn't grip. 'Best bring a chalk bag; a really big chalk bag.'

Somehow focussing on the little technical details of the climb calmed him but there was no getting away from the fact that actually going to where the demon was breaking through was a very different proposition from helping Eldritch to lay spells on the mine openings to catch it when it emerged. It hadn't seemed such a big deal earlier. Aidan smiled wryly at the thought. Eldritch had caught him off guard when he had said there was no way he could be allowed to go down the mine and from that point he had been so wrapped up in convincing Eldritch that he needed expert help his mind had glossed over what it was that they were going into the mine to do. And then of course, Eldritch had been so adamant that he could prevent the demon manifesting that, despite his teasing the wizard, Aidan hadn't given serious thought to what would happen if he couldn't. It was only now, away from Eldritch's cocksure attitude, that Aidan could admit to a growing unease that things would not be as simple as the wizard expected. Once before a man had tried to contain the demon and six men had died as a result. No doubt William Wynn-Jones had thought he could stop it but had he realised it would be at the cost of his life and five others? Now Aidan found himself wondering what would happen if Eldritch had underestimated the demon's strength. For the first time he was beginning to realise that there was a very real chance that things might go wrong and it occurred to him that if they did the consequences were likely to be deadly.

Aidan slipped his hand back around Gwyn's. Despite Doctor Carmel's optimism he could see little sign of an improvement in her. Her bruises had darkened over the last twenty-four hours although perhaps her face was a little less swollen, the skin drawn slightly less than drum-tight across the high cheekbones, but she showed no sign of waking even when he stroked her fingers and called her name. She had always slept so lightly. He recalled how she had always caught him, no matter how quiet he had been when he crept out of the spare bedroom late at night, confronting him in the kitchen, her hair tousled over the shoulders of her oversized t-shirt but her green eyes alert and cat-like in the light from the open refrigerator door. The thought brought a smile to his lips even if it didn't quite manage to reach his eyes. *Please be alright,* he prayed silently. He raised her hand and softly placed a kiss onto her fingers wondering briefly why it felt that he had done this before.

'I'm sorry that we missed the last nine years, Gwyn,' he told her, holding her hand against his cheek. For a moment he thought he caught the faintest scent of lavender and beeswax on her skin and it knotted his throat closed so he had to swallow hard to continue.

'It would have been good to have had more time to get to know each other again, to have the conversations we should have had as adults.'

He gazed down at her, this woman who had been his mother's best friend and who had been there from the very beginning of his life.

'You're the only link I have to her now Gwyn. The things I'd have asked her as an adult I can only ask you.' He swallowed again. 'And now there won't be time.'

His hand strayed to touch the tendrils of her hair, curling like nightfall across the pillow. Someone had thought to catch it up in loose bunches and it made her look like a deranged schoolgirl until his eyes strayed back to her face and the mottled black and purple.

'Why didn't she want me to know?' he asked at last. 'What happened between her and James that makes you so sure I'm William's son and not his?'

He looked down at the bruised and swollen face. He had been so angry with her this morning he could almost have inflicted those injuries himself, but somehow it no longer seemed to matter.

'Take care of yourself Gwyn.'

Very gently he placed her hand back on the sheet, straightening the fingers and giving them one last squeeze before he bent and softly kissed her forehead. As he straightened up he looked at her for a final time.

'You're meant to wake up at this point,' he chided her gently, but her eyes remained closed and, after a moment, Aidan reluctantly walked away.

There was no sign of Doctor Carmel when he reached the front of the ward. Instead one of the nurses he thought he recognised from yesterday's vigil was sat at the desk. Aidan stopped in front of her and pulled a slightly dog-eared envelope from his jacket.

'I'm going to have to be away for a few days. Can you give this to Miss Hughes when she wakes up? You know, when she's well enough to be reading things.' Slightly embarrassed he held it out to her. 'Could you tell her I'm sorry that I'm not going to be there?'

'Of course we will.'

The nurse took the envelope from him and wrote a note on it.

'When are you due back?'

She glanced up as she finished writing, but Aidan had already gone.

CHAPTER 15

Eldritch stood at the window for a long time after the ruddy glow of the car's rear lights had faded into the twilight. On the far side of the valley the sky over the hills still held the last of the day's light in soft apricot hues and the broad bands of hedging and occasional stands of trees were distinct lines of brown and green, not yet blended into one monochrome shade with the fields. But here, in the valley bottom, the little straggle of houses that made up the heart of Caeglas was already sunk in shadow. Even as he watched lights were coming on in several of the houses, casting warm, whisky-coloured promises of comfort into the encroaching dusk. Eldritch shifted slightly, leaning his weight against the thick stone wall. If he stretched out his senses he could feel the subtle change in energies that denoted the turning of day into night. It was a sensation he had been aware of from his earliest days, one that he took for granted, but it occurred to him now that he couldn't remember the last time he had looked up and watched the stars come out. It was something Helen had loved to do. Until now he hadn't realised he had stopped doing so.

There will be other nights to do this, he promised himself, but even so he remained at the window, watching until the first pinpricks of light appeared before he pulled the curtains to and walked slowly back into the kitchen.

He was glad that Aidan had decided to go to the hospital.

208

In all honesty he would have liked to have gone with him but it was true that there were preparations he needed to make and what he had planned was best tackled alone. It wouldn't be easy. As he made a fresh pot of coffee Eldritch acknowledged the fact. What he was about to attempt was something only a handful of people knew how to do and of those fewer still would think it worth the risk. Even at his best it wasn't something he would undertake lightly and Eldritch knew he was currently very far from his best. Not that he would have admitted it to anyone but his mind and body ached with tiredness. He had slept only fitfully and that, combined with the effort of creating a power sink to aid Gwyn's healing and the physical drama of yesterday evening, had taken its toll on an already battered system. Even today's minor expedition into the hills had tired him. No, trying this now was bordering on madness. But facing the demon in such a state would be worse.

It was that which swayed him. *Not,* he told himself, *that it's going to come to that.* But if it did, if they reached the boundary too late for him to strengthen it and the demon did manifest, then he would need every last ounce of power he could draw upon to defeat it. At that point the risk of what he was about to attempt would be justified a dozen times over.

Absently Eldritch pushed the scrub of hair back from his face, his fingers lingering for a moment to rub his temples where the first niggling tension of a headache was starting. He had played down the likelihood of a confrontation for Aidan's sake, hoping he might convince the younger man to leave him alone to seal the boundary, but the truth was that all his senses were telling him it would be a close run thing. It had started again last night, the growing sensation of pressure building inside his head, the nagging awareness of the demon's presence rising like the onset of a migraine or the premonition of a coming storm. Even if he didn't care about the chaos the demon would wreak when it escaped, the crawling sense of it in his mind was almost enough to drive him to enter the mine just to be rid of it. He grew still, his hands dropping down to rest on the worktop in front of him, as he wondered what the demon's victims felt. If it was anything like this he could understand how it might control them. He shuddered and straightened, dismissing the idea as maudlin. He might be reacting to the demon's presence but it wasn't controlling his actions, not unless it wanted to be destroyed. Irritated with himself Eldritch poured his coffee. There was a lot to be done. It was best that he got started.

Upstairs in the small bedroom he laid out the things he would need; little twists of salt and sulphur, the shining obsidian disk and the red nightlight that would mark his protective circle. *No blood tonight, Aidan,* he thought with a fleeting grin as he put the latter down. Next he added a shallow brass bowl, no larger than his cupped hands, and a box of matches. He looked at the assorted items spread out on the bed and, satisfied everything was as it should be, he fetched the final element from the bottom of his bag. It looked innocuous enough; a little sachet of herbs and powders scarcely big enough to cover the palm of his hand, seemingly no different from any of the herb and incense mixes Rowan displayed in a bowl by her till. Yet Eldritch knew instinctively that he would never find this particular mixture among them. Even on their limited acquaintance he was willing to bet it was not the sort of thing that Rowan would approve of. *And for good reason,* he reminded himself. The last thing Llancathan needed was one of its amateur mystics dabbling in what he was about to do.

He considered the sachet again, turning it in his fingers. The herbs it contained would open every energy channel in his body, laying bare even the deepest reservoirs of his power. At the same time they would sharpen his arcane senses to preternatural levels, enhancing his awareness of energy and his ability to manipulate it until he could reach out and pull it to him. In such a heightened state, should he choose to, he would be able to suck the life force from man or animal, twisting and warping and pulling their energies to him until they were sucked dry and he was filled to overflowing, power shining from him like a god. Such an act was not power sharing, as Aidan had volunteered to do, nor the willing gift of power that Gwyn incorporated into her healing. It was power stealing; the violation and rape of another's essence. Eldritch knew of only one man who had taken that path. His grandmother had told him the story as a warning, even as she had taught him the technique that had led that man into corruption. And – though he knew she loved him as dearly as she had her own son – Eldritch had never doubted her when she said she would hunt him down and kill him if he ever chose the path that his uncle had taken.

Don't worry Grandma, that's not going to happen.

Even now, aware of how desperately he might need such additional power, Eldritch could not conceive of taking that route. But there was another option. Those individual life forces were not the only energies that would be opened up to him. Nestled deep within the earth were greater and deadlier reservoirs of power, ancient channels of energy that, due to their very strength, were capable of overwhelming anyone foolish enough to touch them.

Eldritch took a deep breath, holding it for a second and then releasing it in a sharp exhalation along with the tension that had been building in his body. He closed his eyes and let his head drop forward, stretching his neck and the tight muscles across his shoulders. This was what he intended to do; to tap into the great silvery power channel he had sensed girdling this valley, buried deep within the bones of the mountains. Even without the herbs to open and focus his mind it was within his ability to reach it. With them however, he should have the control necessary to siphon off some of that energy and recharge his own reserves. At least that was the plan. He opened his eyes and regarded the sachet with renewed determination. Yes, it would be risky – the trace of a wolfish smile crept to the corners of Eldritch's mouth at the thought – but so was going up against a demon.

Putting the sachet to one side Eldritch took a long swallow of coffee. The caffeine would keep his fatigue at bay while the herbs did their work and he accessed the power he needed. He would pay for it later of course. At the very least his dreams would be foul tonight. Eldritch smiled grimly at the prospect. No matter how bad the after-effects they would have some way to go to outdo the dreams that had haunted him last night. He shuddered and ran a hand over his face, wiping away the thin film of sweat that had sprung up with the memory. Would that he could wipe away the images as easily. He had woken repeatedly throughout the night, his heart hammering with the violence of his emotions as time and again he dreamt of tearing the demon apart with his bare hands. It seemed that every time he closed his eyes he fell immediately into the same dreams; the same ghastly images marching across his retinas, the same smell of blood and corruption filling his nostrils and congealing on his tongue. And each time the anger and hatred built within him, becoming so strong that it reached through to infect the first moments of his waking. Thank God he slept alone. He didn't care to think what he might have done in those first blind moments of consciousness had there been someone asleep beside him.

He swallowed convulsively, the bitterness in his mouth no longer solely due to the coffee. It was hard to envisage being capable of inflicting the carnage he had seen. A shiver wracked him and he shook his head as though he could shake loose the memory, for that was not the worst of what had come to him in the blackness of the deep night. Much though he might wish to deny it, he knew that when the blood lust passed and he came back to himself – when he looked up coated in gore, with the blood dripping thickly from his hands and little gobbets of flesh clinging to his fingernails – the bodies he had been rending were human. One – a young man with light brown hair – had been flung casually against the wall, eviscerated. But the one that disturbed him most lay like a broken doll in a storm wrack of dark hair, one emerald eye staring sightlessly up at him from the ruin of her face. At that point in his dreams he had covered his face with bloodied hands and wept. Only sometimes the sound he heard coming from his throat wasn't sobbing. Sometimes he thought he laughed instead.

Angrily Eldritch tore his mind away from the memory. They were dreams, nothing more, just as the periods of blackness, those momentary lapses of concentration when he would come back to himself with no recollection of what he had been doing – almost as if for a few heartbeats his body had belonged to someone else – were nothing more than tiredness. He pushed a hand up under his hair, kneading his fingers into the tight muscles of the back of his neck. It seemed a long time since he had slept properly with neither pain nor nightmare haunting him, but after tomorrow everything would be fine. He held that thought before him like a talisman, allowing himself to savour just a little of its promise. Tomorrow would see the end of the battle. It would finally be over. All he had to do was get into the mine. Holding to that thought he drained his coffee and set to work.

Rolling back the rug Eldritch bent to touch his fingers to the pine floorboards, letting the energies of the room come to him. He could feel tiny threads of magic, old wards and protections faded almost to nothing by the passage of time and the constant wear of life energies brushing against them as those who had lived here came and went, unaware of their existence. As he traced them he thought he felt the faintest echo of Gwyn's power in their faded ribbons, coming to him like a hint of vanilla and lavender as though he had touched some ancient fabric and in doing so had released the scent trapped within its folds. The impression was gone almost immediately but it warmed him to think that she had been here, a dark-haired guardian angel, lending her strength to keep those who dwelt within these walls safe. He realised he was smiling as he pulled the net of his senses back, as if some measure of that protection could cling to him in the whispery echoes of those long ago wards. It was nonsense, of course. Even had she been here, hale and whole, he would not have wanted her involved in what he did now, in the same way that he would not countenance drawing on Aidan's nascent power tomorrow. No more lives would be put in danger because of him, he promised silently. He would depend on the strength of his own flesh, his own power, as he always had done. What he was about to do would ensure he was strong enough to face the demon's menace alone.

Working quickly now, as the caffeine hit his system, Eldritch placed the markers of his circle around him; salt and sulphur for north and east, obsidian for the west and, facing him, the red nightlight marking the south. In front of this he placed the brass bowl, the matches and the sachet of herbs. Finally, he slipped his grandmother's ring from the chain around his neck and put it beside the bowl. That was it; everything was ready. Leaning over he switched off the little bedside light, plunging the room into darkness before he struck a match and set it to the nightlight.

'Once in darkness, now in light,' he intoned softly. As he did so he reached out and with a sweep of his mind closed the circle around him, sending the energy of light through each of the cardinal points, binding it to them and joining each one in an unbroken chain.

'Let light prevail in this circle this night.'

A thrill of adrenalin twisted his stomach as he picked up the sachet and tore it open with his teeth, pouring the herbs out into a small conical pile in the brass bowl. Breathing shallowly he struck a second match and touched the flame to the herbs, watching intently as he waited for them to catch. The tightness in his stomach increased as they started to smoulder, the first curls of smoke rising towards him. Swallowing against the sudden dryness in his throat Eldritch closed his right hand around his grandmother's ring.

No going back now.

Deliberately he bowed his head over the makeshift censer, his hair falling in a curtain over his face as he inhaled deeply, drawing the narcotic fumes down into his lungs. Bitter and slightly acrid their scent was very unlike that of the incense Gwyn used. It caught the back of his throat and against all his better instincts he felt a sudden regret that – crazy and irritating though the witch was – she wasn't there to help him. But he had no time to pursue that thought for in the same moment his perceptions shifted and the world as he knew it came apart.

Unprepared he would have fallen into madness. Even knowing what to expect he felt as though his head would burst from the overload of sensations. He shut his eyes in reflex as his vision blurred sending a dozen red and gold flames swimming in front of him and clapped his hands to his ears as the roaring of blood through them almost deafened him. It did no good. The images still danced on his retinas and his head filled with noise as though he could hear the very plates of the earth grinding together. His mouth swam with saliva and his stomach cramped with nausea. Every inch of his skin burned as though suddenly all his nerve endings were on fire and he had to fight the urge to dig his nails into his flesh to try and end it.

Hold on!

He might have screamed that aloud as the wave of sensations pounded him, sweeping him to the very edge of sanity. And then everything stopped. In one heart-rending instant there was nothing; no sound, no sight, no feeling, not even an awareness of up or down or the feeling of breath in his lungs. For what seemed like an eternity Eldritch existed in a void as his normal senses shut down and then the world snapped into focus again but utterly different as he perceived it through the lens of his power.

Like the sensory overload that had preceded it, this too had the potential to overwhelm. All around him the physical reality of the room seemed as gauzy and insubstantial as if it had been made of tissue paper. Walls, furniture, the floor on which he sat; all were nebulous and intangible and his mind slipped past them as though they barely existed, but his magic – that was something entirely different. He could see the circle he had cast as a rippling veil of blue and violet light all around him as though from somewhere he had learned to weave strands of mist and moonlight and the clear cerulean blue of a summer sky. It flowed around him, pulsing with his heartbeat like a living thing and beyond it the faded echoes of magic that clung to the house were visible as a scattering of pastel rainbows, strewn across the ghosts of the walls like sequins in the fabric of a long discarded gown. It was breathtakingly beautiful and in that moment all Eldritch wanted to do was to stare at it, to thrust his hands into the shifting silks of the veil and plait them or to gather up those strange, faded relics of magic and feel them running through his fingers like handfuls of bright jewels.

Yet even as he threw his head back, laughing with delight, the discipline of years of training kicked in and he caught himself. Shaking his head like a man waking from an enchantment he drew a long shuddering breath, gathering his senses. It was beautiful – beguilingly so – he acknowledged that, but he had no time to waste in daydreams. His body could not sustain the strain of remaining in this state for long; he had to press on. Focussed again he sank his mind down through the house slipping through it like a ghost. In the kitchen below him he felt the animal consciousness of the bitch, Sula, silver-edged, watchful and guarding. He sensed the quickening of her interest as he brushed past her and moved swiftly onwards, sinking his mind deeper, passing from the house and down into the earth. Little silvery trails of energy flickered against him as he encountered the hundreds of tiny life forms that lived on and in the soil. Deeper he went, plunging on, leaving behind the domains of earthworm and ant, reaching down into the crystal flecked bones of the hills themselves. These were rocks so ancient they existed almost beyond time. Old when mankind had first called the gods into being, the collected power of millennia was contained and focussed within them. No wonder that the boundary with the Unseen Realm could be accessed so easily in these hills. And there – finally – beneath those ancient bones of rock, was the serpentine glitter of the energy line.

Eldritch had heard various explanations as to why such energy channels existed; theories that sought to explain how they had formed and what sources of energy continued to feed them. They ranged from the hard-core science of quantum physics to rambling dissertations involving aliens and UFOs, but whatever one believed or whatever name one chose to call them by – energy line, power channel, ley line or whatever – there was no denying they existed. One might as well refute the existence of the ocean on the grounds of not understanding where the water came from. In his mind Eldritch gave a derisive snort. He knew some people who would take that very stance but he himself was a pragmatist. Such theorising was all very well but one didn't need to know the why behind an ocean to be able to sail on it.

Nor to drown in it, he reminded himself as he continued to sink down towards the ancient reservoir of magic rolling and heaving in a dense, glittering stream below him. As fierce and as savage as wild fire, the closer he drew to it the more aware he became of the intensity of its power. Without conscious decision his progress faltered and he found himself staring down at the electrum and quicksilver maelstrom, partly awestruck and partly appalled that he had had the temerity to think he could draw power from such a source.

Gwyn had it right, you are an arrogant son of a bitch. Yet even as he chided himself he gathered his courage and pushed closer.

As he did so he realised that the energy stream was not the uniform flow it had first appeared. Within that roiling mass were currents and eddies, areas where the flow was, if not gentle, then at least less fierce. It was a fineness of perception that would have been beyond him had it not been for the drugs heightening his senses but the realisation gave him confidence that what he sought to do was achievable. Even though he was close to his limits, his consciousness stretched in an almost impossibly thin strand back to his physical body, he could do this. Selecting one rivulet of energy that was finer than the rest he reached out towards it. His nerve endings sang from the presence of so much power. He could feel it in his mouth, not as a taste but as a sensation – like biting down on tin foil – and smell it like ozone after a lightning strike. And then suddenly he was touching it. The contact took him by surprise as though the energy had somehow bunched under his hand, reaching up to meet him as if it were alive. He gasped as it brushed against his consciousness like a thousand bee stings jabbing into his flesh and then laughed as a sense of elation overcame him. Power surged, sweeping like a tidal wave into the wide open channels of his body. It filled his energy reserves and then spilled over, running through his flesh, molten and consuming. In that instant he felt overwhelmingly alive, every inch of his body burning with power, every cell incandescent. He could do anything. He was invincible!

His fists clenched convulsively and pain stung his right palm, sharp and sudden, somehow reaching him even through the ecstasy. Mortified, Eldritch realised how completely he had been seduced by the thrill of controlling so much power. Except that now, as the dregs of intoxication drained away, he knew that he wasn't controlling it at all. The energy might be flowing into him but all he was doing was surviving that contact and even that situation would not last. What his arcane senses perceived as ecstasy felt very close to agony when he turned his awareness back to his physical self.

Distanced though he was by layers of altered perception he could feel his body still sat, head bowed over the censer, a sacrifice forsaken and abandoned to the thrall of the drugged smoke. Muscles strained as the power surging through him set nerve endings on fire and his heart hammered against his ribs as he fought to draw breath into a chest clenched tight as a fist. Deep within his core he could feel the pressure mounting as energy poured relentlessly into him and he knew that, even with the drugs cushioning his system, he could not survive this for long. Yet he could not release his connection to the energy line. Not yet. Not until he had charged the matrix in his grandmother's ring.

Oh, but this would be harder than he had thought. Now that he was connected to the power line he understood that if he opened a channel directly into the ring, as he had intended to, he would blast the crystal matrix apart. Instead he would have to use his body as a buffer, constraining and slowing the flow of power within his own flesh whilst he fed it gradually into the ring. The degree of control required would be impossible without the drugs he was using and, even with them, the thought of what was needed appalled him. It would be so hard. In the depths of his soul Eldritch grinned humourlessly. It wasn't as if he would have very long to live with the failure if it all went wrong. With that thought he brought his awareness back to the ring clenched in his right fist.

In a dimension beyond its physical form the crystal matrix of the ring opened up before him. Calmly he reached out to it, keying his mind into its familiar patterns. Immediately he felt its emptiness clawing at him, reaching out to the power of the wild magic churning through his flesh, yearning for it as if for some long absent lover. Combined with the almost unbearable need to release the pressure building within him it was all he could do not to give way before it. Yet somehow he did resist. Though his body was locked rigid with the struggle, as calmly and steadily as if he had been feeding the ring from his own reserves Eldritch allowed the tiniest thread of power to flow from him into its jewelled matrix.

He ignored the screaming in his flesh as the power mauled him, turning his back on the voices that told him to give in before he was consumed. Instead he let that measured flow continue as if he had all the time in the world to fill the ring. The sensations within his flesh went beyond agony, beyond anything he had endured before until there was nothing left to him to describe what was happening. Courage was not enough to endure it. In the end it came down to stubbornness and a single-minded determination that he would not be beaten, ground out from the core of every cell in his body. While every sense cried out to him that his flesh was being torn apart Eldritch focussed his consciousness ever tighter and a smooth stream of power slowly filled the ring while he held back the whirlwind.

Then finally it was done. Under his touch Eldritch felt the crystal matrix resonating with the power that filled it. Almost howling with concentration he pulled his mind free, breaking the connection so there was no danger of the wild magic damaging the ring. Too tired for exaltation he barely acknowledged his triumph, understanding that the battle wasn't over until he too was free of the energy stream. Already he thought the sharpness of his senses was fading, the greater acuity beginning to wear off, and he knew the danger he faced was frighteningly real. With his system no longer cushioned by the drugs he would be unable to tolerate the wild magic. His flesh would burn for real as the energy erupted through him, carving new channels through his body as it burst from him. Eldritch had no idea whether he could survive such a conflagration. In a way it scarcely mattered for what he was sure of was that his own power would not, and he would rather die than live crippled.

The wild magic flowing into his body was like an anchor weighing him down, tying him into the energy line. Each golden needle of power was now a fishhook lodged in his flesh, the act of pulling free an ordeal as painful as if his skin were being sliced open with razors. There were too many of them, their hold on him too deep, but desperation lent him strength. Feeling through the overstretched thread of his consciousness the breath beginning to sear in his lungs he gathered himself for one final effort. Catching up a handful of his own power he hurled it into the energy line. The backlash was like being hit by lightning but even as it flayed him, leaving him certain his flesh must be hanging shredded from his bones, some small part of him registered the reassuring hardness of floorboards beneath him as he snapped back into his physical body.

With some effort he opened his eyes, noting with genuine surprise that his skin was whole and not the mess of bloody strips he had expected. Had he hurt less he might have smiled but then the first shudder wracked him and he had just sufficient presence of mind to dismiss the circle around him before a wave of disorientation followed. The room flipped suddenly from solid reality into ghostlike flimsiness and back and for some time after there was nothing but madness. Reality became fluid, washing in and out like the tide, and Eldritch's consciousness went with it, carried along as helplessly as a leaf in a flood. His body flushed hot and cold as the energy levels within him swung wildly, leaving him to ride out the agony of withdrawal shuddering and trembling like a man with ague. But gradually the extremes grew less intense and he began to stabilise. Eventually the waves of fever and chill subsided and he found the strength to push himself first onto all fours and then upright. He had been warned about this too; that while his psychic energy levels would be enhanced, the physical strain on his body would leave him exhausted.

Couldn't you have been exaggerating the downside just once, Grandma?

Staggering with weariness he dragged himself to the window and flung it open, sucking in lungfuls of cold night air. The sweat on his face turned icy as it dried and he was aware of his shirt clinging damp and uncomfortable to his body. But, though he shivered again, he remained where he was, leaning on the sill breathing cold, clean air into his lungs as he grounded himself. Only when he was certain the night had swept away the last lingering bitterness of smoke did he turn back into the room. Then he took the brass bowl into the bathroom and washed the now cold ashes down the sink.

CHAPTER 16

'I didn't think they bandaged broken ribs these days.'

Eldritch paused on the little landing, folding his arms and leaning casually against the bedroom door. His tone was nonchalant but under the dark fall of hair his eyes held a question and the first trace of concern.

'They don't,' Aidan said, not bothering to look up as he wound an initial loop of broad crepe bandage around his chest, holding the end in place with his elbow while he did so. 'Anyway, they're not broken they're cracked. It's a big difference.'

'Ah.'

The undisguised scepticism brought Aidan's head up.

'If you're going to stand there watching you can at least do the decent thing and give me a hand. Come and hold this.'

He cocked his head on one side, watching as Eldritch crossed the room towards him. The upstairs windows had been open when he had come home last night and Eldritch had had the slightly furtive air of a teenager who had been smoking in his bedroom. Whatever he had been doing – and he had steadfastly refused to be drawn on the matter – he had looked shattered, all but falling asleep on the settee as Aidan relayed the news from the hospital. He looked little better this morning and if it weren't for his absolute insistence that they had to get down into the mine as soon as possible Aidan wouldn't have considered letting him climb anything more taxing than a flight of stairs.

'And how are you feeling?' he asked pointedly. As if his words were a tonic, Eldritch straightened perceptibly.

'Me?' Raised brows telegraphed innocent surprise at the question. 'Never better.' The wizard took the end of the bandage and held it flat against the younger man's ribs. 'Here?' he asked before Aidan could enquire any further about his health.

A little kink of irritation appeared between Aidan's brows as he gave Eldritch a hard stare. This close there was no disguising the lines of sleeplessness carved in his face but all he did was smile and Aidan knew that even if he asked again his enquiry would go unanswered. For a moment he wondered whether he should slip the wizard a Mickey Finn with a couple of painkillers in his coffee but reluctantly dismissed the idea. Not only would Eldritch never forgive him but the consequences might just be worse than letting him attempt the mine, regardless of the state he was in. Visiting Gwyn in the hospital last night had reminded him that this wasn't the academic exercise he had spent all week convincing himself it was. Mostly he had managed not to think too closely about the thing that had attacked them on Saturday night, but since his visit to the hospital his mind kept sliding back to it. Like a child watching a scary film, he found himself opening his fingers a crack and peeping through, and the thought of that creature fully loose in the world because he had prevented Eldritch tackling it wasn't something he wanted on his conscience. Not that he would feel wonderful if the wizard keeled over halfway down a caving ladder or, worse still, while confronting the demon. But that was a matter for Eldritch's judgement, not his. Unhappy with the answer but unable to see any alternative, Aidan dropped his gaze to the bandage, temporarily conceding defeat.

'Yeah, that's great,' he muttered. 'Now, hold it tight and don't let it slip.'

He wound a crepe loop swiftly around his chest, waiting while Eldritch moved his fingers out of the way and then followed it up with another, overlapping it expertly until he had six neat rows of bandage encircling him like shiplapped timber from his armpit down to the bottom of his ribcage.

'I take it you've done this before,' Eldritch commented as he stood back and watched Aidan work.

'Oh yeah, two or three times. I took the first of my Dan gradings with cracked ribs.'

The way Aidan said it made it sound like a badge of honour.

'It's nothing worth worrying about. The doctors don't do anything with them because bandages just restrict the movement of the chest and make the muscles stiffen up.'

'So why the Tutankhamen impersonation today?'

'Because the one thing this will do is remind me not to do anything too quickly, which is well worth it. Thank you,' he added, taking the safety pins that Eldritch held out for him and fastening the end of the bandage in place. 'There, that should hold.'

He surveyed his handiwork with an air of satisfaction.

'I won't be wearing them long enough to stiffen up, but they'll give me that little extra support, given what we're going to be doing.' Aidan picked his t-shirt off the bed and pulled it over his head. 'Bandages help when you sneeze too, or laugh.' He tucked the t-shirt into his hiking trousers and glanced up at Eldritch with a sly grin. 'So when you tie yourself in knots on the ropes this morning I'll be able to enjoy it to the full.'

'Thank you for that vote of confidence.' Now it was

Eldritch's turn to scowl. 'I'd still rather we were going straight down the mine.'

Aidan shook his head emphatically.

'Not a cat in Hell's chance. We've been through this already and the answer's still no. You've never done any caving or climbing before so you're going to make mistakes. It's inevitable,' he said with a shrug. 'But it's not a problem. You can make all the mistakes you need to this morning and then hopefully you won't make them later when we're doing it for real.'

Eldritch remembered the conversation as he stood, sweating and frustrated, at the bottom of a twenty foot slab of sheer rock, and wondered if Aidan were being deliberately malicious. For all his earlier talk of using the ropes course they had spent precious little time on ropes. Mostly Aidan had had him climbing up and down a narrow wire ladder fixed to one of the trees, supposedly to get him used to a climbing harness and safety rope and the fact that in caving terms a ladder consisted of rungs barely wide enough to grip with both hands and thinner than his little finger. After what seemed like an eternity of going up and down, coming to terms with the way the wretched thing twisted and moved every time he so much as shifted his weight and learning such tricks as feeling for the rungs with his feet rather than looking for them, he was tired and ready to scream. His shoulder ached, his back ached and the palms of his hands were burning from gripping the metal rungs. When Aidan had finally announced he was satisfied and called a halt he had been so grateful he could have kissed him, but instead of finishing the lesson they had walked through the forest to where this godforsaken chunk of rock poked unexpectedly out of the hillside and the lesson had started again.

Wiping the sweat from his eyes with the back of his hand Eldritch tried in vain to recall how Aidan had shown him how to re-rig the rope so he could climb back up it.

'I've just abseiled down this,' he complained, turning to glare at Aidan who was stood quietly to one side, ready to take up the slack in the safety rope when Eldritch started climbing. 'Tell me again why I need to know how to climb up it.'

'Because what goes down must come back up again,' Aidan explained patiently. 'Unless you're intending to stay down the mine and keep the demon company?'

He unclipped the safety rope from his harness and came to stand beside Eldritch.

'More people have died coming down Everest than have ever died climbing up it,' he commented matter-of-factly. 'You have to plan for getting out as well as getting in and you need to know how to do it yourself in case anything happens to me.' His eyes locked on Eldritch's. 'Because if it does you're the one who's going to have to go for help.'

'Nothing's going to happen to you,' Eldritch scowled. 'If there's even the slightest hint that the demon's breaking through I want you out of there before it does. And, as I won't have time or breath to waste arguing with you if it does happen, I want you to promise that if I tell you to get out you won't ask questions you'll just do it.'

'All the more reason why you need to know how to get out on your own,' Aidan replied, sidestepping the issue of any promise. 'So, let's get on, shall we?'

He glanced at his watch and his smile slipped.

'Ten o'clock,' he commented, almost absently. 'Matt should be in Manchester by now. His flight's at two.'

He dropped his head and scuffed the toe of his boot into the loose soil.

'And?' Eldritch prompted.

'And... I don't know... it just seems weird, that's all. Matt's off to New Zealand. Jane's away all week at a conference. Here we are, getting ready to confront a demon, and none of the people who actually mean anything to me have the faintest idea what's going on. Even Gwyn's only going to find out when she wakes up.'

'Would you have told either of them?'

'You've got to be joking. I don't want either of them caught up in this. Besides, they'd think I was nuts.'

Eldritch laughed.

'So where's the problem?'

'I just hope there isn't a nasty surprise waiting for them when they get back.'

'Meaning you hope everything goes as planned in the mine?'

'Don't you?'

For a long moment Eldritch didn't answer. Then he said, 'You don't have to come with me. You've shown me what to do. I can manage on my own.'

Aidan laughed derisively.

'Don't be daft. I've shown you the basics of abseiling and you know enough not to panic and fall off the first time a ladder tips under you. That doesn't make you a caver. No, it's alright.' He shook his head as though dismissing some thought from his mind. 'I'd be lying if I said I was looking forward to this but I'm not scared, I'm just...'

Aidan bit his lip as he searched for the right word. When he couldn't find it he shrugged.

'This is way outside anything I've ever done before,' he admitted finally. 'But you know what you're doing with the demon and I know what I'm doing to get you down there so, one way or another, we're in this together. Besides, if Gwyn's got it right demon hunting's in my genes.' He laughed again and this time there was genuine amusement in his voice. 'So if I don't screw up on the caving side and you promise not to screw up any of the hocus-pocus stuff, we'll be fine.'

'*Hocus-pocus* stuff?'

One black brow raised skywards as Eldritch considered this assessment of the situation. He looked at Aidan as if trying to fathom the real feelings behind his words but then he too shrugged, his expression softening.

'I guess we'll be fine then.'

'Can you sense it?'

Aidan wasn't sure why he was whispering but somehow the situation seemed to warrant it. Crouched beside Eldritch he peered into the dark hole that punched through the wall of the pit. Daylight lit the first few feet of the scree slope of soil and rock that spilled out into the tunnel but it took the beam of his hand torch to pick out the bottom of the slide. There was little more to be seen other than that tumble of debris, the angle of the hole cutting his view to a yard or two of tunnel, the rough cut walls and floor springing into prominence as he played the beam round the shaft then sinking back into the obscuring darkness as the little circle of light moved on. It all looked reassuringly ordinary, no different from a dozen and one caves he had ventured into in the past save that the regularity of the walls and floor told him that this cavern was man-made, yet the hairs on the back of his neck stood on end as he considered that he and Eldritch were the first people to view this subterranean world for over one hundred years.

'Oh, it's still there alright.'

Eldritch too kept his voice low but Aidan didn't miss the note of unholy enthusiasm in that husk of sound. He glanced curiously at his friend. The wizard had been fretting with the desire to find a way into the mine ever since they had linked it to the demon and the discovery of the pit had left him restless as a cat before a storm. Aidan was still somewhat amazed he had managed to keep him away from it for long enough to do even the cursory amount of training they had managed that morning so he was surprised to see a stillness had settled over Eldritch now. He wasn't foolish enough to mistake it for calm for there was tension there, underlying that sense of poised self-possession, but it was as if now they were finally here, wheels had been set in motion and everything had taken on an inevitability that the wizard was content to let play out rather than race to the finish.

'But no change since yesterday?' Aidan asked hopefully. Eldritch's eyes remained focussed on the tunnel but what he was seeing Aidan could only guess. His head moved almost imperceptibly as he shook it.

'It's stronger.' The grey eyes flicked briefly to Aidan's face and then away again. 'What can I say? It's not manifested yet but it's getting very close.'

Aidan felt his own eyes drawn back to the darkness.

'So does it know that we're coming?'

'Oh, I should think so. The thing I can't tell is what it's able to do about it.'

'Hmm, that's reassuring.'

'Isn't it just?'

A saturnine smile curled the corners of Eldritch's mouth, the first expression he had shown since they had abseiled into the pit. He turned towards Aidan and Aidan started slightly as he felt something brush against the edges of his mind. He glanced around him, unsure what he had just experienced, and then glared accusingly at Eldritch as he guessed. The wizard inclined his head in the briefest of acknowledgements.

'You've got your shields up. Good. Make sure you keep them that way all the time we're down there. Don't let them down for an instant, not until I tell you that the boundary's sealed.'

Unreadable in their charcoal-dusted sockets, the grey eyes narrowed.

'Even then you'd be better keeping them up if you can. There may be some residual psychic energy floating around down there. Probably nothing that will cause you serious harm but it might feel quite uncomfortable if you walk into it.'

'Thanks for the warning.'

'My pleasure. Now, are you ready to go in?'

The question had Aidan smothering a grin. He had been right, Eldritch wasn't as calm as he appeared.

'Before we do I've got a tip for you. When we're in there don't touch any wood you might see. I think we'll be okay in the main tunnels. From what I've read I don't think they had to use props and beams like they did in coal mines but I'm not so sure about the bracing round the vertical shafts. Just remember that any woodwork down there is going to be over a hundred years old so God knows what state it's going to be in. It's probably stable while it's left alone but the last thing we need is to dislodge something. You don't know what we might bring down.'

He backed up the warning with a stern glare anxious to impart the deadly seriousness of what he was saying. Eldritch needed to understand that the mine itself had the potential to be just as deadly as the demon. He watched as Eldritch digested this new information.

'Nice. Are you sure you still want to come with me?'

'Not really,' Aidan answered, truthfully, 'but I'm going to. This is the only way I know for sure I'm going to get all my gear back.'

And with that he flipped on the lamp on his safety helmet, took a firm hold of his rucksack and pushed himself feet first into the darkness.

Scrambling down the loose slide of rock and earth to join Aidan at the bottom Eldritch was shocked by how confined the tunnel was. In his mind he had envisaged the mine adits – those tunnels built for access and drainage – as being like the corridors of a building and of a similar size but the space he found himself in was only slightly wider than the span of his arms. The walls seemed to press very close around him and he had to duck his head to avoid cracking the top of his helmet against the tunnel roof. For a moment a sense of claustrophobia wiped out all awareness of the demon from his mind.

'Okay?' Aidan asked.

'Of course.'

Eldritch made a play of adjusting the set of his helmet and glanced around him.

'Cosy, isn't it?'

Aidan grinned.

'I've been in a lot worse,' he said and as Eldritch shuddered at the thought of just what that might have entailed he continued blithely, 'Come on, if we've got this right Number Two shaft should be about quarter of a mile that-a-way.'

He jerked his head to indicate the way they should go as if umpteen tonnes of earth and stone blocking the tunnel behind them left them any choice in the matter.

It was unnerving how quickly the mine closed in around them. Following Aidan through the darkness Eldritch knew they could have gone no more than a hundred yards but when he turned back to look there was no trace of the thin smear of daylight that had marked their way in and the place they would have to find again if they were ever to leave. It was as if that link to the outside world was already closed to them and they were sealed here in this subterranean labyrinth with no way out. All he could see in the beam of his helmet lamp was the dark rock of the tunnel walls stretching away behind him until they ended abruptly in darkness at the edge of the lamp's beam. There, where the shadows and light met, it seemed – just for a moment – as though the walls were moving, closing in, and Eldritch felt his stomach clench even as he told himself not to be so foolish. Rock did not move silently on cat paws in the dark. If there was a cave-in it would come with a crashing exclamation of noise and dust, not a subtle shifting that stopped the moment he played the light directly on it. Somehow the thought was not as comforting as it should have been. Eldritch snarled inwardly, chiding himself for the way the closeness of the rock made him want to bow his head and hunch his shoulders as if doing so could possibly help him if the roof did come down.

Mention fleas and everyone scratches, he told himself. There was no reason to believe the roof would suddenly fail, he was just letting his imagination run away with him. Angrily he jerked his mind back to the one thing he knew he should be concentrating on; the demon. He should be worrying about how close it was to manifesting, not the unlikely chance of the roof falling in. Taking a deep breath Eldritch forced all other concerns from his mind and as he exhaled focussed his attention on the demon. The realisation came to him that he barely had to extend his senses to feel it. Its presence lay in the air like musk or the taint of long ago corruption, thick and heavy and so close it seemed to be all around him. That surprised him for he had thought to use that sense as an additional guide through the tunnels but the curious whispering he heard in his head had no direction to it. Closing his eyes he turned, trying to refine that contact, to narrow it down. Perhaps if he risked opening himself to it more he could achieve what he wanted…

'Are you okay?'

Eldritch spun round, startled by the voice behind him, and Aidan took a step backwards, flinging up a hand to shield his eyes as the beam from Eldritch's helmet lamp played across his face.

'I hadn't realised you'd stopped. Is something wrong?'

'No, nothing.'

Irritation made the wizard's voice curt; irritation that he had been unable to pinpoint the demon and a creeping sense of shame at how uncomfortable the confines of the tunnel made him feel. Aidan, who had been so against their coming into the mine seemed almost relaxed now they were inside it whereas he, Eldritch, couldn't stop his palms sweating and his gut twisting within him every time he remembered the thousands of tonnes of rock above his head. He had never thought of himself as claustrophobic – hell, he had travelled on the London Underground for years without a problem – but this was different. This was almost malevolent. He realised that Aidan was watching him carefully. *Probably waiting for you to show the first signs of freaking out,* a voice in the back of his mind taunted him. Deliberately he straightened and immediately cracked his head on the tunnel roof.

'Damn!' he swore, grabbing at his head though the safety helmet meant that the impact had hurt nothing more than his pride. At least Aidan had the decency to try to smother his grin, rather than laughing in his face. Very carefully Eldritch drew himself up as far as the roof would allow.

'I was trying to get a bearing on the demon,' he admitted with prickly ill grace. 'But I couldn't. It's too close. It feels like it's all around us.'

He had expected Aidan to scoff at his inability to manage something so simple but instead the younger man nodded thoughtfully.

'Maybe that's because it's below us,' Aidan offered. 'Even if you've got a good sense of direction it's pretty hard to focus on up and down. It's not something evolution's had to equip us for.'

'I wonder if the miners developed it.'

Eldritch's defensiveness subsided in the face of Aidan's acceptance and he found himself giving voice to the words almost before he was aware of having thought them.

'Maybe they did. I've known cavers who reckoned they always knew how deep they were,' Aidan mused. 'But me? No.

I guess I've never spent long enough underground.'

The swift grin that followed Aidan's words told Eldritch that he hadn't kept the shiver of distaste from his own expression but all Aidan said was, 'Come on, we should get going.'

As he turned to lead the way further into the tunnel Aidan glanced back at Eldritch.

'So, when you go back to London – once all this is over – are you going to start that Ph.D. you talked about? After all, you've finally got me to take you down a real mine.'

Eldritch laughed, a short barking sound that echoed back at them from the walls.

'Now there's a case of be careful what you wish for, if ever there was one,' he acknowledged and then, in a different tone, he added, 'I'm sorry about that. I had my reasons for doing it and at the time I thought they were good ones, but it was wrong.'

Ahead of him in the torchlight he saw Aidan's shoulders twitch in a shrug but Eldritch thought he heard a smile in Aidan's voice under the soft burr of accent.

'Forget it. You can buy the beer tonight if you're that cut up about it.'

'Watch your footing, it's getting wetter along here.'

In the confines of the tunnel it was easier to go in single file than to walk two abreast and for the moment Aidan led. He spared a glance back over his shoulder as he picked his way carefully over the slick rock.

'Still having fun?'

Eldritch glowered back at him.

'No one told me I was meant to,' he growled. 'Should there be this much water?'

The sweep of his helmet lamp across the walls revealed little trickles where water was seeping out from the rock. The floor underfoot was slick with it and the roof dripped constantly.

'I'd say this is pretty normal.'

Aidan splashed through a puddle having given up trying to step round them. They were so frequent now it was no longer worth the effort and in a few cases it was barely possible.

'When the mine was working they'd have had to run pumps to keep the lower levels from flooding but I don't suppose they'd have spared this a thought, not unless it got a lot wetter.'

They walked in silence for another minute and then Aidan stopped.

'Ah,' he said and then he added in a resigned voice, 'it's just got a lot wetter.'

CHAPTER 17

The beam of Aidan's helmet lamp glittered on a sheet of water that lay from wall to wall across the tunnel floor. It also stretched as far ahead of them as the light carried. Quite literally there was water for as far as the eye could see. For a few moments there was silence as the pair of them eyed the disconcerting sight.

'How deep is it likely to be?'

'Difficult to say. The tunnel's sloping a fair bit here. This might be a natural sump that collects water and we'll be able to walk through it or we may be in for a swim.'

'A swim?' Eldritch's eyes flicked to the roof of the tunnel and then back to the water. He swallowed heavily. 'What happens if the water comes up to the roof?'

'Then we have to decide if we can hold our breath for long enough to get through it or we try to find a way round... except that we haven't passed any side passages so I don't think there is one.'

Eldritch looked at Aidan, appalled.

'You're joking, right?'

Almost as though he couldn't help himself his eyes strayed back to the water.

'No, you can see for yourself on the map.' Aidan paused, taking a long look at Eldritch's taut face and shook his head. 'You're really not enjoying this, are you?' he said, sympathetically.

Eldritch tore his eyes from the water and stared at Aidan as if he had gone mad.

'If by "this" you mean going up against an ancient elemental that a week ago came within a hairsbreadth of killing me, well there are other things I'd rather do with my time,' he ground out. 'But someone's got to stop it manifesting and you and I are pretty much the only ones available.'

Aidan dropped his gaze but not before Eldritch had marked the look of pain that crossed his face. The wizard winced inwardly. For all his discomfort he hadn't intended the words as a barb.

'She'll be okay you know,' he said quietly and Aidan flashed him a half smile but said nothing. Eldritch returned his gaze to the water.

'If, however, you're talking about crawling around in the pitch black with God knows how many million tonnes of rock hanging over my head and then – as if that weren't bad enough – having to face the prospect of drowning as well as being crushed in a cave-in then no, I'm not enjoying this. I'd rather stick pins in my eyes.'

There was a short silence following his words and then Eldritch sighed like a man who was already regretting what he was about to say.

'So what do we do? Wade in and hope for the best?'

In the end the water proved to be nothing more than a glorified puddle. They went carefully, testing the footing at each step, but at no point was it much more than ankle-deep. As the tunnel curved gradually round to the left the beams of their head torches caught the edge of dry ground ahead of them. Another minute of splashing and they had dry rock under their boots once more.

'There, that wasn't so bad now was it?'

Eldritch scowled at Aidan but didn't answer immediately. He was right, of course, negotiating the wet section – even he could hardly glorify it with the term flooded – had proved an anti-climax but for a second or two, when he had first seen the water stretching out ahead of them he had felt a real sense of fear. Part of that, he told himself, was probably tension due to the demon's presence, but it didn't help that Aidan was so damned cheerful about the whole thing. It made him feel he was overreacting whilst doing nothing to allay his fears.

'Let's hope that's the worst problem we encounter,' he muttered gracelessly, pushing his helmet to the back of his head and rubbing his eyes in the hope it might do something to relieve the pressure building inside his head.

'The demon's getting stronger, isn't it?' Aidan asked, the first trace of worry that Eldritch had noticed since they entered the mine, darkening his eyes. Irritated, Eldritch shot him a "what do you think?" look which the younger man ignored.

'Will we be in time to stop it?'

'We have to be,' Eldritch growled, his face set and angry in the torchlight. Then he closed his eyes and shook his head and his voice was suddenly weary as he spoke again.

'I don't know, but we have to be.'

Aidan looked as though he might say more but in the end he settled for a nod and a small, tight smile.

'We should be at the shaft soon. Once we've cleared that we won't have much further to go.'

They pushed on down the tunnel, neither of them speaking. Eldritch had nothing to say and for the moment Aidan seemed to have run out of cheerful banter. At first Eldritch was grateful for the silence, relieved to be left to deal with his fears about the mine and the demon alone, but as the tunnel led them deeper his sense of unease continued to mount until he would have welcomed the distraction of idle chatter. Try though he might to convince himself that the tunnel system was safe the awareness of the weight of rock above them was almost a physical thing pressing down on his shoulders. It occurred to him then that his increasing awareness of the demon and the absolute need he had felt to enter the mine could be nothing more than a siren song, wordlessly luring him to his death. Yet even as he considered the possibility he knew he would still have answered the call. He was the only one who could destroy the demon. Knowing that didn't make him feel any happier about the mine but it gave him an inkling of just how much he was prepared to risk in order to stop the demon. Maybe that should have made him proud. Eldritch wasn't sure, he just knew that he wanted to get this over with, so when the torches picked out the edge of an abyss cutting across the tunnel floor he greeted the sight with relief.

Staying a safe distance back from the edge Aidan brought out his map of the mine.

'This is it,' he said, consulting the paper as if he hadn't already committed everything written on it to memory.

'If we're right this is Number Two shaft and it drops down to the twenty-five fathom level.'

He looked up from the map with an expression that was as wicked as it was serious.

'Of course if we're wrong and the pit brought us in further along the adit than we thought then this is actually the engine shaft and we'll find ourselves dangling off the end of the ladder with another hundred and fifty feet of nothing underneath us.' He cast his gaze round the tunnel but if the answer to that conundrum was there his knowledge of mining was insufficient to decipher it. The shaft bisected the tunnel, dropping away into darkness below them like an entrance to one of the pits of Hell. Aidan grinned at Eldritch in the torchlight.

'My advice is, don't step off the ladder unless you're damned sure there's floor underneath you.'

Eldritch thought about that while Aidan removed the caving ladders and ropes from his rucksack. Strangely enough the idea of dangling over a precipice on two pieces of wire and a series of metal bars barely larger than the average pencil scarcely bothered him. Heights he could deal with. It was the building sense of pressure and the closeness of the rock around him that he found stifling. In the enclosed space the noise of Aidan hammering bolts into the tunnel floor was a physical assault on his senses, the sound bouncing back at him from the walls until he flinched away from it. There was no doubt in his mind that the demon had long been aware of their presence but even if that weren't the case it must certainly know now. Surely the sound was loud enough to penetrate the Unseen Realm. His ears ringing Eldritch found himself imagining what it must have been like when the miners were working these seams; clusters of men labouring by candlelight in the dust and the damp, breaking the load with pit spikes and sledgehammers and sheer physical strength. They must have talked to each other as they worked, even just to share the information necessary to do their job, and Eldritch knew people too well to believe they hadn't shared other things too; it was what human beings did. But how had they managed to make themselves heard? It came to him then that he too was hearing another sound. In between the hammer blows he realised that Aidan was whistling softly to himself. He listened in disbelief. The noise was fairly tuneless but it was the implication of it that confounded him.

'You're enjoying this, aren't you?' he muttered when Aidan finally put the hammer to one side and inspected his handiwork. His tone turned the words into an accusation. 'Despite everything you know about the demon, despite the risk of it manifesting and what could happen if it does, you're actually enjoying this.'

Aidan looked up from where he knelt on the floor. A shrug accompanied his slightly sheepish grin as if apologising for it.

'I suppose I am.'

'But the demon… If I was you I'd be scared stupid by the idea of what we're up against.'

Aidan gave him an odd look.

'What makes you think I'm not?' he asked softly. When Eldritch snorted irritably he countered, 'The thing is you've said you can stop the demon and I trust you. I know you're not happy being this far underground – that's nothing to be ashamed of, a lot of people would feel the same – but you're not worried about the demon. Concerned, maybe,' he amended with brutal honesty. 'You know you could be in for a fight, but you reckon you can take it.'

Aidan paused, his head tilting to one side as he treated Eldritch to the same detailed scrutiny he had just given the climbing gear. Finally he said, 'It was whatever you did last night, wasn't it? Whatever it was you reckon it's given you an edge.'

He didn't wait for Eldritch to confirm or deny the supposition but nodded as if he could see the pieces of a jigsaw puzzle slowly coming together in front of him. Then he looked up at Eldritch again.

'So until you tell me it's all gone pear-shaped what's the point me wasting my energy worrying?'

'And it's as easy as that?'

Puzzlement replaced the irritation on Eldritch's face.

'Not easy, no,' Aidan admitted. His expression turned provocative; half teasing, half challenging. 'It takes years of hard work to get as laid back as I am. As for the rest of this,' he waved a hand negligently at their surroundings, 'This is what I do for a living. Okay, if I'm honest, I prefer my climbing to be over rocks rather than under them, but no, this doesn't bother me at all. It's not as if these tunnels are that narrow. You should try the show cave at Dan yr Ogof over in the Beacons. There's a squeeze there that goes on for over three hundred feet. It takes an hour to get through and part of it's so tight that you have to relax every muscle down before you can get through.'

His grin returned to full strength as he savoured the memory of that particular challenge and the satisfaction of surmounting it.

'It's worth it though,' he said with relish. 'When you reach the cavern on the other side it's fabulous.'

Then he stopped, noticing that Eldritch's face had turned a sickly white at the very thought. Perhaps caving stories weren't the thing to be sharing given the circumstances.

'I don't suppose it helps much, because I know these things

aren't rational, but these rock formations are among the most stable in the country. There wasn't a single cave-in in this system while they were mining here. Or at least none that didn't involve blasting powder and some fool with a fuse.'

Eldritch digested this information. He ran one hand over his face, wiping away the thin film of sweat that clung there.

'You're right,' he said after a moment. 'It doesn't help in the slightest.'

Somehow he managed a rather feeble grin of his own.

'But thanks anyway.'

With a sensation somewhere between dread and anticipation knotting his stomach Eldritch gripped the first rung of the ladder and swung his legs out over the void. Behind him Aidan stood braced, his own climbing harness securely roped to what he had referred to as a ground anchor, ready to pay out the safety rope as Eldritch descended or to check it if something went wrong and he slipped.

'See you down at the bottom,' he murmured. Aidan nodded and offered a thumbs up and a final warning.

'Remember, don't just step off the ladder when you get to the end. Make sure there's some ground there first.'

One... two... As he lowered himself down the ladder, feeling for each rung with his feet as Aidan had taught him, Eldritch counted to himself. *Twenty-five fathoms. That's fifty metres, which is one hundred and fifty feet, give or take, and the rungs are about a foot apart... three... four...* Each time he moved his right hand to the next rung he counted, repeating the number to himself as he brought his left hand down to join it. Then he moved his feet. The rungs weren't wide enough for him to get both feet on one so it was a case of stretching down with one foot, transfer the hands, right, left, shift his weight and stretch down with the other foot, trying to keep his weight central so the ladder didn't tilt and swing. *Slow and steady*, he told himself. *Make sure of each hand and each foot before you move, just the way Aidan showed you.* When he reached fifty he paused, left arm hooked through the rungs to give his hands and right shoulder a rest, and risked a glance down but he could see nothing beyond the ladder snaking away below him into the darkness.

'Is everything alright?'

Aidan's voice sounded echoey and a long way above him as he called down.

'Just catching my breath. Everything's fine.'

Gathering himself Eldritch shifted his grip and started down again. *Fifty-one... fifty-two...*

At one hundred and forty-three the feel of the ladder changed. Under his questing foot the rung kicked forward unexpectedly and with a jolt of adrenalin Eldritch realised why; he had run out of wall. Below him the ladder hung in free space where the shaft cut the twenty-five fathom level. If they were right he should be able to see the tunnel floor directly below him. *And if we're wrong then there's a very long drop and not a lot of ladder,* but he refused to think any more about what that would mean. Cautiously he glanced down, half expecting to see nothing but continuing darkness below him. When the beam of his helmet lamp picked out a rock floor, solid and substantial and barely six feet below him he could have jumped from the ladder in sheer relief. Discipline stopped him – that and the thought that Aidan would never forgive him if he sprained an ankle doing something so stupid – but for a moment there was the ghost of a smile on his lips as he scrambled down the last few feet to the floor.

The smile had gone by the time Aidan joined him. Eldritch sat with his back to the wall, his long legs drawn up to his chest, his folded arms resting on his knees, as he watched the firefly gleam of the young man's helmet lamp slowly descending towards him.

'What kept you?' he demanded as Aidan paused on the ladder above him and tipped him a jaunty salute. He made no move to get up.

'A hundred and fifty feet of ladder, perhaps?'

Aidan, who had come down the ladder noticeably faster than Eldritch, made short work of the last few feet, coming to stand over the wizard's bunched up form.

'What's eating you all of a sudden?'

Eldritch tipped his head to look up at Aidan and answered with an expression of disgust.

'Can't you feel it?'

Scorn and disbelief mingled in his voice.

'No,' Aidan answered slowly. 'But then I've got my shields up, just like you told me to.'

Eldritch swore venomously.

'Yeah and I've got my shields up too but I can still feel it.'

Almost unnoticed his hands crept round his upper arms as though he could hug away the sandpaper rasp grating along his nerves. The Unseen Realm was so close here. Awareness of it dragged across his mind like barbed wire. It was no longer just a general consciousness of the demon's presence. Here he could feel the boundary weakening, the wall between the Mortal World and the unreality of nightmare growing thinner as the demon strained against it. Every minute he had waited for Aidan to descend had been another minute in which the demon strengthened its assault. Inexorable as the tide, its power was growing, swelling to the point where it could breach the walls of reality and break through and the knowledge of it doing so was eating through Eldritch's body like vitriol. His eyes scoured Aidan's face, seeking even the smallest understanding reflected there. Shielded or not he refused to believe that a sensitive person could fail to register some awareness of what was happening. His own head felt like it would split apart under the pressure, yet he could find nothing but puzzled concern in Aidan's face. A cold feeling settled in Eldritch's gut and he hauled himself to his feet, firing his words like a cobra spitting poison.

'Come on, we've wasted enough time. Let's get going.'

CHAPTER 18

Somehow, despite Eldritch's impatience, Aidan once more found himself leading the way. In itself that didn't bother him, but he was worried by the change in Eldritch's attitude. The prickly bravado, the "I'm fine, stop asking" attitude with which the wizard had tried to disguise a perfectly reasonable dislike of being underground, had morphed into something uglier. He seemed to take it personally that Aidan was unaffected by the atmosphere on this level of the mine and, although Aidan was trying to be generous and put it down to a growing unease over the demon, he didn't have to like it. His expression hidden by virtue of the fact that he was in front of Eldritch, Aidan scowled into the darkness. In truth he wasn't sure what he felt about this level of the mine. Since Eldritch's outburst he had been aware of a tightness between his shoulder blades and a growing feeling that something wasn't right, as though if he turned quickly enough he would see movement caught in the edge of the lamp beam, but that could just as well be an awareness of one hundred and eighty pounds of angry wizard walking in the darkness behind him as anything supernatural. He wondered if he lowered his shields he might feel what it was that Eldritch was so concerned about but felt utterly disinclined to try. Even the thought that he might do so made the hairs stand up on the back of his neck. His brush with the avatar had left him with a healthy respect for the demon's ability for non-physical forms of attack and he had no desire to risk opening himself to them. Whatever Eldritch could sense that was making him so jumpy he was welcome to it. Aidan's fingers strayed to the small silver-bound disc of amethyst and quartz hanging on a thong around his neck. It had been a last minute whim to bring Gwyn's seal with him but he was beginning to think that a wiser head than his had influenced him to pick it off the nightstand this morning. For the last two weeks it had guarded his dreams. Now he wondered if it might be guarding his waking too.

Something on the adit floor caught his eye, interrupting his thoughts, and he turned his head to catch it in the beam of his helmet lamp. A heavy iron rod, the length of his arm, lay abandoned against the wall, one end shaped into a chisel-like edge, the other splayed out and battered from repeated blows with a sledgehammer. In any other surroundings it would have seemed unremarkable but Aidan regarded it with a sense of wonder.

'Take a look at this. I think it's a pit spike. The miners used them for breaking up the rock.'

'Yeah, fascinating,' Eldritch muttered, neither stopping nor looking as he pushed past and carried on walking. Despite Eldritch's attitude Aidan bent to examine his find more closely, awed by the fact that a hundred years ago someone – possibly even his grandfather – had been using it.

'For God's sake...'

Eldritch's anger echoed back down the tunnel but in a moment's rebelliousness Aidan refused to be moved. *You can wait a minute,* he thought. *Maybe it'll cool you down a bit.* Ahead of him the footsteps faltered and stopped and Aidan smiled a little to himself in the darkness knowing he had won. He waited a few seconds and then condescended to look up. His heart froze.

'Eldritch?'

On his feet now he saw Eldritch leaning heavily against the tunnel wall, his head hanging, one arm pressed against the seeping rock, the other clutched protectively around his chest. In the torchlight the little Aidan could make out of his face was grey and drawn. He seemed to be fighting for breath, his eyes closed, his face contorted in pain. Aidan was at his side in an instant.

'Eldritch?'

Getting no response, he put his hand on the other's shoulder, feeling the muscles under his hand tense as Eldritch jerked against him.

'Get... out... of here.'

The words were forced out between gritted teeth.

Damn it, he's having a panic attack. So it hadn't been the imminent encounter with the demon that had been bothering Eldritch – he had been wrong. Aidan moved closer, offering the comfort of warm, human contact against the overwhelming dark and the oppressive weight of rock over their heads. He couldn't see Eldritch's expression now, the man had pressed his face into his forearm like a child covering his eyes in a game of hide-and-seek, but he could feel him trembling.

'It's alright. It's okay. Everything's going to be fine.'

Simple words that he might have used with a child, or an animal, everything concentrated in the pitch of the voice to soothe and calm even if the words themselves couldn't reach him, while all the time wondering what they would do if Eldritch couldn't bring his fear under control. Under his hand he could feel the tremors increasing and Aidan cursed himself for not foreseeing this. Oh, he had been aware of Eldritch's discomfort almost from the moment they had entered the mine, of course he had, but the wizard had seemed to be keeping his feelings under control. He might not have been enjoying the experience but enjoyment wasn't a prerequisite for coping and Eldritch had seemed to be coping. Yes, the water had shaken him but he'd pulled himself together and he'd handled the descent down the shaft as well as any experienced caver. Besides, he had been so keen, so adamant that they must come down here. In the face of such determination it had never occurred to Aidan that the wizard might be genuinely claustrophobic.

Unable to think of anything else he could do Aidan wrapped his arms around the trembling form, trying to find some means of reaching through the terror. As he did so Eldritch reached behind him blindly, not lifting his head from the wall. His fingers caught and closed on Aidan's jacket and with unexpected strength he pulled Aidan against the rock wall, his head coming up so Aidan saw the wild eyes, the pupils huge and dilated even in the lamplight. For one moment their eyes met.

'Get out of here!'

The wizard pushed Aidan from him, the sudden force of it taking him off balance and sending him staggering backwards, then Eldritch crumpled, doubling over, his arms wrapped tightly around his belly. A long, whimpering, 'Nooooo!' sounded as though it had been torn from his throat.

Aidan sprang forward, but even as he reached out to steady the other man Eldritch uncoiled, coming up from his half crouch, knocking Aidan's hands aside, his own fastening around the younger man's throat. For a moment Aidan couldn't react, his mind stalled equally between the drama of Eldritch's collapse and the sudden viciousness of his attack, then his back slammed into the tunnel wall, his head whipping backward with an impact that would have knocked him senseless if he hadn't been wearing a helmet. As it was he felt his knees go and for a second the throttling hands around his throat were all that were holding him up, pinning him against the wall even as they deprived him of breath. Reflex took over then and he straightened, not fighting the grip round his throat but driving his fist into the side of Eldritch's face, connecting hard. The stranglehold on his throat slackened and now he moved, twisting sideways as his forearm came down, almost without conscious thought, smashing into Eldritch's arms and knocking them away. He had no time to do anything else because Eldritch lunged at him again, but this time Aidan was ready and he blocked the outstretched arms, driving a knee into Eldritch's stomach as he sidestepped the other's attack. It wasn't the cleanest of techniques but Eldritch doubled over and Aidan used the opportunity to put more room between them. Breath rasping in his bruised throat, he backed away, giving himself space and options, his eyes never leaving his opponent. He was aware as never before of the cavernous darkness opening up at his back and the closeness of the tunnel walls to either side.

'Eldritch? For God's sake, it's me, Aidan!'

Don't talk to him boy, hit him! In a quiet corner of his mind Sensei commented acidly on his failure to follow up his advantage. *Walk away before the fight if you can but after the first attack you don't stop until your opponent's on the floor and he's not about to get up again.* But he couldn't do that! Not yet.

The form in front of him straightened, turning once more towards him and a thread of ice ran down Aidan's spine at the sight. Blood dribbled from the corner of Eldritch's mouth and ran unnoticed down his chin, but it wasn't that which scared Aidan. There was something unnatural in the way Eldritch's head swung, turning side to side, as though whatever looked out through Eldritch's eyes couldn't quite see him, as though – like a hound – it was questing for his scent.

'Eldritch?' he tried again, desperate to reach the man he hoped was still there beneath the mindless thing that confronted him. But he was no longer certain that was possible. The flash of torchlight reflecting off metal that hadn't been there an instant before gave Aidan a second's warning as the thing that had been Eldritch lunged at him again. *Knife! Where the hell did he get that from?* But there was no more time to think. He sidestepped again and felt the sting as the blade scored his arm where Eldritch had anticipated his move and followed him through it. *Sloppy! This is no time for mucking around!* Aidan backed away hastily and as Eldritch followed, slashing wildly at him, his foot connected with Eldritch's wrist in a swinging roundhouse kick. It was a heavier impact than he had intended, adrenaline and the unaccustomed weight of his boots adding momentum to the technique – *Sorry Sensei. I guess I should have tried practising with my boots on just like you kept telling me to* – and he felt Eldritch's wrist go as the knife flew out of his hand, clattering against the tunnel wall to fall somewhere in the darkness beyond the lamplight. Eldritch didn't so much as flinch, clawing at Aidan's face even though from the angle of his hand his wrist was surely broken.

If there had been any doubt left in his mind Aidan knew

once and for all that this was no panic attack. Pain and shock would have brought Eldritch out of that but the wizard showed no sign of even feeling the damage Aidan was inflicting on him. Instead he lunged forward, his eyes wide and staring, his face contorted into an inhuman snarl that bared bloodied teeth. Aidan knocked him back with a kick to the stomach. What little strategy he had consisted of keeping Eldritch at a distance. As long as he could do that, he told himself, he wouldn't have to hurt him. But he didn't dare think what would happen when he could no longer manage to do so. Eldritch reeled backwards and then, instead of coming straight back at him as Aidan had anticipated, he straightened. He gestured with the broken wrist and Aidan doubled over as white-hot agony seared through his ribs. From somewhere beneath the pain and the shock came the understanding of what was happening. So this was what it meant when Eldritch said he could throw pain! Aidan clamped his teeth on a scream. For a moment that was all he could do but his mind was clear and defiant. *You don't know anything about karate if you think that's going to stop me.*

He stayed doubled over, nursing the pain, but his eyes were fixed on Eldritch and when the attack came he was ready. The thing that controlled Eldritch was fast – far faster than the man himself would have been – but Aidan was trained to this and his body knew he was fighting for his life, even if his mind had yet to accept the fact. He straightened explosively, refusing to acknowledge the fire in his chest, and drove Eldritch back with a solid battery of kicks to the stomach and chest. The last one sent Eldritch hard into the wall, his head cracking backwards against the rock, and the unnatural pain in Aidan's ribs fell away. In the momentary respite Aidan edged back, putting distance between himself and the wizard. He risked the swiftest of glances at his arm and was shocked to see the sleeve of his jacket gaping open and his hand covered in blood. Despite all his training he felt himself go cold. *Bloody hell, that was sharp! I thought it had barely touched me.* The world swam and he jerked his eyes back to Eldritch and didn't look down again. *Shame you didn't block it a bit faster then,* he told himself, trying not to feel the blood dripping from his fingers. He forced himself to focus on the positives. Yes, it hurt, but he could still clench a fist, still use his arm. It might look messy but it wasn't going to kill him. *But it might have done,* whispered a treacherous voice inside his head. For a moment everything went very still as the thought took root. *He could have killed me!* His mind wailed in outraged protest. The other voice was more brutal. *He's trying to kill you!* it roared and then Sensei's voice broke in over the top, silencing Aidan's mental debate. *Don't talk about it – take him out! Do it now, while he's still dazed and you've got an advantage.*

I can't do that, Aidan thought, despairingly. *He's the only one who knows how to stop the demon. The only one who has the power to do so.* And perhaps that was the point. But there was no more time to think. Even as he argued with himself, the thing that had been Eldritch pulled itself up from where he had slammed it into the rock face and launched itself at him once again. And this time Aidan stepped in to meet it. This time he knew what he was going to have to do. More real than the sawing pain of breathing with ribs that surely were broken now, or the burning sting of sweat in the knife slash on his forearm and in the gouges Eldritch had clawed across his throat; more real than all those things was the knowledge of what he was going to have to do. He had no more options. He was going to have to take Eldritch out.

Reality seemed to slow as though he stood in the dojo watching Martin, with his fists the size of hams, stepping in towards him, knowing exactly the form of attack and how he would defend himself. Seemingly of its own volition his arm came up over the outstretched hands clawing for his face, even as he took a half step sideways, moving beyond their reach. The inside edge of his forearm hit Eldritch across the throat, connecting with flawless accuracy, and he felt the man jerk, his head snapping back as his momentum continued to take his body forward. But for Aidan there was no thought as to what he had just done. He had moved beyond that. For him there was only the absolute purity of movement, the harmony of muscles and breath moving together in the deadly perfection of technique. He continued his step around behind his opponent – he no longer thought of the thing attacking him as Eldritch – right arm still against the throat, left arm reaching round, grasping his own wrist, twisting, tightening the knuckles just so against the side of the neck, knowing he had all the time in the world to do this. He stood in the perfect stillness at the heart of the whirlwind feeling the frantic struggling, the clawing at his arms and then at his face, grow more desperate and then finally stop. As unconsciousness dropped the sudden full weight of the body through his arms he kept the lock in place, cutting off the blood to the brain, counting slowly... one... two... three, knowing the consequences of what he was doing. Then he released his hold, stepping back in case, against all odds, Eldritch had been feigning. The wizard slid through his arms, sprawling in a boneless heap on the tunnel floor. He did not move.

Aidan staggered backwards until his shoulders encountered

the tunnel wall behind him. He half turned, almost clinging to the rock as his body sagged. The adrenalin that had carried him through the fight was rapidly draining away to be replaced by the familiar post-fight enervation he knew from tournaments. All of a sudden he was aware of how much of him hurt. It wasn't just his ribs, which were punctuating every breath with sharp needles of pain, it was everything from the back of his head, where Eldritch had first slammed him into the wall, to his bruised throat and the clawed gouges on his hands, not to mention the long cut on his forearm. Belatedly he realised it was still bleeding and clamped his hand over the wound, holding his forearm up against his chest. It occurred to him then that it might be blood loss that was making him feel sick and dizzy and he decided he should probably sit down. *Purely as a precaution,* he told himself, so he was shocked when doing so turned into rather more of a collapse than he had intended. He felt his body slip down the wall almost as though he wasn't quite connected to it and wondered vaguely if he would manage to get to his feet again. Even if he did he wasn't sure what difference it would make. Eldritch had been the one with power. He had been the one who knew how to fight demons. Aidan had no idea how he was going to do this on his own.

For some time he sat there simply nursing his arm. He wasn't sure if it was shock or simply a reaction to what he had just done but, although he knew he had to work out what he was going to do next, he felt so tired he couldn't string a coherent chain of thoughts together. It was as if his brain had been disconnected. Part of him noted this with amazement. He had always considered "too tired to think" a fanciful description but now he felt as though his brain was empty. It was as though he was standing in an empty room with blank, white walls and no matter how hard he looked there was nothing there. His head tipped forward and the beam from his helmet lamp fell on the crumpled form of the man who had been his friend, spilled across the tunnel floor like a discarded suit of clothes. That, he remembered, was how Eldritch had described those possessed by a demon; the mind destroyed and the body nothing more than a garment for the demon to use. He closed his eyes, sickened by what he had done and then forced himself to open them and face the consequences of his handiwork. He had had no choice but knowing that made it no easier to accept. It hadn't been Eldritch who had attacked him, but it had been Eldritch who had paid the price.

'Christ, Eldritch! How did you let it get you? You were the one who kept warning me to keep my shields up.'

Aidan stared at his friend's still and bloodied face as another memory flickered, just under the surface of his mind. It was something Gwyn had once said, something about shields. He could almost hear her voice in his head but the detail of what she had spoken of eluded him and try though he might to pin it down nothing he could remember of her lessons on shielding seemed relevant now. Yet the feeling remained that he was missing something; that Gwyn had told him something important if only he could remember what it was. But his brain refused to cooperate and reluctantly his attention returned to the man on the floor. There, in the dark and with no one to see him, Aidan smiled sadly. It seemed he had spent a great deal of time like this, watching Eldritch either asleep or unconscious, waiting for those grey eyes to flicker open as wakefulness returned. And then it came to him. The conversation with

Gwyn hadn't been part of a lesson on shielding. It had taken place in the Red Kite hut after Eldritch had scried for the demon. As he and Gwyn had watched over the unconscious wizard she had spoken about there being a link between the demon and Eldritch.

'Oh dear God, she was right. She said it had a way through your shields. That's why she made you wear those bracelets.'

Guilt clenched like a fist around his heart and he dropped his head into his hands, for a moment unable even to look at Eldritch.

'But she never actually told you that, did she?' he groaned. Or perhaps Gwyn had done so and Eldritch had been too arrogant to believe her. Aidan raised his head and eyed the wizard.

'So you wore them to humour her and then, because you didn't know any better, you left one with her at the hospital.'

He shifted forward clumsily and checked Eldritch's wrists. 'And the other one...'

The memory came to him of Eldritch in the Land Rover, rubbing the marks the bracelet had left on his wrist when Aidan had grabbed his arm. Try though he might he couldn't recall seeing the amethyst bracelet on Eldritch's wrist after that. *Crap!* Aidan sat back, wiping a hand over aching eyes and shook his head, not wanting to believe.

'How did we screw up this badly?' he asked. Yet somewhere in the back of his mind an idea was building. Gwyn had said something else, about channelling and possession being different, at least initially. Aidan turned the thought over scarcely daring to acknowledge where it was taking him. If he was wrong... He licked his lips tentatively and pushed the thought away. *Don't go there. Not until you have to.* Even so, he would be stupid not to take precautions. Turning his head he swept the beam from his helmet lamp over the floor, looking for the gleam of metal in the arc of torchlight. It should be somewhere close. He had last heard it clattering against the tunnel wall as it spun from Eldritch's hand. Methodically he quartered the tunnel floor even as he steadfastly refused to think about why he was doing it. But the thought he had pushed away was simple; if he was wrong he was going to need Eldritch's knife.

CHAPTER 19

He came back to himself slowly, like a swimmer surfacing through layers of dark water. At first there was only a dim awareness, the merest spark of consciousness, of knowing that he *was*. For some time that was all but gradually other sensations began to creep in, impinging upon his consciousness, telling him more of the world waiting patiently for him to join it. One of the first things he became aware of was the cold. It lay over him like a shroud, its icy touch seeping through cloth and flesh to lodge in the marrow of his bones until his whole body ached with it as though from a beating. Instinctively he tried to curl in on himself, to huddle up and cling to what little warmth he had. That was when he discovered the second truth about his world; muscles cramping in the cold were not the only source of discomfort in his body. Eldritch cried out as the waveshock of pain all but swept him back over the brink of unconsciousness.

Grimly he hung on, clinging to the pain – awful companion though it was – instinct telling him that while he could feel it he was still himself. Somehow the thought seemed desperately important. He held it to him like a talisman as he lay there, animal-still, not daring to risk even the slightest movement, lest it rip him apart. But finally the crisis passed, the wave of agony receding to drop him drained and gasping on the far side of nightmare. For a while he lay waiting, panting softly, afraid to do anything more than breathe lest he trigger a second avalanche of pain, but as nothing happened he gradually relaxed, the strung tension draining from him leaving him enervated, his long body wrung like a cloth. Even thinking was hard. His mind felt woolly and disjointed as though his consciousness had withdrawn to some far corner of his brain from which it had yet to return fully. But while his body hurt, and his mouth tasted of blood and the sour bitterness of bile, slowly he came to understand that the worst of his torment centred in his right wrist. The rest of him ached solidly but the wrist was the core; a black, sickening mass of pain that throbbed in time with his heartbeat.

Eldritch groaned as he pieced together the scale of his predicament. From the unyielding angles jabbing into cheek, shoulder and hip he could tell that he was lying on rock and that, along with the cold and the dank, stale smell of the air, had to mean he was still in the mine. But what had happened? Something – and he couldn't quite fathom out what – was pinning his arms behind him and he knew with absolute certainty that any attempt to extricate them was going to be excruciating. If nothing else his earlier ill-judged movement had taught him that. Yet he had no memory of what had brought him to this state. He could feel no weight of stone pressing down on his body, nothing to indicate that the cave-in he had feared had happened, but somehow he had been hurt and something was restraining him and he felt utterly disinclined to try moving again until he had a better idea of what that might be. Cautiously he opened his eyes or at least he thought he did. Just to be certain he closed them, screwing them tight, but when he opened them again there was still nothing but Stygian darkness to greet him. The sinking of his heart told him that he had been holding on to the minute hope that, against all expectations, somehow he was no longer underground. Two further things occurred to him then. The first was that whatever had happened to him he had somehow lost his helmet and lamp. The second was that without them he had no means of finding his way through the mine. Not, he reflected grimly, that that meant anything if he couldn't move.

And what had happened to Aidan in all this? Tentatively Eldritch tried to call out but the only noise he managed was more like an animal mewling in pain than human words. His throat felt raw and swollen and his mouth very dry. What he wouldn't give for a drink. Recognising that the thought wasn't helping, he resolutely pushed the idea away, chewing at his tongue to bring a little saliva to his mouth. It wasn't much but it was all he could do. Carefully he swallowed and called again.

'Aidan?'

The rasp of his voice sounded weird in the darkness, the name echoing strangely back from the tunnel walls, desolate and lonely, like the cry of a gull far out to sea. As the echoes faded Eldritch strained his ears to catch the smallest whisper of sound, but there was no reply. He became aware of the silence of the mine around him; silence so absolute that it was almost palpable. He could feel it seeping back in the wake of his voice, flowing into the pockets and hollows of the shaft, lying heavy and still over the stone of the tunnel floor like water, dark and ancient as the source of an underground spring. Against it the soft sigh of his breath was like the ripple of a stone cast on its surface, insignificant and ephemeral. Like one of the great elementals the silence would swallow up the noise of his life and his passing as surely as it had taken the names and the banter of the men who had worked these ancient seams. He was alone.

With a sigh Eldritch subsided, letting his head settle back to rest against the tunnel floor as he tried once more to make sense of what had happened to him. He remembered wading – *well, alright then, splashing* – through water and flushed with embarrassment at the memory of how much it had unnerved him. He spared a second to wonder at that for he had never been claustrophobic before, but then dismissed it as irrelevant. At least claustrophobia was one thing he didn't have to face. Then, after the water had come the long climb down to the twenty-five fathom level where he had waited for Aidan.

'Dear God, no!'

He wasn't aware that he had spoken aloud but it was as though a sluice gate of images had suddenly been released in his mind; Aidan's face, hazel eyes shocked and startled under the yellow rim of his helmet as his hands closed around his throat; the young man doubled over, defenceless against the pain blasting through his body; and then finally him advancing on Aidan a bloody knife in his hand and an absolute, aching desire to kill ripping through his heart. For a moment Eldritch rode the tide of images and emotions, feeling again the pressing need, the hot, burning bloodlust that had filled him. *Sweet Lord...* What had he done to Aidan? Try though he might he could recall nothing beyond that image of the knife in his hand and the absolute certainty he was going to plunge it hilt deep in the younger man's heart.

'Aidan?' he cried out again fighting the certainty that no answer would be forthcoming. Even before the first echoes came back to him he was focussing his inner senses, struggling against the lingering heaviness that clung to his mind like cobwebs, to push his awareness out into the darkness desperately searching for some trace of the young man's presence. Eldritch's brain felt leaden, his arcane senses as crippled as his voice, but still he tried. And then it came to him that not only could he not sense Aidan's presence there was something else missing from his mental landscape. Eldritch's breath caught and this time it had nothing to do with his damaged throat. He realised he could no longer hear the demon in his head.

For a second he was motionless, checking in with all his arcane senses, but it was true. All sense of the demon had gone. A chill like ice water washed through him and had he been standing he would have fallen as every muscle went weak with shock. As it was he sagged against the rock floor, understanding running through his veins like poison. There was only one explanation for what he now felt – the demon had manifested. He had failed.

'No!'

His howl of denial blended with one of agony as he tried to wrench his arms free of whatever was trapping them. Pain drove through him like fire and he clamped his teeth together on a scream, muscles spasming along his jaw as he steeled himself to ignore it and try again. There was no option; he had to get free.

'I wouldn't do that if I was you.'

For a moment time seemed to stop. Eldritch froze, every muscle locked rigid. Even the scream died in his throat along with his breath as a feeling of ice knotted in his belly. A minute ago he would have given anything to hear that voice. Now he could only regret that he hadn't succeeded in killing his friend.

Aidan! Eldritch wanted to throw his head back and howl in grief, because of course it wasn't Aidan sitting in the dark beside him. Aidan was as dead as if his body lay on the tunnel floor with four inches of sharpened steel driven through his chest. The thing that crouched beside him now, shielded so tightly that even knowing it was there Eldritch could detect it only as a dead space in his senses, was the demon.

'Aidan?'

Even saying the name choked him. The demon wasn't stupid; it would have stripped the knowledge of him from Aidan's brain. It must know that he had guessed what it was so it could only be playing with him. But if that gave him more time he would let it. He had to believe he could still defeat it if he could only keep it from killing him for long enough.

'What's going on?'

His voice sounded hollow and he could almost see the cruel smile glittering in the demon's eyes at his attempt to play the confused innocent. A cold sweat crawled over his skin.

'My hands are—'

'Tied. Yes, I know they are. I was the one who tied them,' the demon cut across him and Eldritch flinched. Aidan would never have managed such cruel indifference.

'And I really wouldn't recommend struggling. Your wrist's broken. Things like that can be very painful – if they're not treated carefully.'

Eldritch tried not to react to the covert threat and to pretend instead that this really was Aidan he was talking to, but it was so very hard. What would be a normal reaction to a situation so obviously abnormal?

'So sort me out something that will do as a sling. This is

crazy. I can't go anywhere with my hands tied behind my back.'

The demon emitted a short, humourless snort of sound but when it spoke again its voice was frigid.

'Strangely enough that's the idea.'

'Aidan! For God's sake we don't have time for this. Let me go.'

The light in his eyes was sudden and blinding. Eldritch jerked his head back only just controlling the automatic reaction to fling up an arm to shield his eyes.

'And why exactly would I do that?' The demon's face was pushed into his own, close and intimidating. 'So you can stab me in the back?'

His eyes screwed up against the light, Eldritch tried not to flinch away.

'That wasn't me. That was the demon.'

'Oh, I know all about the demon.'

Yes, you would, Eldritch thought, but he didn't dare say it out loud.

'We've got to stop it before it manifests,' he insisted, his eyes watering. Unexpectedly the demon straightened. It sat back on its heels contemplating him, its head tilted to one side in a perfect counterfeit of Aidan's gesture. For his own part Eldritch allowed himself the barest morsel of relief, grateful simply that the helmet lamp was no longer burning in his eyes. At a range of inches the light wasn't just bright it was hot.

'Do you know what this is?'

The demon scarcely seemed to move but all of a sudden it held a knife in its hand, the blade throwing back lamplight like captive stars. Eldritch didn't have to see the handle to know it was his. He licked his lips, unsure whether or not to reply. The demon held the knife casually and then, with lightning speed, it lunged, driving the point against his throat, cold and deadly, where his pulse hammered so close under the skin. Eldritch had a millisecond to anticipate what it would be like to feel his throat parting under the blade and then the pressure was gone. Mischievously the demon traced the knife tip down his chest to his belly. All the time its eyes never left his face.

'I *could* leave you here, on your own. You're right; you're not going anywhere while your hands are tied.'

Again there was that little tilt of the head, that leftover piece of Aidan's body language, as if the demon were inviting comment, and Eldritch felt grief for the young man tighten around his heart. The demon observed him for a moment and then continued.

'But you're not as helpless as you look, are you? I'm sure you'd find a way to get free. Oh, it might take you a while but you'd manage it eventually; use a little of your magic perhaps? You could do that, couldn't you? But I wonder how well you'd manage to concentrate with a knife in your guts, eh?'

Eldritch stiffened, adrenalin widening his eyes. He knew the demon read the horror in his face and behind Aidan's innocent hazel eyes it was laughing at him.

'Aidan, please… I don't know why you're doing this.'

Still he managed the pretence; even here at the gates of death. 'What do you want me to do, beg?'

He would if he had to. *While you have breath you have possibilities*, that was what Helen used to say, but Eldritch knew his possibilities ended here. There was just one option left to him now; if he had the courage to take it. He turned his head away from the demon's unflinching gaze.

'Look at me.'

The sensible thing would have been to obey. Eldritch kept his gaze focussed on the rock of the tunnel floor.

'Why? So you can gloat over me? So you can tell me I'm beaten?'

Slowly and deliberately he closed his eyes, drawing his senses in, beginning to reach within him for his power. This was the one choice he had left. It was known as a final strike; the last option a wizard had, to take all the power in his body and release it in a single instant, letting it rip from him in an inferno that would destroy him and his enemy together. Eldritch swallowed. It was the one possibility that remained when all others had been stripped away, an action for when every single hope had been extinguished.

Perhaps he had known it would come to this in the end. When he had first heard of the final strike he had dismissed it as irrelevant; a young man with a young man's arrogant belief that he would never find himself in such straits. Since he had destroyed the demon in Helen there hadn't been a day when he hadn't thought of it, wondering why he hadn't taken that path then. Maybe he hadn't truly believed he had lost her until it was over, that only when he was left alone in the aftermath of their final confrontation, only then did he understand. Deep inside him he felt the last knot of resistance loosen as he made his decision. He would do it. In the still and silent darkness behind his closed eyes he wondered at his own sense of calm.

'I said look at me!'

A hand fisting in his hair pulled his head around and Eldritch tried not to scream as the movement ground his broken wrist into his back. Sweat slid along his skin and the edges of his vision blurred. His grip on the fire and diamond threads of his power slipped and it was all he could do to hang onto consciousness. As his vision cleared he saw the demon staring down at him.

'Tell me about her.'

For a moment Eldritch couldn't make sense of the request.

'Who?' he asked dully, stupid with pain and shock and stumbling to get even that single word past the agony lancing through his skull.

'Tell me about Helen,' the demon said, nastily. Its eyes narrowed, shining hard as amber in the torchlight. 'Tell me about how you killed your wife.'

For a moment anger wiped everything from Eldritch's mind, even the pain of his wrist. He trembled with it and the power that had run from his grasp like water rose up in him again. *Yes,* he told himself, feeling the force of it swell within him. *Use it.* Use the anger, use the pain. Use them both to breach the walls within him. He needed only a little more time. Light-headed and dizzy as he was he had to be certain he had opened even the deepest channels of his power. Inside his mind Eldritch smiled grimly to himself. He might have failed in all else he had done but in this one thing he would succeed. All he needed was to buy himself that time. It wasn't as if he would have to live with the shame for very long.

And so Eldritch did what the demon had asked. The words came reluctantly at first, his voice halting as he stumbled over what he would say, his mind divided between the telling and the raising of his power. Yet once he had started the story seemed to take on a life of its own, the words coming more easily, the details he thought long buried rising up in his mind and finding their way unbidden to his tongue. He described how he had set his trap with layer upon layer of spells, each wrought with infinite care, each meticulously built on the last so as to hold a demon that knew all his strengths and weaknesses. As he spoke he broke through the lingering muzziness in his brain, reaching past the cold and the bone-deep ache of his body, stretching out to every last fragment of his power that anger and desperation had laid bare and carefully garnering them to him. In a voice that shook he told how he had watched as the thing controlling his wife's body had writhed and screamed and fought him, one moment taunting him, one moment begging him in Helen's own voice, pleading with him to understand that she still existed, that she was still there, trapped like a fly in amber within her own mind but ready to be set free if he would but follow her instructions.

'And even as she begged and screamed I burned the demon out of her.'

He stopped suddenly, his chest heaving, the words congealing in his throat, thick and heavy with the horror of what he had done. Even now, knowing he was about to die, he could not bring himself to speak of what had come after.

'And then?'

'There is no *and then*, you bastard. What do you expect? You know there's no happy ever after, not after one of your kind had taken her!'

Eldritch was shouting now, his voice breaking with emotion, but he no longer cared. He stopped, panting for breath, oblivious to the hot tears falling on his cheeks. The power he needed was there, seething like magma just beneath his skin, aching to be released. With his hands tied he would be unable to direct it; he would just have to let it rip from him and trust that the demon would be consumed in the resulting conflagration. Bowing his head to his chest, Eldritch gathered himself for this final act. In his heart there was no fear only a curious, empty calmness and a hope that it would be over quickly. He felt a moment's grief; for Aidan and the friendship that might have been, and for Gwyn who would never know what had happened and he prayed silently that she would forgive him. Then he pushed all extraneous thoughts away – it was time. Raising his head he locked his eyes on the demon's face and took a last deep breath, reaching within to open himself to one final eruption of power... and something strange happened. The demon looked back at him, an expression of very human puzzlement on its face.

'One of *my* kind?'

Its brows kinked together and then unexpectedly it laughed.

'Oh, that's rich.'

The voice was incredulous but purely Aidan's as was the comment that followed which would have had even a farmer blushing. The lips twitched as if unable to decide what emotion they should convey. 'You think *I'm* the demon!'

Uncertainty hit Eldritch like a wave of ice water and he froze on the very brink of annihilation. The power raged and churned within him, ready to be set free with a single thought. He had only to slip its leash and it would rip from him, growing and expanding until he and the demon were at the heart of a maelstrom of magic. No flesh could stand against it; not his and not the demon's. They would be torn apart and the reign of the demon would end. Eldritch had made peace with what he was about to do and yet, on the strength of that laugh, he hesitated, drawing back from the brink, the fingers of his mind closing around the swirling mass of power and cleaving it to him. What if he was wrong? But even if he wasn't, with his power poised and ready, the demon couldn't kill him quickly enough to prevent him unleashing the final strike. Not, he reflected, that a quick death was likely. Not at the hands of a demon. It wasn't their way. Holding that thought to him like a talisman Eldritch nursed the power within him and dared to wait for what would come next.

'Well I guess we know one thing at least. You're not channelling the demon anymore.'

The knife was prominent in Aidan's hand and Eldritch watched it warily. He forced himself not to flinch as his companion leaned over him.

'Hold still. I'll try not to jar your wrist but this might hurt a bit.'

Both knife and hand disappeared from Eldritch's limited field of view and a second later he felt the binding round his wrists part. He gasped as his arms dropped.

'Sorry about that. Do you reckon you can sit up?'

Aidan's arm was already under his shoulders, easing him upright and Eldritch nodded, not quite trusting himself to speak. Cradling his bad arm against his chest, he shuffled backwards under Aidan's prompting until he could prop himself against the tunnel wall. Though the rock at his back was damp and dripping it felt better to be sat upright than lying bound and helpless on the floor. As Eldritch considered this a water bottle was thrust into his left hand.

'Rinse your mouth out first, then take a couple of sips. It'll make you feel better.'

Eldritch did as he was told, watching silently as Aidan carefully picked the remains of the rope from round his right wrist. In the glow of Aidan's helmet lamp it already looked black and puffy, the blue and red rope cutting into the swollen flesh. Eldritch swallowed hastily and the power within him surged, ready to break free. Grimly he reined it back.

'How can you be so sure?' he asked finally, putting down the bottle and offering his left wrist. 'How do you know I'm not demon-touched?'

Much though he wanted to believe that this was Aidan he was talking to bitter experience had taught him caution. Instinct warned him that this could yet be a part of the demon's Machiavellian game playing. Aidan sat back on his heels, absently twisting a piece of rope between his fingers. The knife had vanished but Eldritch had not forgotten the demon's earlier threat to use it.

'You said that demons were good actors,' Aidan said after a moment's silence. 'I figured it didn't matter how good a demon was, it wouldn't be able to counterfeit a physiological reaction to pain or fear.'

He nodded briefly towards Eldritch's wrist and when he raised his head his expression was rueful.

'Yanking you around like that; you went all white and sweaty. That was when I knew.'

Perhaps he guessed at Eldritch's confusion for he added, 'That's a classic reaction to pain. When you were channelling the demon you didn't feel a thing I did to you.' He gave a little shrug. 'Sorry I had to play rough, but it was the only way I could be sure.'

'It looks like you weren't the only one playing rough.'

Eldritch's eyes were drawn to the sleeve of Aidan's jacket. Slit from elbow to wrist the fabric gaped as Aidan moved revealing the white flash of a field dressing tied around his forearm, a pencil thin line of rust marking its surface. For the first time he noticed the dried blood crusting Aidan's hand from cuff to fingertips and Eldritch remembered his waking vision of advancing on Aidan with a knife. *Even if I just scored him that must hurt.* So must his ribs – not that you could tell by looking at him. Eldritch sagged a little against the tunnel wall and shook his head.

'You're a good actor yourself,' he said wearily. *Too good?* Aidan gave another careless shrug and Eldritch's heart twisted with despair. What Aidan had said was right; pain meant nothing to a demon. So was his companion's seeming lack of discomfort now just Spartan discipline or something altogether more ominous? Eldritch felt the power shift within him at the thought.

His head throbbed with the effort of holding it ready and he knew he would be unable to do so for much longer. Very soon he would have to make his decision and either use it or let it ebb away, back into his core. The way he felt now he wondered if he would be able to summon it again. With a start he realised his eyelids had been sliding shut and he forced himself to sit up straighter. Aidan was watching him closely but said nothing, which of itself seemed strange. Eldritch pushed his good hand through his hair, sweeping the damp tendrils of it back from his face. He so wanted to believe Aidan's story. His explanation made sense and yet there was still one very good reason for doubting him.

Eldritch felt a cold growing inside him that had nothing to do with the damp, nor the creeping chill of the mine. It clutched with icy fingers around his heart. The game was almost over. He had one more card to play and if what he said next forced the demon to reveal itself Eldritch knew his only option was the final strike. Feeling sick and shaky, but determined to finish what he had started, Eldritch tightened his grip on his power one last time. Steeling himself for this final confrontation he locked his gaze with Aidan's.

'Aidan, the demon has manifested. I know it has. I can't hear it any more.'

As he spoke he watched Aidan's face intently but his words brought almost no response; neither protestations of innocence nor the sudden lunging attack he had feared. Instead Aidan scowled briefly and then sighed.

'And you think it's gone into me,' he said levelly. It wasn't a question but Eldritch's lack of response gave all the answer that was needed. Still Aidan made no attempt to deny the accusation. Silence fell between them, pregnant with the possibility of sudden and devastating violence. It was Aidan who broke it.

'You know it's going to make stopping the demon a damn sight more difficult if neither of us is prepared to trust the other,' he observed wryly.

Eldritch said nothing. His control stretched almost to breaking point still he refused to release his hold on his power until he had a satisfactory explanation for what his senses were telling him. Yet he was very much afraid that Aidan could not give him one. Sweat stood out on his face, despite the cold, stinging his eyes and blurring them and still he held the power of destruction in his trembling hands.

'You can't hear the demon any more because of what's currently tied round your neck.'

Very slowly, as if he guessed a wrong move would bring a cataclysm down upon him, Aidan raised a hand to his own throat, tapping the hollow between his collarbones. After a moment Eldritch tentatively put his own hand up, mirroring the gesture. Under his fingers he felt the smoothness of crystal, surprisingly warm against the chill of his skin.

'This is Gwyn's,' he said, wonderingly, recognising the signature of her magic sealed within the stone. His hand closed around the small disk and for a moment it was as if some of its warmth found its way into his flesh, strengthening him. No demon could have touched this. He raised his eyes to Aidan's and the young man nodded as though he had seen that understanding reflected in their silver-grey depths.

'Now do you believe me?'

The words were half question, half statement of exasperation but as Aidan spoke the tension seemed to drain from him, his whole posture changing as he relaxed, and Eldritch realised that the young man had been as wary of an attack as he himself had been. No wonder he had refused to admit to any weakness from his injuries. And he had taken that caution as a sign of possession.

'Dear God, I could have killed both of us!'

The implications of what he had so nearly done washed over Eldritch, stealing his breath, and for a second the world swam, blackness sweeping in from the edges of his vision. He was distantly aware of hands on his shoulders and he forced himself to open his eyes, looking up into Aidan's concerned face hovering inches from his own. Carefully he shook his head and thankfully the world didn't shift with it.

'No, it's okay. I'm alright. Just give me a minute.'

The hands dropped from his shoulders and Aidan moved away, giving him space.

'Thanks.'

Closing his eyes Eldritch took a long, deep breath, centring himself. He could feel the warmth of Gwyn's seal hanging in the pit of his throat, could sense the power emanating from it, seeing it in his mind's eye like a rose and violet haze spreading out along his skin. Now he knew it was there he wondered how he could have failed to sense it before. He must have been more shaken up than he had realised. Yet without the proof of that tiny piece of crystal hanging round his throat he knew he would never have accepted Aidan's assurances that he wasn't possessed.

Looks like you've saved my neck again, woman. Mine and the Boy Wonder's.

Oh, but she was going to be insufferable when he told her. That thought stopped him in his tracks and Eldritch wondered at it as he realised this was the first time he had considered any future beyond the coming confrontation with the demon. It occurred to him then that since they had found the pit he had subconsciously accepted that he wouldn't be coming back. The understanding chilled him. Actually it had started before that, he realised, on that first night at Aidan's, when he had no longer been wearing Gwyn's bracelets. From the blood-soaked imagery of his dreams to this morning's morbid claustrophobia the demon had been there, shaping his thoughts. Only now, with that malign influence blocked, could he understand how much impact it had had on him.

Seems I owe you more than I thought.

Chastened, Eldritch reached within, opening his mind and letting the power he had raised ebb slowly back into the deep energy channels of his body. As it went the tension eased from him and a degree of self-belief returned. Instinctively he reached out and touched the power in Gwyn's crystal weaving its dancing light into his shields. Deep within him something lifted, lightening as he realised he no longer had to face this task alone. In truth he hadn't been alone since the afternoon he had gone to Gwyn's house to talk to her, to ask in fact, for her help. And despite everything he had done since she had given it unstintingly, her and Aidan both. The thought warmed him, even against the chill of rock and stone. It had happened without him realising and against all of his intentions but they had become a team; and as a team they would see this through together.

Opening his eyes once more he caught Aidan's expression. 'What's wrong?'

'You're smiling,' Aidan accused him.

'And I'm not allowed to?'

The echoes of an earlier conversation came back to Eldritch and he found they only made him want to smile more. Watching him Aidan smirked, the lopsided grin pulling at his mouth and casting his face in a mischievous expression that gave Eldritch a glimpse of the multitude of troubles he must have got into as a boy, no doubt many of them aided and abetted by Gwyn.

'It's the first time you've smiled since we came down here. Proper smiling I mean, not like you're contemplating how nice it's going to feel to rip someone's throat out.'

'Hmm.' Eldritch considered this. 'Perhaps I am – smiling that is,' he agreed, but didn't feel inclined to offer any explanation. Aidan could formulate his own and indeed he did.

'There you are, I told you caving's fun. Maybe I'll get you down the Dan yr Ogof squeeze after all.'

'Don't push your luck, kid,' Eldritch growled, a theatrical scowl wiping the smile from his face though it was still there in his voice. Then he added, 'Come on, we need to get going.'

But as Eldritch started to get to his feet Aidan put a hand out to stop him.

'Easy Tiger, before we go anywhere I need to take a look at that wrist.'

Eldritch paused.

'I'd really rather you didn't.'

There was no trace of a smile in his voice now.

'Yeah, that's what you said last time and look where that got us – you passed out on the floor.'

A passable version of Gwyn's "don't argue, I know best" look accompanied Aidan's pronouncement but Eldritch faced it down without flinching. He had forgotten the downside of teams was that the other members seemed to think they had a say in the decision making process. Sometimes they were mistaken about other things too.

'That was different and you know it,' he said coldly, but somehow Aidan failed to understand that that was the end of the debate.

'Right, and as soon as you start waving your hand around you're going to realise just how different it is. You've got a broken wrist. Why else are you holding it jammed against your chest other than you're afraid to move it?'

Aidan stopped as if finally sensing his argument was falling on deaf ears. He pursed his lips thoughtfully.

'Okay then, let's put it to the test. You use your hands to direct power, don't you?'

He took the narrowing of Eldritch's eyes as an affirmative. It was all the response he got.

'So go on,' he challenged. 'Pretend you're going to throw some power at me. You're so sure it's not a problem then do it now. Better that than finding out you're not up to it when we're hip-deep in manifesting demons.'

For a moment Eldritch did nothing. The very air seemed to congeal around him as he glared at Aidan. It didn't help that he knew Aidan was right; he didn't want to move his arm unless he had to, but even more he didn't want Aidan fooling around with it. Yet from the stubborn set of Aidan's shoulders he knew he was going to have to prove his point. He vented a tiny snort of breath like a bull that had had just about enough of the matador's cape-waving antics. Very well, if that was what it would take for Aidan to leave him alone. He summoned a little thread of power, just for authenticity – and the fact that it wouldn't hurt to test Aidan's shields – and flung it at Aidan.

Pain made the breath hiss between his teeth but with an effort of will Eldritch managed to stop himself flinching.

'There,' he said when he could speak without his voice catching. Sweat sheened his cheeks; a fine beading that stood out above the dark stubble, glittering slightly as the muscles along his jaw knotted in the yellow lamplight. 'Absolutely fine.'

His eyes dared Aidan to call him a liar. Aidan nodded carefully.

'Of course it is,' he agreed, his voice and expression

deadpan. 'But perhaps it would be best if I had a look at it, just in case?'

In the end Aidan proved to be a more than competent first aider, something Eldritch realised he should have remembered from the last time he had had need of his skills. He was also inventive, cobbling together a splint from two rungs taken from the bottom of the caving ladder padded with the hacked off sleeve of his own sweatshirt – *It doesn't matter; it's already ruined.* The whole lot was then fixed in place with a field dressing and a triangular bandage, the final remnants of Aidan's small first aid kit. As Aidan worked Eldritch's good hand strayed back to the small crystal disk hanging round his neck, rubbing its smooth surface between his fingers.

'So tell me why you happened to have this.'

Aidan looked up briefly from his bandaging.

'Gwyn gave it to me after John's death. She said it would stop the dreams I was having.' He smiled mirthlessly. 'I didn't know anything about the avatar then, but she did. When I made the connection between what had happened to you and the fact that you weren't wearing her bracelets anymore I figured it might help. It seemed worth a try anyway. If it hadn't worked I really would have had to leave you hog tied.'

'While you did what exactly?' the wizard asked curiously, dropping his good hand so he could hold the end of the bandage while Aidan knotted it tight.

'God knows,' Aidan muttered vehemently. 'I hadn't worked that part out. I'm just glad it did the trick.'

'You and me both,' agreed Eldritch. He leaned his head back against the rock wall, watching Aidan from underneath the dark fall of his hair.

'So really you'd brought it with you as additional protection against the demon? You should have it back,' he offered. Aidan's head jerked up and he looked at him, horrified.

'You've got to be joking. You're the one with the demon-sized hole in his shields, not me. You can give it back when this is over but for now the best protection it can give me is if it stops you channelling the demon. Don't even think of taking it off.'

In the white face and flaring nostrils Eldritch read Aidan's anger and understood too the other emotions that it covered. He was very aware of the mottled bruises already rising on the young man's throat and the clawed scratches that covered his hands. Nor had he missed the careful way Aidan was moving. He had fought for his life earlier. Neither of them was in any shape for a rematch. All that and more went through Eldritch's mind as he met Aidan's gaze yet one thing pricked at him more than his guilt.

'The thing is, if I can't feel the demon I can't tell if it's manifested.'

Regardless of how much he might need the additional protection afforded by the seal, no longer being able to sense the demon left him feeling vulnerable.

'It hasn't.'

'How do you know?'

'Because I can feel it,' Aidan glowered. He fiddled with the bandage, adjusting how it lay across Eldritch's palm. 'Or at least I can feel something,' he amended. As he spoke his shoulders hunched as though to ward off a blow. 'I don't know how to describe it; it's like the feeling you get when a fight's about to kick off or being in the mountains when bad weather's coming in.'

He looked up at Eldritch as though he expected scorn but Eldritch understood only too well.

'Like pressure?' he asked and a little frown creased the skin between Aidan's brows as he considered this.

'Like something's squeezing the back of my head, yes.'

He licked his lips and Eldritch caught a sense of his discomfort. Once more he thought he should give the seal back but before he could make the offer Aidan continued.

'It's been there in the back of my mind, pretty constant ever since I took the seal off but now I'm thinking about it it's changed. It feels as if...'

'As if what?' Eldritch prompted, the hackles rising on the back of his neck. Aidan glanced down the tunnel, not the way they had been going but back towards the shaft where the ladder hung, invisible in the darkness beyond the range of the torch beam. He bit his lip and turned back to Eldritch, his face unhappy.

'It feels as if something's coming.'

Eldritch raised an eyebrow. For a minute he had feared that Aidan was sensing the demon manifesting. If he had said this trouble was coming at them from deeper in the mine that might have been the case but the idea of something coming from outside was ridiculous. He relaxed a little, reminding himself that Aidan was untrained. Sensing the demon was a major achievement for him; he couldn't be expected to be able to pinpoint its location too.

'By the pricking of my thumbs something wicked this way comes?' Eldritch asked, not quite keeping the note of amused scepticism from his voice.

'Um, more by the tightening of my balls actually.'

Aidan looked faintly embarrassed by the admission, his companion's scepticism seemingly having bypassed him entirely. Eldritch laughed at Aidan's chosen imagery.

'Nice. Thanks for sharing.' He shook his head, dismissing Aidan's concerns. 'Are we set to go now?'

Aidan nodded and then paused. An odd note came into his voice. 'Can I ask you something?'

'Sure. What is it?'

Yet Aidan didn't answer.

'Aidan?' Eldritch prompted him and still the silence stretched between them. Then, just as Eldritch was certain that the younger man had thought better of whatever it was he had been about to ask, Aidan finally spoke.

'The feeling you got from the demon – not just now when it took you over but before that – Gwen said you could hear it almost as if it was talking to you. Is that true?'

The question took Eldritch by surprise and for a moment he bristled with indignation. As much ashamed by the fact that the demon had managed to control him as by the desires it had put in his head, his initial reaction was to refuse to answer. What right did anyone have to ask him such a thing? Then he remembered the bruises encircling Aidan's throat and knew that Aidan had earned that right. His anger subsiding, reluctantly he made himself find the words for something he would far rather forget.

'It was just a feeling at first, nothing more. Just a feeling that if I stopped and listened hard enough I'd be able to hear someone talking to me.'

He remembered doing just that, standing in Gwyn's garden and straining to catch the sound of voices on the wind.

'The first time I really got a sense of anything definite was with Griff in the car park. When he went for you I thought I could stop the fight by throwing pain. So I did, but once I'd done it I felt this…'

His words faltered as he tried to find a way of describing what he had felt.

'This blood lust, I suppose. I don't know what else to call it. I didn't just want to stop him I wanted to hurt him. Badly. I wanted to make him beg for his life and then kill him anyway.'

He gestured vaguely with his good hand, his face tight with disgust.

'The thing was I knew if I gave into it it wasn't going to stop there and part of me liked that idea very much.'

He looked down as though studying his jeans, filthy and splotched with damp and grime. After a moment he continued more quietly.

'Then when we saw Gwyn in hospital I wanted to hurt whoever did that to her.'

Finally he looked up and met Aidan's gaze. He held it, waiting for judgement.

'I think that one might have been a natural reaction,' Aidan said, his lips tightening in a grim smile. 'I felt pretty much the same.'

For a moment he too fell silent, seeming to withdraw slightly. His face hardened and Eldritch knew he was seeing the still form in the hospital bed. Then Aidan grimaced and visibly put the image aside. His focus returned to Eldritch.

'But was it always negative thoughts that the demon put in your head?'

'It was like having a little voice in the back of my mind that kept suggesting I use my power to do things no sane person would want to do,' Eldritch said softly. 'Well, perhaps you might want to do some of them,' he amended, dipping his head. 'But any sense of decency would stop you.'

He paused as he made himself remember, feeling the dark tide of disgust that welled up at those memories and scouring it, seeking out the smallest shard of anything that might have been delight or desire. Then he glanced sharply at Aidan as it struck him that this wasn't just an idle question. There had been hesitation in his voice, as though he wasn't certain he wanted to hear the answer.

'Why?' Eldritch asked, his own voice abrupt, and then, because he feared he already knew, 'What have you been hearing?'

'Not exactly hearing,' Aidan said slowly, and now it was his turn to drop his eyes, refusing to meet Eldritch's gaze. 'Or at least not like that, not in my head. It's just that, after I gave you Gwyn's seal I kept thinking…' he broke off, shaking his head. 'It's daft. It was probably nothing more than my imagination, being sat here in the dark waiting for you to wake up so I could find out whether or not the demon had taken you. I'd turned the lamps off to save the batteries and your mind plays tricks with you in the dark.'

'What could you hear?' Eldritch persisted.

'It was very faint but it was coming from down there.'

Aidan jerked his head towards the depths of the mine.

'Aidan!' Had he had two good hands Eldritch might have shaken the younger man. 'What did you hear?'

'Hammering. Digging,' Aidan's voice was deadpan. 'And voices.'

'Voices?'

Eldritch felt his power surge within him, rising to the scald of adrenalin that came in the wake of Aidan's words. Aidan nodded unhappily, the beam of light from his helmet lamp chasing over the rock wall with the movement.

'I think so. It was very faint though, as if I was listening to something a long way away.'

'But they were talking to you?'

The power was there at his fingertips, ready to use. *Dear God, don't let it come to this, not now.* Aidan bit his lip, the corners of his mouth turning down in a scowl of concentration as he considered this. He seemed unaware of Eldritch's scrutiny, his attention turned inwards.

'Well, no, not exactly. Except once, not today but last week, in the hut when the avatar attacked us, I heard a voice in my head telling me to put my shields up.'

There was a long silence as Eldritch digested this and then he sighed and let his power slide away.

'I think it's a safe bet that whatever else that might have been it wasn't the demon,' he said. Experimentally he reached for Aidan's mind but could find no way through the younger man's shields. Mostly reassured he shook his head.

'There's no reason to think that the demon can influence you if you keep your shields up,' he confirmed. 'As for what you were hearing I can think of two possibilities. The first is that you're right. You imagined the whole thing and the fact that it started after you gave me the seal is nothing more than a coincidence. If you listen can you hear anything now?'

He watched Aidan's face as he did as he was told and concentrated, his eyes closed, his head lifted. He didn't think the young man was lying when, after a minute, he opened his eyes and shook his head.

'Not at the moment.'

He seemed to relax a little.

'Well that doesn't prove that you didn't hear something, of course,' Eldritch threw in offhandedly. 'The other possibility is that you're picking up a resonance from the men who died down here; the ones who were caught in William's cave-in. That's what's happened to most people who think they've encountered a ghost. Does it bother you?'

'What, that I might be hearing dead people?' Aidan's voice scaled slightly and he stopped abruptly, taking a deep breath and forcing it back down. 'Of course not. So long as it's not the demon what's there to be bothered about? Hey, they're only dead.'

Eldritch smiled a little at this patently false bravado.

'It's only a psychic residue Aidan, nothing more than an echo. It's disconcerting but it can't hurt you.' Then, because he couldn't help himself, he added, 'Think of it as one of those enjoyable aspects of caving you were telling me about.'

Aidan jerked as though he had been slapped. He opened his mouth to retort and then stopped. The look he gave Eldritch suggested that the wizard might soon be nothing more than psychic residue himself if he kept that up.

'And you can't hear it?' he challenged.

'No. We all pick up different frequencies for these things and I'm not going to lower my shields just to see if I can catch a trace of it. If the thought of it happening again is worrying you, you can have the seal back.'

'Oh yes, and have you turn into Mr Hyde again behind my back? Thanks but no thanks.'

The latter was added a little more graciously, perhaps because Aidan recognised the offer as genuine.

'Are you sure?'

Except for a scowl Aidan didn't dignify that with an answer.

'In that case...' Eldritch said and Aidan sighed.

'I know. We should get going.'

CHAPTER 20

There was something following them in the darkness, Aidan was sure of it. Several times now he had swung round, certain he had heard something behind him or caught a glimpse of movement from the corner of his eye. Of course, when he turned there was nothing to be seen except once when, just for a second, he could have sworn there was a figure at the far edge of the lamplight, gone even as he registered its presence; a man in the dark trousers and dirt crusted shirt of a lead miner. Just one of those psychic echoes that Eldritch had spoken of so casually? Aidan shuddered. He didn't believe in ghosts, he told himself and an echo was just that, the repetition of something that had already happened – past tense, been and gone. It didn't have awareness or consciousness. It wasn't a trapped spirit roaming the earth seeking release or retribution. It was no more real than the image of a candle flame reflected endlessly in parallel mirrors. There was no reason to think that those sad and sombre eyes had been looking at him, no reason at all. But he did.

Aidan rubbed his arms as if doing so could get rid of the gooseflesh prickling them. It didn't help that this whole damn place felt wrong. The hairs on the back of his neck were stood on end as if the air were charged with electricity and crawling over his skin. If this was what Eldritch had meant when he said the presence of the Unseen Realm was very near it was no wonder it had made the wizard so edgy. Even as Aidan considered that he felt again the sensation of someone behind him. With an effort he ignored it and kept walking, but it was difficult. It left him feeling as though he had a target painted between his shoulder-blades and trying to tell himself that he and Eldritch were walking towards the demon, that there was nothing creeping up behind them, did little to help. Aidan balled his hands into fists.

Don't, he told himself, feeling his muscles twitch from the effort not to turn. *Eldritch already thinks you're nuts.*

He hadn't missed the wizard's superior smirk when he had told him what he was feeling even if Eldritch had tried not to sound too condescending as he dismissed those fears. Aidan scowled to himself at the memory. Eldritch knew what he was doing when it came to demons. He didn't. But knowing that did nothing to stop the sensation that something was coming closer. Almost against his will Aidan turned, unable to help himself, and again there was nothing there.

'You're going to get me scared if you keep doing that.'

Aidan started sheepishly at the sound of Eldritch's voice, understanding all too well the undercurrent of irritation that shaded the words. If he didn't feel so nervous he would be annoying himself.

'Are you okay?' The wizard slowed, waiting for Aidan to catch up with him. 'You're looking a bit pale.'

Aidan flushed.

'Yeah, I'm fine. It's just this place is starting to give me the creeps.'

He deliberately made no mention of what he thought he had seen. *Just plain old psychic residue, nothing to worry about.* He didn't need another lecture on how harmless these things were but instead Eldritch nodded sympathetically.

'The Unseen Realm,' he said as if that were all the explanation needed. 'We're very close.'

'Good,' Aidan muttered. Then his head came up and he asked urgently, 'You're not sensing the demon again, are you?'

'No. Gwyn's seal's still working. That's one thing you *don't* need to worry about.'

Eldritch flashed a grin that, for a second, wiped the lines of strain from his face.

'Ah, that's okay then.'

Aidan resisted asking whether *very* close was close enough, whether they would be in time for Eldritch to prevent the manifestation. He understood there was no way of knowing that until they reached the point where the boundary was thinning and Eldritch began to work his magic. Besides, what he really wanted to ask was whether the wizard would be able to complete whatever binding he needed to place on the demon. *He* might look pale, and though he wasn't about to mention it his arm was throbbing and his ribs twinged every time he put weight on his right foot, but Eldritch looked no better. Beneath his helmet the wizard's face was ashen, the shadows under his eyes lending him an almost skull-like appearance. The fresh bruise spreading over the side of his jaw didn't help matters, nor did the blood that had spilled from his split lip and clotted in the stubble on his chin. *He must have bruises on his bruises after the fight we had,* thought Aidan with a twinge of guilt. Surreptitiously he watched Eldritch walking, his right wrist tucked against his chest, his steps stiff for all that his long strides covered the ground. *Great demon hunters, the pair of us.* But they would cope. Eldritch had looked far worse last Saturday and he had still managed a veil on the hut that had defied the avatar. As for himself, well, so long as he wasn't called on to wrestle the demon physically to the floor, he'd be fine. And that was the idea, wasn't it? Stopping the demon before it manifested. He had to believe they still had time to do that. Reflexively he touched his mind to his shields. Like his nervous scanning of the darkness he was aware it was something he had been doing more and more frequently. Stood on the sidelines at a tournament he would be warming up, quietly readying himself for the moment when his name was called and he stepped forward to fight. But how did one go about preparing to fight a demon? Of course it wasn't going to come to that, but if it did the only contribution he could make would be to huddle tight behind his shields and stay out of Eldritch's way.

And you wondered why he didn't want you down here? The voice in his head muttered in disgust. He couldn't argue with it except he knew that Eldritch wouldn't have made it this far on his own.

The physical nature of the mine was changing. As the darkness parted before them like a curtain, opening with the light of their helmet lamps and closing up behind them as they passed, Aidan felt the air grow colder. Even the scent of it was different, he thought, as though the air here was somehow older. It smelled of something beyond decay, like a tomb wherein everything had long since passed from rot and putrefaction into dust. And overlaying that strange, almost sterile odour was something else. It came to him in snatches as though carried by a wind he could not feel against his skin, a hot metallic reek that was a taste as much as a smell.

'Eldritch—'

But even as Aidan spoke his name the wizard was already turning, one hand raised in warning.

'Stay here.' Eldritch's tone brooked no argument and Aidan froze against the tunnel wall, casting wary eyes at the darkness behind Eldritch's back. The shadows seemed to crowd closer and Aidan couldn't help wondering what the wizard had sensed waiting within them. Eldritch turned back and stood for a moment, his head tipped to one side as if weighing something up. Then he slowly advanced along the tunnel, his good hand raised in front of him, fingers spread as though feeling for something in the air.

'So,' he murmured as if to himself. He seemed to have forgotten Aidan's presence behind him but, just as Aidan was considering how long he was prepared to stand there if the wizard simply continued on down the tunnel, Eldritch stopped again.

'So.'

He was still for a moment and then he gestured for Aidan to join him.

'This is it.' The wizard sounded calm but Aidan didn't miss the fact that he neither turned nor took his eyes from the shadowy darkness ahead of him. And as he came to stand at Eldritch's side he understood why. Ahead of them the tunnel ended, but instead of petering out in a wall of fallen rock as Aidan had half expected, it opened abruptly into a huge gallery the sides of which were too distant to be picked out in the torch beam.

Aidan gazed about him in awe. They were called stopes, he remembered; the open spaces left where the miners had removed the ore bearing rock from the lode. He turned his head to sweep the beam of his helmet lamp across that space and his mind baulked at the sheer expanse of it. Surely it shouldn't be this big? Though ore seams could be dozens of feet wide the light from his helmet lantern was lost in the space, even when he reached up and briefly flipped it onto a tight beam. In fact it seemed as though part-way across that void the darkness thickened and swallowed the light leaving Aidan with the horrible sensation that there was literally nothing beyond it. He looked at Eldritch for confirmation of what he was seeing. The wizard's grey eyes met his and they held a strange, fey light.

'Welcome to the borderlands,' he said, the brief incline of his head acknowledging Aidan's unspoken questions. 'This is something that very few people ever get to experience. Thankfully. What you're seeing is a manifestation of the boundary between the Unseen Realm and the Mortal World. It shouldn't exist. In fact it doesn't exist, not in the sense that most people understand it. This is a merger of two worlds; ours as it is now and the demon's, recreated from before the time of the Covenant; a bubble of reality, a no man's land between the two dimensions. It exists here because of the demon.'

Aidan looked out into the darkness and the hairs on the nape of his neck bristled. His body knew this place was wrong, even without Eldritch's explanation. He felt his palms slick with sweat and fear tightened his belly, a deep, visceral fear. More than anything he did not want to step out into that space.

'I'd tell you to go back but it wouldn't be any safer,' Eldritch continued. 'Reality can shift around the borderlands. It's not ideal but it's better now if you stay with me.'

Better, Aidan noted, *not safer. I wouldn't have gone anyway,* he thought, but he said nothing, unsure if it was bravery or cowardice that would have him choose to stay with the wizard. Once more he felt for his shields and this time he could almost see the shape of them glowing in front of him, the gauzy light obscuring the sight of the unnerving blackness. He blinked and the image was gone but somehow its presence steadied him. He had his own protections and they were strong. As Eldritch stepped forward into that strange and altered reality Aidan took a deep breath and plunged after him.

There was a momentary disorientation, akin to hurrying down a staircase and missing a step. For a second Aidan thought he was falling and then his foot connected with the floor, jarring all the way through his ribs, and he caught himself, muffling a sharp gasp of pain behind clenched teeth.

'Okay?' Eldritch's voice was a faint whisper of sound beside him.

'Yeah.'

Aidan forced himself to breathe slowly as he turned to look around him. Oddly the pain helped, giving him another focus that took the edge off the strangeness of this place, like the way he could now make out the rock walls of the stope and was sure he could see further across the cavern before his lantern beam was lost in the darkness. He shifted uneasily, wondering what would happen if he chose to walk across that open expanse. Would the darkness continue to recede before him, pushed back by the light he carried, or was there a point at which this bubble of reality ended beyond which he could not pass? Worse still, might he be able to step inadvertently from this reality fully into the Unseen Realm? He licked his lips, his mouth going dry at the prospect. He had no desire to find out. Rather than think about it too closely he turned to look at the way they had come and was relieved to find he could still see the mouth of the tunnel leading off into the distance. Strangely it seemed further away than he would have thought for surely he had only walked a few steps out into the stope, but there were his and Eldritch's footprints stretching back towards the tunnel, a thin lifeline, fragile as a trail of breadcrumbs, leading back to the real world. But how could there be footprints? Bemused he looked down, only now realising that the surface under his feet was no longer rock, as it had been in the tunnels, but a thick accumulation of dust and grit. The oddest feeling came over him then that he had stood here once before, feeling the ancient void all around him and hearing that silken whisper of sand grains underfoot. Absently he scuffed one boot tip through the powdery residue, watching splinters of quartz glitter in the lamplight as they tumbled amongst the darker fragments of slate and shale. Briefly he closed his eyes. It had been dark then, he remembered. He hadn't been able to see the floor he stood on and he had thought it was sand because of the sound and the feel of it. *But it wasn't sand after all. It was the residue from the blasting.* The thought seemed so natural it took him a moment to place the memory it came with and then he froze, his heart hammering in his chest. This was the place he had come to when Gwyn had first taught him to shield.

No, that's impossible, he thought, and then, *why here?* But deep down he knew. This was where William had called down fire to bind the demon. A hundred years ago his great-grandfather had stood and died here in a welter of Levin fire and falling rock and this was the place he had unknowingly sought to find his shields. Unnerved he cast around him but nowhere was there any sign of rockfall. No debris marred the pale expanse of the cavern floor, nowhere was there anything to indicate that an explosion had taken place here, claiming the lives of innocent men. Impossibly this place seemed to be as it would have been before that fateful morning. It was a bubble of reality as Eldritch had explained, neither of his world nor the other, but an unholy merging of the two.

'It was here, wasn't it?'

Aidan hadn't realised he had spoken aloud until Eldritch said quietly, 'Yes, it was here.'

The wizard didn't ask what Aidan was referring to; there was no need.

'And this is where we'll bind it again.'

He glanced at Aidan and power seemed to radiate from him, darkening his eyes and swirling around him like a cloak. Standing in this strange, unworldly place he looked as though he himself were a part of the Unseen Realm. His pale, angular face was almost ghostly above his dark clothes and the ancient sapphire ring, dangling by its chain from the fingers of his bandaged hand, flashed fire like a captive star. Aidan felt a moment's awe as though he were seeing the wizard properly for the first time. Despite the bruises and the bandages Eldritch looked like a man capable of taking on and defeating a demon.

Aidan scanned the cavernous space around them.

'Do you know where it will come through?'

He was aware that while he had been lost in his own reverie Eldritch had been working, moving back and forth scrying the energies of this place. He could see the boot tracks in the pale dust where Eldritch had paced, the ring on its chain held out in front of him like a dowser's hazel rods. Eldritch nodded.

'I have a fair idea.'

Idly he toyed with the chain around his fingers then slipped it and the ring into the hip pocket of his jeans. He moved away a little and Aidan sensed the power in him shifting. He had the feeling of arcane senses being cast into the darkness, pushing at something, testing it.

'We don't have much time. It's close, very close.'

Eldritch's left hand rose, his fingers smoothing the air in front of him and for a second Aidan thought he saw the far wall blur as though the fabric of space had rippled beneath that touch. He stared but Eldritch carried on as if nothing unusual had happened.

'So much so that I'm not sure I can stop it.'

The wizard shook his head but it wasn't self-doubt that Aidan heard in his voice, just a matter-of-fact stating of the truth.

'The boundary is so thin now. I'm going to try to strengthen it but I can't say for sure that it will hold.'

'And if it doesn't?'

Eldritch turned back and his lips curled in a wolfish smile.

'Then I bind the demon as it comes through.'

The wizard's tone was light, almost mocking, very like his cocksure attitude of old, but Aidan knew this was no idle boast, not when he could sense the power gathering beneath the wizard's hands. He had had glimpses of it throughout the morning but had allowed himself to be distracted; by the wizard's weariness first thing, by his appearance of fear in the mine and his battered state after their fight. What he was sensing now was beyond the physical state. Whatever Eldritch had done last night to prepare for this encounter he believed he could master the demon and Aidan found himself believing it too.

'First things first though, I want you over there, out of the way.'

The wizard gestured to a spot a couple of yards to Aidan's left. Aidan could see little difference between where he was and where Eldritch wanted him to stand but he did as he was told and stepped back.

'Good. I don't want you to move from that spot. Regardless of what happens I want you to keep your shields up and stay out of it.'

The ghost of a smile crossed those saturnine lips as though Eldritch had noticed and correctly read the slight stiffening in Aidan's posture.

'I mean it Aidan. No matter what happens.'

His eyes bored into Aidan's and then he paused, something shifting in his expression.

'Unless it takes me down. If it does, if it gets through my shields and possesses me, then don't hesitate to use that knife on me if you have the chance.'

Horrified, Aidan opened his mouth to argue but Eldritch cut him off.

'I'd take it as a favour.'

Then his expression changed again and he grinned at Aidan, wild and fey once more as he raised a hand to Gwyn's seal, lifting it above the collar of his shirt.

'Not that that's going to happen.'

The wizard clasped the seal for a moment longer before tucking it back against his skin. He closed his eyes briefly as if centring himself and then raised his right hand and sketched a sigil at chest height in the air in front of him. Aidan watched him critically but if the movement hurt him Eldritch gave no sign of it, his face reflecting only concentration on the task in hand. The process seemed much the same as when Eldritch had drawn his protective glyphs on the walls of the Red Kite hut, his long fingers tracing the air, but Aidan felt a small thrill at the base of his spine for this time he clearly saw a trail of phosphorescence follow the wizard's fingers. He shivered, his eyes fixed on the pattern of lines and curves taking shape under the wizard's hand, and the hairs rose along his arms and on the nape of his neck. *Crazy,* he thought even as his pulse quickened at the sight. He should be used to the idea of magic by now, not gawping at it like a child confronted with a stage conjurer, but it was one thing to know in theory it was happening and a very different thing to see it outlined in star fire before his eyes.

The ghostly sigil hung in the air for a second and then faded away and Aidan watched as Eldritch sketched another four signs in quick succession, placing them in a circle around the first as though he were drawing a compass rose in the air. Each one flashed briefly in lines of icy, silver-blue fire and then faded away as the first had done. When the last one was complete Eldritch stood for a moment, holding his right arm briefly against his chest as once more his eyes closed and he took a deep breath. Aidan fancied he could sense the wizard drawing the power from deep within him and felt a strange yearning pull in his blood in response. He fought the urge to lift his own hand as Eldritch raised his, centring his spread fingers at the heart of the now invisible circle. Holding his breath Aidan waited, expecting to see something akin to the veil Eldritch had shaped at the hut, but though the air shimmered briefly where the signs had been no nimbus of light filled the circle. But perhaps it wasn't meant to. Aidan looked at

Eldritch, trying to judge whether things were going according to plan, but it was difficult to tell. The frown tightening his face could just as easily be concentration as frustration and, much though he would have liked to have asked, he knew better than to break the wizard's concentration with a question.

'Hmm.'

Eldritch lowered his hand and for a second stared balefully at the air where the circle had been. Then he moved deliberately to his left. Once more Aidan had the impression of him pushing his senses out into the cavern, probing, testing for something Aidan couldn't sense, then once again the wizard began shaping signs in the air, different sigils this time and more of them, starting low to the ground and set in an arc so the final one was at the level of his head. Each was drawn with swift, flowing strokes that hung like phosphor in the gloom and then bleached out of existence and with each one Aidan was aware of the power within the chamber growing. He could feel the prickly static of it brushing against his senses, the combination of the nearness of the Unseen Realm and the magic that Eldritch was threading through the dark and ancient air. Aidan shifted, feeling edgy and unsettled as a cat before a storm and tried not to think of the lightning that would follow if this particular storm broke. Instead he tried to concentrate on the sigils, trying to memorise their shapes before they sank into the darkness. These were remaining visible a little longer than the first set, or so he thought but Eldritch did not pause to watch them. Before the last had faded he was moving again, this time taking half a dozen long strides to his right before he stopped and drew a third set of symbols, creating another arc of fading star fire rising up from the floor towards the first. As the last symbol was completed Eldritch paused and then swept his hand out in a wide flamboyant gesture and the air sparkled as though he had thrown powdered gemstones across it. But after a moment the glow faded and in its wake the chamber seemed somehow darker and more foreboding.

In that bleak stillness Eldritch's voice was like the soughing of the wind as he turned his head to look at Aidan.

'Well, that was a waste of time.'

He pushed his helmet up and wiped the back of his good hand over his eyes and though he didn't swear Aidan heard it in his tone. Then the wizard's head jerked up and his whole demeanour changed, the momentary weariness dropping away, his body radiating alertness like a hound hearing the far off echo of a hunting horn.

'Keep your shields up,' he barked, swinging back to face into the cavern. 'It seems I'm going to be doing this the hard way.'

CHAPTER 21

It happened so fast that there was no time to be afraid. *The hard way? What the hell does that mean?* Aidan had barely framed the questions in his mind when the air in front of Eldritch began to change. All of a sudden the darkness seemed to press closer around them and Aidan realised he could no longer see anything beyond where Eldritch stood. His hackles rose even as his eyes were drawn to the sight in disbelief. It was as though reality had been sliced open with a knife and nothing existed beyond that point, nothing save a darkness so thick it seemed to absorb the lamplight. He stared at it, his horror tinged with awe. This was a darkness that had existed before mankind had called the gods into being, a dark that existed now between worlds and between lives. And in it something was taking shape. The glossy, obsidian surface seethed and bulged as something within struggled to break free.

He smelled it then; an acrid reek of blood and entrails mingled with the scorched burn of metal. The stench of it made the bile rise in his throat and he clamped his hand across his nose and mouth, fighting not to empty his stomach onto the floor. Breathing through his mouth he watched the writhing mass. Limbs seemed to press against the surface, too many and too weirdly jointed to be anything remotely human. Limbs and a torso and shifting, amorphous shapes, too strange to identify, that bulged and twisted and then vanished. And in front of it all

Eldritch stood unmoving, almost oblivious. The wizard held his grandmother's ring fisted in his left hand and pale blue light leaked from between his fingers. Though the torchlight seemed to be absorbed and smothered by the dark the witchlight gleamed on the shifting, roiling surface of the air, glistening back from it in petrol colours. The dancing patterns of light mottled the angular planes of Eldritch's face, limning them in an otherworldly glow. Here was Lucifer indeed; the Bringer of Light, standing as guardian between the Mortal World and an evil that had existed long before The Fall. As Aidan watched, Eldritch fell back slightly before the coagulating darkness. The air shivered and split and something from the world of nightmare coalesced out of the Stygian gloom.

Aidan stared in horrified fascination at the thing taking shape before him. It came to him then that, although he had known they faced a demon, until now he had had no concept of what that really meant. Why, he wondered, as a cold sweat washed over his body and his breath caught in his throat, had he never thought to ask what it would look like? His heart thundered in his chest and fear threatened to turn his muscles to water as the half perceived form shifted from amorphous shadow into terrifying reality. *How in God's name is Eldritch going to fight that?*

The demon was monstrously tall, towering over Eldritch and with a bulk that dwarfed the wizard's lanky frame. Forcing himself to look at it Aidan felt sure it could literally rip Eldritch apart. But it wasn't just the size and the power of the thing that threatened to overwhelm his senses. Everything about it screamed its utter wrongness. Even the most hardened special effects team would have baulked at creating such a creature. The head was narrow and tapered, somewhere between dog and snake, and with a muzzle that split to reveal long, curved teeth – far too many of them – yellow and bristling and strung with saliva that Aidan suspected would fizz and burn anything it touched. Small in comparison with the size of the body, the head seemed to join directly onto the shoulders with no indication of a neck, for the demon turned its whole torso rather than its head. *That,* thought Aidan, desperately seizing any positive he could find, *could be a weakness in a fight.* If it couldn't turn fast enough its field of vision would be compromised. But something told him that the demon would be able to turn very fast indeed. His hands clenched at his sides as he fought to stop the panic rising to swamp him. Not even in his nightmares had he imagined the details of what he saw before him now.

The demon's arms were huge and grotesquely long. Jointed in too many places they hung almost to the floor and ended in broad, powerful hands – or were they paws? Whatever one called them they were covered in a pallid skin which ended at the wrist making it look as if the demon was wearing a magician's white gloves. Or at least the comparison held until one realised the magician in question would have to have had seven digits on each hand, each one ending in a viciously hooked claw easily as long as one of Aidan's own fingers. Above the wrists the arms, and indeed the rest of the body, were raw flesh. The demon's flayed skin hung from its shoulders like a cape, its underside gleaming like wet leather. The sight of it reminded Aidan uncomfortably of a dissected rat in a long ago anatomy class, with its skin peeled away and all the muscles of its body laid bare. He cringed at the thought, even as his mind noted the similarities, but the rat hadn't moved, its naked muscles bulging and contracting and glistening wetly as they slid over one another. At once both repulsed and fascinated Aidan watched the torso snaking from side to side, sinuous and graceful for all its size. It was awful yet there was something obscenely beautiful in the hypnotic, ophidian movement that drew and held the eye.

What arrogance had led them to believe they could best this monstrosity? But, even as he struggled with his own fear, it occurred to Aidan that, however overwhelming he found the demon, Eldritch seemed curiously unbothered. The pale blue witchfire burned steadily in his hand, its glow lighting a face that, while pale, was almost preternaturally calm. Aidan's gaze flicked from Eldritch's motionless form to the writhing shape of the demon and back. Shabby and battered, his right arm encased in a mess of grubby bandages and splints Eldritch looked an unlikely hero and yet... *He knows what he's doing... He knows what he's doing...* Half reassurance, half prayer Aidan breathed it to himself like a mantra as he fought the instinct that told him to turn and run. *Dear God, let it be true...* because the alternative was too awful to contemplate.

Eldritch also watched the progress of the manifestation, though with a good deal more detachment than Aidan. It helped a little that he had dealt with demons before though this was the first time he had seen one as it crossed between the two realities. It was, he decided, something he would be happy never to experience again. Yet fearsome though the demon's appearance was he knew he was safe for the moment. It couldn't touch him until the manifestation was complete, just as his own magic couldn't reach it while it was in this halfway state. Besides, it wasn't as if the body he was seeing had any real substance to it though he guessed from the choked sound of Aidan's breathing behind him that his companion hadn't realised that. Eldritch smiled, feral and wolf-like. However solid it might appear a demon remained ethereal until it took a host. Or at least that was the theory. As he eyed the wet, shining muscles and the greasy drape of flayed skin hanging from the powerful shoulders he had to admit that it all looked very real. It smelled real too; the hot metallic stench of demon overlain by the copper of blood and raw flesh filled his nose every time he inhaled. Even the sound of it when it moved, the sibilant hiss of powdered rock and the leathery flap of its skin against those naked muscles were details he wouldn't have thought to conjure. All in all it was one hell of an illusion. He was going to feel more than a little stupid if the first thing it did was slice him open with one swipe of those hook-clawed hands while he stood there expecting them to pass straight through him.

At which point it will be over to Aidan and his Bruce Lee act, Eldritch thought. *Best hope it doesn't come to that.*

Poor Aidan. For all that he and Gwyn had tried to prepare him for this, the young man hadn't really understood what they were facing. Very few people would. Yet he hadn't broken down or run. He had spirit. Eldritch continued to watch the demon with hooded, almost lazy eyes. Perhaps the boy genuinely was the last Child of the Covenant as Gwyn thought. He let out a little snort of breath partly amused, partly condescending. Well, there wouldn't be a need for a Covenant when he had finished. He was going to destroy this demon once and for all. He tensed slightly as the demon twisted, its body shuddering like a snake shedding its skin, and a little more of it slid free of the dark.

Behind him he heard Aidan smother an exclamation and he almost laughed. It would be soon now, very soon. The instant the last of that glittering darkness sloughed away the demon would be free to strike and its attack would be viper-fast. Eldritch's lips curled, his expression reckless and cruel. All he had to do was ensure he moved faster.

Yet there was no time for introspection. It was so close. The last threads of darkness were falling from the demon's sides; in a second it would be free. And then it was. The demon lunged for Eldritch. He heard Aidan's frantic warning but made no attempt to avoid the reaping hook sweep of its arms. As though overcome by terror he stood there, rooted to the spot, and the sickle-shaped claws sliced into his body… and passed harmlessly out the other side. Pure illusion they left no mark on him. All he felt was a fizzing static as the demon's energy passed across his shields; unpleasant, but infinitely better than having to explain to Aidan why he'd stood there and let himself be disembowelled. From what he could hear behind him he was in for some explaining anyway. Aidan had an interesting turn of phrase when he was frightened; quite educational and sufficient to have had Gwyn reaching for the soap and water had she been there to hear it. Eldritch laughed then, feeling the mix of power and adrenalin surging in his blood. Tiredness dropped away from him and he forgot the pain of bruised muscles and even the throb and stab of his broken wrist, spinning as the demon blurred to rematerialise on his right side, looming over him with its multi-jointed arms spread wide and yellowed teeth snapping as it lunged for his face. The stench of its breath rolled over him and this time he felt the spatter of its saliva burning his skin but he stood firm knowing that neither sensation was real. *You're going to have to do better than that. You can't terrify me into dropping my shields.* Even so he shut his eyes as the jaws closed around his head. Illusion or not, there were some things it was better not to see. Far more tangible was the wave of arcane power that accompanied the illusory bite. Fully shielded though Eldritch was the force of it drove him backwards, knocking the breath from his lungs like a sucker punch under the ribs. Instinctively he called the cold phosphor of Levin fire to his hand and flung a handful into the demon's face. The creature reared back, its head sinking into its shoulders and its muzzle splitting open in an enraged hiss.

Didn't like that, did you?

As if in answer a hammer blow of inhuman rage smashed across Eldritch's shoulders. Though the demon didn't seem to move the weight of it fell on him like an avalanche, the force of it driving him towards the floor. His knees buckled and it seemed his brain would burst under the pressure as his eyes bulged and a swirl of red swept across his vision. He felt something give within his head and cried out even as he drove his arm up in a warding gesture. Fire burst from his spread fingers searing into the demon's body and for a heartbeat a darker shadow seemed to writhe and twist in the burning light. Then, as rapidly as it had hit him, the pressure vanished. For a second just keeping his feet underneath him seemed a major victory but Eldritch gritted his teeth and forced himself upright. Panting softly he eyed the demon. It had backed off a little and, rather than attacking again, it was watching him, its sulphur coloured eyes small and vicious above the fanged nightmare of its muzzle. Eldritch sniffed, dabbing absently at the blood trickling from his nose with the back of his hand. *Not quite so easy as you thought, is it pal?* The hammer of his heart against his ribs steadied as his breathing eased and returned to normal. Still the demon made no move against him. He could feel its confusion and the burn of its anger that he had withstood its initial attacks. *Fair enough*, he thought, he was getting angry too. He squared his shoulders, taking a step forward and the demon snarled at him. Eldritch snarled back and kept moving. Now it was his turn.

Power surged within him; the hot magma of his own magic called up from the marrow of his bones and the cold sapphire energy stored in the matrix of his grandmother's ring, brittle and sharp as ice crystals carved from the heart of a glacier. Together they merged in his blood, boiling and seething as he opened himself to them and his body sang with the fierce, wild energies. In front of him the demon hissed defiantly, coiling back on its haunches like a snake ready to strike, but it gave ground as he stepped toward it and he thought he saw a new wariness in its eyes as it watched him. Eldritch smiled nastily. The demon was powerful but so was a wizard at full strength and one with access to an external power source was doubly so. *And this time you don't have that, do you?* Eldritch's smile broadened. There would be no one raising power for the demon now, not now that it had manifested. Now it was reliant on the negative energies it could create itself; all the fear and hatred and pain that were in its nature to generate. Eldritch took another long stride, moving closer. Whoever the demon had been able to influence previously, whoever had butchered Tom Owen's sheep or attacked Gwyn or run him and Aidan off the road, they no longer mattered. This was one confrontation they wouldn't be able to change the outcome of. This time it really was just him and the demon and Eldritch knew who was going to win.

He laughed as he flung a casual handful of Levin fire at the demon, laughed again as it twisted away and the lance of power that streamed from his left hand seared along its other side. He was playing with the demon, taunting it, goading it, and part of him was enjoying it immensely. Of course in a very real sense the demon was also playing with him. For all his senses screamed at him that it was real, he hadn't forgotten that the heavily muscled body rearing above him, with its cape of flayed skin swinging from its shoulders like the broken wings of some monstrous bat and the grave-reek scent of it fouling the air, was a pretence. He could throw every ounce of power he possessed at it – indeed that was what the demon wanted him to do – and it would achieve little, while the demon was still in its ethereal form. And yet it *was* there, somewhere, cloaked within that illusion, elusive and ephemeral as a trace of smoke hidden within the shells of a Russian doll. It had been pure luck that he had caught it squarely with that earlier bolt – a fact that might just have saved his life – but Eldritch believed you made your own luck. So he laughed and flung fire but camouflaged behind those carefully judged, oh-so-casual-seeming attacks his arcane senses were extending, seeking that which was his real target.

And there it was, as he had known it had to be; a dark energy pulsing and flowing at the base of that hideous body. His laughter died as his senses brushed against it; even that briefest of contacts leaving him feeling tainted and unclean as though he had shoved his hand into a midden. And the demon felt him too. Anger and hatred and a fierce and terrible yearning for destruction welled up and reached towards him like the fingers of something long dead rising cold and pallid from the bottom of a deep and fathomless sea. Faster than he had imagined possible the sensations surrounded him, groping and clawing, somehow reaching him even through his shields so he felt those emotions coursing through his body as though they were his own. This, his mind screamed, was what awaited him. If his shields failed and the demon took him these dark emotions would be the last thing he ever knew. Pulse racing and sweat gluing his shirt to his back Eldritch pulled back and the demon's energies surged after him, hungry to devour and destroy. He had an instant to wonder if he should have done things differently, a moment when he knew he had misjudged its strength and he was about to pay with his life, then the wave of corruption broke over him, slamming against his shields and burning like vitriol against the edges of his senses. In that instant he might have prayed but even prayer was beyond him as the darkness poured over his mind... and then Levin fire erupted through the darkness like a white phosphor beacon.

Got you!

The demon screamed as the wizard's magic engulfed it and tried to jerk away but it was too late; it was caught. It had taken every atom of self-discipline Eldritch possessed to let it come for him, to wait and to hold and do nothing until it was on top of him, until he knew he could reach it. He straightened, pouring power through the illusion of the beast and straight into the demon's essence. In a strange double vision he saw the starburst of fire blossoming like a flower against the blood-raw flesh of the demon's side and wrapping it in a net of luminous threads that clung to the gory surface, while at the same time

317

his inner eye showed him a cage of living silver forming around a writhing mass of black smoke. The beast bucked and twisted, clawing at its own flesh as though it might rip itself free from the clinging threads, and the smear and spatter of its blood turned the long fingered hands crimson. All this Eldritch saw and disregarded, concentrating his senses on the dark essence that coiled and swirled at the heart of that twisting shape. The filigree cage was holding but in places the dark smoke-like form massed against those gossamer fine bars and when it drew back the silver was blackened and crumbling. An integral part of the power net he had created Eldritch felt the echo of that corruption in his own flesh, the sensation like tiny mouths biting and tearing at his arms, his chest, his sides. He knew then that it wasn't going to be enough. Unless he strengthened the binding the demon would break free before he could destroy it. Reaching within he pulled more power to him, dragging it up from the marrow of his bones and cast a swift second handful of shimmering threads at the demon. But he had lost the advantage of surprise. As the power streamed from him the demon countered, blocking it with a power burst of its own.

The two magics met, splintering against each other in a nebula of blinding white light and this time it was Eldritch who reeled back from the impact, hands raised to shield his eyes as for an instant the darkness of the mine burned as bright as magnesium. The beast reared up, its muzzle splitting wide and saliva spattering from its many fanged jaws as it roared triumphantly. Then it curled inwards, its long arms knotting around the burning threads linking it to the wizard. The black smoke seethed along them, and the lines of silver fire flashed the cherry red of heated steel. Eldritch cried out as a battery of sensations poured through the link, slicing into him like hot wires driven into his brain. He stumbled, clutching at his right shoulder as it erupted in a screaming mass of pain and suddenly he was back in the forest with the avatar's jaws clamping down upon him. In that instant he felt the heat of blood running down his arm, could see the tall, dark shapes of pine trees spinning away from him, their sharp, resinous scent filling his nostrils as he fell backwards, the weight of the avatar crushing against him. When the avatar ripped its head back he felt his flesh tear and his vision tunnelled, the sick weakness of shock overtaking him. Instinct screamed at him to fight, to call power, to raise his arm and defend himself, but instinct was not enough. *What does it matter, anyway?* A seductive voice murmured in his head. It would be easier if he just let it happen. In a moment it would all be over. The avatar's fangs would sink into his throat and everything would end in a welter of blood and a last desperate attempt to draw breath as his life bubbled out of him. The voice crooned, soothing and reassuring. It was better to give in, to stop fighting and let it happen. In front of him he saw the jaws opening, the once black muzzle now red and dripping. His muscles locked, paralysed, and in that final instant all he could do was wait for his death to descend.

Heat seared in the pit of his throat. This wasn't right! *It wasn't like this. This didn't happen!*

'No!' Eldritch hurled the word out like a battle cry. His chest heaved as he sucked in the breath that had so nearly been his last and his eyes snapped open. The demon was rearing over him, the smoky black essence fully visible now as it poured out of the phantom shape, the oily, dark tendrils reaching hungrily to engulf him. A curse broke from him but his body was reacting while his mind was still catching up on the details. Arms that had fallen limply to his sides came up and in his left palm the sapphire ring blazed. All around the wizard the air shimmered with an unearthly luminescence as though the power that crackled from him had set its very molecules dancing. Eldritch straightened and all of a sudden it seemed it was he who towered over the demon. He stepped forward and the darkness fell back before him.

CHAPTER 22

Looking back Aidan could never say for certain what it was that warned him. Perhaps it was an unexpected movement in the air or a sound where there should have been nothing but silence. Mostly he reasoned that it was nothing more than the instincts Sensei had spent years honing in him that had unconsciously registered the danger, but sometimes, when he lay awake at night, playing the images back to himself in the darkness, he thought he had heard a voice crying out his name. It was a detail he shared with no one but that was why, at the very moment Eldritch was stepping forward to confront the demon, instead of watching the wizard Aidan was turning to look behind him. It was a simple enough thing but it probably saved his life. Given the force it had behind it, had it hit him square on the pit spike would have gone through his helmet and skull alike, splitting them open like a machete through a watermelon. As it was, the blow that glanced off the side of his helmet knocked him stunned and disorientated to his knees and when a heavy form barrelled into him he went sprawling gracelessly across the floor.

He hit the ground heavily with no attempt to break his fall, the knife-blade stab of pain from his ribs driving the breath from his lungs. Teetering on the edge of unconsciousness he felt as much as saw the steel-capped boots thud down scant inches from his head and had just enough wit left to curl in on himself, arms wrapping round his head and his knees drawn up to protect his belly and ribs. Dazed he might be but it had been drummed into him what happened to a man who was floored in a fight and though his aching body protested the movement instinctively he curled himself tighter. But to his intense surprise the boots he had expected to pulp his flesh into a bloody mess against his bones sailed past him, not even pausing in their stride, and disappeared.

For a moment Aidan held his breath and waited, not sure he dared believe he was safe but when nothing further happened he shifted, uncurling painfully and tentatively raised his head. What he saw turned his embryonic relief into cold fear. Adrenalin gave him the strength to push himself up onto his knees but all he could do was scream a warning as the dark shape reached Eldritch and fell upon him like a whirlwind.

'Griff! No!'

It made no difference. Wrapped in the deepest layers of his spell casting Eldritch was beyond hearing and words alone were never going to stop Griff. The heavy pit spike swung wildly and Eldritch spilled forward like a broken stringed marionette, long limbs folding beneath him, the light from his helmet lamp tracing a choppy arc through the darkness as he fell. Still on his knees Aidan watched as Griff straddled the wizard's body and horror flooded through him at what he knew would happen next. Worse was the understanding that there was nothing he could do to prevent it and the knowledge rooted him to the spot though his mind screamed obscenities at him for not being able to drive his battered body to his feet. But even if he could stand he would never get across the stope in time. The realisation tore at him as the farmer's arm lifted, the movement as effortless as if the spike weighed nothing in his hand, and Aidan waited for the blow that would crush Eldritch's skull. Bile rose in his throat, choking him. His friend was going to die, his brains spattered across the pale dust, and he would watch it happen, just as he had watched John's death in his dreams, helpless and unable to prevent it. Blackness danced on the edges of his vision and he swayed, fighting the oblivion that reached to claim him, bitterly conscious that the last thing he could do for Eldritch was to bear witness to the manner of his death.

The spike began to swing. Aidan stiffened, unable and unwilling to tear his eyes from the tableau in front of him. The breath locked in his throat, his view of the world contracting to the murderous arc the spike would travel and he felt the last seconds of Eldritch's life trickle through his fingers. Over the ringing in his ears he heard Griff's laughter, vicious and hateful, filling the chamber. When the sound of it abruptly stopped Aidan thought his mind had snapped. Then something moved in the shadows beyond Eldritch's body and with the swift, surging hammer of his heart came the recollection that a sudden and violent death was not the worst thing to be feared in this place.

Dwarfing both the wizard's crumpled form and the man who stood over him the demon rose up from the darkness. Huge to begin with it seemed to grow, its arms spreading wide from the broad barrel of its chest, its flayed skin splaying out behind it, the slippery folds billowing and flapping as if lifted on some unfelt wind. Aidan saw Griff's head tip up to stare at the nightmare creature as it moved closer. The pallid, clawed hands flexed and grasped sending the naked muscles of the arms bulging and sliding over each other, wet and glistening and filling the air with their raw blood stink underlain with the must of the tomb. The iron pit spike fell unnoticed from Griff's suddenly slack fist, thudding softly into the powdery dust at his feet and a thin, keening wail sounded from his throat. Perhaps, now that it was too late, the farmer understood that Aidan's warning had been meant as much for him as for Eldritch.

For his own part Aidan scarcely dared breathe as he watched Griff watching the demon. It was bigger now, surely, than when Eldritch had faced it, or was it just it seemed that way without the presence of the wizard to stand against it? Aidan's gaze dropped to the crumpled shape, lying like little more than a spill of dark clothing in the pale dust, and a cold weight settled over him. Eldritch was beyond helping anybody. Movement caught his eye and he looked up once more as the demon swayed, a lazy, sinuous sliding of flesh over flesh. In the darkness it seemed to Aidan that a strange, greasy smoke was oozing from its body, the tendrils of it coiling around its flesh and partly obscuring it until it seemed as though the demon moved within a forest of midnight-shaded wraiths.

Whether Griff noticed such details Aidan could not say. The farmer made no attempt to flee as the demon came nearer but rather stood, staring up at the grotesque form as though mesmerized. He made no sound now but his body shifted; small, helpless movements that mimicked the demon's own. A thousand images went through Aidan's mind as he watched that stocky shape in its familiar green overalls, the memory of all the torment Griff had inflicted on him over the years, the petty hurts and casual violence he had suffered at the hands of this man and his friends. Griff had come close to crippling him once and only minutes ago would certainly have killed him, but for a caving helmet and a split second of luck, yet despite all this Aidan found his mind wheeling frantically, trying to think of something he could do to prevent what was about to happen. But there was nothing. Even as his brain raced through and discarded a dozen suicidal options the demon's body arched still further upwards, spreading like a cobra hood in its clouds of black, writhing smoke. It rose above Griff and Eldritch, inexorable as an ocean wave, and then it fell on them.

All thoughts went out of Aidan's mind as he watched it happen, too stunned to do anything else. The demon dropped over Griff like a cloak, its body wrapping around him, the oily black smoke engulfing their two forms. Half-hidden within it the farmer screamed, a hideous but strangely muffled sound, his hands going first to his head and then to his body, flailing and clawing as though he could swat away what clung there. Staggering sideways he tripped, his heel catching on Eldritch's prone body, and came down on his knees almost on top of the wizard but he pushed up again almost immediately, lurching away as though a hideous drunkenness had descended upon him. Aidan watched in horrified fascination as the merged shape of farmer and demon went staggering across the floor. The black haze hanging around Griff's head and torso obscured the details but through it he caught glimpses of Griff's arms still flailing wildly as he lurched across the stope. And through it all his screaming never stopped. Aidan did not dare close his eyes but he clamped his hands over his ears, and still the noise cut through him. Never in his life had he heard anything like it and he prayed he never would again. He hadn't known a man could scream for so long.

Then suddenly both screaming and movement stopped. The

silence that filled the stope was somehow worse; pregnant and waiting. Griff was still standing, his knees sagging, his body hunched over and his arms curled about him. Still on his knees Aidan eyed the farmer warily. Of the demon there was no sign but he didn't dare hope that that was a good thing. Carefully he pushed himself upright, his eyes never leaving the hunched form. While he was unsure what to make of this turn of events there was one thing he was certain of; whatever would happen next he wanted to face it on his feet. Yet still there was no movement from Griff. Aidan was aware of the throb of his heartbeat pounding like distant surf in his ears. He wasn't afraid he told himself, as he rubbed sweating palms on his thighs and licked his lips tentatively. No, he was just being cautious. Fifteen feet separated him from the farmer. He had no intention of getting any closer.

'Griff?'

His voice sounded out of place and very loud in the silence but it drew no response from the farmer; no movement, no sound, nothing. Aidan waited but as the last echoes of Griff's name faded into nothingness against the cavern walls he swallowed dryly and tried again.

'Griff?'

Slowly the farmer straightened and in that moment Aidan wondered what it was that had changed. It was still undeniably Griff's body that stood there and it was still Griff's face that looked across at him and yet, for an instant, he could have sworn the eyes that lifted to his flashed sulphurous yellow. Like a wolf about to fall upon a sheepfold Griff smiled.

'Oh sh—'

There wasn't time to throw himself sideways. There wasn't

even time to swear as the Levin bolt hit him squarely in the chest and he went over backwards, the world slipping away from him as though he had been hit by a truck. He didn't even feel his body hit the ground, just found himself staring stupidly up to where the beam of light from his helmet lamp splashed dimly against the far-off ceiling. He was vaguely aware that his hands and feet had gone numb while the rest of his body was a mass of fiery pain. *You're in shock* some hyper-rational part of his mind told him but the observation seemed rather academic as though it were a comment made about someone else. He couldn't quite recall why it should mean anything to him.

He would have let himself drift but somehow there was another voice in his head, demanding his attention.

Get up, boy. You have to fight it.

There was something familiar, almost comforting, about the voice but neither the soft burr of accent nor the odd, rather archaic term of address left Aidan in any doubt that he was expected to obey its instructions. Reluctantly, and because he knew the voice wouldn't leave him alone until he did so, he tried to move but his muscles only jerked spastically at the attempt, sending his limbs twitching uselessly in the dust. For an instant panic rolled over him, rising like bile in his throat to choke off his breath; panic and the old, old fear of being paralysed, trapped in his body, unable to move. He would have sworn that he had put it behind him, that it had no place in his waking world for all that, thirteen years on, it still surfaced occasionally in nightmares. Yet lying in the dust he tasted that same bitterness and felt the familiar terror clutching at his heart. Desperately he pushed it back down. He wasn't paralysed he was just shaken up. He'd moved, hadn't he? Just not quite as effectively as he would have liked. Besides, if he was paralysed he wouldn't be able to feel whatever it was that was digging into his hip, hard and painful where his jacket was bunched up beneath him. What was it anyway? There hadn't been any rocks of any size on the floor. Then he remembered the knife he had taken from Eldritch and how the wizard had told him to use it on him if the demon had got the upper hand... *I'd take it as a favour...* Had the situation been less serious Aidan would have laughed at how simple Eldritch had made that sound. A shame, he thought, that the Englishman had neglected to mention the small matter of the demon throwing Levin bolts. Still, it was a weapon Griff didn't know he had... if he could reach it. His teeth gritted in concentration Aidan struggled to drag one outflung hand towards his pocket. His muscles were starting to respond but the movement was hideously slow and he shook with the effort. A sudden weight pinning his wrist to the floor had his eyes flying open in shock.

'Going somewhere, Cripple?'

Energy hit Aidan like the back of a hand across his face. His head snapped sideways and his mouth filled with the warm thickness of blood flowing across his tongue. For a moment he wondered if this was how he was going to die. Then he heard Griff laughing and gave an involuntary grunt of pain as the pressure on his wrist increased.

'What's that Cripple? Speak up, I can't hear you.'

The boot ground harder against bone and this time Aidan could barely choke back a scream as the pressure sent fire knifing through the nerves of his arm, his fingers clawing into a helpless fist.

'What, nothing to say for yourself? You never were any fun.'

The pressure on his arm eased a fraction as Griff leaned forward, leering down at him.

'The witch fought harder than you,' he sneered. Aidan felt bile rise in his throat at the words.

'Gwyn?' he croaked.

'Gwyn? Gwyn?' Griff mocked, his face dancing. 'Didn't you realise? She put up quite a struggle for an old bitch but she didn't fight half so much after I'd smacked her head into a rock a few times.'

He grinned, his eyes wide with delight.

'Hitting her was fun. I liked the feel of it, all bloody and warm as her head split open.'

The mad eyes seemed to turn inward and in the lamplight a strand of drool glistened on Griff's lips as thought the demon within him were salivating at the memory, like a gourmet recounting the details of a fine feast. Then his eyes found Aidan again and he leaned closer.

'She was tougher than you though. She didn't waste her time snivelling and crying. What do you say, best of three?'

Aidan saw Griff's hand rising to send a third bolt of energy blasting through him, the boot on his wrist crushing down, holding him captive. He should have been afraid but stronger than any fear or any sense of self-preservation was the anger boiling through his system. With it came adrenalin, scalding the last traces of numbness from his body. In an explosion of rage Aidan twisted, rearing up from the ground. He didn't bother trying to free the wrist pinned under Griff's foot, didn't spare a thought for the knife in his pocket, he was consumed with a visceral need to pound that sneering, gloating face to a pulp with his own hands. *Just one good punch.* The thought was a barely coherent war cry ringing through his mind. *Just give me one solid punch and I'll knock that sick laugh right down your throat, you bastard!* Left-handed his fist connected with Griff's face and he felt the flash of his own satisfaction as flesh spread and burst under his knuckles. The pressure on his wrist vanished as Griff reeled backwards, his hands going automatically to his split and broken features.

'That's for Gwyn!'

Aidan's legs were rubbery underneath him, his knees not quite ready to support his weight. Still he let momentum carry him forward, his fists connecting with Griff's jaw and sinking into the farmer's unprotected stomach even as his own legs folded. He staggered, somehow managing to stay upright, as Griff too caught his balance. The farmer's hands dropped away from his face and Aidan found himself staring at the spread of split flesh and mucous that his fist had made of Griff's nose. His gut clenched. A normal man would have been on his knees after taking such a blow but Griff seemed not to notice the blood bubbling from his ruined features and Aidan remembered that the possessed felt no pain. As if reading his thoughts a ghastly smile split the farmer's face, exposing blood rimmed teeth. Then the expression changed, hardening into something more deadly.

'That was a mistake, Cripple.'

Griff's voice was clogged and nasal but there was no mistaking the threat it carried. Aidan felt a cold thread of fear pulling at the base of his spine as he realised that Griff had been playing with him. What had gone before had been entertainment, the casual cruelty of a young boy pulling the wings off flies for fun. What would come next would be utterly serious.

'You're going to pay for that.'

It might be true but Aidan felt no regrets. His fingers closed around the smooth wooden handle of Eldritch's knife, his mind absolutely clear on what he was going to have to do. The demon might still take him but he was going down fighting. Yet even as he was drawing the knife from his pocket Griff gestured and invisible bonds locked around his body.

'You're going to die screaming.'

Shocked, Aidan tried to lunge for Griff but it was as if his limbs had been wrapped in chains of iron and lead, holding him captive. He tried again, fighting to overcome the power that restrained him, fighting he knew, for his life, but to no avail; for all his efforts his body remained frozen and unresponsive. Griff took a purposeful step towards him, cold promise in his eyes. *Damn it, no! Not like this!* Aidan cast a despairing glance at the knife ready in his hand but though he strained until the blood pounded in his ears his arm refused to move. The cold bitterness of defeat washed over him and he realised then that it was over. The demon had him trapped, helpless as a fly in amber. All he could do was to school his face into an expression of stony indifference as the demon closed in, but he couldn't stop his heart pounding frantically as Griff's hand reached for his wrist. Nor could he keep himself from screaming as he felt his flesh ignite under the demon's touch.

The pain was like nothing he had felt before. As it swept through him Aidan's world tipped sideways, blurring out of focus, but not before he saw his skin blackening and blistering underneath those heavy fingers, fingers that remained whole and unharmed even as his own flesh charred down to the bone beneath them. Aidan's nostrils filled with the acrid stench of singed hair and the peculiarly sweet smell of burning meat, the two scents mingling nauseatingly with the odour of stale cigarette smoke and animal sweat that clung to Griff's overalls. Cold sheets of sweat slid down his body and his stomach heaved, his mouth swimming with saliva. As his agonised cry choked into a whimper Aidan's final thought was to wonder vaguely which he would do first; pass out or throw up.

In the end he did neither. Even as his vision tunnelled and blackness washed over him, Aidan felt the grip on his wrist slacken and release. A moment later power slapped him round the face, jolting him back to awareness and he blinked, his mind fuzzy with the aftermath of pain and horror. Somewhat to his surprise he found he was still standing, his arm raised in front of him and Eldritch's knife clenched uselessly in his fist, his body a freeze-framed study in how not to attack a demon. Surely he should be on the floor? He remembered the feel of his muscles curdling, shock turning them to water, but no – it seemed the power that had bound him still held him rigid. Apparently he would remain upright until the demon decided otherwise. The demon! Focussed once more Aidan's eyes sought and found the hated green-clad form. Griff was watching him, waiting – patient as the farmer had never been in life. As Aidan's eyes met his a small, satisfied smile curled the corners of his mouth. For a moment he held Aidan's gaze and then deliberately his eyes dropped to Aidan's outstretched arm and though he said nothing his meaning was clear. *Look,* the gesture said. *Look and understand what I can do to you,* and while Aidan's initial instinct was to do nothing that the demon wanted after a second his eyes dropped and he too looked at what the demon had done.

He had thought he was prepared for what he would see but

the sight that greeted him shocked him to the core. He had felt his flesh burn, had seen it blacken beneath the demon's fingers, splitting and curling from the bone and yet when he looked now the wrist the demon had seized was whole and unharmed. Aidan stared at his arm wide-eyed in disbelief. Pain still throbbed along his bones, gnawing at the marrow like a dozen rats, but the torment that had had him screaming aloud had left not a mark upon his body. Shakily Aidan raised his eyes to meet the demon's. He hoped the fear he felt didn't show on his face.

'So,' Griff said. 'Now you understand.'

He eyed Aidan's frozen form.

'No one's going to come. No one's going to save you. Now it's just you and me.'

He put a hand up and wiped the blood from his upper lip then held his fingers up in the light, studying the oily gleam of blood along their edges. He looked at Aidan and very deliberately he lowered his head and licked the blood from each finger.

'Do you know what time it is?'

His voice had changed, once again becoming teasing, almost mischievous, but Aidan found it no less frightening. He swallowed, knowing that whatever the answer was he wasn't going to like it. Griff laughed as if reading his thoughts.

'It's playtime.'

Slowly he began to walk around Aidan, circling him lazily, a predator closing in on an already wounded prey. Unable to do so much as turn his head Aidan followed him with his eyes as far as he could, desperate to keep him in sight for as long as possible. His heart was pounding, his breath coming in frantic, panicky gasps as Griff moved behind him and all Aidan could think of was those fingers reaching unseen towards him. He bit down on his lip until he tasted blood, anything to stop the whimper climbing from his throat and waited, listening intently, trying to track the whisper of the other man's footsteps in the soft, powdery dust or catch the rustle of cloth that might tell him where Griff was, but no sounds came to him over the panting of his breath. For agonising seconds he waited and then, as he was almost beginning to wish the demon would strike, a flicker of movement snapped his eyes to his right and Griff moved back into view, coming to stand silently in front of him once more.

The possessed man's eyes seemed huge, the pupils dilated as if from drugs with the pleasure of what he was doing. Yet still he said nothing, simply waiting, poised, dragging out the moment and the knot of fear slowly tightened in Aidan's belly at the awful certainty of what was to come. Adrenalin racked his nerves towards breaking point and finally Griff moved closer, leaning into him, his gore smeared face flushed in the torchlight, his sulphurous eyes gleaming in anticipation.

'Say goodbye Cripple, while you still can!'

Almost lazily he reached again but before his fingers could close once more on Aidan's flesh the farmer's body jerked sharply and he spun round, a roar of disbelief and anger rising from his throat.

Looking like something risen from the grave Eldritch stood on the far side of the stope. His face was ashen and coated with dust as were his clothes, more grey now than black, as if he had truly dragged his body free of the earth, but his eyes glittered dangerously as he treated both demon and captive to a long, measuring stare.

'How like a demon,' the wizard drawled. 'Not even fully in the Mortal World and already stopping to torture someone to death.'

He snorted derisively.

'A bit premature aren't we? What happened? Did you let yourself be overcome by your host's feelings? By his emotions?'

The last word was flung like an insult and once more that cold grey gaze raked the demon. Eldritch's lips tightened briefly in a thin moue of disappointment as though he had hoped for better, then he shook his head, a small negating gesture. Contempt filled the dark shadows of his voice as he spoke again. 'You're wasting your time, you know.'

Griff make a strange noise deep in his throat.

'Careful, wizardling. If I want to I can kill him before you can possibly stop me.'

As if to prove the point Griff curled his fingers and the bands of power holding Aidan tightened, python-like around his chest, squeezing the air from his lungs. He gasped, eyes widening as suddenly he found himself struggling to breathe. An immense weight seemed to press against him, as though he stood chest-deep in wet concrete, and it took all his strength to push against it to be able to take even the shallowest breath. It took no great genius to know he wouldn't be able to maintain the effort for long.

'Eldritch!'

Somehow he found enough breath to choke the name out, half plea for help, half warning – as if the wizard needed to be told there was something wrong. He could see that for himself, surely? Yet to Aidan's shock Eldritch made no move to help him. In fact he gave no sign that he even registered Aidan's distress.

He remained where he was on the far side of the stope, watching silently, his face cold and distant under its patina of dust. Aidan stared at the wizard, horror and confusion mounting inside him. When Eldritch finally spoke his words were addressed to Griff but they hit Aidan like a fist in the gut.

'Go ahead.'

Had circumstances been different Aidan would have marvelled at just how much indifference Eldritch managed to cram into those two words. The wizard's gaze flicked briefly over Aidan's frozen form and then away again, the brevity of the glance only serving to underline the dismissal carried by his words.

'The stakes have changed. Sorry Aidan.'

For the briefest moment the grey gaze flicked back to him and something akin to regret showed on the wizard's face but it was gone before Aidan could be sure he had seen it.

'You served your purpose getting me down here; but now?' Shaking his head he turned back to the demon. 'Collateral damage,' he said, one shoulder rising in a dismissive shrug. 'Every conflict has it. He doesn't matter any more. Covenant or no Covenant it makes no difference – you're free. Now I'm the one who's going to stop you going any further, not him.'

He's bluffing. He's got to be bluffing. Aidan clung to the possibility but fighting to draw air into desperate lungs he couldn't be certain. The wizard had always been a reluctant team player, his tendency to treat people as resources to be used and discarded being one of the more unpleasant facets of his character. Images of the man he had met on the hillside above the Bite crept back to him; the man who had thought nothing of leaving Gwyn unconscious and alone or of manipulating him into returning to the site of John's death. Was he going to die because it was simply more expedient for Eldritch to let the demon kill him? *Look at me you bastard!* He willed the wizard to turn towards him, to give him the smallest indication that this was just a ploy, but Eldritch's eyes remained locked on the demon and he didn't so much as glance Aidan's way. Aidan exhaled the barest trickle of breath and the smothering bands closed a little tighter around his chest. *Damn it Eldritch, whatever game you're playing you'd better finish it quickly or I'm not going to be around to see the end result.* But in his heart Aidan wondered if perhaps there was no game and he cursed himself for a fool for ever being stupid enough to trust the Englishman. It seemed it wasn't a mistake he would have the chance to make again. The pounding of blood in his temples made his head throb, the sound of it staccato as the rat-tat-tat of an execution drumroll and through the noise he heard Eldritch say, 'Kill him if you want to. It won't stop me binding you.'

Aidan had no breath to spare to curse the man but the thoughts churned within him, a dark maelstrom of rage and grief and an indescribable yearning to carry on living, to feel the touch of sunlight and living air on his skin one final time. His eyes turned back to the wizard, burning with silent reproach. In the darkness of the stope a faint phosphorescence seemed to gather around Eldritch's hand, the pale nimbus of light shimmering over the stained and tatty bandages that wound from his knuckles to his forearm. The wizard shifted and for a moment Aidan thought he glimpsed lines of fire trailing from the long fingers as Eldritch flicked out his hand like a gladiator spreading a weighted net. Black spots surged in a wave across his vision making it hard to tell what was real but Griff seemed to see it too for the muscles of his shoulders bulged and twisted, like a dog bristling before a fight and once more he growled, an ugly, inhuman sound, deep in his throat. He spun on his heel to face Aidan and from the look on his face Aidan knew he was about to die. Then the wizard called out again, as if as an afterthought, 'Or perhaps you should leave him until after we've fought.'

His voice was silky, almost teasing.

'No point wasting a good death if you're so sure you can take me.'

For several seconds Griff did nothing, neither moving nor speaking, his eyes feral and mad above the shattered nose and blood crusted chin and Aidan waited for the killing bolt or for the invisible force to cut off his breath for good. Then something changed, some tension eased and Griff sneered, 'You'll keep, Cripple,' and turned back to Eldritch. 'I'm going to enjoy this, wizard. I've already mastered you once. What makes you think you can best me now?'

He made a sudden gesture and Eldritch flinched, his right shoulder hunching as though pain had driven through it but then he straightened and from Griff's angry hiss Aidan judged the demon hadn't expected him to be able to.

'You'll have to do better than that.' Eldritch's voice grated slightly but then steadied. 'Or had you forgotten I can beat you magically? I'd have bound you already if it hadn't been for your host.'

Griff's laugh was a thick, ugly sound.

'I think it's you who's forgetting something, wizard.'

He held his hands out, palms up as if examining the calluses and the thick, powerful fingers and then slowly he clenched his fists, tightening them until the knuckles popped.

'But I'll enjoy helping you remember.' The relish was evident in his voice. 'You may think you're stronger than me magically. Well, we'll see about that, but you've forgotten you're no match for me physically. You weren't before. You certainly aren't now.'

As he spoke Griff flung a handful of Levin fire towards the wizard and as Eldritch raised his hand to deflect it he charged at him, barrelling across the stope and howling like a berserker. Aidan saw Eldritch make a fast gesture with his right hand but Griff didn't so much as break stride. Horrified, Aidan guessed that the hastily thrown bolt had gone wide but even as he realised that Eldritch had made a fatal mistake something hit him in the chest like a mule kick and the power holding him prisoner dissolved. As he sucked in a huge lungful of breath he heard the wizard scream, 'Aidan! Now!' and he reacted instinctively, flipping the knife in his hand and sending it cartwheeling through the air before he had time to question what he was doing. The spinning blade cut through the torchlight, a bright and deadly silver mayfly. It dug into the flesh between Griff's shoulder blades and the farmer jerked just as Eldritch hit him with a blast of wizard fire. Griff spun round under the impact and a second bolt hit him, blazing through the hilt of the knife like lightning through a conductor. Griff's arms spread and his back arched as though he had been shot. He choked – a wet, bubbling sound – his mouth working, his fingers clawing as if to cast one final spell, then he collapsed face down barely a yard away from Eldritch's feet. He did not move.

CHAPTER 23

'Are you okay?'

Aidan started at the sound of the familiar voice beside him. He tore his gaze from the empty husk of flesh that had once been Griff Howell, scarcely able to believe that it was finally over.

'Aidan?'

For a moment Aidan could think of nothing to say. He stared at the wizard, hugging his arms protectively a little tighter around his chest, still unable to draw a full breath without pain lancing through his ribs. In the last few minutes he had been more scared than he had ever been in his life. Every inch of his body ached, his spirit felt bruised and torn and it was starting to sink in that he had just helped to kill someone. He could do nothing about any of that but there was one score he was going to settle before he did another damned thing. He fixed Eldritch with an accusing glare.

'You told him,' he wheezed, 'to go ahead and kill me. You said that I didn't matter.'

Aidan couldn't quite manage a shout but the Englishman would have had to have been brain-dead not to hear it in his tone. 'Did it never occur to you that he might do just that?'

Eldritch was silent. Close up he looked truly awful but Aidan didn't feel much inclined to sympathy. He clutched his ribs and continued to glower.

'Yes, well… I'm sorry about that.' The wizard had the grace to look sheepish. 'But telling him I'd really rather he left you alone didn't seem like such a great idea either.'

'Why didn't you just zap him?'

'I couldn't. He was too close to you.' Eldritch gave a little shrug as Aidan's eyes narrowed, taking this for a lie. He winced and absently put up his good hand to rub his shoulder. 'Double vision,' he muttered. 'I'd just as likely have hit you. I couldn't see straight enough to risk it. Still can't,' he added, more than half to himself and then glanced away as if he had said more than he intended. 'Anyway, it worked.'

He turned back, familiar wolfish grin firmly in place. It slipped a little as he took in Aidan's expression and above it his eyes grew still and serious.

'You must have known I wouldn't let him kill you, surely?'

A worn look flitted across Eldritch's face when Aidan failed to answer.

'I see.' He nodded once to himself and his tall frame seemed to slump a little. His gaze slid away from Aidan's. 'I'm sorry.'

A cold knot of tension he hadn't known he carried unwound itself from somewhere within Aidan's chest. Its easing seemed to take with it all the adrenalin, anger and fear that had kept him going through the fight with Griff, leaving him drained and empty. He swayed, suddenly lightheaded, and a hand under his elbow steadied him.

'Get out of here Aidan.' Eldritch's voice was tired but calm. 'Wait for me back in the tunnel. I can deal with this now.'

For a moment Aidan almost followed the wizard's suggestion. It seemed such a reasonable course of action he very nearly nodded and went but then he sighed, letting the idea go.

With an effort he gathered himself mentally and physically. They had started this together. He wasn't going to leave Eldritch to finish it on his own. Once more he looked across the stope towards Griff's body.

'Is he...?'

Despite his good intentions his voice broke, the words congealing in his throat. He shook his head, wondering at his own confusion. It wasn't as if Griff had meant anything to him. All his life the man had been a cruel bully and Aidan had no doubt that if he hadn't thrown that knife Griff would have killed him and Eldritch both. Hell, his initial reaction at seeing Griff fall had been relief so strong it had bordered on elation. So why did looking at that crumpled shape tug at his conscience? Telling himself he was being stupid, Aidan straightened as much as his ribs would allow and forced himself to look again at what was left of Griff Howell. A strong, heavily built man in life, in death Griff's body looked somehow smaller and oddly vulnerable, the limbs sprawled untidily, the feet in their heavy work boots sticking out at odd, uncomfortable angles. From this distance the dark patch on the back of his overalls seemed more like shadow than blood. The beam of Aidan's helmet lamp paused spotlighting that small, insignificant stain as he considered this. It hardly seemed enough to mark the ending of a life.

'He is dead, isn't he?' He was pleased his voice didn't shake.

'He was dead the moment the demon took him, Aidan. He just hadn't stopped walking around, that's all.'

The wizard didn't so much as glance at Griff but his grip on Aidan's arm tightened and his cool grey eyes fixed on Aidan's, drilling into him as if by force of will alone he could make him accept the truth of those words.

'You didn't kill him; the demon did. Don't ever doubt it.' For an instant a look of regret as deep as pain marked the wizard's face. 'It doesn't matter who or what they were to you; when a demon takes them they cease to be the person you know.'

Eldritch dropped his hand and then swiped it across his face, dragging at the skin as if to wipe away something that clung there; cobwebs perhaps or old memories, the image of a slender woman prostrate on the floor, first weeping and pleading for mercy and then spitting fury like a hellcat. Understanding swept through Aidan, bleak and bitter as ashes, but before he could think of anything to say Eldritch spoke again, his voice very close to normal.

'If you're asking me if it's over, then yes, it is, very nearly.' His lips twitched as if he meant to smile but couldn't quite remember how to do so. 'The demon won't stay in Griff's body now he's dead. The power I put through it will have stunned it but I need to set a power net to bind it as it leaves him. Once it's bound I can destroy it. It won't take long.'

Put like that it seemed so simple but nothing so far had gone completely to plan. Was there any reason to think that the tide had turned in their favour? Aidan rubbed at his arms. The air seemed colder now, finding its way through the slits and tears in his clothing to strike like ice against clammy skin. He shivered. More than anything he wanted this to be finished but there was one more thing nagging at him.

'What about the boundary?'

Fragments of earlier talk about the importance of restoring the barrier between the Mortal World and the Unseen Realm flickered through Aidan's head. With them came the guilty understanding that this was no small task he was asking the wizard to complete. Yet overriding that guilt was the absolute certainty that they had to prevent anything else coming through the hole the demon had opened up. He could only hope that Eldritch still had the strength to do it.

The glitter of gold and precious stones drew his eye as Eldritch raised his hand. Incredibly his grandmother's ring still dangled there, suspended from the chain wrapped tight around his fingers. Eldritch regarded it with a certain grim satisfaction, the way in other circumstances another man might have looked at a favoured weapon.

'Don't worry about the boundary. There's just about enough juice left in here to finish the job.'

His long fingers folded over the ring, tucking it away again. Relieved, Aidan dragged up the energy to laugh.

'Good old Grandma. Just promise me you won't pass out when you've finished because there's no way I'm carrying you home. Not today.'

He stopped as he realised Eldritch was no longer listening to him.

'What? What is it?' he asked as the wizard swore viciously under his breath. A surge of adrenalin swept the tiredness from his system. 'Eldritch!' he demanded sharply but still he got no answer.

'No. You can't do this. Don't do this to me!'

'Do what? What are you talking about?'

But even as he spoke Aidan realised Eldritch's words weren't meant for him. Anxiously he cast around, looking for some clue as to what was happening, the beam of his helmet lamp cutting through the darkness like a spotlight. And then he saw it.

On the far side of the stope Griff's body was moving. Aidan's initial thought was that they had been wrong, that Griff wasn't dead. How could there be any other explanation? But as the body hunched itself up, the limbs clawing inwards towards the torso he realised that these were not the movements of an injured man. In the shadowy darkness the whole surface of Griff's body seemed to be writhing as if below the overalls his flesh boiled with maggots like a week-old corpse. Aidan stared in disbelief. It had to be a trick of the light. Unthinking he took a step forwards and a hand like a steel clamp fastened on his arm, jerking him back.

'No. Get out of here Aidan. Now!'

There was no mistaking the horror in Eldritch's face, nor the determination burning through the washed out tiredness that had been there a moment earlier. He cut off Aidan's half-formed protest with an angry shake of his head, his chin jutting, his eyes hard. From the corner of his eye Aidan saw the thing on the other side of the stope roll onto its knees. Its body bowed so far forward that its hair tangled in the dust but slowly its hands moved, fingering their way along the ground until they were underneath its shoulders and its arms straightened pushing itself back onto its heels. All the while its skin jerked and twitched. Aidan gasped as Eldritch shook him, hard and sharp, dragging his attention back.

'Am I talking to myself?'

The wizard's voice was clipped, cold and accentless, which only served to emphasise the anger underlying his words.

'I can deal with this. You can't. Now go!'

As if the matter were decided Eldritch stepped back. He threw a brief glance across the stope and then raised the hand holding his grandmother's ring to his chest, the knuckles whitening as they clenched tight around its delicate shape. As the wizard's head bowed over his fist Aidan caught a glimpse of his eyes rolling back in their sockets to leave only a tiny crescent of white under the dark lashes. He realised that Eldritch was pulling power from the ring, not gradually as he had when he had drawn the veil at the Red Kite hut, but dragging it into him in one final burst, like a man sucking in a lungful of air before plunging into a torrent he knew could drown him. Thirty feet away Griff Howell's body was getting to its feet.

Had he been able to drag the wizard with him at that point Aidan would have gladly turned and run. He didn't know why, after all the things he had witnessed since he and Eldritch had entered the mine, he should find this so disturbing but there was something fundamentally unnerving about the sight of what he knew to be a corpse dragging itself upright. Yet frightened though he was there was no way he was going to leave Eldritch's side, not while the wizard was locked in a trance and defenceless. He darted a swift sideways glance at his companion but the wizard was motionless, head bowed over his grandmother's ring. What he was doing might take seconds or minutes, Aidan had no way of knowing. His teeth worried at his bottom lip as he considered this, fighting down a very real urge to reach out and shake that still form. Seconds they might have but he doubted very much that they had minutes. Griff's body was straightening, the shoulders still jerking and twitching as the head started to lift. Aidan felt his own fingers twitch in response and clenched his hand into a fist to stop himself reaching for Eldritch's sleeve. He held his breath as the head started to swing towards him. For a moment their gazes seemed to cross and yet Aidan couldn't say the corpse looked at him. He wasn't close enough to read an expression in the flat, dead eyes and there was none discernible on the broken features. Griff's dark blond hair hung in dusty strands across his face but there was nothing of Griff left in the slack-jawed emptiness. Now all that was left was the demon, waiting somewhere within that cooling flesh. Could it still see through those curiously staring eyes or did it have other senses with which to probe and search for its enemies? Aidan didn't know but he held himself very still as he returned that blank gaze, not even daring to breathe as he hunkered down behind his shields, hoping no thread of fear, no echo of the fast race of his blood would reach the demon and betray him.

When the eyes swung past him he thought he had got away with it. As the head continued its slow mindless sweep he thought it had missed them and they were safe. Then suddenly Griff's head whipped back towards him and beside him Eldritch jerked upright, his eyes snapping open. The wizard started to move and then he must have registered Aidan's presence for he whirled, his face paling with rage.

'What are you doing here?' he roared, the dark edges of his voice seething with power. Aidan didn't answer. Behind the wizard's back Griff's corpse broke into a lumbering run. It moved with a flat-footed gait, its feet slapping down and its legs not quite seeming to bend as they should. It wasn't nearly as fast as Griff had been while alive but nor was there much ground for it to cover and it came at them with the inexorability of a small avalanche. Somehow Aidan found his voice.

'Look out!' he yelled and reached out with the intention

347

of dragging Eldritch aside. But Eldritch knocked his hand away with a speed and ease that later Aidan would remember and marvel at and then, perhaps because he was the only thing standing between the monster and Aidan, the wizard did something totally unexpected.

It was a sight Aidan thought he would remember for the rest of his life. The demon-ridden corpse was almost on top of them but as the wizard whirled to face it he made no attempt to blast it with Levin fire. Instead he spread his arms wide and though he neither gestured nor seemed to call his magic in any way a pale nimbus of blue and violet fire flared into being around him, throwing back the shadowy darkness. Unearthly and beautiful, the witchlight danced along Eldritch's skin turning its pallor into luminous splendour and striking sparks of turquoise and silver in his eyes. In that moment the lines of weariness and pain that had marked his face seemed to drop away as his flesh glowed, lambent with power. He seemed more like an elemental than a man, moving in the heart of his own lightning storm as he met the corpse's charge head on, making no attempt to dodge, no attempt to sidestep the lumbering form. Eldritch was a good four inches taller than Griff but the farmer was heavier and had momentum behind him, yet his corpse seemed to bounce off Eldritch when Aidan's every instinct told him it would roll over the wizard like a freight train. Aidan's amazement deepened as Eldritch lunged forward, catching the corpse's flailing arms, his hands locking around its biceps and pinning its arms to its sides. As he did so the glow lighting his flesh shifted. Where his hands touched the green overalls it brightened, spreading out from his hands and sliding over the corpse, engulfing its flesh in a glowing veil of light. The corpse began to buck and twist as the light spread over it but Eldritch hung on. How he did so with a broken wrist Aidan had no idea but the wizard's face showed nothing but a grim concentration as he held the writhing form at arm's length, smothering its struggles in a blanket of power. Gwyn had said that Eldritch was more powerful than anyone she had ever met. Aidan hadn't taken much notice at the time, not really knowing what she meant. New to the concept, nothing he had seen the wizard do seemed to justify that belief, but now he saw and he understood why the demon had tried to destroy him.

For all its deadly ferocity the struggle was almost silent, the only noise being the gritty slur of the combatants' feet on the dusty ground, so the sudden rent of tearing cloth was startlingly loud, filling the stope like a gunshot. All across Griff's shoulders the fabric of his overalls ripped apart as the flesh beneath bulged outwards, seething and writhing, the skin unnaturally taut and shining greasily in the witchlight. For a second more it strained outward and then it split open, flecks of blood and flesh spattering outwards as it erupted in a mass of writhing, snakelike protuberances. Medusa-like they coiled and squirmed over the dead man's shoulders, probing the air with blind, seeking heads split by sickle-shaped mouths. Needle-fine teeth glinted as they struck out at Eldritch snapping at his hands, his arms, his face. Where they struck his coat they seemed unable to do any damage but they latched onto his hands, tearing bloody crescents from his skin. He turned his face aside as one went for his eyes and it caught his cheek instead but though he shuddered as it fastened onto his flesh still he held on, his face determined in the pale glow of witchlight and the fire spreading from his hands flared even brighter. The demon began to struggle harder, twisting against Eldritch's grip, its movements becoming more frantic as it tried to get away from the cold sapphire flame. But Eldritch would not let it escape. In one swift move he pulled Griff's corpse towards him, his arms encircling the writhing shape and crushing it against his chest. Even as the snake heads lunged at his face fire burst from him. For a moment the wizard's entire body seemed to burn as bright as magnesium. Aidan flung up a hand to shield his eyes from the blinding light. The very air seemed on fire and he had the impression of a shadowy form being flung across the stope. Then darkness fell across the scene like a curtain.

CHAPTER 24

Gradually the world came back into focus and Aidan blinked owlishly, trying to separate shadow and shape from the chaos of violet and white after-images still dancing across his retinas. The amber wash of torchlight seemed very dim after the lightning flash of Eldritch's power, the darkness beyond it that much deeper, but he could just make out the wizard's tall form standing like a coalition of shadows in the beam of his helmet lamp. Of the demon he could see nothing. He hoped that was a good thing. Holding that thought in his mind like a touchstone he looked again at Eldritch. The wizard was very still, his head bowed, his body motionless. Was he listening for something? Waiting? Re-gathering his power to cast another spell? There was no clue in the turned back and Aidan was loathe to break the silence and risk distracting him. Yet the more his vision cleared the more uneasy he became. In the last moments of his battle with the demon Eldritch had seemed all but invincible. Now he stood with his right arm hanging at his side as though it weren't so much broken as ripped half from its socket.

As if feeling the weight of Aidan's gaze Eldritch straightened and Aidan caught his breath. The fluid, predatory grace with which the wizard had stepped forward to tackle the demon was gone, burned away along with the power that had blazed through him. Instead Eldritch moved with the painful stiffness of a man grown old before his time. Seeing that, Aidan was almost prepared for the ashy pallor of Eldritch's face as he turned, but not for the expression that haunted the grey eyes. It pierced him like needles of ice and he shivered without quite knowing why. Feeling the grinding weariness in his own body Aidan registered that aching loneliness as exhaustion. It was only later that he would realise it had been despair.

His eyes still locked on Aidan's, Eldritch took a single step forward. Then whatever energy had been keeping him upright drained away and his legs folded underneath him, dropping him to his knees. Aidan's breath came out as a curse as he lunged forward to stop the wizard going face down in the dirt, but though he swayed dangerously Eldritch remained upright, his body hunching protectively, his right arm in its cocoon of filthy bandages and splints cradled tightly against his chest.

'Eldritch?'

His hands were poised ready but Aidan resisted the urge to grab and catch, unsure where he might touch without causing the other man pain. At the name the bowed head raised fractionally, the grey eyes lifting though Aidan wasn't sure if they focussed on him.

'Hey.'

He reached out and very gently closed his hand on the wizard's left shoulder. Eldritch stiffened slightly under the contact and Aidan sighed. He knew better than to waste his breath asking if the man was alright.

'I think you cut yourself shaving,' he offered, pointing to where blood dribbled unnoticed down the wizard's face. Slowly, and without a word, Eldritch raised a hand to his cheek. Lifting it away he stared at the blood on his fingers like a man waking from a dream. Aidan watched him slowly coming back.

'You realise we have to stop meeting like this?' He gave the shoulder a careful squeeze and dropped his hand. 'People are starting to talk.'

For a moment there was no reaction and then as if from nowhere a smile stole over Eldritch's face. It was like the changing of a chameleon's protective camouflage. Even the greyness of fatigue gave way before it.

'Let them,' he husked. 'There's nothing else for them to talk about round here.' Slowly Eldritch let his head fall forward. He took a deep breath that became a sigh as he lifted it again and with surprise Aidan realised he was stretching some of the tension from his neck and shoulders.

'Don't look so serious Aidan. The demon's finished.'

The words were spoken so casually that at first Aidan didn't know how to take them.

'We though it was finished before.' That came out before he could stop it, the scepticism heavier than he might have intended. 'Before it did that whole zombie reanimation thing and then that... that whatever it was with the snakes.'

Just saying it had his skin crawling. Despite himself Aidan shuddered. *The demon's finished...* Was that really possible? He knew he should be elated but instead he found himself torn between the desire to believe that what the wizard said was true and fear that the demon might somehow be able to rise once more. *Shows just how tired you are,* he told himself. He looked again at Eldritch. The wizard was still holding his arm against his chest but he seemed a little straighter and a little less drawn than he had been only a moment ago. Perhaps there was reason to believe.

'You're certain it's over?'

Eldritch nodded and only the briefest tightening of his lips suggested that that might have been a mistake.

'I wove a binding around its essence that trapped it within Griff's flesh and then I blasted it apart.' A degree of satisfaction edged the tiredness from Eldritch's voice. 'Now all I have to do is to seal the boundary and the demon and this whole sorry episode will be history.'

'Well.' Aidan let out his breath in an exhalation that was part sigh and part short huffing laugh as the tension left him. He glanced around him, not sure what to say. Ridiculous though it was after all that had happened, this felt like an anticlimax. He shook his head, laughing at himself for having such a thought and his eyes came back to the wizard's. 'Best get on with it then and we can go home.'

The corner of Eldritch's mouth twitched and a trace of mockery slid into his voice.

'In a hurry are we? And here's me thinking you liked being underground.'

Something shifted in the back of his eyes, a hint of coolness, gone before Aidan could say for certain what it was.

'There's only one thing. I need you out of here before I do it.'

'What?'

Taken aback Aidan stared at the wizard, uncertain he had heard correctly but when Eldritch merely looked at him he asked, 'Why?'

'Because I say so?'

Eldritch paused, a small moue of irritation tightening his lips as he realised a fuller explanation was going to be needed. Finally he clicked his tongue in disgust.

'Closing the border will release a lot of psychic energy,' he said, tersely. 'I'd really rather you weren't caught up in it. In fact, I think you should have this back, just in case.'

He reached up and lifted the flat disk of amethyst and rose quartz away from his throat.

'Won't you need it?'

Aidan couldn't think of what else to say. The casual dismissal had left him deflated. After all they had been through he would have expected more.

'I'll be protected by the wards I put in place for the closing. It's better that you have it. Then when all this is over you can give it back to Gwyn.'

As if that decided it Eldritch started picking ineffectually at the knot, one-handed, but after a moment he bowed his head for Aidan to take over.

'Oh.'

Aidan started to oblige and then he stopped as something niggled at him. Perhaps he was being overly sensitive, but even so.

'You never said anything about psychic energy being a problem before,' he challenged. 'When you were going to use the power stored in your ring to close the boundary, you didn't say anything about me having to go then.'

Rather stiffly Eldritch straightened up and glared at Aidan. His voice was cooling towards glacial as he said, 'As I recall we were interrupted before I got to that point. Anyway,' he added, 'I had more energy to play with then. I would have been able to keep you safe.'

Again there was that flicker of something in his eyes, that old wariness and the unwillingness to share what was really going on inside his head. *He's lying,* thought Aidan and though the idea shocked him that shock made him no less certain he was right. What he couldn't understand was why.

'So, how are you going to seal the boundary?'

There was a sore spot there and Aidan nudged at it like a man digging at toothache.

'It doesn't matter.'

Had he been standing the wizard would have turned on his heel and stalked away. Even kneeling he managed to give the impression of doing so. Certain now that Eldritch was holding something back Aidan poked a little further.

'I know it doesn't matter but how are you going to do it?'

'This is no time for a lesson in magical theory, Aidan. I need to do this and I need to get it over with. And right now you're stopping me doing that.'

A brief and brittle anger flared in Eldritch's eyes and then it was gone. All of a sudden he was the cool and aloof stranger, the man who held himself apart, using people like tools but never trusting them to know what he was doing. He contemplated Aidan down the long, bony length of his nose, his lips curling sardonically and his voice was as sharp as his expression as he offered up the tersest of explanations.

'Seeing as you're so anxious to know, I'm going to change the physical nature of the boundary where the demon broke through. Doing so will take a great deal of energy and I'd rather you weren't anywhere in the vicinity at the time.'

Aidan frowned. Eldritch was speaking the truth – he could hear it in his voice, in the edge of irritation and the slightly condescending tone he adopted as though he were lecturing a particularly dense four-year-old. And yet still his instincts told him there was some detail that he wasn't being told; something that the wizard was deliberately keeping from him. He looked around him trying to imagine what the wizard was planning. In his mind he saw the demon stepping out of a wall of glittering darkness that stretched across the stope but when he looked at where it had happened there was nothing there but rock dust and open space. How could Eldritch change that? He eyed the cavernous darkness, struggling to see the missing piece of the puzzle, trying to understand, and as he did so a second image formed in his mind. He saw another man standing there, younger than the wizard – in fact closer to his own age – a man far too young to be contemplating what he was about to do. There was something strangely familiar about the wiry, compact form clad as it was in a miner's dust caked trousers and pit shirt. Aidan could not see the other's face for his back was turned to him, but he sensed the cold desperation that must have filled it as fire streaked from those upraised hands and rock and debris rained down around him. The sensation of being caught up in that maelstrom of falling rock and choking dust was so real that Aidan jerked back physically from the image – be it a vision, genetic memory or just some scene conjured from his own imagination – his heart pounding frantically. His eyes saucered as they locked on Eldritch's, a mixture of shock and something akin to awe chilling his skin.

'Wait a minute. You're talking about bringing the roof down?'

It was a question but Eldritch remained silent, his face enigmatic beneath its mask of blood and bruises. Yet within that aloofness there was also an air of expectancy as though he were waiting for Aidan to form his own answer and from there to make one final connection.

357

'But what about you? How are you going to get out?'

And then it dawned on him. Even as he said the words he knew. For a minute the knowledge silenced him, the enormity of it rendering him beyond words. Kneeling in the dust he fought to get his emotions under control. Somehow, briefly, he managed it. When he finally opened his mouth he didn't shout, he didn't even protest, not at first. Very quietly Aidan said, 'You're not intending to, are you?'

'It's called a final strike.' Eldritch said, his voice surprisingly calm and level, as though he weren't describing the thing that was going to kill him. 'Every living thing carries within it an energy, a life force if you will, the essential energy of life. That's why there's power in sacrifice.'

His lips quirked into a brief, rueful smile.

'A final strike is an act of self-sacrifice. When a wizard has used all his power, when he's exhausted every other option and has nothing left, then he can choose to use his own life force as a final source of power. I used the last of my power and what was left in the ring to finish the demon.'

He shrugged, a small lopsided gesture barely noticeable in the darkness, as if the consequences of that act were of no great importance.

'There wasn't any choice. It had to be stopped. But the boundary still has to be closed and I don't have the strength left to do it any other way. With a final strike I can bring the roof down. It should disrupt the physical elements of the boundary sufficiently to seal the hole the demon ripped in the ether.'

The wizard smiled, dark and feral. 'I don't have to worry about falling rocks. They won't be a problem for me.'

'But it's going to kill you.'

Perhaps it was Eldritch's attempt at black humour that triggered it but horror pressed down on Aidan, making it hard to breathe. The bitterness he felt at Eldritch's fatalistic stance surprised him. His fists balled as he fought the urge to pound them into the Englishman, to beat some sense into him. Perhaps Eldritch understood for his voice was almost gentle as he said, 'Just go Aidan. It's for the best. Please don't make it any harder than it is.'

Aidan wasn't in the mood to be gentle.

'No. Absolutely not.' He glared fiercely at the wizard, his nostrils flaring. 'You can't do this. I'm not going to let you.'

'Aidan... please.'

'You can't do this,' Aidan reiterated angrily yet still Eldritch's voice remained calm.

'I can't *not* do this. It's what I am. I can't risk anything else crossing the border.'

'Even if it costs you your life?' Aidan retorted bitterly.

'Even then.'

A stillness settled across the stope. In it Aidan could hear the ragged draw of Eldritch's breath.

'I tried, but this is the only option I have left. Please.' There was a tiredness now in the wizard's voice, 'Just go.'

Something in that quiet insistence cut Aidan to the quick. He gritted his teeth, steeling himself against the desperation he could sense underlying Eldritch's words. Eldritch was wrong, there had to be something else they could do. He wasn't about to let the wizard throw his life away. How would he ever explain it to Gwyn?

'No.'

The tiniest tremor ran through Eldritch's frame. When he shook his head his whole body swayed.

'What else do you want of me?' A weary bitterness filled his voice, sending it scaling upwards. 'Do you think I want it to end like this?'

A look of pain crossed his face and he dropped his head, swallowing convulsively as if choking down some further remark. For long seconds he remained unmoving, a huddled, somehow lonely shape hugging his pain to him. Then he straightened and though his eyes were dark as storm clouds they were calm once more.

'I'm sorry. This isn't your fault. None of it is. The demon was far stronger than any I've encountered before. I knew that as soon as I fought the avatar. I should have realised then that I couldn't hope to tackle it on my own and manage to seal the boundary if it did manifest.'

The wizard paused, his expression becoming distant as though he were reviewing his own actions and when he spoke again he could have been talking to himself.

'But somehow, after that fight, I knew I could beat it. It seems stupid now but I was convinced that if I could only find where it was breaking through I'd be able to destroy it.' He laughed, a soft husking of breath, mocking the hubris revealed by those words. 'I was wrong.' The grey eyes came back to Aidan's once more. 'I think that was the demon's influence. It wanted me to think that so it could lure me to it. I was the host it had chosen.'

He laughed again but the sound was bitter. 'Perhaps if Gwyn and I had been able to do this together...'

Abruptly Eldritch stopped as if acknowledging the pointlessness of such speculation and he looked away into the darkness.

'Then wait for her.'

If that was all it would take it seemed a simple enough answer to Aidan. Eldritch shook his head, a small movement but it had him hissing in pain. For a moment his breathing went ragged but then he continued.

'I'm sorry Aidan, I can't. I daren't. The boundary is still open. I daren't leave it that way. Stretch out your senses,' he added, as Aidan started to argue, 'just for a second. Then tell me that I'm wrong.'

He didn't much like the idea of dropping his shields but cautiously Aidan did as he was told and his face paled as he felt the immediate prickle of unseen energies dancing over his skin. He had thought the Unseen Realm would be still after the demon's manifestation, but he could feel things pushing against the darkness, things that whispered to him in chittering, malevolent voices and his mind crawled with the absolute certainty of what would happen should any of them cross. With a cry he slammed his shields back into place, his arms wrapping round himself as though he could hug away the sensation of those darkly massing energies pushing and probing and seeking for a way across the void.

'You can feel it,' Eldritch said and there was no triumph in his voice, just a weary matter-of-fact tone that suggested he would have given much for it not to be so. Aidan swallowed, forcing down the sour taste of fear that threatened to choke him.

'What is it?' he asked, his voice little more than a thread of sound in the darkness. As he spoke his eyes strayed back to the boundary as though expecting to see some new horror begin to coalesce out of the Stygian gloom. Reluctantly he tore his eyes away to look at Eldritch. 'What's out there?'

The wizard gave the tiniest of shrugs.

'Things that you don't want to know about. Things that will make the demon seem quite tame by comparison.'

He too glanced at the boundary and Aidan saw the way his face tightened as if in pain.

'A lot of power has been used here. It draws things that will seek to use the residue of that energy to come through. The boundary is wide open at the moment. It won't take much for one of them to find its way across.'

Eldritch shuddered in a way that, under other circumstances, might have had Aidan asking what had walked over his grave. But as he stared into the shifting curtain of darkness, trying to decide if the movement he thought he saw was the beginnings of some alien shape manifesting or just his eyes playing tricks with the dark and the shadows, the question seemed too close to the bone. He watched the wizard make a small dismissing gesture as if to avert evil and then raise his head defiantly.

'I'm not going to let that happen,' he promised.

Aidan said nothing. Faced with this new understanding he could no longer find it in him to argue against what the wizard intended to do but the knowledge was bitter as ashes. In silence he waited for Eldritch to continue.

'There is one downside to a final strike – apart from the fact that it will kill you, of course.'

Gwyn would have recognised Marcus Eldritch's tendency to use humour to mask his feelings but Aidan flinched as though a lash had been laid against his bare skin. Still shaken by what he had felt when he had lowered his shields he could not bring himself to smile at Eldritch's perverse attempt at humour.

'You need to know this Aidan.' There was a gentle reproach in Eldritch's voice.

'A final strike isn't a subtle form of energy. The force of it can be directed but I won't be able to use it to cast the bindings I'd normally seal the boundary with.'

He paused to wipe a hand across his face and Aidan saw that it was shaking. He realised then what Eldritch had been trying to conceal with that brief burst of humour and felt ashamed.

'The physical disruption should be sufficient to make the boundary snap back into place but if it doesn't at least nothing from the Mortal World will be able to get near it. Even so, when you get back to the surface don't let anyone else come down here and as soon as she's up to it ask Gwyn to set wards on the entrances, just as we planned. That will make it as safe as it can be.'

The wizard stilled, his gaze dropping and turning inwards momentarily, then his eyes sought Aidan's one final time.

'This is the best I can do Aidan. I want you well away before I finish it. I don't want to take you with me.'

A dozen conflicting thoughts jostled for dominance in Aidan's head.

'There'll be questions asked about what's happened.' It wasn't what was uppermost in his mind but it won him a little more time to come to terms with the awful decision he had just made. 'Sooner or later someone's going to put two and two together and ask what happened to Griff.'

'Say whatever you want. There's no body for them to find. Tell them you'd taken me down the mine as part of the research for my book. Tell them that Griff came down after us and when

I saw him I went crazy, that I killed him and nearly killed you when you tried to stop me. That knife wound should make it pretty convincing. They may have questions but they won't be able to prove anything different. Blame it on me. It's not so far from the truth anyway. No one has to know what really happened.'

Eldritch's mouth quirked slightly as though he was struggling to reconcile his words with his feelings.

'Except Gwyn,' he added. 'Tell her I'm sorry.'

For a second the wizard was silent, having said all that he intended to. Then he straightened perceptibly. He seemed to be drawing all his energy together.

'Now go.'

For a long moment Aidan studied Eldritch, marking the pallor of his face and the fine tremor that shook his limbs like palsy and that even now he was struggling to hide. He was aware as he did so that his heart was pounding and his palms were slick with sweat. He swallowed, trying to bring some moisture back to a throat that had gone uncomfortably dry. *Say it now. Say it before you chicken out and it's too late.* Could he really do this?

'How long have I got to get clear?'

Perhaps thinking he heard acceptance in Aidan's voice Eldritch's expression softened. Relief lifted some of the strain from his face.

'I can't give you long; five, maybe ten minutes at the outside. I know it's not much but I daren't wait any longer. I can't win against what's out there Aidan and it only needs one of them to work out the way and then they'll all cross. I daren't let that happen.'

'Ten minutes,' Aidan mused as though he hadn't heard anything else Eldritch had said. *You can still back out.* But he couldn't. His lips pursed thoughtfully as he eyed Eldritch and he took a deep breath. His head came up and there was more than a hint of defiance in the tilt of his jaw.

'Would a second life give you enough energy?'

The words came out more like a challenge than Aidan had intended but he had had to force them past the tightness in his throat.

'What are you talking about?' Genuine puzzlement tinged the wizard's voice.

'A second life, surrendered willingly. Would that give you the controllable energy you need to seal the breach?'

Eldritch's eyes went wide and shocked in the lamplight. He stared at Aidan aghast, his mouth open but saying nothing as though the sheer horror of what Aidan had proposed had stolen the words he needed from his brain.

'Aidan, no! You don't know what you're saying.' The wizard shook his head as though denying what he had heard. 'You can't. You've got to get out of here.'

But Aidan knew exactly what he was suggesting and he noted that amongst the protestations Eldritch had not said it was impossible. To his surprise he found himself laughing, a deep, genuinely amused belly laugh that had him clutching his ribs, as the tension left him. He waved off Eldritch's one-handed attempt to steady him – the wizard was in no shape to help anyone.

'Oh, so it's alright for you to be all heroic and self-sacrificing but not for anyone else? I'm sorry but it doesn't work like that. You're going to bring the roof down and you're talking of me getting out of here? Perhaps you haven't noticed but I'm in no state to run and even if I were I don't trust you to be able to do it.'

He sobered then and straightened, wincing as pain stabbed him from too many places, and looked appraisingly at his companion.

'Oh, you'll bring the roof down alright but you'll probably collapse the entire level when you do it. Ten minutes head start isn't going to make a blind bit of difference.'

A smile brightened his face then, sweet and almost innocent, despite the knowing look in his eyes. He reached out and rested a hand on Eldritch's arm.

'If I'm going to die I'd rather do it here, with a friend, than be crushed to death in the dark on my own. At least this way my death will mean something.'

For a second there was absolute silence between them. In that stillness Aidan thought he could hear the faintest whisper of sounds, sibilant and hateful, coming through the darkness from where the boundary lay. He told himself he was imagining it, but as he turned his head to listen he saw Eldritch do the same. As one they turned back to each other.

'You're crazy,' Eldritch stated bluntly.

'Is that a yes?'

'Aidan...' Eldritch didn't have the energy to fling his hands up in exasperation but his tone communicated the gesture just as well. 'You're too young to throw your life away.'

'And you're so much older than me, aren't you?'

Eldritch answered the words, seeming not to notice the undercurrent of feeling – half teasing, half challenging – that ran through Aidan's voice.

'It's not that, it's just…'

He stopped, perhaps sensing he wasn't getting through. When he spoke again his voice was barely more than a whisper.

'What about Gwyn? She'll never know what happened.'

For a second Aidan's composure slipped and a look of intense sorrow passed over his face. He didn't reply immediately but his eyes were suddenly full of a dozen emotions too raw to give voice to. Eldritch watched him, his own expression unfathomable, but if he had anything more to add he let it slip away, unspoken. For a long moment they regarded each other and in that still, bleak silence Aidan knew they were both aware of the pressure building within the boundary, the stray tendrils of energy brushing like tentative, questing fingers over their skin. He shuddered as feelings of greed and loathing and a deep, lusting hunger picked at the edge of his consciousness raising the hackles on the back of his neck and sending a cold and sour sweat trickling down his spine. The understanding of what those sensations meant haunted his voice when he finally spoke.

'When I went to the hospital yesterday I left a card for her, for when she wakes up. I put a letter in with it, just in case. If we don't come back…'

He struggled to find the words. Even now, with the decision made, he couldn't quite bring himself to vocalise it. Instead he shrugged, awkward and one-sided, favouring his ribs.

'She knows the score, she'll understand what happened.'

He dropped his gaze, not wanting Eldritch to read on his face all the things he couldn't bring himself to say out loud.

'She's never going to forgive me for this.'

Aidan looked up and there was a hint of mischief at the corners of his mouth.

'So what's she going to do about it? Kill you?'

Eldritch's expression lurched from shock to disbelief and from there into a kind of bemused appreciation. He wiped his good hand across his mouth, his long fingers smearing sweat, dust and blood into a savage-looking war paint. Beneath it his skin was almost colourless but his eyes were resolute.

'I'm sorry. I didn't want it to end this way.'

Acceptance and an iron strong resolve strengthened his voice.

'Me neither. But look at it this way; if you don't seal that boundary it's not going to matter if I get out of here. One of those things is going to find its way across and Gwyn and I will be the ones who have to deal with the consequences. If you reckon they're stronger than the demon what hope have we got?' There was something close to horror in Aidan's eyes as he contemplated that vision of the future, then he took a deep, shuddering breath and dismissed it. 'Better that we end it here, today,' he said, his voice soft but utterly determined. 'End it properly. I don't want any more like John on my conscience.' Cinnamon and grey eyes locked. 'What do we do?'

'I need you to drop your shields so you're open to me. Don't worry,' Eldritch added, understanding the concern that jerked Aidan's head up and flared wide in his eyes. He did not blame the younger man for his reaction. They both knew there were good reasons to be afraid of doing what he had just suggested.

'I'll put my shields round you first so you'll still be protected. I want you open to me, not to any other influence.'

At his words Aidan's breath whistled out in an exaggerated sigh of relief.

'That's good,' the younger man said. 'I mean, dying's one thing but having my brain eaten by some demon from another dimension... that's not something I want to risk.'

A shaky grin acknowledged the thinness of the joke and said all that was necessary about a situation in which dying could be considered a preferred option.

'So I drop my shields and then you're free to create your link or mind-meld or whatever you call it?'

'Something like that,' Eldritch agreed, 'and don't worry, I haven't eaten anyone's brain in, oh, years. They play havoc with my cholesterol levels.'

The wizard also knew the value of humour in avoiding other, less pleasant emotions and the swift flash of his smile lifted years from his face. Then just as quickly he sobered.

'I'm going to use you as a power source, just as I would use the power stored in a crystal or a gemstone,' he spoke matter-of-factly as he outlined what he planned. 'Draining your power will give me enough to shape the wards and bindings to seal the boundary. The energy of the final strike will activate them, the hole will close and the boundary will be as strong as if it had never been breached. Stronger, even, because I'm going to bring the ceiling down and seal this whole area physically. No one will be able to open it again.'

Aidan shot a quick, calculating glance upwards, the beam of his helmet lamp splashing over the rough-hewn surface of the rock suspended above their heads.

'So it turns out you were right to be worried about a cave-in.'

He did his best not to imagine what would happen when that rock shifted and poured down on them like water. He had often suspected he had too much imagination to be brave. His eyes returned to Eldritch and this time there was no sidestep into humour. The wizard hesitated, his lips quirking as though he was unsure whether what he had to say would help. His voice was almost gentle when he finally spoke.

'Neither of us has to worry about the rockfall Aidan. Our energies will be linked so when I commit to the final strike your life force will be released with mine.' He gave Aidan a small, tight smile. 'I don't know if it will be painless, but I can promise it will be quick.'

Silence closed in in the wake of Eldritch's words. The pair of them stared at each other. *We who are about to die,* thought Aidan. He worried at his lip, feeling he should say something meaningful, should make some clever response, but he could think of nothing. Finally he said, 'It's been nice knowing you Marcus Eldritch. You're not such a bad bloke for an Englishman.'

An appreciative grin chased the fatigue from Eldritch's face.

'You're not so bad yourself, for a pigheaded Welshman.'

For a moment longer they looked at each other.

'Let's do it then.'

Gritting his teeth Eldritch nodded.

'Help me stand up.'

CHAPTER 25

It was, Aidan supposed, a little like blood loss, the feeling that his strength was draining quietly away, flowing out of his body in a slow and inexorable stream, and he could do nothing to stop it, even if he wanted to. As he stood and watched Eldritch shaping the first sweeping sigils of ward and binding he could feel the subtle pull of energy being drawn from him, flowing through the link that tied him to the wizard. At first he simply noted the sensation, still sufficiently curious about what was happening to take interest in such details, but each time Eldritch completed one of those strange, arcane symbols he felt another, stronger pull, like a hook snagging in his flesh and tearing away a piece of him. Each time he was left a little more empty, a little more hollow, and as the emptiness grew a sense of lethargy began to overtake him, seeping into his muscles and tangling his bones in ribbons of frost and lead. A siren voice called to him, soothing and seductive, dulling his senses. It wrapped around him like strong arms, offering comfort, luring him towards the floor. *Sleep,* it whispered and icy fingers dragged at him until only a stubborn sense of duty kept him standing. Pigheaded Welshman indeed, but Aidan would not leave Eldritch to face the last minutes of his life alone in the darkness. If only he weren't so tired.

At his side his right hand twitched, his fingers unconsciously following the symbols the wizard was shaping.

Another sigil completed and set like a glowing talisman upon the surface of the seething dark, another fistful of energy torn from him. Aidan swayed forward as though this time his very flesh was being pulled with it. He staggered a little, fighting to keep his balance and Eldritch paused as though feeling the echo of that strange tearing within his own body but he did not look back. The boundaries between them seemed to blur as, through the link, Aidan sensed the other man gathering himself, pulling together the shards of his own strength, holding them together with little more than willpower and his own brand of stubbornness and pride. Nearing the limits of his own endurance Aidan still had enough awareness left to be awed by the wizard. A few minutes ago he wouldn't have given anything for the man's chances of standing unsupported, let alone being able to perform the complex magic that would seal the boundary. Yet even as he watched Eldritch straightened, raising his hand once more and another sigil began to take shape beneath it. A sense of disorientation swept over Aidan and for a moment it was his hand that was outstretched and his fingers that brushed the air and left traces of phosphor and moonlight in their wake.

With a start Aidan jerked back, his eyes saucering, his heart pounding. He could have sworn… but the hand he raised in front of him was his own once more, though he fancied he could still feel the ghost of ragtag bandages wrapping it from wrist to knuckles. Slowly, almost clumsily, he dragged leaden fingers over his face, trying to focus once more on what Eldritch was doing, but it was getting difficult to follow the wizard's movements in the gloom. Perhaps his lamp battery was dying for surely it was getting darker? Aidan's eyes slid closed and it seemed hardly worth the effort to open them again. His hands and feet were icy cold and a grinding weariness buckled his knees and dragged his body to the floor. It came to him then that he was dying. Strangely the thought no longer held any fear. The demon had been defeated and soon Eldritch would close the boundary, locking it tight against the evil that would otherwise be free to pass through to wreak chaos and havoc on a defenceless world. In his heart Aidan knew he could never have let that happen and though it would cost him and Eldritch their lives it was a price worth paying. *We all die*, he thought hazily, *sooner or later. Perhaps this is a good day for it.* And it came to him that the old wisdom had nothing to do with the date or the time and everything to do with what was accomplished by that death.

This, he realised, was the essence of the Covenant; that someone was willing to lay down their life so that others might live. This was the power that had sealed the beast away for so long. A small smile played over Aidan's lips as his head drooped sideways, his cheek pressing into the soft powdery dust. He relaxed, letting it pillow him. It was becoming hard to breathe, the air in the mine growing soupy and thick until it was a struggle to draw it into his lungs. The last of his energy was draining into the link and through it he was aware of the wizard, feeling him falter as he struggled to hold his strength together. The echo of pain throbbed in the bones of his right wrist and his head exploded with the sudden stab of migraine lancing through the back of his skull. He felt his shoulder muscles cramp and a dozen burning torments where the demon's teeth had carved little crescents from his flesh and he no longer knew whose pain he was feeling. A terrible cold was sweeping through his body. He struggled for breath which would not come.

And then somehow he was no longer in the link but standing a little way off, looking at the scene in front of him with an odd sense of detachment. He recognised the two figures, the one lying crumpled on the floor of the stope, drained of all but the palest flicker of life, the other still standing though the silver-blue flame of his wizardry had sunk to mere embers, smoked and shrouded in the dark, muddy red of pain, but they were not what drew his attention. Instead Aidan found himself staring into the darkness beyond the wizard. Where previously there had been nothing to see now the air seemed in some way tangible and almost alive. It danced and shimmered, rippling as though a curtain hung there, woven out of darkness and sprinkled with a million tiny specks of diamond light. Aidan's breath caught as realised what this had to be. He was seeing the boundary; the veil that existed between the Mortal World and the Unseen Realm. He eyed the strange, glistening expanse of it warily, finding the sight both fascinated and repelled him. For all its unworldly beauty there was something about that expanse of softly folding darkness that he found deeply disturbing as though some part of him knew it was not meant for mortal eyes. Yet that was not the worst thing about the boundary. For there, in the centre of that strange, shifting curtain, just beyond the tips of Eldritch's outstretched fingers, lay horror beyond reckoning.

It's a hole, Aidan told himself frantically, *nothing more than a hole*, but his soul knew differently and his skin crawled as he fought not to back away. It was a hole, indeed, but one that had been torn through the very fabric of reality and there was such a wrongness in its existence that he could barely bring himself to look at it; even glancing at it from the corner of his eye made him sick. How Eldritch could bear to stand so close to it Aidan could not begin to imagine. Nor could he have explained what it was about it that terrified him so but in those formless, shapeless depths lay horror and terror and the condensation of every nightmare he had ever known. Such a thing should not exist. Briefly he closed his eyes, denying the sight of it, but its image seemed carved indelibly onto his retinas. He found himself imagining it spreading; the utter blackness that defied all light, the creeping, almost sentient nature of that un-space – feeling it reaching for him, extending long, slithering pseudopodia of darkness, sliding towards him. With a choked off cry he snapped his eyes open, his heart hammering against his ribs, his breath almost strangled in his throat. The darkness seemed just as it had been mere seconds ago but his skin quivered at its imagined touch. Aidan swallowed queasily. This then was what the demon had ached and hungered for, for all the long years it had been held by the Covenant; a rent in the fabric of the boundary that kept the Mortal World and the Unseen Realm apart. And – *dear God!* He shuddered at the thought of it – this was what Eldritch was going to seal.

It seemed an impossible task and yet seal it he would. For all around that yawning void, woven onto the shimmering fabric of the boundary were the sigils the wizard had created. It was hard to look at them and not see the horror that gaped in their centre but when he did Aidan was once more staggered by what he saw. There were the shapes he had watched Eldritch sketching, but whereas previously their ghostly phosphor images had hung in the air for the briefest of moments before sinking into the dark and vanishing, now he could see them in their entirety, layer upon layer of them as intricate as snowflakes, stitching the veil between the worlds together. For a moment, as he gazed at them, he could forget the horror of the hole ripped through the boundary. Instead he found himself marvelling at their individual beauty and at the pattern they created. They looked so fragile, so delicate, their forms as insubstantial as a lacewing, and yet when they were imbued with power the subtle, shifting energies that linked them would come alive and they would swell and multiply and pull the boundary closed. How he knew this Aidan wasn't sure but know it he did, as well as he knew the moves of a basic kata or the shape of the hills that surrounded his home. Unbidden their names came to him, beautiful and archaic, filling him with an aching melancholy as he heard Eldritch singing them into being with his mind. There were the flowing lines of Keth that brought strength, the strange, spiky angles of Sho for protection and the gap in the pattern that could only be meant for the sweeping curves of Roc whose name promised safety. And mingled with those traditional wards of closing he saw Bel – sanctuary – and Mir – silence. He noticed Jain whose wheeling spiral held eternity and Ahrn, the rune of ending that he knew now had once been traced over the eyes of the dead. There were others there as well and in their shining, shifting shapes he glimpsed a portion of the wizard's intent and in that moment his soul wept.

I can't win against what's out there, Eldritch had said, but he could and would seal the boundary against it, whatever the personal cost of doing so. Yet as he stood and watched the wizard dragging up the strength to complete the binding Aidan cursed the naïvety that had let him believe it would be as easy as Eldritch had said. He should have known the lengths Eldritch would be prepared to go to and now he could see it, could read the story of it in the sigils Eldritch had chosen. Having taken the energy that he, Aidan, could offer and with his own magic spent, the wizard was calling on the only resources left to him. Eldritch was taking the jagged red energies of physical pain, the muddy ashes of exhaustion and the cold, burning rawness of grief long buried and now freshly reawakened and laying them on his spirit like flensing knives. With nothing else to call upon the wizard was tearing his body and soul apart and layering them into the breach.

'Damn you! Why didn't you tell me?' he cried, wanting to reach out and grab hold of those charcoal-clad shoulders as if by doing so he could shake sense into the wizard, as if even now he could offer some measure of comfort. But Eldritch could not hear his disembodied voice and Aidan knew it would have made no difference if he could. His hands dropped impotently to his sides.

'Damn you,' he murmured again, his voice soft, his own shoulders slumping with defeat. In a few minutes it would no longer matter, he told himself, trying to find anger to force back the grief he felt for his friend, he would be dead and so would Eldritch, but he couldn't stop himself wondering how much of Eldritch's spirit would remain, its essence tied inextricably to the sigils, tangled and trapped in their sweeping curves and sharp, savage angles, forever a part of the boundary.

He passed a hand across his eyes, telling himself that it must be sweat that was making them sting.

'Let it go,' he told himself. Eldritch was doing what had to be done and if he needed to remind himself why he had only to look at the horror gaping at the centre of the ring of sigils. Even now the forces the wizard sought to contain were massing behind the boundary. Aidan hoped it was nothing more than his altered perceptions but it seemed to him that the stray energy leaking through the breach was increasing. Surely the half-heard whispers of sound were louder now as though whatever was responsible for those darkly malevolent voices had slipped closer. Partly to take his mind off Eldritch he found himself listening to them, trying to judge how close they were, even as he willed the wizard to hurry up and finish the binding. Did they know – those creatures that Eldritch had said were worse than the demon – that even as they sought to find a way through the boundary a human wizard was trying to repair the breach? Could they sense what Eldritch was doing and, if they could, what might they do to try and stop him? Before he could so much as question the wisdom of such thoughts Aidan felt the energies behind the boundary shift as if something there had felt the touch of his mind and reacted to it. There could be no possible breath of wind, no stray draught here in the stope, yet for a second he would have sworn the air around him stirred, brushing like invisible fingers across his skin, reaching out, feeling for him. He froze, his mind crawling with horror as something from within the darkness regarded him.

It's okay, they can't get you. They can't get through your shields.

Yet even as he repeated it to himself, over and over again like a mantra, still he thought he could feel those slithering tentacles of consciousness reaching out for him, their oily ropes of thought seeking to wrap themselves around his mind. There were words there, in the darkness, sliding across his consciousness, probing, testing. Panting with fear Aidan willed himself not to hear them as they caressed him with promises of things he had never before wanted, sly and needling, yet sweet as honey-laced strychnine, seductive and seducing.

Eldritch will stop them. They can't come through once he's sealed the boundary.

But the voices in the darkness told him that the wizard was going to fail.

Lies!

Aidan almost shouted it aloud, yet as he spun to look at the wizard his heart sank. The voices might have been premature in their claim yet Eldritch was plainly faltering. Under the long, outstretched fingers Aidan could see the fragile, spun-glass shape of Roc, the last sigil of the binding, shimmering and struggling to form. Eldritch's whole body shook with effort and the ragged draw of his breath sounded loud in the stillness and laced with despair.

For a moment Aidan watched, feeling the wizard's desperate struggle as though it were taking place in his own body. Surely there was something more he could do, something more he could give? He looked from Eldritch to his own supine body. The link between them pulsed feebly, like a dying heartbeat, but no energy flowed along it. Eldritch had taken all Aidan could offer. All that would flow along it now would be the final spark of life force released as Aidan died. And understanding that Aidan knew what he had to do. With a sense of calm inevitability he looked down at his chest and studied the gleaming strand he had known he would find there. The thread was as fine as spider silk and palely luminous, more as though it had been spun from moonlight than from silver, despite what myth and legend might have had him believe. His heartbeat

379

quickened as he followed it with his eyes, tracing it back to that still form on the stope floor. He knew exactly what the thread was. He could only hope he guessed right in what would happen when he broke it. Hesitantly he licked his lips. The strand was as fine as gossamer. It seemed he should be able to take it in his hands and snap it as easily as taking his next breath. Carefully he lifted his hands towards it. There was no panic, no fear driving him, just a last, desperate prayer that this would work.

'Don't do it, boy.'

It seemed to Aidan that he had been aware of the presence beside him for some time; that the man who stood watching him, even as he himself watched Eldritch sealing the boundary, had in some strange, indefinable way always been there, watching and waiting for this moment. He remembered the figure he had glimpsed in the tunnels, caught at the very edge of his torch beam, and the voice he had heard in his head the night he and Eldritch had fought the avatar. Slowly he turned knowing already what he would see. He found himself looking into a face that, though it was more different than alike, still somehow reminded him of his own. The eyes were the same, he thought; a light hazel flecked with green and gold. Right now they glittered with a kind of righteous indignation that Aidan could not understand. Even as he puzzled over that the other man spoke again.

'Do you think he's worth it? Do you think any of them are worth it?'

The voice was sharp, at once both angry and contemptuous, and Aidan could not tell if those emotions were directed at him or Eldritch or the undefined "them".

'They're not. Not one of them is worth you throwing your life away.'

'William?'

Ghostly apparition, trapped spirit or simply one of Eldritch's psychic echoes, Aidan knew of no one else this could be, yet the resentment radiating from the other man threw him. He couldn't reconcile it with his perception of the quiet hero who had given his life to imprison the demon. Confusion made him hesitate over the name, the syllables suddenly heavy on his tongue as if some part of him would resist tying his ancestor to this embittered stranger. For a moment they stared at each other and in the sharp and sudden silence Aidan thought he saw something shift in the back of those amber eyes. But it wasn't the softening he might have hoped for. He felt certain that William must know who he was but there was no acknowledgement of kinship there, not even the recognition of shared purpose. If anything William's expression seemed to become more hostile until Aidan wondered if he had been naïve to think that the presence of his wizardly ancestor could possibly be a good thing.

It was William who broke the contact, abruptly turning away from Aidan to stare at Eldritch, glowering at the wizard as he pulled the last painful strands of magic together to finish the binding. Aidan half expected the Englishman to react to that scrutiny, so intent was William's focus, yet Eldritch continued his work, seemingly unaware of his disembodied audience and the fierce gaze drilling into the back of his head. His attention was focussed so completely on the spell he was weaving that nothing would have distracted him. Silently Aidan urged his friend on, sending his encouragement to that lone, struggling figure. Sharp words, spat into his face, jerked him back.

'Are you afraid of me, boy?'

William had barely seemed to move and yet suddenly he was pushing up against Aidan, his face so close that for a second Aidan could have sworn he felt the other's breath on his cheek. His first instinct was indeed to back away, to put a safe distance between himself and his unnerving, and just possibly unhinged, companion; his second was to push William back. Gritting his teeth he did neither. "Don't pick fights with drunks or madmen", was one of Sensei's oft-quoted rules for a long life, but it was something else that made him hold his ground, stubbornly staring into those angry eyes. Was he afraid? He wanted to say no but his heart was hammering too hard against his ribs for that to be the truth and somewhere deep inside he understood that William would know if he were lying. What that mercurial character would do then he could only guess but he knew that only the truth would do. Even so it surprised him to hear himself say, 'I don't know. Maybe.'

Unnerved perhaps; that he would admit to. Still there was no discernable reaction from William. Aidan scowled, the corners of his mouth kinking down as he shrugged defensively.

'A little,' he added grudgingly, the words as sour in his mouth as if they had been drawn from him by torture.

'You should be.' Finally William nodded. He sounded slightly mollified as though Aidan's confession had appeased him. 'I have power you can only dream of.'

His heart might be racing but Aidan decided he was now more annoyed than frightened. He and Eldritch had a job to do. One, he reminded himself, that was going to kill the pair of them. He could do without the wizardly posturing and grandiose threats, especially from a man who should by rights be only too ready to help them. William had done so before, hadn't he? Or had all that been in his imagination? Indeed, this whole episode might be nothing more than some bizarre fever dream, conjured up by his dying brain cells gradually succumbing to anoxia, as his breath slowed and stilled and finally ebbed away.

'I know what a wizard can do,' he said. His voice held neither fear nor anger, just a simple statement of fact.

'Do you boy? Do you really? I wonder.'

Aidan shook his head, baffled. William's eyes glittered, almost feral in the darkness. He could feel the anger bubbling under the other's words but it made no sense to him – unless this really was all happening inside his head.

'I don't understand.'

'That's because you don't know what you're doing!'

The words burst from William in a torrent and this time there was no mistaking where that seethe of emotion was directed though Aidan couldn't comprehend what he had done to earn it. William didn't give him a chance to ask.

'They're not worth it. Not one of them. Why should you throw your life away to save them, boy? Keep your shields up and the beasts can't touch you. You'll be safe and to hell with the rest of them. If I had my time again I'd let the demon take them.'

And finally William's words made sense though Aidan couldn't match them with the man who had sacrificed himself to save his village and his workmates. The cynicism embodied in that short, vicious speech shocked him yet what he felt most was an overwhelming sense of sadness.

'What about Sarah?'

The words came before he could stop them. The memory of that final parting flooded over Aidan, the pain of it as real as if he had lived through it himself; the feel of her cold, thin fingers pressed against his, the smell of her hair and the taste of her skin. All those things he remembered and over them all, stronger than any of them lay the almost unbearable longing to remain there, to turn his back on what had to be done and stay.

'You loved her,' he said hesitantly for it seemed strange to be speaking of love to the ghost of a man who had been dead for a hundred years and then too "love" seemed too small a word for the depth of emotion he had sensed there. Fleetingly he wondered what it must be like to feel so strongly for another and in the next instant realised that it did not matter. He would never have the opportunity. Carefully he put the thought aside.

'You loved her and yet you still sacrificed yourself to stop the demon.'

How could a man who had done that mean the things he was saying now?

'They reviled me.'

The accusation was spat like venom over the top of Aidan's words, cutting off what he was struggling to convey as though William were aware of his thoughts and sought to crush them.

'They cursed my name for what I did that day. I saved them all and not one of them cared.'

Aidan flinched as a lash of hate that was close to madness curled round him. He remembered light on amber glass, the smoky sweetness of Beethoven and the churn of anger in his gut as he read Edward Evans' incriminating account of the mine disaster. How could he defend the behaviour of such people to the man whose very memory they had despised? Then he saw in his mind another hand, thin and strong as Sarah's but still and pale as death against the hospital sheets, and he knew he had to try.

'They didn't understand what you had done. How could they? None of them knew what was down here. None of them knew what would have happened if you hadn't stopped it. They didn't know anything about the demon but they knew their sons and fathers and brothers died when that roof came down on them and they thought that you were responsible. It must have been easier for them to believe that than to accept the real reason for what happened.'

Watching William as he spoke, Aidan thought he saw a slight softening in the hard lines around his mouth, the faintest of questions shadowing those fierce and glittering eyes and he thought he had reached through the bitterness and anger to the man underneath. Softy he added, 'Sarah understood.'

He realised it was the wrong thing to say even as he said it. Something seemed to shut off in William's eyes. His whole body stiffened and his expression turned glacial.

'You think that makes it better, that she understood what was happening, that she knew what I was going to have to do? Well, it doesn't. She understood alright. The problem was she just didn't care. Not when it came down to it.'

As if he read the disbelief in Aidan's face William turned on him.

'Why didn't you know about the Covenant, boy? Something like that you should have known about before you could walk but your parents never told you, did they? No!'

William answered his own question, the one word spat out like a curse.

'You didn't know because she didn't care enough to pass that knowledge on. The others might not have believed her but she knew what happened. She knew! She could have spoken up. She should have done, damn her, but even if she didn't have the courage for that at the very least she should have told our child about the Covenant.'

The miner whirled, turning away to the darkness but not before Aidan saw the grief contorting his features. His next words were little more than a whisper of breath, as though he spoke only to himself, defeated, bitter and betrayed.

'She promised. I held her in my arms that last morning and she promised me. But she never told our child, never told him why it had to be done.'

Silence flowed back in the wake of William's words. Though he wanted desperately to say something Aidan could think of nothing that might offer comfort in the face of such hurt. Indeed he wasn't sure that the words existed that could counter what William had just revealed. How could she have done that? He tore his gaze from William's turned back, staring out into the darkness of the stope, this ancient place, deep in the bones of the earth, where William had given his life. In the depths of his own mind he could feel the link to Eldritch and was aware of his friend shaping the final passes that completed the wards of binding. Soon it would all be over and yet all he could think of was Sarah and that act of betrayal. She had loved William, he was sure of it, her grief at their parting had been every bit as real as William's. And like him, even as she grieved, she had known and accepted the necessity of what he had been about to do. How then could she have turned her back on his memory to the extent that she never even told their child the truth about its father?

But was that what had happened? Doubt wormed its way through Aidan's mind. It might be what the evidence suggested but the memory of that parting, of the tears she had shed, stopped him. *I'll love you 'til the day I die;* she had said and nothing he knew would convince him she had been lying. He turned back to William, wondering if he had the right to say what he was about to but the thought of his great-grandmother — something inside him gave a little lurch as he made that connection — firmed his resolve. William wasn't the only one who deserved the truth.

'My father…'

Aidan hesitated. That was how he referred to James Morgan, the term being an ironic acknowledgement of their relationship, rather than one of respect and never of love. It seemed inappropriate for the man he knew as nothing more than a smiling face in an old newspaper clipping, yellow with age.

'I mean your grandson, the third William Wynn-Jones…' A thought struck him, 'Did you know she called your child William and his son was called William too? I'd have been a William if Mum had had her way but James — her husband — wouldn't agree to it. Her William died before he could have a say in the matter. He may never even have known she was pregnant.'

Was William taking any of this in? There was no movement in the turned back, no lessening of the tension that radiated from it. Aidan carried on regardless.

'So no, I don't know if he knew the truth about you and the Covenant because he never had the chance to tell me. But someone knew. I found the note that they'd left in a Bible along with the clipping about William's death. Whoever wrote that knew you'd sacrificed yourself. They were scared that the Covenant had been broken and what would happen as a result. That was how we found out about it – about the Covenant – me and Gwyn and Eldritch. We pieced it together. Now Gwyn's in hospital – the demon nearly killed her – but Eldritch and I came. Eldritch used all his power to destroy the demon but we're not going to leave the boundary open. We'll both die to seal it and stop anything else coming through.'

Aidan stopped, wondering if William had listened to a word he had said. He could feel the miner's sullen anger seething around him. He hadn't meant to say those final things about what he and Eldritch were about to do but somehow they had come out and if William took them as a boast or a challenge he no longer cared. Finally he was too tired to try to win round that capricious spirit. Instead he felt his own anger building up within him.

'We're leaving loved ones behind as well, you know. Friends and family. I've a girlfriend – Jane. Perhaps what's between us isn't as strong as what you and Sarah had. Perhaps it was never going to be. It's not like we'll have the chance to find out now. But still this has to be done. Eldritch doesn't even come from the valley but he's still willing to give his life to save the people here. That's what it means to him to be a wizard, to be there to protect the people who don't have the power to protect themselves. It's what he does. It's what he is.'

Can't you do anything to help him? But he did not say it. He might have asked that once but he no longer had any such expectation of William.

'Then he's a fool.'

In William's voice Aidan heard the bitterness of all that had been denied him; all the years of life, the miracle of holding his newborn child and the pleasure of watching that boy grow to a man and raise a child of his own. But these were things that neither he nor Eldritch would have the chance to do either.

'Then he and I are both fools.'

The words came out before Aidan could stop them, wearily defiant. Out of the corner of his eye he saw Eldritch lower his hands and he knew that the binding was finally done. For a moment the wizard swayed, exhausted, depleted and Aidan wondered if he would collapse where he stood but finally the dark head lifted and he looked around him, barely seeming to know what he was doing. Slowly he turned to the figure slumped on the floor behind him and a look of sorrow sharpened the angles of his face.

'So he'll murder you to meet his own obsession.'

Aidan jerked at the sound of William's voice. The miner was staring at the wizard and there was madness and mayhem in every line of his body. Aidan was suddenly very scared of what he might do.

'No!'

Without thinking he reached out, grabbing hold of William's arm, surprised at how solid that contact felt, how warm the suggestion of flesh was under his hand.

'He wanted me to leave. He even tried to trick me into going, but I knew there was something wrong. He didn't have the energy left to ensure the boundary was completely closed.

Using my energy with his was the only way to make sure it was properly closed, but that wasn't his suggestion; it was mine. It was my choice. No one forced me into this. Call me a fool if you want to, but I believe in what we're doing.'

For an instant he locked eyes with William and then deliberately he turned back to watch Eldritch, daring the elder wizard to make a move against him.

Across the stope Eldritch staggered to where Aidan's body lay and knelt clumsily by the still form, his left hand reaching out to touch the younger man's shoulder. His right, wrapped in its ratty mess of bandages, hung at his side.

'I'm sorry Aidan.' The deep voice was husky with pain and exhaustion, the wizard sounding as though it hurt even to speak. 'It won't be much longer.'

Aidan looked at his battered friend with affection. He turned to William and the anger that had blazed in his eyes a moment before softened, changing into something that was gentler and somehow rather sad.

'Maybe I am a fool for that. Or maybe I'm living up to the memory of what my great-grandfather did.'

Through the link he felt Eldritch gathering himself, the wizard reaching deep within to where he would sever the links between flesh and soul. In a strange duality of consciousness Aidan was aware of gritty dust under his face even as his disembodied self stood watching that final tableau. Blackness reached for him as energy poured through the link. He felt Eldritch's consciousness tangling around his own and he was sucked into spiralling darkness.

CHAPTER 26

Aidan coughed feebly. The air around him seemed to consist of nothing but dust. He could taste it, smell it, feel the fine grit of it raw in his throat, half choking him as he breathed in. He coughed again, trying unsuccessfully to clear it from his lungs and managed to do little more than send pain lancing through his chest. If this was the afterlife, he thought hazily, it had little to recommend it. But at least he wasn't alone. Someone was moving beside him, fumbling in the dark. A hand brushed his arm, fell away, then reconnected and latched, long fingers tangling in his sleeve and gripping it like a drowning man clinging to a lifebelt.

'Aidan?'

Scratchy and almost unrecognisable a voice rasped his name and despite the weary weight of exhaustion Aidan felt his heart lift. Dead he might be but he had company and there was only one man it could be. He groaned a response as he rolled over and spat dust from his mouth. The whole world seemed to be coated in the wretched stuff.

'Are you alright?'

'Give me a minute.' He clutched his ribs protectively as he dragged himself to his knees, fighting against the renewed need to cough, afraid that if he gave into it this time it would rip his chest apart. 'Urgh!' He tried unsuccessfully to work up enough saliva to spit again. 'Yeah. You?'

'I think so.' There was a moment's hesitation and then Eldritch's disembodied voice added plaintively, 'I can't see a damn thing.'

Hidden by the darkness Aidan grinned, though not unsympathetically. After all they had been through he wasn't sure he would ever feel completely happy in the dark again, either.

'Just a moment.'

He fumbled for the switch on his helmet lamp and breathed his own sigh of relief when the light came back on, dim and murky but light none the less. He swiped a hand over the lens and the light brightened slightly though the air around them was a thick haze. Dust, noted Aidan, resignedly. So where the hell were they? For a moment he wondered just how much he wanted to know. Maybe he should lie back down for a while and worry about that later, but curiosity won over tiredness and he straightened up, bracing his hands on his knees as he looked around him. Not that there was much to see. Through the murk he could just make out hewn rock walls on either side while to the front a slope of fallen rock blocked the way from floor to ceiling, a height of less than six feet he estimated. They were no longer in the stope, a quick, panicky glance behind him showed the walls running back into the dust-clogged darkness. A proper tunnel then, rather than a pocket in the stope wall. *Thank God for that...* He swallowed down the lump that had risen in his throat and offered up a very genuine prayer of gratitude. As his heartbeat slowed to normal he turned back to where Eldritch – a grey shadow in a world of grey – was also examining the rockfall.

'You did it then.' Aidan's voice rasped uncomfortably but

the sound reassured him that he really was alive. He gestured at the cascade of broken stone. 'You brought the ceiling down.'

'I… I don't know.'

Eldritch eyed the rubble dubiously as though, despite all evidence to the contrary he rather doubted its existence. Like Aidan he was covered in fine, powdery dust. 'I suppose I must have done but if that's the case why aren't we dead?'

'It did work, didn't it?'

Eldritch nodded, understanding that Aidan wasn't asking about the rockfall.

'Oh yes. The boundary's closed. You can feel it.'

Perhaps "you can't feel it" would have been a more accurate way of putting it. Aidan realised that the zinging feeling along his nerves had gone. He tried reaching for it but there was nothing there and it wasn't because he was shielding; he simply didn't have the power left to do so. How had Gwyn put it – "Not enough power to shield a small rodent" – he groaned softly, knowing now just what she had meant.

Beside him Eldritch had stopped eyeing up the puzzle of the rockfall and was looking around him, assessing their surroundings much as he had just done.

'This is one of the tunnels, isn't it?'

Following Aidan's example he had turned his helmet lamp back on and the light bounced off the fog of dust particles, an eerie glimmer in the darkness. 'So how did we get here?'

'You really didn't do this?'

Aidan had thought it must have been some trick that the wizard had pulled off but Eldritch shook his head, his brows lowering in a look of genuine puzzlement.

'No. Well, not that I know of,' he amended. His eyes closed

as he considered the possibility, fighting to dredge up some meaningful insight from his memory. After a moment he began to speak, his voice strangely flat as if describing a film running through his head.

'I started setting the seals on the boundary. You passed out about halfway through. I carried on, finished the binding and I was just about to release the final strike and then…' The wizard stopped, baffled. 'Something happened.'

Again the pause as Eldritch searched through memories hazy with pain and exhaustion.

'There was a surge of energy through the link. I felt it sweeping through me, like touching wild magic, and I thought that was it, that was the final strike, but then…' He looked around him once more, gesturing helplessly with his good arm. 'Then we both wake up here.'

'You couldn't have released the final strike and we both somehow survived it?'

Eldritch shook his head sending dust particles dancing.

'A final strike's not like that. It's the conscious release of all the energy – all the life force – from the body. By definition it's not something you *can* live through.'

'And yet somehow we did.'

'Even if that were possible why aren't you unconscious? I drained your energy to the point where you passed out. There's no way you should just wake up after that.'

Aidan glared at the fallen rock wall as though he held it personally responsible for the mystery.

'Well, something must have generated the energy you felt. It wasn't me and it certainly wasn't you.'

How could it have been when Eldritch had been forced to

resort to the dark energies of pain and grief simply to complete the binding. Even as the thought came Aidan wondered how he knew that. As if in answer he had a sudden memory that surely couldn't be real of standing and watching the wizard spinning strange and haunting shapes from quicksilver and starlight. And there beside him... no! His eyes went wide in the darkness. Surely not! But he knew it was the only possible answer.

'It was William,' he said softly, his voice fading away in wonder. From the corner of his eye he caught Eldritch's confused look but ignored it. He opened his mouth to speak and then stopped, not yet ready to talk about such things; not here, not now.

'I'll explain later. Right now I think we should get out of here.'

Wearily he straightened up, bracing himself on the hewn rock, and then stopped as an awful thought struck him.

'I hope to God he put us in the right tunnel.'

'Oh Christ!'

Like the start of a prayer for deliverance Eldritch's words echoed back from the dripping walls as his torch beam glinted on the metal rungs of the caving ladder disappearing up into the column of darkness that was Number Two shaft. *Well*, thought Aidan, coming to stand beside him, *at least that settles whether or not we're in the right tunnel*. Eldritch turned to him, his eyes haunted.

'I'd forgotten about this bit.'

Aidan hadn't. He had been thinking about it all along the half mile of passageway, wondering how he himself was going to find the strength to manage the climb, let alone how he was going to get Eldritch up it. Under any other circumstances he wouldn't have allowed either of them try it but as the only way out of the mine was up that ladder there really was no other choice.

'I don't think I can climb that.'

Though Eldritch tried to keep the defeat from his voice Aidan read it in the slump of his shoulders and the way his left hand tightened convulsively where it held his injured arm tucked against his chest. The wizard's eyes were fixed on the floor as he spoke. After that first horrified glance up into the darkness he had avoided looking at the ladder and in the pale glow of the helmet lamps Aidan could see that he was trembling with exhaustion. The practicalities of the climb would remain a moot point unless he could convince Eldritch it was possible and that, Aidan conceded, might be the hardest task of all.

'It's not a race. We're going to take this slow and steady.'

Aidan checked the rope knotted to Eldritch's harness and then checked it again for good measure. One final time he laid out how they were to tackle the climb focussing on keeping his voice calm and above all confident.

'You're going to reach up with your good hand, get hold of the rung above your head and then you climb two, maybe three rungs until that hand's level with your chest. Then you let go and grab the next rung above your head.'

Holding the wizard's gaze with his own he nodded, willing the other man to agree with him.

Believe me. You can do this.

'You climb a ladder with your legs, not by hauling yourself

up with your arms so all your hand is doing is steadying you. It's your legs that are doing all the work. I'll be holding you in tight on the safety rope so whatever you think you can't fall off the ladder when you let go to move your hand to the next rung.'

Eldritch closed his eyes and swallowed convulsively. He looked pale and shaky and though he nodded when Aidan asked if he was alright Aidan knew he was lying.

'Think of it this way; there's…' He did a quick calculation in his head, 'About one hundred and fifty rungs—'

'One hundred and forty-three to the point where the shaft intersects with the tunnel,' Eldritch corrected him, his voice absolutely neutral. Aidan grinned.

'Like I said, about one hundred and fifty rungs. You move up three rungs each time so you only have to do this fifty times. It's not that hard. All you have to do is keep moving up the ladder. Fifty times; that's all it takes. I know you can do that.'

'Yeah,' Eldritch's answer was little more than a huff of breath as though he barely had the energy to respond, let alone climb one hundred and fifty feet through the dark one-handed. Aidan squeezed his shoulder and put every ounce of reassurance he could muster into his voice.

'Of course you can. Okay, I'm going up. When I'm at the top I'll give two pulls on the rope to let you know I'm ready. You do the same back and I'll take up the slack and you can start climbing.' He caught the wizard's eye. 'Fifty times. You can do it.'

'Simple,' murmured Eldritch.

'You're doing fine. One more and you're half way!'

In the years that he and Matt had run Red Kite Adventure

Training Aidan had helped more people than he cared to think about clamber up – and indeed down – cliffs, across rope walks and Tarzan swings and over, under or around any number of seemingly – to them – insurmountable obstacles. From overweight executives with wobbly thighs and beer bellies to desk-bound computer nerds who looked as though they had never seen daylight and would break in half if pushed, he had a way of encouraging them so that somehow, almost without their realising, they overcame their fears and perceived limitations and achieved what they had previously thought was impossible. Many of them considered what he did close to miraculous but Aidan knew that a big part of that success was down to being very good at judging just how big a challenge someone was capable of tackling. As he watched and sweated over Eldritch's progress up the ladder, waiting for the first firefly glimmer of his helmet lamp in the darkness and willing his friend closer, he was painfully conscious that this time he had no control over the challenge that had been set. Nor would there be any way of helping if Eldritch did get into trouble. The safety rope would keep the wizard from falling but he didn't have the strength to haul him up with it. Rarely had he felt so helpless. All he could do was to keep up the stream of encouragement and hope that Eldritch was listening to him. 'That's it. You're over two thirds now. Not much further. Just keep going.' And when Eldritch's strength gave out and it was only sheer stubbornness that kept him clinging to the ladder, he did the only thing he could.

'Don't you dare give up on me, you coward!' Aidan roared, choking back fear and forcing anger into his voice instead. 'Do you hear me? If you've got a death wish you come up here and tell me about it. I'm not having you giving up just because you think you're tired. Call yourself a wizard? You're pathetic! I've seen five-year-olds with more guts than you.'

In a voice pitched to cut across hillsides he kept up the tirade, hurling abuse and curses until Eldritch's face appeared directly below him, ashen and sweating, his eyes closed except for a thin bar of white at the bottom of the lids, and his good hand locked convulsively around the final rung of the ladder. Aidan seized it and, clamping his teeth against the howl of protest from his ribs, dragged the wizard almost bodily over the lip of the shaft.

For some time Eldritch lay unmoving, stretched out on the cold, damp stone like a corpse on a slab, his feet still hanging out over the abyss. When he could breathe again without flinching Aidan shuffled himself over and began working on the wizard's shoulders, rolling and kneading the rigid flesh as best he could until eventually the fine trembling that coursed through Eldritch's body began to ease and he stirred enough to raise his head.

'You bastard!' He coughed weekly, like a man trying to find sufficient energy to throw up. 'You utter bastard!' With his good arm he somehow managed to lever himself onto his side and from there rolled onto his back. He looked up at Aidan in the yellow wash of torchlight. 'Thanks.'

The next stage was both easier and much, much worse; easier because at least there was no vertical ascent, just a long, almost imperceptible slope to keep climbing; but worse because the two of them were utterly spent. Even the ankle-deep water in the wet section seemed to suck at their feet as though it was five times as deep and they were having to wade through it.

'We're doing fine.'

It was a mantra grated out through clenched teeth, a charm whispered against limbs that were weighted with exhaustion and pain.

'Fine?' A panting breath added punctuation. 'We're bloody marvellous.'

On the far side of the water Aidan's foot caught on a rough piece of the tunnel floor and he staggered. Too tired to compensate he came down flat-footed and the impact jarred through his ribs like a knife. He would have gone down but someone – it must have been Eldritch; there was no one else there – hauled him upright and kept him there. God alone knew how. He could feel the arm under his trembling with the effort and knew if he didn't get his legs solidly underneath him he would bring them both down. There was no question in his mind that if that happened they would lie there 'til they rotted. *Go on boy. You can do it.* He wasn't sure if the quiet voice inside his head was real or only in his imagination but he felt the smallest surge of energy flow through him, whether from that presence or from some unguessed at reserve. Gritting his teeth he pushed himself upright. Then it was he who was steadying Eldritch. For a moment the two of them stood swaying, leaning on each other like a pair of drunks on a Saturday night bender.

'Come on. We're getting out of here.'

By the time Aidan realised that the faint glow outlining the stones ahead of them wasn't solely down to his helmet lamp he wasn't sure who was supporting who. Perhaps they took it in turns. Aidan could never remember. One thing he was certain of; neither of them would have made it without the other. He was stumbling blindly and Eldritch's feet were barely tracking as they dragged each other forward. He could feel the spastic trembling of muscles pushed to the limit of endurance but he couldn't have said whether the shaking was in his body or Eldritch's. In the end it scarcely mattered. There was daylight up ahead – they had made it. He would have sworn Eldritch was barely conscious but the arm draped around his shoulders tightened briefly.

'Is that what I think it is?'

Hope brightened the hoarse whisper and Aidan felt the wizard straighten slightly as if drawing strength from that dim glow. He felt a similar lift in his own spirits. Like two tattered moths, drawn onward by the light, together they staggered the final few feet towards the promise of freedom.

CHAPTER 27

The afternoon was damp and grey, a thin, half-hearted drizzle falling from a sky the colour of cinders. Lying flat on his back, with the spatter of rain dampening his face, Aidan decided he had never seen or felt anything so delightful. If he had had the energy he would have got to his feet and danced. As it was he wondered if he would ever have the strength to move again. It took a concerted effort just to turn his head to look at the silent form stretched out beside him. It wasn't an inspiring sight. Marcus Eldritch looked very much like he felt. With his long limbs sprawled haphazardly the tall man looked less like a demon-slaying wizard and more like a recently deceased corpse. Seen in daylight the only colour in his dust-smeared face was the mottled blue and purple bruising spreading through the stubble on the side of his jaw and the clotted scarlet of a demon bite that stood out as livid as a brand on his cheek. Aidan winced at the sight of that particular memento of their day's work. When it healed Eldritch was going to have another scar to add to his collection. Fleetingly Aidan wondered just what adjective Gwyn would choose to describe it. The thought brought an amused huff of breath followed swiftly by a wave of sympathy for his comatose friend. They would both have some explaining to do when they saw Gwyn again. Somehow the idea seemed rather comforting.

As if feeling the weight of Aidan's gaze Eldritch cracked one eye open and regarded the younger man.

'If anyone had told me I'd be pleased to be lying in the mud in the pouring rain...' he began, lifting his head slightly as if he were luxuriating in the caress of moving air and the fresh smell of rain and mountains. In other circumstances Aidan would have delighted in taking Eldritch to task for describing a little drizzle as pouring rain, a distinction that surely even a dull-witted city slicker should be able to understand. Now he simply nodded his agreement.

'You okay?'

The city slicker thought about this for a while.

'I feel like I've been run over by a steamroller,' he conceded. 'But so long as you don't expect me to actually do anything for a few hours, yes I'm okay.' He shifted his shoulders fractionally, a soft grunt of effort accompanying the movement as he settled himself a little more comfortably on the stony ground. 'Feels good, doesn't it?'

The twitch of his fingers encompassed the open space around them before they folded back onto his chest. Slowly his eyes slid shut.

'Good?' Aidan retorted. He grinned and threw an earlier response back at the wizard. 'It feels bloody marvellous.'

Eldritch laughed softly at this but didn't open his eyes. For a while there was no sound save the brittle whispering of the wind stirring the grasses that clung to the pit edge, twenty feet above their heads. Finally Aidan cleared his throat.

'You know that bit about not doing anything for an hour or two? We do still have to get out of here so don't go falling asleep on me just yet.'

He wasn't sure the wizard had heard him but after a moment Eldritch turned his head and regarded Aidan balefully.

'Can't you just leave me here and come back for me later?'

'It's tempting.'

So was the idea of staying where he was for a few more minutes. Aidan found himself smothering a yawn at the very thought. He knew he would soon be asleep if he did.

'But once I get home I'm planning on doing nothing more strenuous this evening than hitting the Unicorn for a pint.' *And maybe not even that.* He would take Sula for a walk to make up for leaving her shut in the garden all day and he'd ring the hospital to get the latest news on Gwyn. Then he'd call Jane and find out how the conference was going. He smiled to himself. It would be good to talk to her without having to skirt around what he and Gwyn and Eldritch were doing. But after that he might just settle for a long bath and then bed. With a start he realised his eyes had closed and he had been starting to drift. Shaking his head in a vain attempt to clear it Aidan forced himself to sit up.

'Given the choice between the Unicorn and coming back up here to retrieve your scrawny carcass, well, it's just not going to happen. Sorry. I promise you can sleep all you like when we get back to the car.'

'If it weren't for having to explain it to Gwyn I'd turn you into a frog,' Eldritch muttered. He scowled grumpily, like a teenager told he has to get out of bed, but when Aidan showed no sign of relenting he sighed and extended his good arm.

'Give me a hand up and then you can tell me how I'm going to climb a rope one-handed.'

'You'll be surprised,' promised Aidan as he helped the wizard to his feet. For a moment Eldritch said nothing but he eyed the far wall of the pit with a puzzled expression.

'I'm going to be bloody amazed, Aidan. The rope's not there.'

'Perhaps you should have tied it better,' Eldritch suggested dryly, nudging the loose tangle of climbing rope with his foot. He leaned against the pit wall and folded his arms across his chest, managing to project a thin air of disappointment with the world. While deep down Aidan knew the wizard was trying to disguise the fact that he barely had the energy to stand, still the supercilious tone riled him. He was bitterly tired too and he wasn't about to accept that this final misfortune was anything to do with him.

'I did tie it better,' he snarled, thrusting the end of the rope towards Eldritch so he could see for himself. 'Someone cut it.'

Eldritch snorted, a sound that could as easily have been derision as agreement.

'Griff.' His mouth twisted as if the name left an unpleasant taste behind. 'It must have been.' He tilted his head back against the slate and stared up at the grey sky. 'After everything else that's happened I should have guessed the demon would have had one final trick up its sleeve.'

Aidan shook his head, unconvinced.

'But why would the demon have persuaded him to cut the rope?'

'To make sure we couldn't get out?'

The sarcasm in Eldritch's tone suggested this should have been obvious. Aidan bridled.

'And exactly how was he going to get out, then?' he retorted caustically. A bitter mix of exhaustion, anger and frustration roiled in the pit of his stomach and the urge to lash out at something, just to relieve that tension, was very strong. 'For that matter, how did he get down here if he cut the rope?'

'I imagine he hung from the edge and dropped.' Eldritch twisted round, craning his neck to look up at the pit rim. 'At full stretch he'd knock at least eight feet off the drop. Once you do that it's not so far. As for getting out again, perhaps the demon was planning on using magic to rejoin the rope.'

Aidan had opened his mouth to argue, more out of principle than anything else, but at the wizard's words he shut it again. He glowered at Eldritch, his expression torn between reluctant curiosity and angry disbelief. Finally curiosity won.

'Is that possible?' he asked grudgingly. He gazed up at the pit edge as though he could see beyond the windswept grass to where the remainder of the rope presumably still hung from the ground anchor.

'Oh yes. It takes a fair bit of power but technically it's not that difficult.'

'So you can do it, then?'

'Aidan, right now I don't have the energy left to tie the damned thing in a knot.' The wizard's shoulders twitched in a small, rueful shrug as Aidan swore. 'I'm sorry.'

Aidan glared at him for a moment and then shook his head tiredly.

'No, it's not your fault.' He had the grace to look apologetic. Then, realising he was still holding the now useless rope, he flung it down in frustration. 'Damn him!'

'I think he managed that all on his own,' Eldritch said quietly.

Aidan's mouth thinned, either in agreement or annoyance, but he made no comment. Instead he asked, 'So what options do we have?'

Maybe there was something that the wizard could do.

'I've got my phone. Can't we call someone to come and get us out?'

Left-handed and awkward Eldritch fumbled with the inside pocket of his jacket.

'Don't bother. You won't get a signal up here.'

Aidan pulled his own mobile out and showed the display to Eldritch. Then he waited with thinly veiled impatience as Eldritch stubbornly withdrew his own phone and checked it. He didn't bother asking the result; Eldritch's growl of frustration told him all he needed to know. The words "I told you so" burned on his lips but with surprising restraint he bit them back. Addressing no one in particular he said, 'You wouldn't believe the number of idiots we pull off these hills who think that all they need in an emergency is a mobile phone so they can call for help. It comes as quite a shock to them when they find there's no network coverage. Sadly it doesn't help us either.'

He kicked half-heartedly at a clump of mud and grass.

'The stupid thing is that normally I could climb something like this in my sleep.'

And there it was; the thing that was galling him most – admitting that he wasn't up to a simple free climb. It was no more than twenty feet, it should have been easy. But not in his current state. He half turned, bracing himself for Eldritch's sarcastic response. The wizard had every right to vent his feelings. Aidan knew he had let them both down.

'You're joking.'

There was neither scorn nor sarcasm in the wizard's tone. If anything he sounded amazed. Aidan glanced at him suspiciously, uncertain how to take this.

'No.'

From the corner of his eye he watched Eldritch weighing up the wall and saw the dark brows wing skywards.

'You're seriously saying you could climb that without a rope? In God's name, how? It's sheer rock.'

Somehow the wizard seemed to have missed the point. At the very least he should have been disappointed, but as Aidan waited for the penny to drop he realised that Eldritch was genuinely shocked, not by his inability to make the climb now, but by the thought of his ever being able to do so.

'You might as well try climbing the side of a house,' the wizard continued. Indignation momentarily replaced the tiredness in his voice as though he half suspected Aidan was winding him up. In spite of everything Aidan found the corners of his mouth twitching. Climb the side of a house? He and Matt had once been arrested for doing more or less that, although at half past midnight – and more than slightly drunk – perhaps they shouldn't have chosen the side wall of the Post Office as the place to prove a point. Still, a bet was a bet and Kevin James had been adamant that they couldn't do it. He also suspected Bethan Hughes had known from the outset that he and Matt weren't really moonlighting as cat burglars although it hadn't stopped her arresting the pair of them for attempted breaking and entering. Despite their current circumstances the memory brought a grin, swift and mischievous, and then Aidan laughed out loud at the confusion on Eldritch's face. He shook his head, refusing to be drawn.

'That's a story for the Unicorn,' he promised. 'The thing is that most of the time when you're climbing you're not using a rope to help you up the rock, it's just there to stop you falling too far if you come off. The actual climbing's done on whatever hand and footholds you can find.'

Warming to his topic Aidan ran his hand over the grey-black rock with an almost affectionate air. It was far easier to talk about climbing than about being trapped.

'This is slate. See all these fracture planes where it's sheared – there's plenty of grip there. It's a bit rougher up the top. That last couple of feet where it's only soil – there won't be any handholds there so you'd have to get as high as possible on the slate so you could reach over the edge and pull yourself up. Apart from that it's a pretty easy climb.'

Aidan paused to consider the rock face in more detail. 'Start out here and follow the fracture up diagonally to the right and you've got hand holds there and there.' Though he pointed to where he meant he could tell from Eldritch's frown that the wizard couldn't see what to him were clear grab points. 'The next one's a bit of a stretch but get your foot up onto that crease there and you'd be well away.'

Thoughtfully he eyed the different textures of the rock judging the span from one point to the other. His fingers flexed. The fractures in the slate were fresh and sharp. They would provide plenty of grip but it would be rough on his hands. Normally he would tape them before climbing on such a surface. He'd probably cut them to ribbons... He stopped suddenly, realising where his thoughts had led him and his smile disappeared. He laughed sourly.

'Who am I kidding? So what if I could climb this easily on a normal day? Today's not normal. I'm wrecked.'

To demonstrate he raised his arm and there was no missing the fine tremor that shook it, even though he tried to hold it still. With a look of disgust he let it drop to his side.

'All the strength of freshly chewed string,' he mocked. 'Even if that weren't the case my ribs wouldn't take it. The first time I put my weight on my right arm my side will go into spasm and I'll come off.'

It had very nearly happened to him on the caving ladder. Two-thirds of the way up, wanting to get the ascent over and done with he had overstretched, reaching for a higher rung. A simple enough mistake but the immediate stab of cramp had nearly taken him off the ladder. Free climbing on a rock-face he wouldn't have been so lucky. Wearily he shook his head, irritated by his own stupidity. Eldritch was quiet, his face unreadable and after a moment Aidan turned away. Damn Griff, damn the demon and most of all damn his own feeble body for letting him down! It should have been so simple. Almost without conscious thought he stretched his hand out again, feeling the smooth, almost silky texture of the slate under his fingertips. *The bones of the earth,* Matt had once called the slabs of rock protruding from these Cambrian hillsides, an unusually poetic description for the normally blunt speaking Kiwi geology graduate. They had been climbing over near Cadair Idris at the time and the path that took them back to the campsite had meandered down a slope marked by great angular uprisings of stone that jutted from the thin soil very much like shards of bone from an open fracture. Halfway down the valley Matt had left the path to go and stand by one of those great, grey sentinels.

'These rocks are amongst the oldest things on earth,' he had proclaimed. 'They were old even before the Dreamtime.'

Aidan wasn't sure why the words had come back to him

now. He must be more tired than he thought, slipping into a daydreaming half-sleep even while he stood leaning on the rock, but he remembered how Matt's strong, blunt-fingered hands had run over the lichen covered slate as he spoke, caressing it as though it were a lover's cheek.

'What wonders have they seen, eh Adi?'

Aidan smiled wryly at the memory. What wonders indeed? Today he and Eldritch had faced something not so much out of the Dreamtime as from the realms of nightmare. Yet they had lived to tell the tale. But now, if someone didn't find them, they were likely to succumb to exposure. They had been lucky so far but he was aware that above them, beyond the sheltering pit walls, the wind was picking up and the sky had darkened to the colour of a bruise. The drizzle that had greeted their emergence from the mine might have stopped for now but there was a lot more rain in those clouds. It was going to become very unpleasant when it finally fell.

Aidan's gaze skimmed once more over the traverse he had mapped on the pit wall, surveying each hand and foothold, noting in his mind where he could take his weight on his feet and where he would be reliant on that vulnerable right arm. It wasn't so bad, he thought. Mostly the footholds were good. There was only one place where he would have no other option than to take his weight solely on that right side, just there, not far from the top of the slate where the fracture line petered out and he would need to get across to those final few holds and boost himself over the edge. Could he do it? It would only be for a few seconds but it was a long reach to that next grip and if he had misjudged it… His hands went sweaty at the thought of what would happen next and he flinched as though the pain had already stabbed him. He wasn't a coward, he told himself. He was only being realistic about what was likely to happen.

Movement glimpsed from the corner of his eye caught his attention and he turned, almost grateful for the distraction, to see Eldritch folding his long frame down to the ground, back against the pit wall, his head hunched down into the collar of his coat and his arms folded against his chest as if for warmth. As he watched, the tall man shivered, his face tightening in pain as he shifted the arm he held cradled against his body. Swollen and black fingers protruded from the mess of bandages and splints. The wizard hadn't complained but it was obvious he was in no shape to sit out a storm, waiting to be rescued. He needed to be in hospital having that wrist sorted out properly.

Unaware that he was being watched Eldritch wiped his good hand over his eyes, the muscles along his jaw bunching as another shiver jarred his body. Feeling useless Aidan bit his lip and turned away. More than anything he wanted to be able to tell his friend it would all be okay. After all, this was the sort of situation he rescued people from. This of all things was something he ought to be able to make right. But there was only one thing he could do now that would help. Even as his mind shaped the thought Aidan understood that he had made his decision.

'Dear God,' he whispered, appalled at the realisation of what he was about to attempt. Weariness that was close to physical nausea pulled at his bones and he leaned his forehead into the cold, grey rock, wishing with all his heart it could be otherwise. He would attempt the climb but it didn't change the fact that everything he had said to Eldritch was true. He would fall. Given the state he was in how could he hope not to?

Distractedly he wondered how bad it would be. Would he feel his ribs being driven like knives into his lungs or would the impact kill him outright?

Don't, he told himself, trying not to imagine those last seconds of life; the bubbling rasp of his breath as he laboured to pull air into lungs that were filling with blood. *It doesn't matter.* He wouldn't let it matter because – like Eldritch choosing to seal the boundary even at the cost of his own life – saying no wasn't an option. There was too much at stake to live with himself if he didn't try. Self-consciously he swallowed, trying to calm the clenching in his gut as he turned back to Eldritch.

'Give me your car keys.'

The wizard's head jerked up and he looked blearily at Aidan, momentarily nonplussed by the request.

'What?'

'Your car keys. Give them to me. I may get a signal down by the road but if not I can get help a lot faster if I can drive back to town rather than walk.'

Aidan watched Eldritch's expression change as the wizard realised what he was intending to do.

'Aidan—' His voice held a note of warning but Aidan cut him off.

'Yes, I know, "It's bloody mad and I don't have to do this".' The little voice in his head was telling him the same thing but Aidan didn't intend to listen to that either. Peripherally he was aware of the sharpness in his tone but he didn't much care. He didn't need to discuss what he was doing he just needed to get it over with. 'Except we don't have any options left. We can't just sit here and wait for someone to trip over us. It could be days before anyone comes. If we're going to get out of here one of us has to make that climb and – let's face it – it's not going to be you. No offence intended.'

'None taken,' Eldritch responded dryly. 'I always suspected you were mad. Now I know it.'

The ghost of a smile tugged at the corners of the wizard's mouth but it was gone in an instant and it never came close to touching his eyes. They were deadly serious as they locked onto Aidan's, grey as a winter sky and equally unforgiving. Meeting their gaze it seemed to the younger man that everything he feared about the climb – everything he had deliberately left unsaid – was laid bare for Eldritch's judgement. It wasn't a sensation he took kindly to.

'Are you going to give me the car keys or not?' he snapped.

'Sit down.'

When Aidan didn't react Eldritch muttered something under his breath. Painfully he pushed himself to his feet all the while fixing Aidan with that strange, calculating look. 'I said, sit down.' He put his good hand on Aidan's shoulder but even fit and well the wizard would have found it difficult to push Aidan to the floor. Stubbornly Aidan squared his shoulders and stayed where he was.

'For the love of God, Aidan, will you just do what you're asked for once?' Though he swayed with exhaustion a flash of temper sparked in Eldritch's voice. 'If you're really going to try and climb out of here you need help and you know it.'

'What I need,' Aidan said through his teeth, 'are my proper climbing boots and a dose of industrial strength painkillers. Failing that a stepladder would be good. Now unless you can magic up any of those things I suggest you let me get on with it.' He glared at Eldritch but the wizard didn't move. Aidan stiffened. 'I know what I'm doing,' he growled, giving up any pretence of keeping the frustration from his voice.

'And I know what you're doing as well,' Eldritch shot back. 'And without help you're not much more likely to succeed at it than I am. You said it yourself, you're a wreck.'

'Thank you. That's a great help.' Sarcasm dripped from every syllable and Aidan found himself fighting down a sudden urge to show Eldritch just what he was capable of, wrecked or otherwise. 'Let go of me before I make you.'

'Listen you pigheaded Welshman—'

Maybe Eldritch felt the muscles under his hand bunch or perhaps it was the sudden coldness that flowed over Aidan's face but with exaggerated care he lifted his hand from Aidan's shoulder. For a handful of seconds the pair of them glared at each other, bristling like fighting dogs, neither willing to back down, until Eldritch said in a quieter voice, 'Will you just trust me on this?' just as Aidan muttered, 'What is it you want to do?'

They eyed each other sheepishly.

'You could start by sitting down for a minute.'

CHAPTER 28

'I know why you're doing this Aidan.'

'Oh, so you're a mind reader now?' The comment earned him a look that Eldritch must have borrowed from Gwyn. 'Sorry.' He shut up and let the wizard continue.

'I'm not going to insult you by telling you not to try it. I couldn't attempt to climb that, not even with two good arms.' Eldritch spared a swift glance at the slate wall behind them and shook his head. 'But if you're absolutely certain you're going to give it a go the one thing I can do is to boost your energy levels first.'

Aidan's frown was like a physical question mark. He didn't need to say anything; the doubt was there on his face. It wasn't that he didn't believe such things were possible – he had seen enough to accept that both Gwyn and Eldritch could gather up the subtle, shifting energies that suffused their bodies and pass them back and forth like bright handfuls of jewels – but looking at Eldritch now he couldn't see how the wizard had any energy to spare. After all they had been through he knew he hadn't. Yet when he said as much, pointing out that only a few minutes ago Eldritch had claimed he didn't have enough energy to fix a rope, Eldritch's only answer was, 'That was different.'

Aidan's scowl brought an enigmatic smile.

'Aidan, how much energy do you think I need to sit and

wait for you to come back with the cavalry? If you're going to risk your neck climbing out of here the best thing I can do for both of us is to give you a fighting chance of succeeding.' A lopsided shrug accompanied the words, more a suggestion than an actual movement. 'I think I can spare you that.'

He seemed so certain. Aidan sighed.

'You're really sure about this?'

Eldritch didn't answer at once and Aidan had the impression – as he sometimes did with Gwyn – that the wizard was picking through his thoughts like a miser through a hoard of gold, deciding what he would and would not share. Then Eldritch grinned, wild and fey, the sudden brightness chasing the tiredness from his face.

'Just get out of here Aidan. There's no point in us both hanging around to rot.' Fumbling slightly he drew out his car keys and handed them over, his expression turning serious. 'Best take these now. I can't guarantee how long the effects will last so you need to start climbing as soon as it's done, okay?'

'Yeah, sure.'

Aidan turned the car keys in his hand still not entirely convinced that this was the right thing to do.

'I mean it Aidan, it's important. Don't waste any time hanging around, just go.'

'Okay.'

Consciously pushing aside his sense of unease Aidan stowed the car keys in his pocket. Now it was his turn to be serious.

'It's going to take me half an hour to walk back to the car and another half hour to get back into town if I can't get a signal. We'll be able to get the mountain rescue team landy most of the way up here so I should be back within two hours, two and a half at the most.' He glanced at his watch. 'It's going to be dark by then but don't worry, we'll still be able to get you out.

'The thing is though, it's going to get cold so try and keep moving around, even if you don't feel like it.' He looked the wizard up and down, judging just how tired he was. 'Especially if you don't feel like it,' he modified his instruction. 'At least you're out of the wind down here but if the rain starts – and looking at the sky it's going to – you'll be better off waiting back in the tunnel.'

Aidan offered a stern look in response to Eldritch's disgusted huff of breath. 'I don't want to be coming back to find you half dead from hypothermia. Rather than get soaked out here go back into the tunnel. You've got both the helmet lamps. The batteries should be good for another couple of hours each.' He eyed the wizard, weighing up how much of this advice he was likely to heed, and added pointedly, 'Take a leaf out of your own book and do what you're told for once.'

Eldritch's head inclined briefly, acknowledging the hit.

'Yes Mother. Let's just do this, shall we.'

Moving stiffly Eldritch edged round to sit beside Aidan.

'You don't need to do anything, just close your eyes and relax.'

Though still slightly dubious about the whole idea Aidan did as he was told.

'If I relax too much I'm going to fall asleep,' he protested, smothering a yawn. 'See?' he said, opening his eyes again and regarding the wizard accusingly. Eldritch gave him a superior smile.

'That's not a problem. Now close your eyes and relax.'

As if to show Aidan what to do Eldritch closed his own eyes.

So now we're both likely to fall asleep. That's really not a good idea.

Aidan scowled briefly at the wizard although from the little frown line creasing the skin between Eldritch's brows he had to admit the other man looked to be concentrating hard rather than relaxing. Aidan supposed he was gathering together whatever dregs of energy he could spare. For a moment longer he studied him curiously but it felt intrusive and rather rude to be watching someone so closely and after a moment Aidan gave in and shut his eyes.

'Wake me up when you've finished,' he muttered and caught the amused huff of Eldritch's laugh in response.

A second later he felt the light weight of a hand against his chest and then a similar pressure over his solar plexus. He could also feel an edge of metal digging into his sternum; one of the splints bracing Eldritch's wrist, he guessed. It was uncomfortable enough that he thought he might say something but even as he considered it he was distracted by an odd tingling sensation in his skin. He twitched away from it and an exasperated voice said, 'Stay still, Aidan.'

'It tickles. It made me jump.'

'It's only energy. Relax.'

Aidan didn't need to see the wizard rolling his eyes heavenwards; Eldritch's tone said it all.

'Sorry.'

Sheepishly he settled back down again and did his best to obey although how he was meant to relax when what felt like an army of ants was crawling over his chest and side he wasn't sure. Well at least he wasn't likely to fall asleep, he thought ruefully, biting his lip to keep from protesting as the sensation spread. Even without the invasion of invisible ants he was beginning to feel as if he had drunk too many cups of coffee late at night. His head was starting to buzz and an odd restlessness, more intense than any caffeine high, niggled at him, flowing through his body and replacing the feeling of fatigue that had so recently been dragging at his limbs. His skin prickled and crawled as though it wasn't quite attached to him. No, thought Aidan, there was no danger of his falling asleep now. Nor would he waste any time hanging around once Eldritch had finished. He wanted nothing more that to be up and moving, burning off this odd fizzing energy that filled him. Fighting to stay still he found himself counting in his head, anything to distract himself. He was almost at one hundred when he felt Eldritch's hands slide down his chest and fall away.

'Finished now?'

Anxious to be up and moving Aidan opened his eyes just in time to see Eldritch slump sideways. Startled he jerked forward, grabbing at the wizard and catching him before he went face down in the mud.

'Eldritch?'

The wizard's body sagged in his arms, limp and heavy with the boneless weight of a corpse.

'Dear God, what have you done?'

Awkwardly he shifted so he could lay his friend down. A coldly logical corner of his mind noted that while his ribs protested the movement the pain seemed somehow remote as though cocooned beneath a layer of anaesthetic. Irritated with himself Aidan pushed the thought away. It hardly seemed relevant now. Fingers digging frantically under Eldritch's collar he searched for a pulse while his own heartbeat hammered.

'Come on, don't do this to me.'

A tiny flicker of life stirred beneath his fingertips but only when he felt a second beat and then a third did he dare to relax even slightly. For a moment he had truly believed that Eldritch was dead. Silently he numbered the beats, like a man counting over the beads of a rosary, stringing them together like talismans while his mind raced. He could guess what had happened; that in seeking to boost his energy levels Eldritch had drained his own to a dangerous level. Studying his friend's face – slack and curiously vulnerable looking under the hotchpotch of blood and bruises – Aidan wondered if that had been a conscious decision or the miscalculation of a man already stumbling on the edge of exhaustion. Neither scenario offered him any comfort. A hot rush of anger clogged in his throat at the thought that Eldritch would do something so reckless, followed swiftly by guilt that his friend had done so to protect him.

'You stupid bastard,' he addressed the unconscious man. 'Why do you think it's always up to you to save the world?'

Yet in the angry bitterness of his words lay an awareness of the dilemma he now faced. He could do as they had agreed; leave Eldritch and go for help, but the help he had intended to fetch would be of little use, not when the only hope of saving the wizard lay in finding someone able to replace the vital energies that Eldritch had given away. If Gwyn were conscious... but the chances of that were too slender to give Aidan any comfort and underlying that knowledge was the all too real fear that if he did leave Eldritch would be dead by the time he returned.

Uneasy with the possibility Aidan tried desperately to think of an alternative. He could stay and try to channel some of that borrowed life-force back into Eldritch. It would mean he wouldn't have the strength to climb out of the pit but by doing so he might just keep Eldritch alive for long enough for someone to find them. Even if no one did come, by morning he should be sufficiently rested to be able to make the climb on his own. For a moment Aidan considered the idea, testing it out, holding it before him like a tiny glimmer of hope, but then he sighed and the sound was like the final exhalation of a dying man. He knew he was fooling himself. In his heart he understood that Eldritch wouldn't live until morning. The storm would be on them soon and at some point in the cold and the dark his loosening grip on life would fail and his spirit would slip quietly away. If he stayed with Eldritch all he would be doing was delaying the inevitable.

For a second he sat very still, considering his decision. Then resolutely he lifted his hand from Eldritch's throat and the pulse beating slowly beneath the cold, pale skin. Carefully he rolled the unconscious man onto his side, tilting his head back to ensure he could breathe, and stood up. He knew what he had to do. One last time he looked down at the still body, allowing the sight to harden his resolve. Eldritch had made his choice and now it was up to him to honour it. He refused to believe that it might already be too late.

The first part of the climb was as straightforward as he had described it to Eldritch; perhaps not quite so simple that he could have completed it in his sleep, but demanding no more than basic climbing skills and a belief that a diagonal ledge of rock a few thousandths of an inch wide equated to sufficient foothold to scale an otherwise vertical rock face. Aidan was confident in both his climbing and the slate's ability to support him. It was his own body he was dubious about but as he inched his way along the fracture line, using his hands mainly for balance and to steady himself against the slate he found he was able to move surprisingly easily, buoyed up by the borrowed energy fizzing through his body. It felt good to be moving, to be doing something constructive, and in spite of all his worries it felt good simply to be climbing. This, after all, was his passion and his joy. Under other circumstances it would have been easy to give himself up to the pleasure of pitting himself against a rock face for no other reason than he could but the muffled ache in his ribs reminded him that there was more at stake today. What Eldritch had done had not healed him. Crabbing his way towards the end of this first traverse, fifteen feet above the pit floor, Aidan knew he daren't put his borrowed strength to the test with a misjudged hold or a slip that meant he had to catch himself on his injured side. He was under no illusion as to what would happen if he did. So he made himself concentrate and do things absolutely by the book, testing each hand and foothold before he shifted his weight and he forced himself to ignore the nagging sense of urgency in the back of his mind that goaded him to go faster.

'Slow and steady,' he murmured as he sidled his feet along the thin lip of slate, each time gaining a few more precious inches of height. He thought he had never been so aware of the rock under his boots and fingertips. He was also aware that his ribs were twinging slightly through the numbness Eldritch had layered over them. Gritting his teeth Aidan hoped it was because he was breathing more heavily and not because Eldritch's magic was starting to wear off. It would be just typical of this whole affair if that were the case for he was now at the part of the climb where he really needed that help. Five feet above his head the edge of the pit was tantalisingly close but the fracture line that had taken him this far petered out mere inches beyond his right foot. A few feet further along the pit wall another fracture extended up to where the slate itself gave way to topsoil and then finally the thin moorland grass. If he got to that point he would be within reach of the pit rim and should be able to haul himself out, but first he had to get across to that second traverse and to do that he was going to have to take his life very literally in his hands.

Aidan took a moment to rub his forehead along his arm, wiping the sweat from his eyes. He could see the first handhold; this one a hole in the slate rather than a protuberance. It was a long stretch but he reckoned if he shifted so he was balanced on the very last inch of the fracture line he could get his right hand to it and jam his fingers in. He swallowed and tried not to think of what that stretch would do to his side or that that was the simple part of the manoeuvre. There were no footholds to help him so once he had that handhold he would have to take all his weight on his right arm until he got his left hand across and then he would have to repeat the process to get onto the final traverse. His breath tightened in his chest at the thought and deliberately he turned his attention away, looking up at the slashed line of the pit brim. *That's where you're going. That's where you've got to get to.* He studied the line of the traverse that would take him there picturing his hands and feet finding the holds unerringly, his right foot hitting that final stub of rock from which he would kick off and push himself up over the edge. Concentrating on that goal he imagined how it would feel, the thrust of muscle propelling him upwards, getting his hips level with the edge so he could fold forward and anchor as much of his body as possible onto the ground beyond the pit. Then he could drag himself fully clear. The wind would hit him, cold and fresh, and he would be free. For a second Aidan homed in on that moment, building for himself the sensation of the wind tugging at his hair, the grey-green mountain grass coarse and prickly against his palms, the peaty smell of damp earth, solid and reliable under his cheek and cradling his body. This was his own magic, his own spell, willing that future into being. He would do it. He *could* do it. In his mind's eye it was already a reality and all he had to do was to step into it. His breathing steadied and settled and he refocussed his eyes on the rock face to his right. He was ready.

Cautiously feeling for the lip of rock under his feet Aidan edged forward until he was poised on the very end of the fracture, his right foot protruding partly into thin air. It was a precarious position, balanced on less than a finger's width of rock and in the back of his mind was the knowledge that if his feet slipped now he would fall just as certainly as if his ribs gave way. He wished again that he was wearing proper climbing boots but even as he sent that vain protest into the ether he took a half breath, gritted his teeth and reached out, stretching against the immediate protest of bruised muscle and cracked bone until, almost at the limit of his reach, his fingertips found the crevice he was seeking and he jammed them into the crack in the slate. He risked another breath, feeling the muscles of his side tighten, not quite cramping but suggesting they weren't far from doing so for all the magic Eldritch might have worked on them. Not daring to think about what might happen next Aidan pushed off from the ledge. His weight shifted, momentum took him and then he was hanging from his right hand. He cried out as pain sliced through the numbness blanketing his ribs, ripping it away. Sweat burst from his skin and his grip started to loosen but his left hand was already jamming into the slate, his fingers crammed in, overlapping his right hand, pressing it into the slate and taking some of the weight from his injured side. The raw edge of rock bit into his fingers and he barely registered it, smearing his feet against the slate to find even the smallest amount of purchase as he pushed himself upwards, reaching for the next handhold. His breath came in short, panting gasps and sweat stung and blurred in his eyes.

He couldn't do this. He had been crazy to think he could make the climb and Eldritch had been a fool to believe him. Now Eldritch was dying and he was halfway up a rock face with the last dregs of energy draining away, running like blood from his side. A dull anger washed through him; anger at the wizard and himself and at the circumstances that had pushed them to their choices, but it was insufficient to drive back the weight of fatigue dragging him down. It sucked at his body, pulling against his feeble grip on the rock. Vaguely he thought he might as well let go and get it over with; he was going to fall anyway. Why delay the inevitable? Yet though his muscles shook with effort and every breath cost him as though he had been racked, still he kept moving, some visceral mix of stubbornness and survival instinct keeping him clinging to the rock. He could barely see the holds he had mapped out. They swam in his vision, doubling and trebling and then blurring into amorphous grey but his hands found them anyway and his feet followed. He made a mangled, inarticulate cry of protest as be brought his right foot up onto a tiny nub of rock and his ribs stabbed as he pushed upwards. Suddenly, disorientatingly, there was no more rock in front of him. For a moment he thought he must be falling and then he understood, folding himself forward to clutch at the ground as he kicked and scrabbled to get himself over the edge to safety. On his hands and knees he stared down at the coarse grass between his fingers, panting and dizzy with the effort. His stomach churned and he thought he might be sick but he knew he had to get his feet underneath him. He had managed the hard part. He mustn't stop, not now. He shut his eyes against the blackness that poured into his vision. The blood pounding in his ears was like the sea, rushing in to engulf him, and for a moment he fancied he could hear voices within its surge, strange and distorted, calling his name. He pushed the thought away, ignoring it like everything else and gritting his teeth he forced himself upright.

He managed one staggering step as his energy slid away from him. Vertigo tipped him sideways and he started to fall but somehow he didn't hit the ground. Something caught him round the chest, the impact enough to drive the air from his lungs in a pain-filled gasp. He opened his eyes and was shocked to see people around him; faces he knew, hands easing him down onto the scrubby grass. A bedlam of voices was calling out orders.

'Huw, I need a blanket and the first aid kit. Tom, Kat – get the ropes rigged.'

'For goodness sake stay still.'

That last one was addressed to him as he struggled to sit up.

Aidan stared up at the fierce looking Valkyrie leaning over him and wondered if he was seeing things although, if he was going to conjure an image of Hazel Jones, he could at least have done so without the pinched frown line between those finely shaped brows and the scowl that narrowed her otherwise enviable mouth into a thin and formidable line. Yet for all that he thought he had rarely seen anything more welcome. He briefly considered telling her so but even as lightheaded as he felt he still knew better than to do that. The leader of the Plynlimon Mountain Rescue Team wasn't renowned for her patience and from the look on her face it had already been sorely tested. Probably something to do with a real casualty turning up in the middle of a training exercise, he thought, although he couldn't recall any exercise having been planned. For a moment his tired brain stalled, stumbling over the idea that he could have forgotten something so fundamental, but then he refocused. There were far more important things to worry about now.

'Hazel, thank God you're here. I need your help.'

He tried again to lever himself upright but a rush of dizziness and Hazel's palm planted firmly in the centre of his chest defeated him.

'It's going to be a whole lot easier to help you if you stay still, Aidan. Why don't you start by telling me what happened to you.'

Her cool blue gaze raked over him, the elegant hitch of her eyebrows an unspoken comment on everything from his grime-caked clothing to the assortment of raw gouges and bruises that decorated much of his visible skin. But even as Aidan started to protest that all of that could wait Hazel was already stripping back the sleeve of his jacket. It was only when she caught his hand and slapped it over the sodden bandage, telling him to put pressure on it, that he realised his arm was covered in blood. He stared at it in fascination, surprised by the warmth as the slippery wetness oozed between his fingers. There was an awful lot of blood. No wonder he felt so dizzy he thought, as he watched his fingers turning red.

'Aidan!'

The sharpness of Hazel's voice brought him back.

'Talk to me. Are you hurt anywhere else?'

If his hands had been free he would have batted hers away as she fingered back the hair from his forehead to get a better look at his face. Feebly he tried to twist away from the unwanted attention.

'I'm fine,' he mumbled, wishing she would stop fussing. So his arm was bleeding again. So what? Best not tell her about his ribs. 'Don't worry about me. It's Eldritch you've got to help.'

Hazel's lips pursed and she favoured him with a look that suggested she was humouring him but all she said was, 'So where is he?'

'He's still in the pit.'

Speaking was becoming difficult, as though his mouth was full of dust. Aidan swallowed, struggling to find the words. He would have liked to have asked Hazel for some water but there would be time for that later. First he had to get help for Eldritch.

'His wrist's broken so he couldn't climb out. I was going for help—'

Hazel gave an unladylike snort.

'Then it's lucky for everyone that we were already on our way. You need to keep that raised,' she added, lifting his arm which had slipped down across his chest, 'to stop the bleeding.'

She scowled at him as though annoyed by the need to explain herself but for a second Aidan thought he had seen concern on that coolly efficient face.

'You're hardly in great shape yourself Aidan. A broken wrist is no reason for heroics. What else is wrong with him?'

'He's unconscious. He…'

The fear that had driven him up the cliff face caught hold of him again; a cold, leaden feeling that pressed against his chest, smothering the air in his lungs. Hazel and the team could get Eldritch out of the pit but what difference would it make? None of them could give him the help he needed. Only Gwyn could do that. He hadn't realised he had spoken aloud until Hazel said, 'What about Gwyn, Aidan? How can she help?'

'She's the only one who can save him.'

He stared at her, willing her to trust him even if she couldn't understand.

'You've got to tell her about Eldritch. Promise me. Tell her he gave me the last of his energy. She'll understand. She'll know what to do.'

He tried to grab her arm, desperate now to make her realise the importance of what he was saying. Impatiently Hazel pressed his hand back down onto the bandage.

'For heaven's sake Aidan, lie still. I'll tell her, I promise. What about Jane? She's away at the moment, isn't she?'

'What?' Aidan struggled to make sense of Hazel's questions.

'Jane. Do you want me to call her, let her know what's happened?'

'No. No, it's Gwyn who needs to know.'

'Aidan—' Hazel broke off as one of the team came over to join them.

'Ropes are rigged, boss.'

Under his red climbing helmet Huw Price's round face was calm and matter of fact. His tone was businesslike but the glance he shot Aidan gave away his concern at his teammate's condition.

'We've got another casualty at the bottom of that hole but he's not responding to us. Everyone's ready. I can take over here if you want to go down yourself.'

'Okay, good.'

Hazel turned back to Aidan one last time.

'I take it that's your friend Eldritch. Is there anything else we need to know about him?'

Aidan shook his head and momentarily there were two Hazels leaning over him.

'Tell Gwyn. She's the only one who can help.'

Hazel disentangled herself.

'He's all yours Huw.'

'Okay Aidan, let's see if we can make you more comfortable…'

But Huw's words were drowned by the buzzing in Aidan's ears.

'You've got to tell Gwyn,' he mumbled, desperate to make his teammate understand. Huw's lips moved and the concern was plain on his face now but Aidan couldn't make out what he was saying. It didn't matter, he just had to make him understand about Eldritch but even as he tried to make one more effort blackness swamped his vision. Before he could clear it he passed out.

CHAPTER 29

Marcus Eldritch clung to life. Or perhaps it would be more accurate to say that life – in the form of a black-haired witch – clung to him. Released from his own bed after a night of observation Aidan found Gwyn in the artificial twilight of the Intensive Care Unit, grim faced and silent, trickling life into a body that lay too close to death. The doctors had done all they could to stabilise him but, unable to find anything but superficial injuries, they were at a loss to explain Eldritch's condition. *It's down to him now* – a phrase delivered with a shake of the head and a deep frown was all they had to offer. Aidan knew differently – it was down to Gwyn. But as time slipped by, punctuated only by the measured suck and draw of the machine ventilating Eldritch's lungs, and Gwyn slumped ever lower against the bed, he began to face the prospect that even her help might not be enough.

Fighting his way free of the pit he had known that Eldritch would die without help but he had refused to consider that it might already be too late to save him. Now, as he saw the fatigue harrowing Gwyn's face, the dark circles under her eyes blending with the marks of the beating she had yet to recover from, he realised how naïve he had been. He had failed to understand the enormity of what was being asked of her. As a healer Gwyn would do all she could to save the man in her care. If Marcus Eldritch wanted to die he would have to get past her first. But, like a cold hand around Aidan's heart was the fear that in doing so Eldritch might just take Gwyn with him.

She found him on the far side of a wide, windswept plain. He stood with his back to her, the wind whipping his long hair out behind him and catching the white cotton shirt he wore, alternately billowing it up and then flattening it to his body. He had stopped where the scrubby grass gave way to rolling, sandy dunes, stretching down until finally, far in the distance, a silvery glitter of water melded with the sky. Eldritch stared out over that desolate estuarine landscape. Far out on the expanse of glittering mud flats and water pale shapes were just visible, people starting to separate out from the pearlescent haze that marked the horizon. Gwyn wasn't sure whether she was seeing them now because her eyes had adjusted to the strange play of light and water or whether they had only just come into being, slipping into existence like colours returning to the world with the dawn. She wondered if Eldritch saw them more clearly than she could for she knew what they must be; the spirits of his dead drawing close, coming to him to be there at his own passing.

For a moment she watched him watching them, while the wind snapped at his hair and lifted a stinging scour of sand to fling against his face. Though Gwyn raised her hands to shield her eyes and to keep the wind from tearing her own hair into knots Eldritch seemed indifferent to the elemental barrage. Amongst the hard tufts of marram grass his bare feet were scraped and bleeding but if he noticed he gave no indication.

'Eldritch.'

As she had been doing since she started this search, she

called his name again, the wind tearing her words away, but this time it seemed he heard her for he turned his gaze from those pale phantoms to look at her and she was horrified by the exhaustion and utter desolation naked in his eyes. Then he blinked and some of that raw emotion disappeared, buried once more in the depths of his soul. He seemed to come back to her slightly.

'Gwyn?' He spoke her name as though she was someone he remembered from a long time past, his voice puzzled. 'What are you doing here?'

He looked bewildered and Gwyn fought down the urge to step up to him and take him in her arms, to hold him tightly against her as she might a child, afraid that if she did so he might shatter and be torn into dust by the wind, he looked so fragile.

'I came after you.'

Of all the things she could have said she chose the simplest, letting her voice carry her compassion to him. The wind, that had been a constant force since she had come to this place, dropped and in the echoing silence she said, 'I don't think you should be here.'

His gaze had been drifting back to the quicksilver lure of the water and the coalescing shapes of the dead. They were clearer now, distinct individuals though still too far off for her to make out features though perhaps Eldritch could already recognise them. With a visible effort he pulled back from them to focus on the woman by his side. Gwyn wondered if it was she who seemed more ethereal to him.

'I'm so tired, Gwyn.'

Very slowly Eldritch folded his long body to the ground. There was nothing graceful in the motion. He moved as though consumed by a bone-deep hurting, as though every joint in that lanky frame had been reamed out and filled with ground glass. For a moment he sat with his arms drawing his knees up to his chest, huddled and fragile, and then gradually he sank back, stretching out on the gritty scrub of sand and grass. Bruised lids closed over those haunted grey eyes.

Carefully Gwyn knelt beside him. In this world between worlds there was no sign of the injuries she knew his body bore in the physical realm. His right wrist was straight, the flesh unswollen, the open neck of his shirt revealed pale skin unmarred by either the old bruises, fading to an ugly yellow, or the newer ones overlaying them with black and purple. Yet the imprint of those injuries and more besides clung to the wizard. The accumulation of pain and loss from so many battles weighted the air around him, covering him like a shroud. While the physical wounds he had sustained had been tended there had been no peace, no time for healing his spirit. Gwyn could tell it was as much the accumulation of all that had gone before as the damage sustained in this final fight that had brought Marcus Eldritch to this place. Looking now at that pale, worn body Gwyn wondered if she had any right to ask him to return.

Yet it was a question that would have to be answered soon. Neither of them could remain here for long. Eldritch would have to choose whether he would go on and join those shining figures, far out in the shallow waters, or whether he would try and return with her. Even if he sought to come back there was no guarantee that he had the strength to make that journey. Indeed, there was no guarantee for either of them. Having spent most of her own energy in finding him Gwyn knew she was close to the end of her reserves. When she reached them she would either snap back into her own body or find herself lost here in this wasteland, facing her own crossing. Yet even if she had had the strength she knew in her heart she would not try to force Eldritch to return. Now she had found him she wondered if the right thing might be to help him cross towards those who had come to be with him at the time of passing. It wasn't what she wanted, it wasn't what she was risking her life to do, but it might be the kindest act, the one thing she could do for Marcus Eldritch as a friend. Her heart heavy, Gwyn slid her hand into his, feeling the long bones of his fingers like so many sticks through the cold and too thin flesh.

'When we first met you gave me your business card,' Gwyn addressed the still form, 'and I asked you what the "M" stood for. You told me it was for Marcus but that your friends all call you Eldritch.'

In her mind she conjured the moment again; the tall man with his angular, saturnine face and a voice like granite threaded with silver, his true nature hidden behind that deceptive self-mockery. Her senses had warned her that he was more than he professed to be, that he was striving to deceive her with that false charm, to deflect her from recognising all that he was. It had made her want nothing to do with him and time had proved her instincts right. Yet circumstance had thrown them together and she had found there was more to this devil than his false persona, more perhaps than even he wanted to admit.

'I can think of a few other things that "M" could stand for; maddening, meddling, Machiavellian, manipulative, moody, moronic. Even magnificent – on the odd occasion.'

She closed her other hand over his, holding it in both of hers, as she raised it to her cheek.

'But mostly I think it stands for "my friend".'

She was crying now she realised, tears spilling silently over her cheeks and onto their entwined hands. Unusually she let them flow. She shifted, tasted salt as she touched her lips to his fingers.

'True friends – those who know and accept me for what I am – are a rare and precious thing for the likes of me, Marcus Eldritch, and for the likes of you too I suspect. We stand on the front line and too often that's a dangerous place to be; too dangerous to go giving hostages to fortune. If it's time for you to be done with the battle I'll understand, but I'd rather not lose you. Will you come home with me, my friend?'

Her words provoked no answer, no response from the prone figure. After several heartbeats Gwyn sighed. She could see the figures of the dead drawn closer, still a way off but recognisable now; a slender woman and a man who, from his likeness to her, surely had to be her brother, an elderly woman whose small frame burned with power and a young man who wore the uniform of a soldier though she knew him to be a doctor. Slowly they drifted closer.

'I understand.' Gently she squeezed the cold fingers, a wordless gesture of acceptance and farewell. 'Blessed be, Marcus Eldritch.'

She laid his hand back on his chest but as she started to lift hers away his fingers tightened around it and his eyes flickered open.

'You're crying,' he said and his fingertips brushed briefly against her cheek before his hand sank back to his chest. Gwyn shook her head.

'The wind's blown sand in my eyes, that's all. It doesn't matter.'

437

She blinked and the figures surrounding them wavered and were gone.

'Take me home, Gwyn.'

Aidan hated hospitals with a vengeance. Even the thought of those long, antiseptic-smelling corridors, with their bland, mint green walls that some expert somewhere had deemed to be calming, made his skin crawl. Yet despite that he was smiling as he pushed through the heavy double doors and not even the sound of his trainers squeaking on the detested linoleum floors could quell his good humour. This afternoon he was heading for one of the general wards, not the dimly lit limbo of the Intensive Care Unit. This afternoon he wasn't afraid he was going to watch someone die.

He found the ward easily enough, matching the numbers on the corridor signs to the one inked on the back of his hand as a reminder – insurance against a brain buzzing with too much coffee and too little sleep – and his smile broadened as he caught sight of the figure sitting propped up in the bed nearest the window. In the pale autumn sunlight Eldritch's face held scarcely more colour than the pillows surrounding him but his eyes were open and focussed on the woman who sat beside him, her legs folded up underneath her like a displaced pixie forced to make do with a grey plastic chair instead of a toadstool. Aidan stood for a minute unnoticed, content just to watch the pair of them. He had come within a hairsbreadth of losing them both. His hands, hooked casually around his belt, tightened momentarily. Even now it was hard to believe that they would be alright.

Up close the ravages of the last few days were still clear on

Eldritch's face, from the healing scab of the demon bite that emphasised the prominence of his cheekbone, to the yellowing bruises and the dark shadows under his eyes, but he smiled when Aidan told him he was looking better.

'I'm feeling better, or at least I will be when I can get rid of this. It's driving me mad.' Irritably the wizard scrubbed his knuckles through the thick stubble darkening his cheeks. 'It's coming off as soon as I can get to a razor. Although...'

He raised his right arm, encased in a cast from knuckles to elbow and treated it to a look that should have reduced the plaster to dust. It was obvious he wasn't going to be doing anything useful with that hand for some time.

'I offered to do it for him,' Gwyn piped up, her voice full of mischief, 'but he didn't seem very keen on the idea.'

'I can't think why,' Eldritch responded darkly. Knowing what it was to be the subject of Gwyn's humour Aidan took pity on him.

'I've got an electric one you can borrow. You should be able to manage that left-handed.'

Gwyn unfolded her legs and propped her bare feet on the side of the bed.

'I reckon he's growing it to charm the nurses.' She poked the bed's occupant companionably with her toes. 'Have you seen his cast?'

'Oh yes?'

His interest piqued Aidan leaned over to take a closer look and with the air of someone resigned to being teased Eldritch lifted his arm for him to see. Aidan's eyebrows rose. Whether due to the stubble or otherwise it seemed the wizard's charm was indeed working well on the medical staff. In the short time he had been out of intensive care Eldritch had amassed quite a collection of messages including an offer of the use of a hospital bed for distinctly non-medical purposes. Even a certain Lisa Carmel had added a get well soon prominently across his knuckles. Aidan wondered if the good doctor always added a flourish of three kisses after her name and smirked at the thought.

'This isn't so much a plaster cast as a little black book.'

He sat back and eyed the wizard with his battered face and the stray tendrils of hair tangling haphazardly over the pillows at his back. The hospital gown Aidan had last seen him in had been replaced by a plain white t-shirt – a definite improvement – but it was still difficult to imagine Eldritch turning anybody's head. Aidan wasn't sure whether to be amused or envious.

'How come I didn't get nurses fawning all over me?'

'Can I help it if they think I'm such an obliging patient?' Eldritch's expression was perfectly deadpan but Aidan caught the trace of wickedness that had slipped into his voice. 'Besides, you have to have a suitable bit of your anatomy that they can sign.'

Gwyn, who had been helping herself to one of the patient's grapes, made a muffled choking noise and had to be slapped on the back until she could breathe again. Aidan decided it might be best to change the subject.

'I brought the local paper in for you. Thought you'd be interested seeing as we made the front page.'

He held up that day's edition of the *Cambrian Times* where the words "Mine Rescue Success" were emblazoned in bold red capitals.

'Mine rescue?' Gwyn queried. She selected another grape

from the bunch but made no move to eat it, rolling it instead between her thumb and forefinger as though it were a large, black worry bead. 'But you'd already made it out of the mine.'

'Ah, but "big hole rescue" doesn't make such an exciting headline.'

Eldritch shook his head in disgust.

'Do I want to know what they've written in the article? Irresponsible thrill seekers endanger selves and local search and rescue team?' he suggested.

'If it's your standing with the nurses you're worried about, don't be. Surprisingly we come out of it quite well. Mind you, it probably helps that it was one of Hazel's cousins who wrote the article. That and Hazel was a little creative with the truth. She probably didn't want what I was doing to reflect badly on the team. Listen to this.'

He started reading.

'*The Plynlimon Mountain Rescue Team were in action on Saturday when they were called to help two cavers who had got into difficulty while exploring a newly revealed section of mine workings.* So far you can't argue with it but you'll like this next bit. *Marcus Eldritch, an experienced caver* – like I said; a little creative – *was taken ill whilst investigating the tunnel as research for a forthcoming book. He and his companion, Aidan Morgan, managed to make their way back to the point at which they had entered the mine where Mr Eldritch collapsed. They were then helped to the surface by members of the Mountain Rescue Team who had been alerted by a member of the public. Hazel Jones, the leader of the team that carried out the rescue, rejected suggestions that the pair had been irresponsible in entering the mineshaft, stating that they were both experienced and were well prepared. "Aidan had left word of what they were doing with a friend and when they didn't return at the specified time she immediately raised the alarm".'*

Aidan lowered the paper and looked across at Gwyn.

'I haven't thanked you for that.'

'You're welcome.' She turned her head, including Eldritch in the comment. 'Both of you. But next time you might consider telling someone who's conscious rather than leaving a note in a get well card. What if the nurses had forgotten to give it to me or if I hadn't woken up in time?'

A stranger might have heard only the irritation but Aidan wasn't fooled. He understood it was the fear of what might have happened that was making her voice sharp. His eyes met hers over the bed.

'If you hadn't woken up it wouldn't have mattered who else I'd told. You were the only one who could help.'

Gwyn pursed her lips as though disapproving but unable to think of a suitable rejoinder. In the bed Eldritch cleared his throat.

'What else does it say?'

'Nothing much; a bit of background about local mining history and the obligatory warning not to go exploring any workings on your own. Don't try this at home, kiddies.'

'There's nothing about Griff?'

'Ah.' Aidan had intended to skip over the other article on the page, the one with the headline "Local farmer still missing". 'Only that a quad bike belonging to missing farmer Griff Howell was found close to where the rescue took place. Police investigating his disappearance say there's no connection between the two incidents.'

He raised an incredulous eyebrow but any comment he had

been about to make was lost as Gwyn said softly, 'It's better that way. I suppose the demon must have focussed its influence on him after John's death, once Aidan was protected.'

She glanced at Eldritch, her head tilted, bird-like, to one side and he nodded.

'Each time he gave into it it would have tightened its hold on his mind. By the time I encountered the avatar he would have been almost completely under its control. It may be that the demon was intending to take him as its host before it managed to get a link to me.'

Eldritch gave a small, slightly uncomfortable shrug as though worried they would think he was boasting. 'A host with power would be more of a temptation.'

'Doctors, nurses, demons… Is no one immune to this man's charms?' Aidan asked of no one in particular. 'But despite the link it couldn't influence you while you were inside the wards on Gwyn's house or wearing her bracelets. So at that point the demon changed tack. It used Griff again but this time to try and murder Gwyn and leave you unprotected and when that didn't work it ran us off the road.'

'It had to know that we were getting closer to finding it and at that point it must have decided that an ordinary host and a dead wizard were a better bet than risking me being able to stop the manifestation.'

'Hedging its bets,' Aidan agreed. 'Only instead of being killed in the crash you ended up losing the last bracelet. Which reminds me.' He delved into his jacket pocket. 'The garage recovered the landy for me. This was still in the passenger foot well where somebody,' he looked pointedly at Eldritch, 'dropped it.'

The string of amethyst chips, dark as winter pansies, glittered between his fingers as he handed the bracelet back to Gwyn. She took it with a smile, cradling it in her palm for a few seconds before slipping it onto her wrist to nestle against the circle of rose quartz pearls.

'Hard to believe that such a small thing could have such consequences,' Eldritch said ruefully. 'Without the wards on those stones I was completely open to the demon's influence. All it had to do was call me to it in the mine.'

Eldritch's eyes strayed to the window but Aidan doubted he saw anything of the view beyond the slightly smeary glass. The wizard's gaze was turned inward and his voice was bitter and reproachful as he judged his own behaviour.

'I thought I was in control but everything I did from that point on was tainted; flawed.' His good hand clenched unnoticed by his side. 'If it hadn't been for Aidan...'

Abruptly he fell silent, his gaze dropping to stare down at the sheets until Gwyn poked him again with her foot. He looked at her, his grey eyes troubled, but she only said, 'It seems to me that we all have things we could wish we'd done differently. I for one wish I'd run the other way when I saw Griff coming up the road on his quad bike. Not that I could have outrun him,' her tone became fierce, 'but at least I wouldn't have made it as easy for him as I did.'

She eyed Eldritch and there was both understanding and a challenge written on her face. She would accept no maudlin brooding. 'What's done is done. We can't change that but we can celebrate the fact that we came out the other side more or less intact, which is more than can be said for the demon or for Griff Howell.'

'He must have been called to the mine when the demon realised it could no longer influence me.'

'Poor Griff.'

'Poor Griff my ar—' Aidan stopped short at Gwyn's look and shot her a black one of his own. '*Poor Griff* smashed your head in with a rock,' he reminded her. 'Not to mention having a damn good go at killing me and Eldritch, several times over.'

He shifted, running a hand unconsciously over his ribs. An X-ray had shown no further damage but that didn't stop them aching when he sat for too long in one position. Gwyn reached over and patted his arm.

'And you saw the demon rip his body apart and use his flesh to create its own. He may have asked for what he got but I'm not sure even he fully deserved it.'

'Huh,' Aidan huffed out his breath, unwilling to concede even that much, although on some level he couldn't help agreeing with Gwyn. Griff's contribution to his world had been singularly unpleasant but his death had been brutal.

'You surprise me. I didn't think you were the sort to turn the other cheek.'

From his tone it seemed that Eldritch didn't think much of forgiveness, or at least not in this case. Gwyn arched one elfin brow and looked at him over the top of a pair of imaginary glasses.

'I'm not – that's someone else's religion – but I do believe the world has a way of paying us back for our actions.'

Eldritch laughed.

'That's just so much New Age nonsense.'

'Well even you have to admit there's not much mileage in holding a grudge against someone who's dead.'

Aidan leaned back in the hard plastic chair and let their voices drift over him. Two days ago he had stood face to face with death and with things that were worse by far. Then he had lived on tenterhooks waiting to find out if Eldritch would live or die. He had kept going on too much coffee and too little sleep and the latter was beginning to gain the upper hand in his system. But that was okay. He shifted, easing his head back against the wall. Gwyn was right. The three of them had emerged, if not unscathed, then at least unbroken from the demon's rising.

What doesn't kill you makes you stronger. He heard his mother's voice in his head and smiled to himself. In future there might be other creatures from the Unseen Realm to deal with and for certain there was the nature of his own magical inheritance to explore but for now there was peace and warmth and the wash of friends' voices squabbling – albeit reasonably good naturedly – as they moved from philosophy to some obscure element of demon lore. Aidan laughed softly under his breath, amused that the very phrase "demon lore" now had a place in his vocabulary and let his eyes slip closed. For the moment, at least, all was right with the world.

AUTHOR'S NOTE

I would like to extend my thanks to Professor Tony Brown, of Bangor University, for his kind assistance in putting me in touch with Gwydion Thomas and to Gwydion himself for allowing me to include the quotation from his father's poem, *Welsh Landscape,* in my writing.

As in my first book, *The Demon's Call,* in telling Gwyn, Eldritch and Aidan's story I have taken a few liberties with the landscape of mid-Wales. Not all the features I describe exist outside the murky realms of my imagination. Likewise the names I have ascribed to them are my own creations. My purpose in all of this has been solely to entertain and I hope that those who know and love the area will forgive me.

Some real places are referenced to set the context in which my story takes place but the town of Llancathan and the village of Caeglas are both fictional and any resemblance to real locations – or to the businesses or individuals associated with them – is coincidental.

Any errors in the Welsh I have used are entirely down to me.